For my mum.

Thank you for having me.

Sue Margolis was born into a Jewish family in Ilford, Essex. She studied politics at Nottingham University, and while a student married Jonathan Margolis, now a journalist and biographer. Their first two children were born in Yorkshire, where she also started her career as a BBC radio journalist. Sue and her family later moved to west London and, along with having a third child, she specialised in making offbeat items for Radio 4's WOMAN'S HOUR.

Praise for Sue Margolis's NEUROTICA and SISTERIA, also available from Headline:

'Funny, sexy and hugely warmhearted' Wendy Holden

'A riotous romp . . . Terrific characters . . . It will make you laugh out loud – a lot' *Jewish Chronicle*

'Touching and amusing . . . Hits all the right buttons' *Bookseller*

'Its humour is irresistible' *Jewish Telegraph*

'Margolis's prose is witty and sure . . . a taut and rambunctious tale' *Publishers Weekly*

'An urban Jilly Cooper without the riches. There are the juicy sex scenes to make you hot and fidgety on the Tube, the deliciously evil hyper-bitch and plenty of over-the-top character traits. And, it all comes good in a ridiculously Hollywood happy ending' *Ham & High*

Also by Sue Margolis

Neurotica
Sisteria

Launderama

Sue Margolis

headline

First published in 2001
by HEADLINE BOOK PUBLISHING

First published in paperback in 2002
by HEADLINE BOOK PUBLISHING

10 9 8 7 6 5 4 3 2 1

ISBN 0 7472 68215

Typeset by Palimpsest Book Production Limited,
Polmont, Stirlingshire

Printed and bound in Great Britain by
Clays Ltd, St Ives plc

HEADLINE BOOK PUBLISHING
A division of Hodder Headline
338 Euston Road
LONDON NW1 3BH
www.headline.co.uk
www.hodderheadline.com

CHAPTER 1

Rachel Katz lifted the mike off its stand and jerked the lead away from her feet.

'So yeah, right, anyway,' she began, moving the mike stand to one side, 'what do you think about this new morning-after pill for men?'

She'd hoped for a few expectant chuckles at her opening line, but wasn't too alarmed when none came.

'The male morning-after pill, yeah. It changes their blood group.'

Silence. OK, she thought. It happens.

'You know,' she continued, her trademark deadpan voice not faltering, 'I'm thirty-four years old and still I don't get it. Men – and the emotions thing. I mean, why *are* they so afraid of feelings, so alienated by the remotest display of sensitivity? Let's face it, the only time you'll catch a bloke watching *Oprah* is when it's on nymphomaniacs and where they hang out.'

She paused. Waited for her laugh. Again, nothing. She was beginning to feel uneasy, and more than a little perplexed. She'd tried out the *Oprah* gag on a dozen audiences in the last few weeks and people always hooted.

The family of highly-strung ferrets which usually inhabited Rachel's stomach when she was performing went into a psychotic frenzy of somersaults and backflips.

'Right,' she said breezily, doing her best to ignore the ferrets. 'Just me on that one then.' She smiled at the audience, hoping she might receive a few titters of encouragement in return. But none were forthcoming.

'You see,' she continued, starting to feel mildly nauseous now, 'it's not only the emotional thing fellas can't do. That's just the tip of the iceberg. I mean, practically all my boyfriends have missed the things that are really important to me – my birthday, the anniversary of when we met . . . my clitoris.'

She paused once more. Still not a hint of a hoot. This could not be happening.

She peered at the audience through the smoke and semi-darkness. Sitting round The Anarchist Bathmat's pub tables was the usual mix of pierced and goateed student types, a few yuppies and a smattering of forty-somethings desperate to show the world their humour was still cutting edge whilst forgetting their sartorial style was more cutting hedge.

'Right . . . er . . . OK,' Rachel battled on. 'I was lying in bed next to my boyfriend the other night after we'd made love and I found myself thinking that God just has to be a man. I mean, if God were a woman, She'd have made sperm taste of chocolate.'

Cold silence.

'God, I wish you lot had been here yesterday,' Rachel said, swallowing hard. 'I was in Birmingham.'

Suddenly a woman in the front row began sniffing loudly. Others followed. Then came the sound of somebody crying. By now Rachel's nausea, panic and overwhelming confusion were turning to astonishment. She couldn't understand it. Usually when people didn't like her material, they heckled, went off to the bar or simply ignored her. They didn't collapse into depression. Her bewilderment was such that she realised she'd forgotten the next part of her routine. She had to come up with an ad lib, fast.

''S funny,' she chuckled nervously. 'Right now, I'm having amnesia and déjà vu at the same time. I think I've forgotten this before.'

The whole place was now filled with the sound of people weeping. For the first time in her career and, Rachel suspected, in the history of stand-up comedy, an entire audience had been reduced to tears.

Through the hazy half-light she could see women hunched over tables wracked with noisy sobs. Blokes were biting their bottom lips and gently consoling their girlfriends. A few fellas were even hugging each other. Through her peripheral vision, Rachel caught sight of Lenny, the compère, who was standing to one side of the stage making violent cut-throat gestures to her. She realised she had no alternative but to come offstage.

'Thank you,' she shouted above the din of wailing,

sniffing and nose-blowing. 'I'm Rachel Katz and you've been . . . an audience. Good night.'

Rachel bounded over to Lenny. He was a short, thirty-something Sheffield lad with mad-scientist ginger hair and pink tartan flares. They'd worked together dozens of times, and he and Rachel were good mates.

'Blimey,' she gasped. 'Talk about going down like Sylvester Stallone's dick at a ladyboy convention. Do you mind telling me what was going on? I mean, I've died before, but I've never been mourned.'

'It's OK, Rachel. Calm down,' Lenny said, smiling and gently rubbing the top of her arm. 'It wasn't your fault. You see, the audience couldn't help it.'

'What do you mean, "couldn't help it"? 'Course they could bloody help it!'

'No, they couldn't, honest. You were in the bar with your bloke when Mori Bund, the Jewish Goth hypnotist was on. He put the entire audience in a trance – managed to convince the men that England had just lost the Ashes, the Football World Cup and the Rugby World Cup all on the same day and the women that they were watching the final scene in *Casablanca*. He finished his act positive he'd brought them back. It was only when you went on that he realised they were still under.'

Rachel turned to look at the audience. The crying had stopped and everybody was sitting upright in their seats, their eyes closed and heads flopped forwards. Onstage a gangly, nervous-looking chap with an Alice Cooper face, wearing a black top hat, matching satin cloak and horizontally striped black and white tights and red DMs, was counting loudly backwards from ten.

'You're quiet,' Rachel said to Adam through a mouthful of Big Mac. 'You haven't even told me what you thought of my set tonight – at least, what there was of it. I know it all went a bit egg-shaped because of the hypnosis thing, but weeping punters aside, what did you reckon?'

Adam took one hand off the steering wheel and leaned across to steal one of her chips. He said nothing. He looked thoughtful and uneasy at the same time. She could tell he was building up to something.

'Come on, out with it,' she said good-humouredly. 'You thought I was crap, didn't you?'

He opened his mouth to speak, but she came back at him before he had a chance.

'OK, I know what it is,' she said. 'All my bloke-bashing material makes you feel like I'm getting at you. Come on, Adam, you know none of my gags are personal. Jokes against men get laughs, that's all.'

She began stroking his cheek. 'You've never once missed my birthday,' she purred. 'Or my clitoris.'

Adam smiled. 'Don't be daft,' he told her. 'It never even occurred to me to take any of your anti-men stuff personally. Mind you, it is a bit unrelenting. Why don't you try ringing the changes? I heard this brilliant gag the other day. Now then, how did it go? Hang on . . .

OK, yeah. What do Japanese men do when they have erections?'

'I don't know,' she said, her voice a perfect imitation of a music-hall comic. 'What *do* Japanese men do when they have erections?'

'Vote.'

'Right,' she said with a weak chuckle.

'Oh, well,' Adam shrugged, 'it made me laugh. Still, what do I know, I'm just a dentist.'

'Yeah. You think loose dentures are funny.' She shoved some more chips into her mouth.

'I don't know about that, but I could certainly name you dentists whose bridgework makes me laugh out loud.'

Neither of them spoke for a moment or two.

'I know what's bugging you,' she said eventually. 'You still think I should jack in the comedy, don't you?'

'Look,' he said, bringing his brand new Audi A6 to a stop at a red light, 'with the exception of maybe your mother, nobody would be more delighted than me if you gave it up and went back to journalism. Bloody hell, Rache, two years ago you were a broadsheet features editor earning a bloody decent salary. You had an expense account, a company BMW. Then you just walk away. For what? To spend night after night in seedy smoke-filled pub back rooms getting heckled by drunks.'

'Er, excuse me,' she said. 'For your information, I haven't had a heckler in ages. Adam, we've been through this a thousand times. You know how much I love doing the comedy. You know the buzz I get from standing up there, making an audience laugh with material *I've* written.'

'I can't imagine what it must feel like, performing in front of all those people,' Adam said. 'I'd be petrified.'

'I *am* petrified,' she said eagerly. 'But in a way I love that too. Even before I get up onstage, the adrenalin starts pumping because I know I'm about to take this enormous risk. The audience may not laugh – and that's scary. Then when they do, I get this wonderful sense of triumph. It's like I've climbed a mountain or run a marathon. Journalism could be satisfying occasionally – you know, blowing the whistle on some bent MP or whatever – but it never gave me the rush the comedy does. It didn't come close. In the end it just bored me.'

As she took another bite of burger, mayonnaise started to dribble down her chin. She wiped it with the back of her hand. When she realised all she'd succeeded in doing was transferring the mayo rather than getting rid of it, she began sucking her hand.

Adam winced, and opened the glove compartment. Next to the box of tissues which he always kept in the car in case he had one of his frequent, stress-related nose bleeds, was a container of Wet Ones. He handed it to her. But by now she'd already wiped her hand on her combats. She put the box down next to her feet.

'Thing is,' she went on, 'I must give it a proper go. I can't give up just because once in a while I get heckled.

That's how comics learn. It's part of finding out what material works and what doesn't.' She stopped chewing and watched Adam take a neatly folded yellow duster from the driver's door compartment, open it and wrap one corner round his index finger.

'But you're earning no money,' he said, rubbing at a spot of non-existent dirt on the dashboard.

'I am,' she said brightly. 'I made a hundred and fifty quid tonight.'

'I mean real money. Rache, you have to clean people's houses to make ends meet. And you've got a child to support.'

Satisfied that the imaginary speck was gone, he refolded the duster down the original crease marks and put it back in the driver's door compartment.

'C' mon, Ad,' she said, playfully punching the top of his arm. 'I get by. And you know I'd never let Sam go without. Anyway, it's only till I get famous. D'you want the rest of these chips?'

He shook his head.

She screwed up the burger paper and rammed it down on top of the half-full chip box. 'Plus I've worked it out. I've got all the money I need . . . so long as I die before Monday.'

Adam turned to her and smiled, despite himself.

'Look,' she went on, 'please try and understand. I'm doing something I really want to do, and that means so much more to me than having piles of dosh in the bank.'

By way of response, Adam took the McDonald's rubbish from her lap, twisted round and placed it neatly in the Car Tidy hanging from the back of the passenger seat.

'Floss?' he said a moment later, taking his hand out of his jacket pocket and offering her the tiny white container.

Rachel was used to Adam's flossing obsession. No matter how many times she begged him not to, he still offered it round at dinner parties. She shook her head.

'Fine, but I tell you, Rache, you neglect oral hygiene at your peril. Don't come crying to me when your teeth start to turn yellow.'

'I won't,' she giggled. 'I'll just wear brown to compensate.'

The traffic lights changed and Adam pulled away.

'So,' she purred, moving towards him and trailing her finger over the small bald patch on the back of his head, 'talking of making ends meet, when will ours meet next? It's been ages since you told me to open wide.'

'I'm sorry,' he said. 'Thing is, I'm just so busy at the moment. I've got bloody admin. coming at me from all sides.'

'Yeah, I know,' she said sympathetically. She rubbed his arm affectionately and felt the softness of the expensive navy woollen jacket. Underneath he was wearing an immaculately pressed denim shirt. She looked down at her combats and scruffy Nikes. How the supposedly witty, 'alternative' likes of her, who always looked like

SUE MARGOLIS

she'd thrown something on and missed, had managed to fall in love with a Jewish dentist with a thing about dental floss and shoe trees, she had little idea – beyond a firm belief that opposites really did attract.

'I don't mean to put pressure on you,' she said, 'honest. But I just hate you being in Manchester. I only get to see you at weekends and sometimes not even then because you're so busy. And when you disappear to South Africa for a month, I won't see you at all.'

The following week, Adam was off to Durban to work in his Uncle Stan's dental practice. Adam's father had died of a heart attack when Adam was twelve, leaving no life insurance and very little capital. When Stan, his father's brother, discovered this, he started paying Adam's school fees and put him through university. Despite the geographical distance, they'd always been close and Adam felt he owed Stan a great deal. When he phoned to say he was going into hospital for a hip replacement and was there any chance Adam could take over the surgery for a few weeks, Adam had felt he was in no position to refuse.

'We'll speak on the phone every day. Believe me, Rachel, I'll be busy, you're busy. Four weeks will go in a flash.'

'Yeah, I s'pose. But why you had to go to Manchester in the first place, I've no idea.'

'Come on, you know precisely why. I went because, unlike you, I recognise a sound job opportunity when I see one.'

A year ago, Adam's best friend from dental school had offered him a partnership in his cosmetic dentistry practice in Alderley Edge with a million pound a year turnover and he'd grabbed it like a shot.

She grunted. 'I know. I just miss you, that's all. Look, don't go back tonight. Please stay. It's already gone eleven. Tomorrow's Saturday. What's to go rushing back for?'

'A mountain of VAT returns, that's what. I've been putting it off for weeks. I'd love to stay, Rache, you know that, but I really do need to get back. Anyway, your mother and father are at your flat. I can't bear doing it with them a few feet away on the sofa bed.'

Rachel's regular babysitter had let her down and her parents had offered to look after Sam, her ten-year-old son. Her father tired easily these days and didn't like driving home from Crouch End to Chingford late at night, so when they babysat they invariably stayed over.

'Plus I'm convinced your mother stays awake listening.'

'Don't be daft. Why would she listen?'

'Rachel, your father is over seventy. He wears trousers with elasticated waists and shoes that do up with Velcro. His idea of excitement is allowing himself an extra Rennie after dinner. If you lived with a man like that, wouldn't *you* listen?'

'Maybe,' she said. For a fleeting moment she could see Adam at seventy, soaking his loose change in biological detergent overnight and washing the rubbish before throwing it in the bin.

She put out her arm and squeezed the inside of his thigh. He smiled back at her. A moment later she was trailing her fingers over the outline of his penis.

'That's nice,' he said softly.

She felt his penis begin to stiffen.

'I do love you, you know,' he said, stroking her head.

'Yeah, me too. And listen – thanks for driving down to see my gig tonight. I really appreciate it.'

'My pleasure. Rache, I know I seem a bit tough on you, but it's only because I worry. I hate to think of you struggling like this. Why won't you at least let me give you some money?'

'I've told you before. Because I want to make a go of the comedy on my own. I refuse to live like some kept woman indulging a fantasy.'

He shrugged. 'OK. But when we're married . . . which reminds me – we really ought to sit down and sort out a wedding date.'

'We will. Soon – I promise.'

'You've been saying that for months.'

'I know. It's just that I've been so taken up with the comedy, I haven't had a moment to think about it. Look, we'll talk when you get back from South Africa, OK?'

He turned to look at her. 'Rache, you do love me, don't you?'

'Of course I do,' she said, leaning across and kissing his ear.

'Then we're just wasting time not setting a date. And getting married makes sound practical sense for both of us. We're neither of us getting any younger . . .'

'Christ, do you think maybe the time has come to stop buying giant jars of Marmite?'

'Funn-ee. Rachel, you know exactly what I mean. Look, I'm nearly thirty-six and I want to get my life sorted. It feels like it's time. I want to settle down. I want us to have a couple of kids, a nice house round the corner from the practice . . .'

'. . . membership of the synagogue burial society.'

Adam was starting to get irritated. 'I'm trying to have a serious conversation here. Why won't you listen?'

'I will listen,' she said, smiling a sexy smile, 'but, later. There's something I want to do first.' With that she began unzipping his fly.

'Christ Almighty, Rache,' he gasped. 'What if somebody sees?'

'Ssh,' she whispered as she moved her head down towards his lap. A moment later she was running her tongue over the top of his erection.

Adam whimpered softly and slipped fractionally lower in his seat. Then almost at once she sensed him clenching his buttocks in panic.

'But what if I get so carried away that I crash the car and you end up biting off my knob? Oh God, that feels incredible . . . Look, Rache, just in case this all

13

goes wrong and I end up haemorrhaging, for Chrissake remember to tell the ambulancemen I have thin blood. You know how hard it is to stop my nose bleeds 'cos I have trouble clotting . . . fuck, you're good. I'll need FFP, right? And possibly platelets. Have you got that? Fresh. Frozen. Plasma.'

But Rachel wasn't listening. She took virtually his entire penis in her mouth – just as the Audi entered the Rotherhithe Tunnel.

CHAPTER 2

'No, Coral, listen to me. List-en. I know it seems unbearable now, but you have to calm down and believe this is
just a temporary setback. All of you is beautiful and
valuable . . . Of course I mean it. Coral, this is me,
Faye, your best friend. Would I lie?'

Rachel dropped her shoulder bag on the floor next to
the hall coat-stand and shook her head. Not only was
her mother up at gone midnight, she was yakking on
the phone. She swore that one day the woman's larynx
would seize up. She walked towards the kitchen and the
sound of Faye's voice.

She opened the door. Her mother, mobile phone between
her shoulder and chin, was kneeling on the kitchen worktop
in her lilac candlewick housecoat and a pair of brand new
rubber gloves. A plastic bucket stood beside her. Although
she had her back towards her daughter, Rachel could see
quite clearly that her mother was cleaning the Venetian
blind above the sink. A few feet away, Rachel's father Jack
was standing in his dressing gown stirring hot chocolate into
mugs of boiling milk.

'Dad,' she said, without taking her eyes off her mother, 'do you mind telling me what on earth she's up to at this time of night?'

Jack gave his daughter a 'you know your mother' shrug.

'So, how'd it go tonight?' he asked, giving Rachel a peck on the forehead.

'Not bad,' she told him, taking a Rich Tea out of the biscuit tin and biting into it. 'Sam OK?'

'Good as gold, bless him,' Jack smiled. 'Not a peep since he went to bed. You want some hot chocolate?'

Rachel shook her head.

At that moment her father stopped in mid-stir, clutched his chest and grimaced.

Before Rachel had a chance to react to the clutching and grimacing, Jack let out an enormous belch. Hearing this, Faye immediately swung round. Covering up the mouthpiece, she took the phone off her ear and cocked her head towards her husband.

'He had wheat tonight,' she said to Rachel. 'Now he's paying the price. Coral? I've got to go, Rachel's back. I'll speak to you in the morning. Meanwhile, cheer up and try to get some sleep. Bye. Love to Ivan.'

'Three hours your mother's been on that mobile,' Jack said as Faye stabbed the off button and manoeuvred herself into a sitting position on the worktop. 'I tell you, her head is so full of microwaves, I could use it as a hot-water bottle.'

Faye snorted. 'Jack,' she said brusquely, 'just be quiet and help me down.'

He padded over to the sink, took the bucket of Flash from her and held out his hand.

'That was Coral,' she said to Rachel once she was back on her feet. 'Poor soul, her manicurist took one look at the state of her cuticles and told her there was nothing more she could do for her. So how did it go tonight? Channel 6 discover you yet? Wait . . . don't tell me. I already know the answer. Rachel, I beg you. Give up this comedy nonsense. Look, I know you're funny, Daddy knows you're funny, so what's wrong with just making us laugh and going back to a proper job? Showbusiness is a tough world. So few people make it and I worry about you having no money.'

'Mum,' Rachel said, going over to her mother and wrapping an arm round her shoulders. 'You have to stop worrying. I admit things get a bit tight occasionally, but I'm doing fine. Honest.' She gave Faye a reassuring peck on the cheek.

Her mother shrugged and turned to Jack for moral support, but he'd disappeared into the living room with the mugs of hot chocolate and half a dozen Rich Tea biscuits in his dressing-gown pocket.

'So, where is Adam?' Faye asked, wiping her forearm across her brow. 'I thought he was going to stay over.'

'He's driving straight back to Manchester,' Rachel replied, swallowing the last of her biscuit.

'But he won't get home till three in the morning.'

'He's got to do the VAT tomorrow.'

17

'And to think I've spent hours slaving over a hot Flash bucket. I know how high his standards are.'

Rachel looked round. The pile of washing-up she'd left in the sink was gone, the previously overflowing swing bin was empty, her worktops were clear and the J-cloth on the drainer which had been there at least two months had been replaced with a new one.

On the one hand, Rachel couldn't help taking offence that each time Faye came to the flat the first thing she did was sniff the fridge, wince and then reach into her handbag, from which she would take a pair of Marigolds. On the other hand, since Rachel didn't get much time for housework these days, she was genuinely grateful. She decided there was nothing to gain from pointing out how much Faye's cleaning irritated her. Her mother would only get upset.

'Oh, Mum, I'm sorry,' she said kindly. 'I really am. You've worked really hard and—' Rachel broke off in mid-sentence. 'Mum,' she said with faux casualness, eyeing Faye's rubber-gloved hand, from which there hung a short white string. 'Correct me if I'm wrong, but you appear to be holding a water-logged tampon.'

'Yes, I know,' her mother said excitedly. 'It's my own invention. I always use them to clean Venetians. You take a Tampax out of its cardboard, damp it and run it along the plastic. Works a treat.'

Faye looked round the kitchen, smiled a satisfied smile and took off her rubber gloves. Almost at once she put them back on. She'd spied a significant build-up of green gloop round Rachel's washing-up bottle nozzle. Having rinsed it to her satisfaction and taken off the rubber gloves once more, she suggested they join Jack in the living room. As they walked in he was sitting up in the sofa bed reading *You and the Continental Drift*.

'I tell you,' Jack said, looking at them through Faye's reading glasses, which had gold filigree arms and which he always borrowed because he could never find his own, 'it says here the whole of Europe is on the move. The entire continent. Believe me, it won't be long before Chingford ends up in the Caribbean.'

'So what are you saying?' Faye said, picking up her hot chocolate from the coffee-table and sitting down at the end of the sofa bed. 'That I shouldn't bother buying a winter coat this year?'

The two women burst out laughing.

By way of reply Jack gave an involuntary belch, put Faye's glasses back on the end of his nose and returned to his book.

Rachel perched herself on the end of the bed next to her mother. It was then that she noticed the large mock-leather wedding invitation catalogue lying on the floor next to the bed.

'Mum,' she said, doing her best to keep her tone light, 'what's this?' She picked up the catalogue and opened it.

'You can see what it is,' Faye said quietly. 'The chap at the printers said I could hang on to it overnight. I thought maybe we could look through it together tomorrow.'

19

'I dunno,' Rachel said, shaking her head and giving a half-laugh. 'What am I going to do with you?'

'Adam won't wait for ever, you know. Please, darling, why can't you set a date?' Faye then launched into her usual ten-minute lecture about what a lovely boy Adam was, how much he loved Rachel and how thirty-four-year-old divorced mothers didn't get too many offers of marriage.

'Plus he's well off. You and Sam would want for nothing. Absolutely nothing.'

'I know,' Rachel said gently, 'but I've just been so busy trying to get my career off the ground, I haven't had time to think about weddings.'

'But you had a career. A wonderful career. You were earning good money.'

'Oh Mum, the money thing isn't important . . .'

'Rachel, darling, of *course* it's important. Look at you in this tiny, scruffy flat. How can you say it's not important? I mean, what about this room? Bare floorboards. You can't even afford to put down carpet.'

'How many more times? They're not bare, they're stripped. Stripped is fashionable, not a sign of poverty.'

Faye shrugged. 'If you say so. Why don't you at least let us give you the money to take out that monstrosity over there.' She was nodding at the Victorian fireplace.

'Mum,' Rachel gasped, 'how can you call a white marble fireplace a monstrosity? It's exquisite. You know full well it was one of the reasons I bought the flat.'

'But it's so old-fashioned. It reminds me of my grand-mother's house in East Ham. Rachel, you've got central heating. You don't *need* a fireplace. Of course, I blame your father.' She turned to Jack, who had dozed off with *You and the Continental Drift* lying across his chest. 'When you said you wanted to do English at university instead of something useful like Estate Management, he should have put his foot down.'

Rachel was too tired to get into an argument. She stood up.

'Let's leave it for now,' she said with a yawn. 'Anyway, Adam and I have agreed to discuss wedding dates when he gets back from South Africa.'

'You have?' Faye said, beaming. 'That's wonderful. Let's see, it's November now. A spring wedding would be nice . . . Mind you, the weather's never reliable. July might be better. Then again, people start going on holiday . . .'

'OK, fine, whatever. I'll think about it. Look, I really must get to bed. Let's talk in the morning.'

Faye nodded. 'You know,' she said, reaching up and taking her daughter's hand in hers, 'Me and your father have been married nearly forty years. I know we have our ups and downs, but I really do think being married is wonderful.'

'Mum,' Rachel said with a chuckle, 'you think Chingford's wonderful.'

Just then Sam appeared in the doorway in his old Toy Story pyjamas which were two sizes too small for him. His

21

dark hair looked like a family of mice had been nesting in it and his face was red and creased down one side.

'Darling,' Faye said, 'I thought you were sound asleep.'

By now Rachel had got up and walked over to him. 'You OK, love?' she asked.

'Yeah. I was just thirsty.' He held out a glass of water which he'd clearly just got from the kitchen.

'Come on. I'll take you back to bed.'

'Night, darling,' Faye said.

Rachel now holding the glass of water, they walked down the hall back to Sam's room.

'Mum,' Sam said as she pulled the duvet over him, 'what's ape suzette?'

Rachel smiled and sat down on the bed. 'I think you mean crêpes suzettes. It's a French dessert made with pancakes and booze.'

He nodded slowly. 'Oh, right. It's not made of monkey, then?'

Rachel laughed. 'No. Definitely not. So where did you hear about crêpes suzettes?'

'Oh, it was just something I overheard Grandma say to Grandad. They were talking about weddings or something.'

Rachel frowned a brief, suspicious frown.

'It's a funny idea, though,' she said, 'animal desserts. 'You could have – ooh, I dunno . . . profitermoles.'

Sam started to giggle.

'And mice pudding,' she went on. 'Meringue-utan. Oh, and what about crème camel?'

By now Sam was laughing his head off.

'You're really funny, Mum,' he said.

'Am I?' she said softly, beaming with pleasure.

He nodded.

She leaned forward and kissed him on the cheek. 'Night, night,' she said, switching off the bedside light.

'Night . . . Mum?'

'What is it?' she said.

'How's about low-bat yoghurt?'

Rachel lay in bed, hands behind her head, staring up at the ceiling. Her mother was right: Adam was a good catch. He was successful, well off, good-looking. He also thought the world of Sam. Whenever Adam came to stay at the flat he brought presents for him. Last time it had been fifty quid's worth of rare POKÉMON cards he'd ordered off the Internet. And he had a point when he said they had both reached an age when they should be thinking about settling down. Although Rachel had no intention of giving up the comedy, she was in no doubt that pretty soon she would want another baby, or even two.

So what, she thought, that Adam tidied the bed when she got up in the night for a pee? He was just a bit uptight, that's all. And so what that he was comedically illiterate and found silly schoolboy gags about Japanese accents funnier than her stuff? It didn't mean he couldn't change – that she couldn't change him. She would just have to work on him slowly. The important thing was that in his own, deeply conventional, impeccably tidy way, Adam loved her and she loved him. What was more, his conservatism and caution provided the perfect counterbalance to her quixotic idealism. He kept her grounded – which was precisely what she needed.

Of course it wasn't the electrifying, mind-altering grand passion she'd known when she met Joe, her ex-husband, Sam's father. It was a more sedate, grown-up kind of love based on mutual understanding, care and respect.

One of the first things that had struck Rachel about Adam was his kindness. They'd met at a dental hospital two years ago, just after she'd started out as a stand-up. She'd gone in to have a couple of obstinate, intermittently painful wisdom teeth removed. Teeth aside she was also feeling pain of an emotional kind.

Rachel had been going through a particularly barren patch, romance wise. She'd had a string of hapless blind dates with self-important prats. The only upside was that each had provided her with an excellent source of comedy material – none more so than the American tax attorney she'd met the night before, who had spent the whole of their three-hour dinner talking about himself.

It didn't help that Rachel had misheard him when he'd told her what he did for a living and had spent the first half-hour thinking he was in taxidermy. Having almost reached the end of her tether with this egocentric tosser, she said, 'You can ask *me* questions, you know. I really don't mind.'

'OK,' he said, leaning back in his chair. 'What do you think of me? 'Cos I reckon I'm just your type.'

'No, mate,' she'd retorted. 'Your type's inflatable.' Then she got up and walked out.

She'd just about come round from the anaesthetic when her mother burst into the room pushing an empty wheelchair.

'Rachel, there's this gorgeous Jewish doctor,' she exclaimed, catching her breath about as easily as a teenager in the presence of Brad Pitt. 'I've just seen in the corridor. God, talk about a dreamboat. You have to meet him.'

'Mum,' Rachel had said woozily, through the cotton-wool pads in her cheeks, 'they're all dentists here, not doctors.'

'OK, dentist then. Jewish doctor, dentist – what difference? Come on.'

'What do you mean, come on?'

'I mean, come on and get in the wheelchair. I'm going to take you out there and introduce you.'

Had her brain not been addled by lingering anaesthesia, she would have been horrified by the suggestion, but instead all she said was: 'But Mum – what are you going to say?'

'I'll think of something,' Faye said as she dragged her daughter out of the bed and into the wheelchair. Even in her fuddled state Rachel couldn't help wondering how a

25

sixty-year-old sparrowlike woman of five foot three could possess the upper body strength of a hod carrier.

Rachel caught sight of her face in the dressing-table mirror. Her cheeks were so stuffed with cotton pads she looked like a hamster stocking up for a famine.

'Maybe you should put on some mascara and a bit of eyeshadow. Some blusher wouldn't hurt.'

'Mum.' Rachel's shriek was muffled, but eloquent. Clearly realising she had pushed her far enough, Faye simply put a blanket over her daughter's knees and swung the wheelchair round towards the door.

A moment later they were charging down the corridor, Faye muttering breathlessly, 'I can't see him. He was here a minute ago. How far can he have got in just a few seconds?' Then, as the wheelchair smashed through a pair of clear plastic doors and came out the other side, she screeched to a cartoon halt.

'There he is,' she said in a shrill whisper. 'On the left there. Talking to some other doctors.'

Rachel wouldn't have described him as gorgeous exactly, but he was good-looking in a beaky kind of way. She suddenly became even more aware of her hamster face and decided, unwisely as it turned out, to remove the cottonwool from her mouth. Almost at once she could feel blood starting to trickle down the back of her throat.

'Doctor . . . er . . .' Faye squinted at Adam's identity badge. 'Landsberg. Ooh, any relation to the Hendon Landsbergs?'

Adam smiled and shook his head.

Rachel squirmed with embarrassment. What was more, the taste of blood was beginning to make her feel sick. Very sick indeed.

At that point Adam's colleagues, clearly taking the view that he'd picked up a couple of nutters, made their excuses and left.

Faye cleared her throat nervously. 'Er, look, Doctor Landsberg,' she went on.

'He's not a doctor,' Rachel hissed.

Faye glared down at her.

'Er, look,' she went on. Rachel could have sworn her mother was actually batting her eyelashes at Adam. 'I realise you are a very busy man and I know you didn't actually perform the operation on my daughter, but she's in a great deal of pain and as there's nobody else around just now, I was wondering if you would mind taking a look at her.'

Rachel looked up at Adam and smiled a weak, helpless smile. He returned the smile. He had soft, gentle eyes, she thought.

He crouched down and whispered in her ear, 'It's OK. I've got a Jewish mother at home, too.'

At that moment the nausea took over. Before Adam had a chance to stand up, Rachel had chucked up all over his Edward Green brogues.

He didn't flinch. (It was only once she got to know Adam and his hygiene fanaticism that she realised what a heroic act his lack of flinching had been.) Instead, he fetched a nurse to mop up the vomit and agreed to

27

examine Rachel as soon as he'd cleaned himself up. The following day, just before she was due to go home, he came back with a huge bunch of white lilies.

Dear sweet, kind Adam. She really should start making wedding plans. Marrying him did make sense in so many ways.

Rachel fell into an uneasy sleep. In her dreams a bunch of weeping, pierced-nose feminists, each with Adam's bald patch and each wearing candlewick dressing gowns and rubber gloves, were pelting her with Flash-soaked tampons for daring to suggest that somebody should invent a new intimate deodorant for women and call it Fishguard.

CHAPTER 3

Rachel stared down at the damp patch on the bottom sheet and grimaced. Funny, she found herself thinking, that even the rich and famous leaked when they did it. She threw the huge square pillows on the floor, released one fitted sheet corner and started walking round the bed to do the others. Like many ordinary people, Rachel had long nurtured a suspicion that celebs and royals were, due to a dispensation from on high, excused the unpleasant seepages, emissions and outflowings which afflicted the rest of humanity. Dame Judi farting, Sophie Wessex dropping a floater, or Carol Smillie giving birth through anything other than a tiny, specially constructed orifice behind her ear, were thoughts far too gruesome to contemplate.

What she was forced to contemplate however, was that Otto and Xantia Marx, founders of the planet's most renowned interior design company, OP8 UK, who were about to launch what would surely become the planet's most renowned high street fashion label, OP8 of the People, and for whom she had recently started cleaning five mornings a week, had sex much the same as everybody else. She rolled up the bottom sheet and dropped it on the floor next to the pillows. As she started removing the duvet cover she prayed that when she went into the bathroom she wouldn't find skidmarks on the sides of the lavvy.

Wet patches aside, the Marxes seemed to have very little in common with ordinary people. For a start there was their immense wealth. In interviews, for the sake of good public relations and a desire to continue being regular guests at Number 10, they preferred to play down their multi-millionaire status and made much of their socialist thinker namesake, referring constantly and in the most gushing and exuberant terms to Otto's illustrious Great-uncle Karl. In private, however, Xantia owned a modern art collection to rival Charles Saatchi's and a rowing machine which looked to Rachel like it could sleep eight. Moreover, despite sitting on several government working parties set up to combat inner-city poverty, she wasn't the warmest of souls. On Rachel's first day she'd heard Xantia on the phone to a friend suggesting that instead of feeding the Third World starving they should be taught how to become Breatharians.

But it wasn't simply their wealth and fame which marked them out from the rest of the world. The couple possessed a unique sartorial style which was odd, to say the least. Xantia only ever wore purple muslin saris with stiffened shrouds covering her Day-Glo mauve dreadlocks. Otto had a shaven head and wore purple combats and T-shirts.

Then there was the house. From the outside, the Marx pile looked much the same as all the other grand five-storey Victorian villas overlooking Hampstead Heath. The interior, on the other hand, gave the impression, at least as far as Rachel was concerned, that it had been designed by a couple of thirtieth-century androids who had just won the lottery.

In the eighteen months the Marxes had owned the house, they had knocked down every non-supporting wall, removed the roof and all the floors. The vast, eighty-foot-high shell had then been topped with a glass dome and divided up by four immensely thick, semi-opaque toughened glass platforms suspended and encased by steel wires. Bedrooms were obscured by high metal screens on wheels. Only the bathrooms had doors. Living areas were linked by steel and glass staircases or bridges. These were bathed twenty-four hours a day in bright purple halogen light.

'By dispensing with the notion of room *qua* room,' Otto had expounded to Nettle di Lucca when she arrived to interview the couple for the *Sunday Tribune*'s 'Shitegeist' page, in which famous artists and designers revealed their three pet design hates, 'we have rejected an authoritarian use of power and collective regulation. What we have created instead, with carefully weighed juxtapositions of manmade materials and forms, is a functionalist, timeless idiom of pure universal order. The room is dead. Long live the PIAZZA.'

Nettle di Lucca leapt to her feet in the huge purple

31

inflated dinghy filled with cushions which served as a sofa, almost turning her ankle in her flower-filled Perspex platforms as she did so, and burst into dainty, fingertip applause.

'And three cheers to that say I,' she squealed, breaking off from her clapping to rearrange the two chopsticks which had started to fall out of the half ponytail, half spiky-haired fan arrangement at the back of her head. 'Otto, my darling, those are without doubt the most spiritually uplifting words I have heard since Gwyneth's Oscar acceptance speech.'

Rachel saw and heard all this because she was standing at the kitchen sink at the far end of the downstairs-piazza, wiping over the half dozen or so sets of stainless steel wind chimes which the Marx-Engels had hanging about the place for Feng Shui purposes.

Back in the master bed-piazza, Rachel picked up the dirty linen from the floor and headed towards the bathroom and the aluminium laundry bin, which Xantia insisted she call 'The laundry pod, dahling. The laundry *pod*.' She couldn't put the sheets in the washing machine because the damned thing was on the blink. She'd put in two or three bath towels when she arrived at half eight, as Xantia and Otto were leaving for the day, and after a couple of minutes the thing was shudder-ing and jumping across the floor and sounding like a thousand castanets were caught up in the works. She didn't know whether to call out a repairman or start humming 'La Cucaracha'. In the end she'd consulted

Xantia's *Tradesmen to Call in an Emergency* list and phoned the washing-machine man.

She put the lid down on the laundry pod and turned towards the shower cubiculum. Not only was the Marxes' shower huge and purple-tiled, with spotlights in the floor and surround sound speakers, but it was of the 'carwash variety', whereby electronically powered jets of hot water shot out from the cubicle sides as well as the shower head. So far, whenever Rachel had cleaned it, which could only be done from the inside, she'd got confused about which of the shower settings was which and ended up soaking wet.

Rachel stepped into the cubiculum, picked up a bar of Space NK soap from the tiled floor, removed several Marx pubic hairs which were stuck to it and laid it on the wire soap holder. Then she unhooked the hand shower which she would use to hose down the tiles once she'd Jiffed them.

She moved the chunky metal dial on the wall to what she thought was the correct setting. The next second, as seemed to happen whichever way she set it, needles of ice-cold water were shooting down on her. She yelped and leapt out. Her hair was soaked. Swearing, she grabbed one of the Marxes' oversize bath towels from the heated rail and wrapped it in a turban round her head. It was then that she noticed her T-shirt front. It was dripping wet and clinging to her bra. Swearing again she leaned over the bath, took hold of the fabric and squeezed out some of the water. When she'd finished, the T-shirt was horribly creased and only marginally less wet. She started to shiver. There was nothing for it. She would have to borrow a T-shirt from Xantia's freebie pile in the spare bed-piazza. Young fashion designers and companies in search of her sponsorship sent her T-shirts, trainers and sweatshirts 'by the truckload, dahling, by the truckload'. Naturally Xantia, who loathed the sartorially parochial (which for her included Voyage, Comme des Garçons and Vivienne Westwood), wore none of the items she was sent. On Rachel's first day she had pointed out the freebie pile and invited her to help herself.

'Your sense of style is so natural, so unaffected, dahling,' she smiled, holding a canary yellow Giorgio sweatshirt up against Rachel. 'I'm sure you'll find absolutely oodles of things here to suit you.'

Rachel took off her sodden T-shirt and bra and hung them over the heated towel rail. They wouldn't take more than an hour or so to dry. She would put them back on when she left at lunchtime. Then she headed towards the spare bed-piazza. Under the clothes rail was a pile of plain white T-shirts, each wrapped in cellophane. She had just begun ripping into the packet on the top of the pile when the front doorbell rang.

She looked at her watch. If that was the washing-machine repairman, he was half an hour early. Quickly she undid the turban. A moment later, wearing the new T-shirt, she was dashing towards the glass bridge which connected the bed-piazza to the stairs. She'd almost reached the bottom when the doorbell rang for a second time.

'All right. All right,' she muttered. 'Gimme a chance.' She threw her long damp hair forward and back again, hoping it would fall into some halfway acceptable shape. Through the one-way glass panel in the door she saw a tall bloke in jeans and a suede jacket, carrying a blue metal toolbox. She opened the door.

'Matt Clapton,' he said brightly. 'You phoned earlier about the washer-drier.'

'Hi. Sorry I took so long, I was right at the top of the house.'

'No problem,' he smiled, ramming his keys into the pocket of his 501s.

She stood back to let him in.

'Jeez,' he said, looking round and shaking his head. 'I knew I should have worn titanium.'

She giggled.

'The moment I turned into the road,' he continued, 'I remembered I'd been here before. I plumbed in the washer-drier a year ago. The place was starting to look a bit Skylab then, but this . . .'

His eyes continued darting round. After a few seconds they came to rest. On her chest. She couldn't be sure, but he appeared to be trying to get an eyeful of her tits through the T-shirt. She felt herself blush with pleasure. Rachel always pretended to despise men who leered at women, while secretly acknowledging that a wolf whistle from a huge sweaty bloke in a hard hat and CAT boots, could set her up for the rest of the day. It was only as the look became a prolonged stare that her sense of feeling mildly flattered, particularly as her tits, although still pert, were utterly average 34 Bs, turned to annoyance and discomfort.

'Sorry about my hair,' she said smiling, hoping bland chatter might divert him. 'Must look a sight. I was trying to clean the shower cubicle, got confused with the settings and ended up drenched in freezing water. Look at me. My arms are covered in goose bumps.'

He looked up. 'Oh, right,' he said vacantly, before his eyes returned to her breasts.

'OK,' she said firmly, starting to get irritated now. 'I'll lead the way, shall I?'

He just about managed to tear his eyes away. 'Sure,' he said.

As she watched his gaze drop again, her instinct was to ask him to leave, but she just knew Xantia was the type to throw a major wobbly if she came home to find a pile of dirty laundry and the washing machine on the blink. Rachel needed the money too much to risk getting the sack. Instead she stretched her T-shirt neck, and shoved her hand down inside.

'Here,' she said sarcastically, bringing out the hand and thrusting her open palm at him. 'You seem to have mislaid your eyeballs in my cleavage.'

He came to with a start. 'Oh, God. Sorry, what did you say?' he said, clearly abandoning his sexual reverie. 'I was miles away.'

'I'm sure you were,' she said with an icy smile, bringing her hand back down to her side. 'The utility room is this way.'

'Oh . . . right,' he said.

She turned and headed towards the kitchen. He followed.

'So, you a friend of Xantia's then?' he said breezily.

Blimey, Rachel thought. I catch him ogling my tits and he doesn't even have the decency to look awkward – just carries on as if nothing's happened.

'Nope, just the cleaner,' she replied, keeping her back to him in order to make it crystal clear she had no intention of getting into matey banter with him.

'Oh, I see,' he said.

He put his toolbox on the floor, took off his jacket and crouched down in front of the machine. The Wiener 2500 was a brushed aluminium washer-drier of Laundromat proportions which had cost thousands and had to be especially imported from Stuttgart.

'So what seems to be the trouble?' he asked, looking up at her. She explained about the castanets.

'Probably just needs a few squirts of Oil of Olé.' He looked up at her, grinned and began rolling up the sleeve of his denim shirt.

Right, she thought. He wasn't only a letch, he was a smartarse too.

'You reckon?' she said. Her lips had formed a thin smile.

'No, not really,' he chortled. 'Just a joke. Look, don't

37

worry. You just put the kettle on and I'll have you sorted in no time.'

Typical workman, she thought. First he ogles my tits then he starts demanding bloody tea. He was the kind of cocky git, she decided, who rang 'Dial A Prayer' and asked for his messages.

'Perhaps you'd like a nice toasted tea cake with that?'

'Oh God. No, sorry,' he shot back. 'You said you were cold, that's all. I thought a hot drink might warm you up. I wasn't suggesting or even asking . . .'

''Course you weren't,' Rachel said flatly.

'No, really.' Apparently deciding to give up his feeble protest, he turned back to the machine, released the catch and stuck his head inside the drum.

'So what do you think might be the matter with it?' Rachel asked.

'Probably got a foreign body in the works,' he said. 'I find all sorts.'

'Yeah, like lipsticks, jewellery, bottles of nail varnish?' she said in a barely audible murmur.

He carried on poking around inside the machine.

'OK,' he said eventually, his head emerging from the drum. 'Can't tell till I get the back off, but I might have to send away for a new part.'

She nodded, noting that neither the name of the part nor its purpose was forthcoming. He clearly thought she was too much of a bubble brain to take it in. She watched him stand up and hoik his baggy Levis back to his waist. Two minutes from now, she thought, he'll be dragging the machine out from the wall, all exposed beer gut and hairy arse cleavage, saying, 'I mean, take my girlfriend for example. Loses everything. Mind you, she's about as bright as Alaska in December. If a form says "sign here", she writes "Capricorn".'

'If you don't mind, I'll leave you to it,' Rachel told him. 'I've still got masses left to do upstairs.'

She had just finished putting fresh linen on Xantia and Otto's bed when the phone rang. Her first thought was to let the answer machine pick up. Then she remembered she'd given the Marxes' number to her mother and to Sam's school in case of emergencies. Feeling a sudden swell of maternal panic she shuffle-bottomed across the bed and snatched at the receiver.

'Hello?'

'Rachel, thank God I got you. It's me. I'm at Hylda Klompus.'

'Mum,' she said, 'I gave you this number for emergencies.'

'But darling, this *is* an emergency. A catering emergency.'

'Sorry,' Rachel said, frowning in confusion, 'I'm not with you.' She manoeuvred herself so that she was now sitting on the edge of the bed.

'Look,' Faye said, sounding distinctly harassed, 'all I want to know is whether you'd prefer profiteroles or crêpes with hot cherries for dessert. Of course, if you went for the profiteroles then the cream would have to be non-diary – *if* we had chicken for a main course, that is. Then again we could go for the kosher Chinese option. You know – spring rolls, mango chicken . . .'

'Mum, slow down. I'm finding this about as easy to follow as the Oberammergau Passion Play.'

'Hylda says she's got a Sunday at the end of April which nobody's taken yet, and she'll give us twenty per cent off if we book now.'

'Mum, please. Book what?'

'The reception, sweetie. Yours and Adam's.'

'Our reception,' Rachel repeated tonelessly.

'Yes. Look, I'm in Hylda's lounge. She's gone off to make coffee. If we're thinking about a spring wedding, we have to make some quick decisions.' She lowered her voice to a whisper. 'Listen, Rachel, you can't go wrong with Hylda Klompus. She did your Cousin Geoffrey's bar mitzvah in 1974. Wonderful melon balls. Not too ripe. She's over eighty now, but believe me she can still buffet with the best of them . . . Rachel? Please speak to me.'

Rachel let out a long, slow breath.

'Mum,' she said, doing her level best to control her exasperation, 'I told you Adam and I weren't going to discuss wedding dates until he got back from South Africa.'

'I know. But you ended up saying you would think about whether to have a spring or summer wedding.'

'Yes, think about. That doesn't give you carte blanche to go organising receptions without discussing it with us first. I don't believe this. I bet you've told the entire neighbourhood Adam and I are getting married next spring. You have, haven't you?'

'I haven't, honest . . . I mean, naturally I mentioned it to your father. And, all right, I may have mentioned it in passing yesterday to the girl who waxed my bikini line, but Rachel she's from Chechnya, barely speaks English. Who's she going to tell?'

Rachel shook her head slowly.

'Mum, please . . . you can't start making wedding plans until Adam and I give the go-ahead. Just say thank you to Hylda Whatsit and tell her you'll be in touch soon. Now then, I've got to go. The washing-machine repairman's downstairs and I ought to check how he's getting on. I'll phone you tonight. In the meantime please, please promise me you won't book anything.'

'But, darling, what about Hylda's twenty-per-cent discount? Personally I think we should grab it. I mean, if you don't like the Chinese idea we could think about poached salmon. A bit uninspired maybe, but it always goes down well . . .'

'Mum,' Rachel said, gently, but firmly.

'OK, darling. I promise.'

Rachel walked slowly down the glass stairs, replaying the conversation with her mother and hoping she hadn't been too hard on her. Maddening as Faye could be, she meant well. It was a few moments before she got to the bit where Faye had mentioned waxing her bikini line. Rachel frowned.

'What?' she muttered out loud. 'She's waxing? At

her age?' In the thirty-four years she'd known her mother, Faye had never once mentioned owning a bikini line, let alone one she needed to wax. What was more, Rachel had always thought that when women reached Faye's age things started to get a bit thin on the ground down there.

'Every other sixty-something woman starts losing it,' she said to herself, 'and my mother suddenly develops Velcro inner-thighs.' She reached the hallway. As she wandered into the kitchen, she was still puzzling about the cause of her mother's newfound pubic circumstances.

'Unbalanced load,' Matt Clapton declared, turning to smile at her as he finished putting away the last of his tools.

It was a moment or two before she realised he was referring to the washing machine and not her mother's hormones.

'So,' she said, having quickly gathered her thoughts and feeling overcome by a powerful, almost childlike need to display her wit to this berk with his smug, self-satisfied smile. 'Is that "unbalanced" as in demented, unhinged and in need of therapy?'

He closed his toolbox, stood up. The smile turned into a broad grin.

'No, as in too light, diminutive and insignificant,' he said. 'The thing about your Wiener is that it tends to kick up if the load isn't heavy enough. Drum slips off its bearings, which is what happened here. Fortunately

42

I've managed to get it back. Shouldn't give you any more trouble so long as from now on you make sure it's full before you use it.'

'OK,' she said quietly, irritated that the machine had broken down because of her incompetence. He was probably more certain than ever that women's technical nous began and ended with them spitting on their mascara brushes.

'Right,' she said. 'I'll show you out, then.'

He nodded.

'Oh, by the way, I've left the invoice for Xantia on the worktop,' he said as they reached the front door.

She shot him the briefest of smiles and opened the door. It was only as she stood back to let him out that she noticed a copy of *The Clitorati – Heroines of the British Feminist Movement from Wollstonecraft to Widdecombe* sticking out of his jacket pocket.

CHAPTER 4

'So you don't reckon there's any possibility,' Rachel said, biting into one of Shelley's sugar-free, gluten-free, dairy-free alfalfa and kelp scones and wishing she hadn't, 'that a misogynist letch could be reading *The Clitorati*.'

Rachel's best friend Shelley Peach, partnerless, six months' pregnant sometime actress, hand model and health food freak who rented the flat downstairs, carried on stirring mint leaves round in the tea pot.

'Seems highly unlikely,' she said thoughtfully. 'It'd be like Rosemary West owning a copy of *Women Who Love Too Much*.

'Yeah,' Rachel said thoughtfully as she chewed on the scone, while lying stretched out on her friend's battered lime-green sofa. 'That's kinda what I thought – which doesn't explain why he behaved like an arrogant tosser.'

While Shelley poured the tea into two Elvis mugs, Rachel brought one arm under the back of her head and pondered.

'Right, I've got it,' she said, sitting up and swinging

her legs onto the floor. 'How's about this: he's wandering round WH Smith looking for girlie mags . . .' by now she was waving the remainder of her scone in the air ' . . . notices a book with *Clitorati* in the title, decides it has to be porn, that Wollstonecraft and Widdecombe are a pair of lesbian lap dancers, and buys it.' With that she popped the last of the scone into her mouth.

Shelley gave her a withering look. 'Rachel,' she said, leaning over the coffee-table and handing her a mug of mint tea, 'has it occurred to you that maybe you got him all wrong – that maybe you overreacted? Perhaps he wasn't staring at your tits at all.'

'What do you mean, not staring at my tits?' Rachel said indignantly, through the mouthful of scone. 'Shelley, believe me. His eyes were fixed on my mammaries like the Hubble telescope on Alpha Centuri.' She took a sip of tea to wash down the crumbs.

'Ah, you might think they were, but what if he's cross-eyed?'

'Cross-eyed?'

'Yeah. Why not? It's possible. We had a Domestic Science teacher at school who was cross-eyed. Clarence we called her, after the lion in *Daktari*. She could fillet a mackerel and starch a pillowcase at the same time.'

'Sounds more ambidextrous than cross-eyed.'

Shelley thought for a moment. 'Yeah, you could be right. Maybe she was both. You know, cross-eyed *and* ambiwhatsit.' She paused to swallow some tea. 'But anyway you get my gist.'

'S'pose,' Rachel smiled.

Just then Shelley's cordless phone began ringing in the kitchen.

'Oh, God,' she said, tossing the remainder of her scone back on the plate and leaping out of her armchair, 'that could be my agent.' Rachel knew she'd been on tenterhooks for days waiting to find out if her hands had been chosen to pour the blue menstrual flow in an ST commercial.

'Look, I'll go,' Rachel said, looking at her watch. 'I didn't mean to stay so long. Sam's upstairs waiting to be fed and for me to help him with his homework.'

'OK, but just hang on for a sec while I take this call,' Shelley called out excitedly from the kitchen. 'If I've got this gig, I want you to be the first to congratulate me.'

While Shelley took the call, Rachel sat sipping her tea, her eyes wandering round the room. Shelley had only just finished decorating. Rachel smiled. To say her friend's taste was wacky was an understatement. Common or garden wacky worshipped at the altar of Shelley Peach wacky. For a start both the walls and ceiling were painted deep red. A giant silver disco ball hung from the ceiling, the battered junkshop dining table was concealed beneath a floor-length emerald-green sequinned tablecloth, and opposite the Seventies lime sofa was another, covered in pony skin. The lamp-shades were made of bubble gum pink fake fur and in the far corner, suspended above the Astroturf rug and half a dozen pots of plastic crocuses, was a wooden garden swing. Shelley called it her 'tart's boudoir meets the Teletubbies' look. While Rachel adored the humour and outlandishness of it all, Adam, who had visited chez Shelley only once, had walked into the living room, visibly stiffened and declared in a loud whisper that they had clearly just descended into hell and were standing in Lucifer's garden room.

Adam's visit had been a month or so ago, when the room was still awaiting its finishing touches. Now every surface was covered in glam-kitsch plastic ornaments. Rachel's favourite was a twelve-inch statue of Marilyn Monroe, whose white polythene skirt flew up when a button was pressed in her back. Only most of the time it didn't and her head fell off instead. In Rachel's opinion, Marilyn's sole rival for pride of place was the Elvis loo-roll holder in the bathroom. Every time a piece of paper was torn off, he burst into 'Wipe Me Tender'.

The two women had become friends from the moment they met four months ago – on the Saturday Shelley moved in.

Feeling at a loss because she was gigless that night, Joe, her ex, had Sam for the weekend and Adam was at a root canal symposium in Kentucky, Rachel had spent the morning wandering from room to room in her pyjamas, dibbing and dabbing at bits of housework, trying to decide how to spend her day. By mid-afternoon she was still dibbing and still in her pyjamas. It was then, as she stood staring out of the window at nothing in particular, that she noticed a woman pull up in an exceedingly battered East German Trabant, which had been sprayed fluorescent orange. She was closely followed by what Rachel took to be a hired man and van. The woman was clearly her new neighbour. Curious and having bugger all else to do, Rachel decided to carry on watching.

The first thing she noticed about Shelley was her breasts. They seemed to emerge from the car a full three seconds before the rest of her. It wasn't that they were freakishly huge – probably no more than double Ds, Rachel guessed – they just appeared so because Shelley was five foot nothing and skinny with it. With her cropped copper hair, fuchsia bell bottoms and tangerine and purple tie-dyed top she looked like a multi-coloured umbrella, a substantial section of which was refusing to fold down. Rachel found it difficult to strike up relationships with beautiful women with perfect figures because they always made her feel that she should be listed in *The Guinness Book of Yuck*, but with her out-of-proportion tits and slightly too big nose, Shelley appeared reassuringly imperfect, bodywise. Moreover, her garish style suggested a vivacious, off-piste personality which appealed to Rachel. So, when the removal man disappeared just after six, she went downstairs to introduce herself.

By way of a neighbourly gesture she took with her the week-old supermarket African Violet which had been sitting on the window ledge in the kitchen and still looked new.

'Hi, I'm Rachel,' she beamed as Shelley opened the door. 'From upstairs. I just popped down to say welcome.' She held out the African Violet, which she'd wrapped in some used, but relatively uncreased blue tissue she'd found in one of the kitchen drawers. Shelley smiled weakly. Then, as she took the plant, she promptly burst into tears.

'Oh God,' Rachel said, panicking. She assumed Shelley had realised the African Violet was less than fresh and taken umbrage. Her best strategy, she decided, was to make a quick exit.

'Look,' she said, 'I've obviously called at a bad time. I'll come back later.'

'N . . . no, you haven't,' Shelley sobbed. 'It's just that I'm . . .'

'Oh right,' Rachel said in a distinctly relieved tone. 'Don't tell me. You're allergic to African Violets.'

For some reason Rachel was instantly overtaken by the need to invent a story which would justify her choice of gift.

'I'm really, truly sorry. I had no idea,' she started to gabble. 'Thing is, I got to the supermarket late and all they had left were African Violets or roses meant for training. I know for a fact the roses are crap. My mother's been training hers for years and they still don't know any tricks.'

Shelley immediately began laughing through her tears.

'No, it's not the plant,' she said, wiping her eyes, which were huge and green. 'It's lovely, really. You're very kind. I'm just feeling a bit emotional, that's all. Probably down to the move. I'm Shelley, by the way.' She held out her hand. Rachel noticed her fingers were long and exquisitely manicured. 'Please come in.'

She led Rachel through the chaos of half-emptied packing cases into the kitchen. Rachel stood in the doorway and did a double-take. The work surfaces were awash with packets of organic flours, nuts, grains, beans, seeds, lentils and tubs of sprouting shoots. A box of Planet Organic fruit and veg was balancing on a stool. The kitchen table was covered in books of the *Healing Juices*, *Love Your Liver*, *Blissful Bioflavonoids* variety. On the floor beside the water filter was a box labelled *Masticating Juicer*. Next to this were twenty or thirty plastic tubs of vitamins and diet supplements.

'Wow,' Rachel said, walking in and shaking her head. 'Your kitchen makes Holland and Barratt look like the Pop Tart factory.'

'I know,' Shelley smiled. ''Scuse the mess. You caught me in the middle of loading cupboards.' She picked up the box of fruit and veg, put it on the floor and invited Rachel to sit down on the stool.

As Rachel did so she couldn't help thinking that despite the smiles, Shelley still looked bloody miserable.

'I got into the health food kick,' Shelley said, picking up a packet of millet and a bottle of Tamari and putting them on a shelf in one of the cupboards, 'after a nutritionist cured my thrush. I tell you, before I saw her it was so bad I reckon I had an entire flock of the bloody things roosting down there.'

Rachel giggled and passed her some more packets, which she arranged in the cupboard. While Rachel carried on passing packets and Shelley stored them, they exchanged the usual Where do you come from? What do you do? stuff. Rachel talked about being a stand-up and described the first time she'd died on stage during a routine about misshapen vegetables which looked like willies, and how she'd nearly given it all up there and then.

'At least you don't have these to worry about,' Shelley said, pointing to her breasts. 'Ever since I was a teenager, all I've ever wanted to be is a serious actress. Some hopes. Everybody else gets auditioned for parts, I get measured. So what made you decide to become a stand-up?'

Rachel explained how she'd gone into journalism because it seemed a logical safe option, having done English at university.

'Plus by then I was married and we were thinking about getting a mortgage. So I needed a proper job. Thing was, deep down I always knew I wanted to be a comic. Even when I was a kid. My mum would have the family over for tea and I always ended up standing in the middle of the living room, telling pathetic jokes that I'd got from some kids' joke book or other. Then, when I was seventeen I started going to comedy clubs. I saw people like Jo Brand and Julian Clary ages before they were famous. Pretty soon I was writing my own material – in secret, of course. I never showed it to anybody, just performed on my own in front of the mirror. Then one night, two or three years after I'd left uni, a whole gang of us were out on this hen night and we ended up at a comedy club. They had an open mike night. The girls I was with could see I was desperate to have a go, but I was too scared. In the end, they virtually dragged me up onstage. I remember I did this routine about my cat going to the vet to be neutered and how I felt so sorry for him that I'd taken him out the night before the operation to find a cat hooker. Anyway, the audience laughed. They actually laughed. I couldn't believe it. Pretty soon I started doing the odd pub gig at weekends and finally I plucked up the courage to go professional.' Shelley, it turned out, had been born in Upminster. 'So we're both Essex girls, then,' she said.

'Yeah, but don't forget,' Rachel said, 'when we were growing up, the place still had a definite air of gentility about it. Back then, Essex Girls was a hockey team, not an insult.'

Shelley's face broke into a broad grin. Rachel had a sense she was cheering her up.

'Don't know about you,' Shelley said after they'd filled two cupboards, 'but I could murder a drink.'

Assuming she meant of an alcoholic variety, Rachel nodded enthusiastically. Then Shelley opened the fridge and took out a carton of organic cranberry juice.

'Wonderful for cystitis,' she declared, holding up the carton. 'Totally detoxes your waterworks . . . Oh, and I think I've got a packet of sunflower and pumpkin seeds somewhere.' She began rummaging through the piles of packets.

'Tell you what,' Rachel said, doing her best to sound tactful, 'you still look a bit down. How's about we spike it with some vodka? I've got an unopened bottle upstairs.'

'No, I mustn't,' Shelley said uneasily. 'You see, I'm pregnant.' At this point she burst into tears again.

'Look,' Rachel said, 'I don't want to pry, but if it would help I'd be happy to listen.'

Ten minutes later they were sitting on the living-room floor (the junkshop man wasn't delivering the sofas until Monday), drinking cranberry juice. Although in Rachel's case it was more like cranberry-laced vodka juice.

Shelley took another glug of her drink and started telling Rachel how she was three months' pregnant and that Ted, her thirty-eight-year-old boyfriend, had reacted to the news by ending their relationship and asking her to move out because he said he didn't feel ready for marriage or fatherhood.

'And what does the hypocritical bastard go and do? I'll tell you what he does. He shacks up with a sixth-former who's still in train tracks and has a Saturday job frying burgers. Still, at least he's agreed to support the baby. I suppose I should be grateful.'

Rachel, who by now had forgiven Shelley her health food fanaticism on the grounds that she was funny, open and warm, shuffled across the floor and put an arm round her.

'God, I'm really sorry. What a tosser. Going off with a McSchoolgirl when he could've had you and the baby. 'I dunno why we bother to have men in our lives,' She went on knocking back more of her drink.

'I do,' Shelley said, smiling through her tears. 'It's because a vibrator can't mow the grass.' The pair of them burst out laughing.

A minute later Rachel was telling Shelley how Joe, her ex, a sports reporter on the *Vanguard*, had left her for a cosmetics demonstrator who worked on the Estée Lauder counter at Dickins & Jones.

'Total bimbo, I take it,' Shelley said, hiccoughing again. 'Don't tell me – forty-inch bust and so thick she can't remember the recipe for ice cubes.'

'Not exactly,' Rachel said. 'You see, it was a cosmetics demonstrator by the name of . . . Greg. More of a himbo really.'

'Blimey. So your ex – he's . . .'

'Gay? Oh yes, he's gay all right. In fact, he's utterly euphoric these days.'

'Oh my Gawd.'

'I mean,' Rachel continued, 'even though I've met somebody else now who really loves me and wants us to get married, it still hurts when I think about how Joe left me for somebody with hairy knuckles and a thirty-four-inch waist. Doesn't do much for the old self-esteem. Eight years we'd been married. Of course, I missed all the signs. I mean you would, wouldn't you, in a bloke who was six three and a former rugby wing forward. First the sex trailed off. But I thought that was normal when you had a small child. We were both so exhausted.'

She took a couple more sips of her vodka.

'Then there was the way he used to look through *FHM* and all those other men's mags with a high nipple count. He'd stare at a picture of some half-naked bird and go, "Christ, look at the upholstery on that one" – only he didn't mean the woman, he meant the Conran sofa she was lying on. Even when I came home late one night and found him sitting up in bed poring over the *Colour Me Beautiful* book with a Bioré patch on his nose, the penny still didn't drop.'

'Oh, God. Poor you,' Shelley said.

Rachel shrugged. 'Then a few weeks later,' she went on, 'he just comes out with it. Says he's been living a lie since he was a kid, that the time has come for him to face up to his sexuality and he has to leave. Of course I'm hysterical with shock, but he just carries on packing his bags. All the time he keeps going on and on about how he wished to God he'd been born black and not gay. When I ask him why, he says, "Why do you think? At least then I wouldn't have to tell my mother". Eight years we'd been married and the only person he was truly scared of telling was his mad Jewish mother.' She knocked back the last of her drink.

They spent the rest of the evening fantasising about a world without men.

'No more wars,' Shelley said dreamily. 'Just millions

of happy hairy-legged women getting fat on . . . ooh, what do you reckon – avocado?'

'Nah, I'd rather 'avo box of Ferrero Rocher,' Rachel giggled.

A moment later their schoolgirl giggles had turned to hoots. As they neared the knicker-wetting stage, they clung onto each other for dear life, like mates who'd been friends for ever – which they both felt they had.

Rachel carried on playing with the Marilyn statue and as usual couldn't resist pressing the button on her back. There was always the hope that this time, Marilyn's skirt would fly up and her head would stay on. But, as usual, her head shot off on to the floor. Rachel had just retrieved it from under the sofa, clipped it into place and managed to return Marilyn to the the mantelpiece, when Shelley came bounding into the room.

'*Yesss,*' she squealed, punching the air. 'I got it. I only blinkin' got it. Me and the foetus get to eat for a couple more weeks. That was my agent. Said she'd just come off the phone from the woman from the ST company, who apparently not only adored my hands but thought I sounded good too. Upshot is they've given me a line to say. As I pour the blue dye out of the test tube, you'll hear me in voice-over purring . . .' She paused for effect, '" . . . Flowtex Super Menstrual Mats – don't get caught by a downpour".'

'That's wonderful,' Rachel said, going over to her and giving her a huge hug. 'I'm really, really pleased.' She paused and looked at her watch. 'Look, I hate to walk out just as you've had such fantastic news but I really should be getting back to Sam. Why don't you come up later after he's in bed?'

'No, I can't. I really must sugar my bush tonight. It's so overgrown that if I leave it any longer I'll have to take a strimmer to it.'

Rachel snickered. 'You know,' she said, 'my mother's suddenly started waxing her bikini line.'

'So?'

'Well, don't you find it a bit odd that she's started waxing now? At her age?'

'What makes you think she's only just started? She's probably always done it. She's just never discussed it with you, that's all. For women of our mothers' generation, depilation is a very intimate, private affair.'

'Not for my mother,' Rachel said, as she headed towards the door. 'Words like "intimate" and "private" have never figured in her vocabulary. Believe me, a woman who has always been perfectly at ease discussing optimum turd texture over the breakfast table, cannot possibly have a fear of pubic speaking. Doesn't make sense. No, there's something going on. I just know it.'

'Maybe she's going on holiday and she's treated herself to a skimpy bikini.'

'No, she'd have said something if she were going away.'

'OK. OK. I've got it,' Shelley said, starting to laugh. 'Perhaps she's found herself a toy boy.'

'As if,' Rachel said with a chuckle.

Even from the bottom of the stairs, Rachel could hear
Sam's execrable singing. The atonal racket could curdle
milk, she thought, grimacing. She opened the front door,
came in and dropped her keys into her bag, which was on
the hall table. Then she walked towards Sam's bedroom
and peeked through a crack in the door. He was sitting on
the floor in his blue school sweatshirt and grey trousers
surrounded by tapes and CDs. The headphones he was
wearing were plugged into the ghetto-blaster Rachel had
bought him for his birthday and he was singing along
to the music with all the gusto of a well-oiled Japanese
salaryman in a karaoke club. She shook her head. Like
most of his mates, Sam had just started getting into
music. But whereas his friends were all wearing their
parents down by playing the latest chart-topping crap
at full volume from the moment they got home from
school, Sam was wearing Rachel down by playing Barbra
Streisand.

He knew all her songs by heart. He spent all his
pocket money on Barbra CDs, old records and videos
of her concerts. He could imitate her gestures and facial
expressions, and did his excruciating utmost to reach for
those top notes and hold them just like Barbra did. His
room was plastered in Barbra posters. Until a few weeks
ago, Rachel had thought his mania was nothing more than
an irritating, but amusing – if slightly eccentric – stage
her son was going through. It was Faye who had arrived

to babysit, walked into Rachel's kitchen, come to the end of her usual, 'This place is so filthy it should come with a tetanus jab,' speech and then segued straight into how, in her opinion, Joe and Greg were turning Sam gay.

'Mum,' Rachel had laughed, 'Joe rented him a video of *Hello Dolly* one afternoon, that's all, and Sam fell in love with Streisand's voice. Joe thinks the whole thing's as funny as I do.'

'Really,' Faye sniffed. 'And what about Adam? Does he think it's funny, too?'

Rachel said nothing as she remembered the faintly concerned 'Rachel-this-just-isn't-normal' looks Adam gave her whenever Sam disappeared to play his Barbra CDs.

'He's fine with it,' Rachel said a tad defensively. 'Just like me.'

Faye merely arched her eyebrows.

'Look,' Rachel said, 'Joe may have his faults, but he would never try to brainwash his own son. For a start, Joe's been a West Ham supporter all his life, and yet Sam's turned out to be fanatical about Tottenham. And anyway you can't *turn* a person gay. They're born like it.'

Faye had shrugged one of her you-may-think-you-know-best-but-I'm-warning-you shrugs and hadn't mentioned it since. But the damage had been done. Into Rachel's otherwise liberal, logical and intelligent brain, Faye (not to mention Adam) had sewn the seeds of doubt. It wasn't that Rachel had suddenly become homophobic. She hadn't. Even her ongoing hurt about the way Joe had

allowed their marriage to carry on under false pretences
for so long before upping and leaving her hadn't affected
her open-handed, prejudice-free position on gays. If Sam
grew up to be gay she knew it would take her time to
get used to the idea, but she didn't doubt she would
be there to love and support him. But what, she found
herself thinking from time to time, if she was wrong
and her mother was right? Maybe people – particularly
vulnerable, impressionable children – *could* be 'turned'
gay. What if Joe and Greg *were* encouraging Sam to
'develop his gay side'?

So ashamed was she of what she considered to be
her newfound bigotry, that she hadn't dared voice her
thoughts, even to Shelley.

Now she came into the room and stood in front of
her son. 'So, Sam, what do you fancy for supper?'
she said.

He lifted one headphone off his ear and looked up at
her. 'What did you say?' he said.

'Supper. What would you like?'

'Dunno,' he said, shrugging.

'Come on, you must feel like something. What about
sausages and chips or I could grill you a burger.'

'Yeah, OK.'

'Which?'

'The sausages. By the way . . .' He pulled the headphones down so that they hung round his neck. 'Greg
cooked these brilliant herby sausages at the weekend
and then afterwards we had all these different cheeses

61

from France and Italy with this sweet jelly stuff you put on top. The cheese was all runny and smelled gross, but I still tried it 'cos Greg said it was time I started to educate my palate. He said that meant getting your taste buds used to posh food. The cheese was OK, but the jelly stuff was dead nice.'

'So what was it called, this jelly stuff?'

'Dunno. Can't remember. Kwi . . . something, I think he called it.'

'What, you mean quince? Quince jam?'

'Yeah, that's it – quince jam.'

'Quince,' she muttered. 'He's got you eating French cheese and quince jam.'

'Yeah. What's wrong with that?'

'No, no, nothing,' Rachel said through a forced smile. 'Really. It's fine. Couldn't be finer, in fact.'

Sam shot her a puzzled look. Then he turned on his ghetto-blaster, put his headphones back on and broke into 'Secondhand Rose'.

CHAPTER 5

'No, honest, Adam,' Rachel said, holding her mobile in one hand and the steering wheel in the other, 'I love it. Really. It's a sweet, sweet thought . . . and to have sent it by courier from Manchester. Heaven only knows what that must have cost.'

'A fortune, but who cares? It was for you.'

'So, where did you find it?'

'I was in John Lewis in Cheadle,' he explained, 'looking for a new sock-net for the washing machine, when I saw it and I thought, That is just *so* Rache.'

'Oh it is, it is,' she enthused diplomatically.

'It did occur to me,' Adam then said, his tone a tad uneasy, 'that you might have preferred flowers.'

'Believe me,' she said gently, 'it's great. Flowers would be dead in a week. A plastic shoe-rack is something I can cherish for ever.' Naturally, she would have preferred flowers or chocolates, but she didn't have the heart to tell him and hurt his feelings.

'Yeah, that's what I thought,' Adam went on, relieved.

'I mean, we're past all that sloppy romantic stuff now, aren't we?'

'Oh God, yeah. Absolutely,' she said firmly. 'Look Ad, I gotta go. I'm just pulling up outside Mum and Dad's. I'll ring you tonight when I get back.'

'Right. Love you.'

'Love you, too.'

Rachel turned off the engine and picked up the wedding invitation catalogue from the passenger seat. Her mother had forgotten to take it home after she and Jack stayed the night and had rung in a panic an hour ago, begging Rachel to drop it round. The printer had been on the phone, pointing out that she'd promised to return it first thing Monday morning and that it was now Thursday. If he didn't have it back by the following morning, he said, he would charge them for it.

Rachel protested that it was already gone six and that she had to help Sam with his homework, get him bathed and into bed.

'Why can't Dad come and collect it?' There was no point in asking her mother to drive over. Although Faye had passed her test years ago, she'd only driven a couple of times since, on account of having developed a morbid fear of flyovers.

'He's constipated.'

'Oh, right. So he won't have to stop on the way then, will he?'

'Rachel, stop being so obtuse. He's too frightened to

go far from the loo in case the floodgates suddenly open and he gets caught short.'

In the end, Rachel caved in and Shelley agreed to keep an eye on Sam.

Jack opened the door, the cordless phone clamped to his ear.

'They've put me on hold,' he whispered to Rachel, giving her a peck on the cheek and motioning her to come in.

'Who have?' she asked, stepping into the hall.

'The Royal Opera House. I thought I'd take your mother this weekend. It's a surprise. She can't hear me. She's upstairs hoovering.'

Rachel could hear a distant hum of vacuum cleaner. 'But Dad, you hate opera.'

'Yeah, I know,' he shrugged. 'But your mother loves it and she hasn't been in ages. So I thought . . . 'He broke off and began making stabbing motions at the phone, signalling to Rachel that the person he'd been speaking to had returned. 'Oh right, you've got two in the dress circle for Saturday. Wonderful. Look, miss, I'm not a great opera buff. In fact, just between you and me, I think opera's a load of high-pitched squawking. The only way I can tolerate it is if there are a few decent tunes I recognise. You know, like the Can Can in *Orpheus in the Underworld*. Now then, this *Götterdämmerung* – I'm not familiar with it. Could you hum a few bars, maybe?'

Rachel felt herself go crimson with embarrassment.

'You can't? OK,' Jack went on, 'not to worry. Perhaps

there's a bit that's been used in a TV commercial that I might recognise. You know, like that bit of Elgar they used in the Hovis ad.'

At this he started to hum loudly and tunelessly down the phone, and Rachel escaped to the kitchen and put the kettle on.

While she waited for it to boil and he continued his increasingly ridiculous conversation with the Opera House woman, she sat at the kitchen table thumbing through the wedding invitation catalogue. It wasn't the first time she'd done so in the last couple of days. There had been at least three occasions when she'd found herself opening the catalogue with its padded leatherette cover, embossed with silver wedding bells, and having secret fantasies about white weddings.

Before her first wedding, Rachel and Joe, being old-fashioned, unreconstructed Leftie students at the time, had refused to even consider a huge ostentatious Jewish wedding on the grounds that it was a shameful waste of money. On top of that, Rachel knew full well her mother would hi-jack the entire event and that it would all end in lavender meringue bridesmaids' dresses and tears.

As a result, the couple decided on a secret wedding. Without telling either set of parents, they married in a Register Office late one sodden afternoon in November and spent the evening getting drunk in the pub with a bunch of their university mates. When Faye found out she wept for a week. Each night she would lie in bed with

Jack demanding to know how her only child could have done it to her.

'What sort of a daughter gets married and doesn't invite her parents?' Faye sobbed. 'Ever since the moment she came into the world, I have longed to organise her wedding, yearned for the day I would take her to choose her wedding dress. Now she's denied me all that. How could she be so cruel, Jack? How could she?'

When Jack made the tentative suggestion that Faye's broken heart wasn't entirely due to them being excluded, and that perhaps it had more to do with her realising she would never get the chance now to organise a wedding reception seating plan which ensured that her first cousin Irene, who had supposedly snubbed her at Faye's mother's funeral in 1973, sat as close to the kitchen as possible, she bashed him over the head with a pillow and sobbed all the louder.

It took months of begging and pleading on Rachel's part before her mother finally forgave her. Jack's hurt was noticeably more muted. Rachel suspected he was secretly grateful to have been let off the hook, bill-wise.

A decade or so on, Rachel's opinion of huge lavish weddings hadn't changed. On the other hand, she knew how much pain she had caused her mother by marrying in secret and she longed to make it up to her.

The moment Rachel heard Faye coming downstairs she slammed the catalogue shut. If her mother got the slightest hint that she was up for discussing wedding plans, the woman would be on the phone to Hylda Klompus, making unilateral catering arrangements before anybody could say 'ice sculpture'.

Faye walked into the room looking positively stunning. She was wearing a cream woollen suit with a knee-length pencil skirt and short boxy jacket with a tiny collar and large pearl buttons. Her face was fully made-up and her blonde streaked hair looked like it had been newly cut and blow-dried. The effect was only slightly marred by the vacuum cleaner she was carrying and the faint trace of white powder above her top lip. Rachel also couldn't help noticing her mother's nose was running.

'Hi sweetie,' Faye said, putting the vacuum cleaner down. Then she went over to Rachel, cupped her daughter's face in her hands and kissed her. 'So, how's my gorgeous grandson? Still doing the Barbra Streisand impressions? I tell you – you have to say something to that ex of yours.'

Rachel got a whiff of Miss Dior. She also noticed a tiny plastic bag sticking out of her mother's jacket pocket. It appeared to contain the same white powder Faye had round her mouth.

'Mum, I've told you before,' Rachel said, her eyes shooting to her mother's top lip and runny nose and back to the bag of powder again. 'It's a phase he's going through. Please stop nagging me about it.'

Faye shrugged, wiped her nose with the back of her hand and sniffed. Rachel noticed her mother's eyes were watering. As her gaze returned to the plastic bag, her mind started to race. Christ, she thought, the evidence was truly overwhelming. On the other hand it was absurd to think that a sixty-something Jewish grandmother from Chingford had developed a cocaine habit. Unless, of course, her mother was going through some kind of acute psychological crisis. That could explain the bikini waxing. Perhaps she'd developed a morbid fear of growing old. Yes, that was definitely it. Faye was going in search of her lost youth and she thought waxing and doing the occasional line or two would help her find it.

'So . . . Mum, you look amazing,' Rachel said uneasily, deciding not to mention the cocaine until she'd phoned one of the drug help lines and taken advice about the most tactful way to bring it up. 'That suit must have cost a fortune.'

'It did,' she said, flicking more specks off the skirt. 'God, this bloody stuff,' she went on. 'It's everywhere.'

Rachel could hardly believe how open her mother was being about having spilt cocaine down her skirt.

'Do you know, I've breathed in so much of this stuff,' she said, 'I can feel it going to my head. Plus my nose has started running like a blinkin' tap. I must be allergic to it or something.'

'No, Mum, I don't think you're allergic. That's what it does to most people.'

'Really? That's outrageous. They should be forced to take it off the market.'

'What do you mean, "off the market"? It's not exactly on the market.'

'Don't be ridiculous. I bought it in Waitrose in Buckhurst Hill.'

'What?' Rachel said incredulously. 'You bought it in the supermarket?' She had sudden image of her Jewish mother and some Tommy Hilfigered geezer with wraparound shades skulking next to the wet fish counter.

'Yes,' Faye said, nodding slowly as if to a visiting Venutian. 'Come in, Planet Rachel. That's where we Earthlings buy Shake 'n' Vac.'

'Shake 'n' Vac?' Rachel repeated. '*That's* what's in the little bag?'

'Yes,' Faye said with a puzzled laugh. 'What did you think it was?'

'So it's not?'

'Not what? Faye asked, giving her daughter a bewildered look.

'No, er, nothing. Forget it.' So her mother wasn't some bizarre new breed of suburban smackhead. Rachel's relief was almost palpable.

'I was hoovering upstairs,' she started to explain, 'and I dropped the Shake 'n' Vac container on the marble hearth in the bedroom and it burst. Bloody stuff ended up all over the bed, the dressing table and me. At least I managed to scoop up some of it.' She took the plastic bag out of her pocket and put it down on the worktop.

'So, where are you off to, dressed up to the nines?' Rachel said, anxious to get the conversation back on track.

Rachel noticed Faye hesitate before answering.

'Oh, I'm not off,' she said. 'I've been and come home again. An old schoolfriend took me out for an extremely posh lunch in town. We got talking, went out for tea and I only got back when I called you.'

'Who were you seeing?' Rachel said, giving her mother a bemused look. 'You've never mentioned before that you keep in touch with anybody from your schooldays.'

'Haven't I?' Faye said. She sounded distinctly agitated, Rachel thought. She was also starting to colour up.

'No, you haven't,' Rachel said. She watched her mother pick some post up from the worktop and pretend to glance through it.

'Oh,' Faye said, without looking up, 'I'm sure I must have mentioned my friend Tiggy Bristol – Goldberg that was.'

'No, I don't think so.'

'Yes, I have,' she persisted, laughing nervously. 'I've talked about her hundreds of times. Her husband's a millionaire – made his money in paper. I tell you, Rachel, for them it really does grow on trees.'

'Mum,' Rachel said emphatically, 'I think I'd remember a name like Tiggy Bristol, don't you?'

Faye shrugged.

Rachel sat thinking. She was absolutely convinced that her mother had never mentioned the name Tiggy Bristol. She couldn't be certain, but she was pretty sure that Faye was lying. Her edginess said it all. First there was the bikini-line waxing, now she was inventing stories about who she was meeting for lunch. Rachel was positive her mother was up to something. Precisely what, she had no idea.

'So, where's your father?' Faye said, clearly needing to change the subject.

'Dunno,' Rachel said vacantly. She was still mulling over the Tiggy Bristol issue. 'He was on the phone when I arrived.'

Faye went back to the mail.

Just then Jack came into the room singing, 'Everyone's a Fruit and Nut-case, Crazy for those Cadbury's nuts and raisins . . .' He gave Rachel a don't-breathe-a-word-about-the-opera wink.

Rachel smiled back. She looked at him with his paunch and fawn polyester slacks with the elasticated waistband, and then back to her mother with her size ten figure and exquisitely cut suit.

'So, Jack,' Faye said, looking up, 'have you been yet?'

He grimaced and waved his hand in front of him as if to say, 'Don't ask.'

'The thing is with you, Jack, you don't eat enough roughage. Your idea of a balanced diet is a fried egg sandwich in both hands. I tell you, carry on like this and you'll end up with a colostomy. Look, your sister dropped in that Boots enema this morning. Why won't you at least give it a go? She said your brother-in-law only used it the once. And she sterilised it thoroughly afterwards.'

'Rachel, tell your mother she's mad, will you? Who in their right mind uses a second-hand enema?'

'*I'm* mad?' Faye retorted. 'May I remind you that I'm not the one who sees eating a bit of broccoli from time to time, as a threat to his manhood. Like I told you, she sterilised the enema. Rachel, tell your father he should give it a go.'

Having no desire to be drawn into an argument about her father's bowels, Rachel decided to say her good-byes.

It was only as she pulled up outside her flat, having spent most of the journey home trying to work out if Tiggy Bristol was real or an invention – and if she was an invention, why – that she remembered she'd run out of orange juice. It wouldn't have mattered, except Sam refused to put anything else on his cereal. Each morning she went through the same routine, trying to convince him that milk was food and far more filling than juice, but he wasn't interested. What was more, since cereal was the only thing Sam would agree to eat in the mornings, failure to provide the juice to pour on top of it meant he would go to school on an empty stomach. Since there was more of the Jewish mother in Rachel than she cared to admit, she wasn't about to let this happen. If he went to school hungry, she reasoned, he wouldn't be able to concentrate. It then followed that if his blood sugar got dangerously low, he could pass out. If he passed out, he could hit his head. As she turned off the car ignition, there was no doubt in Rachel's mind that if she didn't find some orange juice tonight, by mid-morning tomorrow her son would be lying on a trolley in the Royal Free Hospital, with concussion.

The 7-11 was a five-minute drive away. She decided to pop round the corner to the pub and see if Terry could spare a carton.

As usual on weekday nights, The Red House was pretty quiet. She walked towards the bar. From what she could make out, Terry, the ex-cabbie, diamond geezer landlord, was the only person serving. He appeared to be pulling a pint for a youngish bloke who was sitting at the bar doing a crossword. She was struck by his pallor – he looked like a blood donor who couldn't say 'when' – and his wild Bob Geldof hair.

Having eyed the hair for a moment or two she decided he didn't use Wash and Go – he used Wash and Forsake. She leaned on the bar, a couple of feet from him. Terry looked up, smiled and mouthed that he'd be with her in just a sec.

'OK, Tel,' Rachel heard the mad hair guy say, 'what about three across? "Exclusively female," ending in U N T.'

Terry continued to pull gently on the pump. 'Aunt,' he said.

'Oh yeah, right,' the bloke said, drawing on his fag. ''Course it is. Otherwise three down: "Largest Antipodean country" would've been Custralia.'

Rachel laughed quietly to herself as she watched him cross out his previous answer. He was wearing a very fitted Seventies-style royal blue velvet jacket with wide lapels. Underneath it was a tangerine-coloured shirt unbuttoned to the chest, with a long twin-pointed collar and frill down the front, plus frilly cuffs in the style of Jason King in *Department S*.

He threw the newspaper and pen down on the bar and grinned. 'Right – finished,' he declared. 'OK, I spent a couple of hours on it yesterday morning after *Kilroy*. Three more in the afternoon. Twenty minutes now. So, that's what altogether?'

'Five hours twenty minutes,' Terry said, picking up another glass.

'Wick-id. My best time yet.'

'So, it took you as little as five hours then,' Terry said, putting the pint glass down in front of him, 'to do the *Sun* crossword.'

'Tel, mock not. You know how dyslexic I am.'

He uttered the word 'dyslexic' with two hard, back-of-the-throat, phlegm-clearing sounds common to consumptive tramps and heavily accented Liverpudlians. 'You know as well as I do, I can't count me balls and get the same answer twice. Right, I'm off to the khazi – the tortoise head's starting to show. Put the beer on me tab.' He stabbed out his cigarette in the ashtray.

It was only when he stood up that Rachel noticed he was tiny – no more than five five – and that along with the velvet jacket he was wearing skin-tight black leather trousers and platforms. What a poseur, she thought. But good-looking, too, in a dishevelled, Byronesque

75

sort of way – albeit a half-pint version. He wasn't her type, though. She'd never found men with pale skin particularly attractive. Unlike Shelley, for whom the warmed-up corpse look was a definite turn-on.

'Terry,' Rachel said, suppressing a giggle, 'who on earth is that?'

''im?' Terry said, grinning. 'That's Tractor.'

'Come again?'

'Tractor. Apparently his real name's David Brown. And David Brown happens to be the biggest-selling make of tractor in Cornwall. So everybody calls him Tractor.'

'But he sounds as if he comes from Liverpool,' Rachel said.

'Yeah, I thought that was a bit strange. Still . . .'

'And does he always dress like that?'

'Always. He reckons the Seventies was the most stylish decade of the twentieth century. To be honest I can't see it myself – all those perms and droopy moustaches. And that was just the women.' Terry burst out laughing.

Just then Rachel noticed a copy of *The Clitorati* lying on the bar. Blimey, she thought. What was it about this book that attracted such knobheads?

'Somehow I don't see him as the kind of bloke who'd be into heavy feminist literature,' she said, turning the book over and glancing for a few moments at the blurb on the back cover.

'Oh no, he's not reading it,' Terry said. He leaned forward and looked quickly to the left and right. 'I probably shouldn't be telling you this, but he uses it to pick up women.'

'To pick up women? You're joking.'

'No, straight up. He calls it 'is "ticket to Tottieville". Says it makes him look intelligent and sort of New Manish. Doesn't seem to be having much luck though.'

'Really?' Rachel said sarcastically. 'You do surprise me.'

Terry chortled. 'So, Rachel. What can I get you?'

She explained about having run out of orange juice and asked if he could possibly spare a carton.

'No problem.' He walked the couple of paces to the fridge. She started to tap her hand on the bar in time to the music. Somebody had just put Abba's 'Dancing Queen' on the jukebox.

'There you are,' he said, putting the carton on the bar.

'Thanks,' she said, handing him a fiver.

He turned towards the till. At that moment, Tractor returned and sat himself back down on the bar stool next to Rachel. She continued to face the row of Optics behind the bar, but out of the corner of her eye she could see him looking at her.

'Great book,' he said, picking up *The Clitorati*.

'So I've heard,' Rachel said, turning to give him a half-smile.

'In my opinion,' he said, lighting up, 'it's a profound and thought-provoking historical analysis of gender conflict.' He drew hard on the cigarette.

77

'Funny,' Rachel said, ostentatiously fanning away the smoke, 'those words are identical to the quote on the back cover.'

'I don't believe it. You have to be kidding,' he said.

'See for yourself.' She reached across and turned the book onto its back and tapped the cover.

'I am gobsmacked. Totally gobsmacked,' he said. 'Who'd have thought it? Well, you know – great minds and all that.'

'You reckon?' she said, smiling. He was a total twonk, but part of her couldn't help finding him entertaining.

He didn't say anything for a moment.

'Funnily enough,' he said eventually, flicking ash into the ashtray, 'I know this great clitoris joke. D'you want to hear it?'

'Er, not really,' she said.

'OK, right. Well, there's this woman walking past this pet shop and she sees a notice in the window advertising a clitoris-licking frog. She's intrigued so she goes in and says to the bloke behind the counter, "Excuse me, I'm enquiring about the clitoris-licking frog," and he says . . .' Tractor paused for effect. 'And he says . . . "Oui, madame."'

Tractor started guffawing. Despite herself, Rachel's lips were quivering

'Get it?' he said, between laughs. 'It's frog as in Frenchman.'

'Yeah,' she said, stifling her giggles. Laughing would only encourage him, she thought. 'I get it.'

'I love this song, don't you?' he said after a moment.

'It's OK,' she said.

'So, er, what's your favourite record then?'

By now Terry had returned with her change.

'Linford Christie's hundred metres,' she said, turning away from him to take her change. 'Cheers, Terry. Bye,' she said, then smiled briefly at Tractor and started walking towards the door.

'Wey hey, Terry, I reckon I'm in there,' she heard Tractor say. 'She really fancies me. She'll be back, mark my words.'

Rachel swung round. 'You know,' she shouted back, 'it's such a shame when cousins marry.'

But Tractor didn't react. Instead he was standing in front of Terry, pointing to his leather-clad crotch.

'Terry, as a mate,' he was saying, 'tell me honestly . . . do my balls look big in these?'

CHAPTER 6

'. . . So anyway, sex with this American bloke was so good, even the neighbours had a cigarette afterwards.'

Once again, the audience hooted. Tonight, unlike a week ago, the punters were lapping up her material.

'But they're a funny lot, Americans,' Rachel continued. She couldn't remember ever feeling this relaxed onstage and she was relishing every moment.

'There they are, the richest, most powerful nation on earth, but not one of them's got a decent haircut. Where does your average American go for a cut and blow dry? Albania? And what about all those ridiculous euphemisms they use for anything lavatorial? I was listening to this woman from LA on the radio the other day – you know the type: thin, neurotic, health food freak who looks like she spends her whole life petrified that soon there'll be nothing left in the world to decaffeinate – anyway, she spends five minutes giving masses of full-on detail about what she and this bloke got up to in bed and finally she goes, "And then he went to the bathroom in my mouth."'

The audience roared.

'So, then this agony aunt comes on and says that women should tell their partners how to make love to them. Yeah, right, I thought. Mine has a major eppy every time I tell him how to drive.'

Shrieks from the women.

'Well, that's my time up for tonight,' she said, putting the mike back on its stand, 'but I'd like to leave the women in the audience with this final thought. Remember, not all blokes are arrogant, egotistical gits. Some are dead.'

Whistles accompanied the laughter and applause. Rachel felt herself beaming.

'You've been a great audience,' she shouted above the din. 'I've been Rachel Katz.' She bobbed her head briefly by way of a bow and jogged offstage.

She'd arranged to meet Adam at the bar at the back of The Anarchist Bathmat when she finished her set, which coincided with the start of the interval. When she arrived, having done a quick change in the loo into the new Ghost dress she'd been out and bought especially (having miraculously discovered some space on her Barclaycard), the area round the bar was teeming with people, but Adam was nowhere to be seen. Tonight, their last night together before Adam went off to South Africa for a month, the night they'd planned to go out for a romantic dinner, he had to be late. She looked at her watch. It was just after half-nine. She'd booked the table at Momo for ten. It could take them ages to find a parking space in the West End on a Saturday night. If Adam didn't turn up in the next few minutes they would miss it. Realising she had no option but to wait, she shouldered her way to the bar, grabbed an empty stool and eventually managed to order a Coke.

She'd been sitting there for a couple of minutes when Pitsy Carter, a pain in the arse Aussie comic, appeared pushing her way through the crowd. Rachel groaned inwardly at the sight of the woman who without doubt headed Australia's most unwanted list.

'Oh, hi Rache,' she said with her usual Aussie matiness, grinning from one tiny bleached pigtail to the other. 'Great set.' She punched Rachel playfully, but too hard. Then she turned to order a beer.

'Thanks,' Rachel said, forcing a smile as she began rubbing her shoulder.

'That last bit,' Pitsy went on, shoving her change into her back pocket, 'you know – not all men are arrogant gits, some are dead – totally cracked me up.'

Pitsy – hipster jeans, sleeveless crop top, fleece tied round her waist, brought her beer bottle to her lips. As she did so she revealed one of the tarantulas of thick black underarm hair which had provoked her secret nickname. Since Pitsy, whose real name was Janeece, described herself as Australia's very own Germaine Greer, apparently having no idea that Germaine Greer was a) already Australian and b) not intentionally funny, everybody assumed she kept the tarantulas for political reasons.

'I was racking my brains to work out where I'd heard

it before,' Pitsy continued, 'then I remembered I'd read it on a bumper sticker a few months ago, but it works so much better when you say it out loud.'

Rachel's first inclination was to punch Pitsy's lights out. Her second was to tell her to shut up and shave. Instead she took a deep breath and smiled.

'Oh, right. Glad you think so,' she said evenly. Although Pitsy always made her feel like she wanted to jump for joy – off a tall building – Rachel had made it a rule never to let Pitsy provoke her. Unlike everybody else on the circuit, who thought Pitsy was a spiteful, dangerous, Class A bitch, Rachel had come to the conclusion that, infuriating as she was, Pitsy merely had a kangaroo loose in her top paddock.

'She's just thick,' Rachel said to Lenny, The Anarchist Bathmat's compère when he'd taken her to one side and warned her to give Pitsy a wide berth. 'Believe me, Lenny, she'd buy a zebra and call it Spot.'

'Thing is,' Pitsy said, taking another swig of her beer, 'I was slightly concerned about your mike technique. When I did my comedy class back in Killadingo, they warned us not to get too close because you pop. And I have to say I detected a fair amount of popping tonight.'

'Popping,' Rachel repeated, unable to stop a trace of iciness creeping into her voice.

'Yeah. It's caused by . . .'

'Thanks, Janeece.' Rachel cut across her. 'I've been in the business a while now. I know what causes it.'

'I'm sure you do,' Pitsy carried on breezily, 'but I

always reckon it's useful to have somebody take you
back to first principles. So, Rache, you going in for the
comedy contest, then?'

'What contest?' Rachel said, more than mildly taken
aback.

'You know, the Joke for Europe Contest. It's being
held at The Gas Station in Islington, the last Sunday
before Christmas.' She went on to explain that the event
was being filmed and sponsored by Channel 6, and that
the winner would be given their own show. 'Plus they
get to enter the Eurovision Comedy Contest in Helsinki
next March. Apparently it's going to be mega. Thirty
countries are taking part.'

Rachel burst out laughing. 'The Eurovision Comedy
Contest? Come on, Janeece, somebody's been winding
you up. The Eurovision Song Contest is already a total
joke in this country. Has been for years.'

She went on to explain that people only watched it
to take the piss out of the naff costumes, the entirely
political voting and because the Slovenian goat-herding
songs which seemed to come up every year were so
gruesome they became good again.

Images flooded into her mind of some Turkish stand-up
in a sparkly jacket and a Michael Bolton haircut dissing
the Greeks with a routine about Ariana Stassinopoulous,
a Greek Orthodox priest and a souvlaki; oh, yes, and the
Swedes getting ten points from each of the Scandinavian
countries for some pathetic gag about being God's frozen
people.

'Well, the song contest may be a joke,' Pitsy said, 'but according to my agent, everybody's taking the comedy competition very seriously. I can't believe you don't know about it.'

'Janeece,' Rachel said, frowning and shaking her head, 'are you absolutely sure about this?'

'Absolutely. My agent mailed me the registration form a few days ago. I sent it in and I've got an audition next week. Didn't yours send you one?'

Rachel didn't have an agent. She couldn't afford one.

'No,' she said with an awkward smile, 'he didn't. Must have forgotten.'

'Well, phone him and ask for one. And make sure you tell him how bloody fucked off you are. You don't pay an agent ten per cent to forget.'

'Yeah, you're right,' Rachel said, giving Pitsy another smile. 'I'll do that.'

'Anyway,' Pitsy prattled on, 'I was a bit worried at first that I might be barred – you know, being Aussie and all that – but it seems like it'll be OK, since both my parents were Brits and I have dual nationality.'

'So, you're going in for it then?'

'Does the Chief Rabbi eat pork? Too bloody right I am. The thing is, as the competition's only open to comics who are relatively unknown and there are loads of us out there, they're limiting the number of entrants to seventy-five. So I'd register quickly if I were you. And don't worry, you can always come to me if you're having problems thinking up new material. I've got stacks of old stuff from when I was doing stand-up back in Killadingo that I'd be more than happy to pass on.'

'Really?' Rachel said faintly through her indignation. There may have been some doubt as to whether Pitsy Carter was a bitch or merely an idiot, but the one thing nobody ever disputed was that she had Van Gogh's ear for comedy.

Pitsy majored in dated, hackneyed gags about menstruation, light-bulb jokes and lame insights into life on her Uncle Frank's sheep station in Killadingo. The latter included a routine about her Aunty Gwen drowning in a vat of Vegemite (complete with sound effects). How she'd found her way on the comedy circuit at all nobody could quite make out. That she'd ended up performing at top comedy venues like The Anarchist Bathmat was even more baffling, particularly as she wasn't exactly a hit with the audiences. But for some reason the bookers loved her. If Rachel didn't know better, she'd say somebody was bribing them.

'Look,' Pitsy said, 'I'm gonna pop outside for a quick ciggie – I'm on in a few minutes. You know, Rache, I'm so glad I've got you to talk to because sometimes I get the feeling people take an instant dislike to me. Have you got any idea why?'

'Perhaps it's just to save time, Janeece,' Rachel said with a kindly smile.

Pitsy gave her a quizzical look.

After Pitsy had gone off for her fag, Rachel drained

her Coke bottle then looked round for Lenny to get the lowdown on the Joke for Europe Contest. As luck would have it she spied him almost immediately, heading towards the bar.

'Hi, Rache,' he said breathlessly. 'Great set.'

'Thanks,' she said, flattered. She was just about to ask him about the comedy contest, but he got in first.

'God, I just found out about this earthquake on the Internet – six point nine on the Richter scale.'

'Blimey, that's pretty huge isn't it?'

He nodded excitedly.

Lenny was the world's only seismologist stand-up. Despite being brought up on a sink council estate by his mum, a single parent with four kids apart from him, he turned out to be gifted academically. In his teenage years he'd developed a passion for rock – although in Lenny's case it was granite and bauxite rather than Motorhead and it seemed natural that he would study geology at university. After three years at Cambridge, where he ended up neglecting geology in favour of the Footlights, he decided to see if he could make it as a comic.

But he'd never been able to give up the geology entirely – in particular his passion for earthquakes. These days he spent much of his time searching out new ones on the Internet and logging their details in a school exercise book. That he could be cool, witty and at the same time a bit of an anorak appealed to Rachel's passion for quirky personalities and the two had been great friends almost from the moment they met.

'You know,' Lenny continued, 'I can't believe it didn't make the papers.'

'Where did it happen?'

'Bolivia.'

'How many people killed?'

'Luckily none at all. It happened in the desert.'

She looked at him and started laughing. 'OK, let me get this straight. You seem to be saying that an earthquake in some remote part of Bolivia where nobody was killed should be front-page news in Britain.'

'But it was massive,' he persisted. 'I just can't believe none of the newspapers carried it.'

'Lenny,' she said, 'let me buy you a beer. Then I'll explain to you what makes a good newspaper story.' She got them a couple of Budvars and they sat down at a table. 'So,' she said, 'Pitsy's been telling me all about this comedy competition.'

'God, didn't you know about it?' he said, sounding both surprised and apologetic at the same time. 'I thought everybody knew. I take it you'll be entering.' He put the beer bottle to his lips.

'Dunno,' Rachel said with a diffident shrug. 'I'm not sure I'm quite up to it.'

'Not up to it?' he came back at her, his accent pure Emmerdale. 'Don't be daft. 'Course you are.'

She blushed.

'I mean,' he went on, taking another swig of Budvar,

'if the competition had come up a couple of years ago, when you started out, I'd have agreed with you. You were bollocks then.'

'You know your problem, Lenny,' she teased. 'You never come out and say what you mean. It's so bloody annoying'.

He grinned at her. 'But a couple of years down the road and you couldn't be more ready. This competition is open to unknowns, and face it, Rache – you're one of the best-known *un*knowns on the circuit. You'd be mad if you didn't give it a go.'

'I dunno,' she said again, looking down into her lager.

'I mean it. This is a great opportunity. You mustn't walk away.'

She asked him if he was entering and he told her Channel 6 were looking for somebody to compère the competition and he had auditioned along with a dozen other hopefuls.

'I'll find out in a couple of weeks,' he said.

She promised to keep her fingers crossed.

'You know, Rache, there's no doubt in my mind that you could win this thing. And even if you didn't actually come first, you'd be bound to come in the top three or four, which would still be brilliant. I mean you'd still get your name known and . . .'

He broke off and looked at his watch. 'Oops. Sorry, Rache, I gotta go and start the second half.'

Lenny reached into the pocket of his tartan trousers

and pulled out a copy of *Plate Tectonics and Crustal Evolution*. He opened it and removed a scrap of paper he was clearly using as a bookmark. He handed it to her.

'That's the name and number of the producer guy to ring at Channel 6.' With that he drained his bottle of beer, put it down on the bar and trotted off.

Rachel sat staring at the piece of paper and mulling over what he'd said about her being mad not to enter the competition. She didn't dare share his confidence about winning, but deep down she knew she was just being modest when she'd said she didn't think she was ready. She was. She didn't need Lenny to tell her how much she'd come on in the last two years. Of course it would be brick shittingly scary performing live on national TV, but she couldn't walk away from an opportunity like this. She just couldn't.

Her broad smile faded as she looked at her watch. Adam was nearly half an hour late. She tutted and then decided to pop to the loo to check her make-up.

By the time she got back, there was still no sign of Adam. She was starting to get worried. Onstage a tiny, bespectacled, bobble-hatted Geordie chap she'd never seen before was singing his own version of 'Doe a Deer', but with different, supposedly hilarious words. Mediocre as he was, the audience, most of whom were pretty pissed by now, appeared to be loving it. So infectious was the laughter that even Rachel couldn't stop herself smiling.

As she turned round to help herself from the bowl of peanuts on the bar (she was ravenous by now), she noticed a familiar figure standing at the far end. The battered suede jacket and 501s had been replaced by a trendy long-sleeved V-neck T-shirt and khakis, but she was in no doubt who it was.

'Omigod,' she hissed. 'It's him.'

Xantia's obnoxious woman-hating letch of a washing-machine repairman was standing at the bar waiting to be served. She prayed he hadn't seen her. What if he came over and spoke to her? Should she cut him dead? She threw a handful of peanuts into her mouth and began munching nervously. She wasn't sure precisely when it had happened, but there was no doubt she was turning into a jerk magnet. First there'd been him – the washing-machine guy – then that Tractor bloke at the pub, now the washing-machine wanker again. What she had done to deserve them, she had no idea.

'OK, folks,' she heard the Geordie shout. 'Now I want everybody to join in. You all know how it goes now. Right then. After three . . .'

Christ, Rachel thought, what if he comes over and tries it on? Why did Adam have to be late? She swivelled round on the stool so that she had her back to him.

'Doe – the dosh to buy my beer,' the audience went. 'Ray – the bloke who buys me beer.'

And what was he doing here anyway? Perhaps it wasn't mere coincidence that he was in the audience tonight. Maybe he had traced her through Xantia and was about to become a real pest or even, God forbid, a stalker.

'Me – the bloke I buy beer for, Far – a long long way to the bar . . .'

She downed another handful of nuts. On the other hand, maybe she was being paranoid and he was a harmless, innocent punter.

'So – let's have another beer, La . . . la-la-la-la-la-la.'

Then again, perhaps Shelley had been right. It was just conceivable that he was cross-eyed like she said and hadn't been staring at her tits at all. If he came over, maybe she should give him the benefit of the doubt.

'Tee – no thanks, I'll have a beer.'

'Hello. I don't know if you remember me,' a male voice boomed over the singing. Rachel shot round. The washing-machine repairman was standing in front of her, holding a pint of Guinness and what looked like a spritzer.

'Which will bring us back to Doe – ho, ho, ho.'

He paused to let the laughter and applause die down.

'I'm the bloke,' he continued eventually, smiling what Rachel took to be a deeply sarcastic smile, 'you trod in the other day – at the Marxes'.' He was much taller than she remembered – six four or five at a guess. And more solidly built.

'Er, excuse me?' she shot back indignantly, her good intentions re. offering him the benefit of the doubt evaporating in an instant. 'I think I had every right to be angry. After all, you were incredibly rude.'

'I'm terribly sorry,' he replied, 'but I don't think I was in the remotest bit rude.'

'Not in the . . . ? I can't believe I'm hearing this. You stood in Xantia's hall ogling my tits. I'd call that rude. What would you call it?'

He looked at her quizzically and took a moment to reply.

'Oh, no,' he said slowly, a penny clearly dropping inside his head. 'Do I feel like a berk. I'd come over here to have a go at you, when it was all my fault. Now I get it. You thought I was eyeing up your . . .'

She blushed. His sandy-coloured hair was fashionably short with long sideburns. She'd not noticed that before.

'Well,' she said. 'Weren't you?'

'No, not at all. I was staring at your T-shirt.'

'My T-shirt,' she repeated doubtfully.

'No, honestly, I was,' he said anxiously. 'You have to believe me. You see, until recently I was going out with this woman who owned an identical top. In fact, she was wearing it the first time we met. It was a painful split and seeing it again just knocked me for six, that's all.'

Rachel began shaking her head. 'But it was a plain white T-shirt.'

'Well, yeah,' he said. 'A plain white T-shirt that had *I'm having a party in my pants, want to come?* printed across the front.'

Rachel's jaw dropped. 'That's absurd,' she said with a half- laugh. 'I think I'd have noticed if I'd been wearing something like that, don't you?'

He shrugged. 'You'd have thought so, but I guarantee that's what you had on.'

'You promise you're not making this up?'

'Absolutely.'

There was a warm openness to his face. She was suddenly in no doubt that he was telling the truth. She stood thinking.

'Oh my God,' she said slowly, realising what must have happened. She'd been so desperate to get out of her top after wetting it in the shower, that she'd simply pulled on the first one in the freebie pile as quickly as she could, without so much as glancing at the front. What was more, even when she'd taken it off to change back into her own dry clothes, she still hadn't noticed the motif.

'I'd got my own T-shirt wet, when I was cleaning Xantia's shower and I'd borrowed one in a hurry. I never looked at the front.'

His face broke into a broad grin. She couldn't help noticing the smattering of freckles over his nose.

'Well, at least we've got that sorted,' he said in a friendly way. 'I really am sorry about what happened. I didn't mean to embarrass you.'

'No, *I'm* sorry for being so unpleasant. Shelley – she's my best mate – she said that because you had a copy of *The Clitorati* sticking out of your pocket, I'd clearly got you all wrong. She reckoned you were most likely looking at something else completely because you were cross-eyed like the lion in *Daktari*.'

'Cross-eyed?' he repeated.

'Yeah. Oh, God I'm sorry, now I've embarrassed *you*.'

'No, you haven't.' He was still grinning this boyish, slightly lopsided grin which she couldn't help finding attractive. 'It's just that I've never been compared to a cross-eyed lion before.'

'Look, I'm really sorry. I shouldn't have mentioned it.'

'Please, it's OK. Really.'

Neither of them spoke for a moment or two.

'So, bit of a coincidence you turning up like this,' she said eventually.

'Not really. I've been coming here since it opened back in the Eighties.'

'Oh, right,' she said, wondering how she could even have considered he might be a stalker. 'I'm Rachel, by the way,' she added politely.

'Yes, I know. I just saw your set.' Another lopsided grin.

'Oh, right. You did tell me your name the other day, but it's gone right out of my head.'

'Matt. Matt Clapton.'

'Hi, Matt,' she said, holding out her hand.

He motioned his head towards the two glasses he was holding. 'Er, I don't think I can quite.'

'Oh, God. No, 'course you can't,' she said, feeling herself go red. 'Stupid of me.' Her hand fell back to her side.

There was an awkward silence.

'I thought your set was great,' Matt said eventually. 'Very, very funny.'

'Really? Thanks.' Rachel started twirling her hair round her finger, the way she always did when she felt self-conscious.

'Yeah. You were brilliant. I mean, it wasn't just the gags,' he was becoming so animated now that the beer was starting to splosh onto the floor, 'but your timing's totally spot on. You had the audience eating out of your hand.'

'Honestly? You really think so?' The hair-twirling got faster.

'Absolutely.'

More silence.

'Well, he said, 'I'd better get going. There's somebody waiting for me at the front there.' He nodded his head in the direction of the stage. Rachel turned to look. All the tables in the front row were empty except one where a slim, pretty woman with long blonde hair was sitting nibbling peanuts. Having finished with the T-shirt girl, she thought, he hadn't wasted any time finding somebody else.

'So, good is it, then, *The Clitorati*?' she said as he moved to go.

'Oh, the book. I haven't read it. When you rang I realised I'd run out of paper, so I ended up writing down your address on the inside of the cover. It actually belongs to my flatmate.'

'Oh well, I hope she's enjoying it.'

'He,' Matt said.

'Oh right. Sorry. I just assumed . . .'

They both hovered awkwardly for a few more seconds.

'Right, well . . . see you then,' he said. 'And I really am sorry about the other day.'

'Yeah, me too. Bye.' As he walked away he turned back to give her another lopsided grin.

Onstage, Pitsy Carter was about to lead her less than enthusiastic audience in the second sing-song of the evening. 'Right, all together now,' she yelled. 'Oh, don't go jogging in a white tracksuit when you've got a heavy flow . . .'

'It was the chilli that did it,' Adam groaned as he continued to press the chapati firmly to his nose. They'd used up all the paper napkins.

'Don't be daft, Ad,' Rachel said, watching his blood seeping out from round the chapati and drip onto the tablecloth. 'Chilli makes people sweat, it doesn't give them nose bleeds. You know as well as I do, it's your mother who caused it.'

Having lost their table at Momo, they had ended up at The Taste of the Raj in Tottenham Court Road. Adam had been suitably apologetic about turning up late. He'd spent the morning clothes shopping. Then, when he got home he'd decided to update his wardrobe catalogue. He kept a meticulous card index file of all his clothes – right down to his socks and pants – which told him exactly what shirt, tie and socks went with which suit. It had been gone six before he knew it. Seeing how genuinely sorry he was, Rachel hadn't the heart to get cross with him.

They'd almost come to the end of their meal when Adam's mother Sylvia phoned him on his mobile in a state of near-hysteria. It turned out that her bridge had come out in a piece of nut brittle during *Hettie Wainthrop Investigates* and she was insisting that since Adam was in London he should come over to Stanmore and fix it right away.

'Mum,' he'd said in a pleading tone, 'it's gone ten and Rachel and I are just finishing dinner. Plus, I don't have any instruments with me. Can't it wait until Monday when you can see your own dentist?'

Apparently it most definitely couldn't. He continued his feeble protest for another minute or two before finally caving in. No sooner had he done so, than blood started gushing from his nose.

'I think it's stopping now,' Rachel said, thinking – not for the first time – what an overbearing old bat Adam's mother was.

Gingerly, he pulled away the chapati.

'Yeah,' she said, leaning forward slightly and peering at his nostrils. 'It's fine.'

He put the chapati on his side plate, on top of the bloodied napkins.

'Oh, by the way,' he said nasally, 'I don't suppose you happened to see last Monday's *Media Guardian*? The *Telegraph*'s advertising for a features editor.'

'Adam,' she said gently, reaching out and taking his

hand, 'We've been over this a thousand times. Comedy is what I do now. It's my life. I am not about to give it up.'

'But this is such a great opportunity. Sixty grand plus a car. It's a decent package.'

'Maybe, but . . .'

'OK, OK,' he cut across her, in a resigned tone. 'Forget about the job. Look, there's something else I want to discuss with you, too.'

'Go on,' she said, wondering what on earth was coming.

'I've just been on the phone to Barry, my accountant. He's adamant we shouldn't delay getting married much longer. Thing is, I've done some pretty profitable share deals this year and it turns out that if we get married before 6 April, I can sell my shares and pass the profit over to you without having to pay Capital Gains Tax. I'd be saving thousands and the money would stay in the joint kitty.'

As he took a calculator from his breast pocket, Rachel threw back her head and laughed.

'Do you know, Adam, I haven't got the foggiest idea what you're on about.' She paused and wetted her lips. 'But that dibby thing you do with your finger on the calculator is like pure sex.'

He grinned at her for a moment or two. 'Rache, what I'm saying isn't even remotely complicated. You just can't be bothered to listen, that's all.'

He tapped in a few more numbers. 'Right, just bear with me a sec . . .'

'Adam,' she said quietly, trailing her finger over the tablecloth, 'there's this nationwide comedy competition happening in a few weeks and I've pretty much decided to enter.'

'Right,' Adam said, putting down the calculator, 'I reckon – at a conservative estimate – I could save twenty grand in Capital Gains Tax if we got married before April. Christ, even you have to admit that's not to be sneezed at.'

'No, I suppose it isn't,' she said. 'But about the competition . . .'

He wasn't listening.

'You don't have to make your mind up now,' he was saying, 'but getting married straight away makes extremely sound financial sense for both of us.'

'All right,' she said. 'I'll think about it.'

He put down the calculator. 'So tell me about this competition.'

She explained.

'It's such a fantastic opportunity,' she said, brimming over with excitement. 'Lenny reckons I'd be daft to pass it up.'

'I dunno, Rache,' Adam said, running his finger idly over the rim of his beer glass, 'I hope you're not over-stretching yourself. I mean, the opposition is bound to be pretty fierce.'

'I know,' she said. 'It's a risk, but it's one I'm prepared to take.'

'Look, I can't tell you what to do. Though I have to

say that in my experience, competitions are for losing, not winning, but if it's what you really want to do . . .'

'It is, Ad,' she said, her face lit up with enthusiasm. 'Believe me, it is.'

'Rachel,' Adam said, 'you didn't tell me Austrians had moved into your building.'

'They haven't,' she said.

'So why is the front door being opened by a bloke wearing Lederhosen and a Tyrolean hat?'

'What?' Rachel leaned across Adam and peered out of the car window. 'Blimey. Who on earth's that?'

'I don't like this,' Adam declared. 'Look, you stay here, I'm going to check him out.' He opened the car door.

'Adam,' Rachel hissed, pulling him back. 'For Chrissake, be careful. He might have a . . .'

'A what?' Adam said. 'A semi-automatic Bratwurst? Don't be daft.'

'I'm not being daft,' she came back at him, 'and I'm not having you confront him on your own. I'm coming, too.'

By the time they reached the door, the man had disappeared inside. It then took Rachel several seconds rummaging through her bag before she found her keys. The moment they stepped into the hall, they spotted him hovering outside Shelley's flat.

'Er, excuse me,' Rachel called out. 'Can I help you?'

The man swung round. He was tiny, with a fair-sized

paunch. He also had a beard and was wearing small gold-rimmed glasses.

'Oh, hi, Rache. Hi, Adam,' he said – except it wasn't the voice of a he. He was a she.

'Shelley?' Rachel said uncertainly. 'Is that you under there?'

Shelley pulled off the beard and burst out laughing. ''Course it is.'

Adam rolled his eyes.

'I've been to a fancy dress party. We had to go as our favourite hero or heroine.'

'So,' Adam said, 'who did you go as? Captain Von Trapp's batman?'

'Hah, hah. Oh, come on – isn't it obvious who I am?'

Rachel and Adam looked at her and then at each other.

'Not really,' Rachel said. 'No.'

'It's easy,' Shelley urged. 'Guess.'

'Nope. Give up,' Rachel declared.

'I'm Dr Joseph Bircher. You know, the bloke who invented Muesli.'

'Oh, right,' Rachel said diplomatically. 'I bet that's a first for a fancy dress party.'

'Yes,' Adam said. 'Very wholegrain, I'm sure.' Then he whispered to Rachel that Bircher was Swiss. Rachel elbowed him in the ribs.

Shelley feigned offence at the wholegrain remark and then invited them in for a drink. Adam made noises about having to get to his mother's, but Rachel said five minutes wasn't going to make much difference.

While Shelley disappeared in search of a bottle of Château Noshit Aussie organic, Adam went to the loo. When he came into the living room, he winced at the décor as if he were seeing it for the first time, flicked an imaginary spot of dirt off the ponyskin sofa and sat himself down gingerly next to Rachel. A moment later Shelley came in, carrying two glasses of red wine.

'The thing about so many wines,' she said, 'is that they put anti-freeze in them to give them a kick. This stuff is totally additive free.' She handed a glass to each of them and then went back to the kitchen to fetch her glass of cranberry juice.

Adam took one sip of wine and pulled a face. 'I can understand why they add the anti-freeze,' he muttered.

This time Rachel kicked him. 'Be quiet,' she hissed. 'Shelley'll hear you.'

Just as Shelley walked back into the room, Adam's mobile went off. It was his mother again.

'I'm sorry, but I really do have to go.' He stood up and kissed Rachel briefly on the lips. 'It's probably best if I sleep at Mum's tonight. I'll pop round tomorrow to say goodbye.'

Rachel smiled, doing her best to conceal her disappointment. They hadn't done it in ages and now they wouldn't until he got back from South Africa.

'OK. See ya.'

He gave Shelley a hesitant, awkward peck on the beard and left.

After Adam had gone Rachel told Shelley about the comedy competition and about having met Matt Clapton again. She listened, made highly encouraging noises about the competition and laughed when Rachel explained the mix-up over the T-shirt, but Rachel could tell her friend was preoccupied.

Eventually their conversation fell into silence.

'You know,' Shelley said eventually, as she carried on swinging on the garden swing and dragging her feet over the Astroturf. 'You're so lucky to have a somebody who loves you.'

Rachel's smile was tinged with guilt.

'I mean,' Shelley went on, 'at this party tonight, there wasn't one bloke who seemed even remotely interested in me.'

Rachel was tempted to say this probably had more to do with the beard and Lederhosen than any innate unattractiveness, but she didn't.

'Look,' she said, 'I know how hard it is to find a decent bloke with all the jerks and wallies out there.' She told Shelley about Tractor, the Seventies remould who'd tried to pick her up in The Red House the other night.

'Oui, madame,' Shelley chortled when Rachel got to the clitoris-licking frog joke. 'That's hysterical. So what does he look like, this bloke?'

Rachel told her.

'So exactly how pale would you say his skin was?'

'Very. You could rent him out for hauntings.'

'Really? That pale . . .' The idea clearly turned Shelley on. 'Plus I've always found that whole Seventies thing rather sexy. I mean it's so cheesy, it actually gets stylie again – a bit like Leo Sayer or Vesta curry.'

'Shelley, he uses *The Clitorati* to pick up women. Is that sad or what?'

Shelley shrugged. 'I think it's sweet in a naff kind of way. Maybe he's just shy and it's his way of hiding it.'

'Yeah, right,' Rachel said dismissively.

'So . . . *did* his balls look big in the leather trousers?'

'I didn't investigate,' Rachel said, giggling and pulling a face.

Shelley pretended to go all pathetic. 'Sorry. It's just that I'm a poor pregnant woman who isn't getting any.'

'Oh, come on,' Rachel said warmly, 'there's somebody out there for you. I just know it.'

'Not who'll take on another bloke's baby.'

Rachel stood up, went over to Shelley and put her arm round her. 'Yeah he will,' she said, hugging her tight. 'Just wait and see.'

'You reckon?' Shelley smiled doubtfully.

'Promise – or my name's not an anagram of Czar Hat Elk.'

CHAPTER 7

'I agree,' Rachel declared. 'They are completely and utterly gross. Sam, look at me – I would never, ever ask you to wear one. And that's a promise. Grandma had no right to start talking to you about pageboy suits – particularly not cherry-red velvet ones. Apart from anything else, it's far too early. Adam and I haven't even set a wedding date yet. But I promise that as soon as we have, you will hear about it from me, not Grandma. OK?'

Sam nodded and carried on eating his Coco Pops, which were floating disgustingly in orange juice. Rachel picked up a half-slice of buttered toast and disappeared once more behind the *Guardian*, but she couldn't concentrate because her mind kept going back to what had happened – or to be precise, *not* happened – when Adam came round the day before to say goodbye.

When he arrived, an hour or so after Rachel had got back from dropping Sam at his best mate Charlie's house, where he was going to spend the day, she had answered the door wearing nothing but a cook's apron and a sexy smile. She had kissed him and led him into the kitchen where she was in the middle of preparing a scrambled egg and smoked salmon brunch.

'C'mon,' she'd purred, handing him a glass of champagne, 'why don't we take all this to bed?'

'Wonderful thought, Rache, but the thing is, my mum cooked me kippers before I left.'

'Oh, right,' she said. 'Stupid of me, really. I might have known she'd cook for you. I should have phoned and checked with you first.'

'Might have been an idea.' He went on to say that tempting as it was, he didn't have time for sex because he had to rush back and get started on his packing.

'Come on, Ad,' she said, putting her arms round him. 'This is the last chance we'll get.' She removed one of her arms from round his neck and began undoing his jeans belt.

'Rache, not now,' he'd said, clamping his hand over hers. 'I really don't have time. It's not just my packing I've got to do, there's a whole load of stuff I must get in the post before I leave, not to mention a pile of bills waiting to be settled.' He paused and lifted her chin, which had fallen almost to her chest. 'Come on, Rachel,' he said softly. 'What's a month when we've got our whole lives to look forward to? Now then, why don't you go and put something warm on. You must be freezing.'

Lying in bed on Sunday night, she'd worked out it was now nearly six weeks since they'd had sex. She decided that going down on him the other night in the Rotherhithe Tunnel didn't count because he hadn't returned the gesture, not that he really could have done at the time without creating a whole new driving offence. Adam seemed to be forever producing excuses for not making love to her. If it wasn't that her parents were in the flat and Faye might be listening, it was that he had to dash back to Manchester. She put it down to him working too hard and did her best to pretend she didn't mind, but she did. She minded a lot. What she couldn't understand was why, when he was so desperate to marry her, he was so off sex. It just didn't make sense. Then, just before it got light, Rachel's emotional pendulum took a more generous-spirited swing. She decided she was being far too hard on him. Everyone knew the sex part of a relationship cooled after a year or so. Look at her and Joe. (For some reason she forgot that sex with her ex had cooled primarily because he was gay.) Adam might not be wildly demonstrative, she thought, but he showed his love in more practical ways.

'Sam,' she said eventually, putting down the newspaper, 'you know, when Adam and I get married, he won't try to take the place of your dad. You do understand that, don't you?'

'He'd better not. 'Cos nobody could ever, *ever* take the place of Dad.'

'But you do like Adam, don't you?'

'He's OK,' Sam said with a shrug.

It was the same response she always got when she asked Sam how he felt about Adam. No matter how often or hard she pressed him, he would never say more than Adam was 'OK', or 'all right'.

'He buys you great presents,' Rachel persisted. 'And those POKÉMON cards cost him a fortune.'

Another shrug.

'And he spent ages the other day helping you with your maths homework.'

'Yeah, except he tells me I shouldn't subtract, I should deduct.'

She giggled. 'Oh, don't take any notice,' she said. 'That's just Adam's idea of a joke.' She went back to her newspaper.

'Mum,' Sam said thoughtfully, 'when you get married, could Barbra come?'

'Barbara who?' Rachel said vacantly, from inside the newspaper. 'Bit of an old-fashioned name for a kid.'

'You know,' Sam said impatiently. '*Barbra.*'

'Sorry, darling, my brain's not quite got in gear yet. I'm not with you.'

'Oh Mum, come on . . .'

Suddenly the penny dropped. 'What?' she said, lowering the newspaper. 'You mean Barbra as in Streisand?'

He nodded eagerly.

'You want Barbra Streisand to come to my wedding?'

'Yeah, can she?'

In an instant her doubts about Sam's sexuality resurfaced. Not that they had ever really gone away. She still had no problem with him growing up to be gay, it was just that she worried about how he'd cope as a teenager.

She knew for a fact that gay adolescents could become very isolated and lonely. Had it been a football hero he'd wanted to invite, she wouldn't have turned a hair. She would have let him get on with it and simply said, 'I told you so,' when all he received by way of a reply was the standard letter and signed photograph. But because of her feelings about his Barbra Streisand obsession she felt compelled to discourage him.

'Sam, don't be daft,' Rachel said with an uneasy half-laugh. 'She's Barbra Streisand mega-rich super star, not Barbra Streisand, cheap nightclub turn, available for weddings and bar mitzvahs. I mean, perhaps she'd sing for Michael Jackson or the President of the United States, but even then she'd charge hundreds of thousands of pounds.'

'No,' Sam cut across her. 'I mean maybe she'd *like* to come – as a guest. She could sit with us on the top table.'

'Oh darling, that's very sweet,' Rachel said, smiling, 'but she doesn't know our family. Why on earth would she want to come to a wedding where she doesn't know a soul?'

'But I feel like I know *her*,' Sam said. 'I can sing all of her songs. I've seen all her films stacks of times.'

'So have thousands of people, Sam. But you can't expect her gratitude to extend to showing up at their weddings.'

'You never know,' he persisted, 'she might come. I could write and ask her.'

'Sam, stop being silly,' Rachel said, beginning to get exasperated. 'You cannot possibly invite Barbra Streisand.'

'Why not?'

'Because apart from anything else we haven't even set a date yet.'

'I could at least find out if she'd like to come.'

Rachel let out a long slow breath. 'Look, if you've had enough to eat, go and put your lunchbox in your school bag'.

'Can't I at least . . . ?'

'No,' she said firmly. 'That's enough. Now off you go. Your dad'll be here in a minute.'

Every so often Sam spent a week with Joe and Greg. They enjoyed having him stay. Sam adored going there because he got spoiled rotten, and it gave Rachel a chance to spend the evenings working on her comedy. Usually they would pick him up on a Monday after school, but today, as Rachel was due at Xantia's half an hour earlier than usual, Joe had agreed to take Sam to school.

Clearly frustrated, Sam got down from the table and ran off towards the kitchen. A moment later the intercom buzzer went. Rachel stood up, went to the front door and lifted the handset.

'Oh hi, Joe. Come on up.'

She left the door ajar and went back to the table to gather up the breakfast things. Her mind returned to Joe and Greg and whether they really could be influencing Sam's sexuality. As usual she did her best to convince herself that sexuality had far more to do with nature than nurture. What was more, she thought, there was absolutely nothing stereotypically gay about Joe which could influence Sam – even if it were possible. He still went to see West Ham every Saturday. He was tall, broad-shouldered and with his dark curly hair and Semitic features he looked more like an Israeli paratrooper than a caricature gay. Greg on the other hand was blond and gamine and just a tad too Liberace for her liking. But then again, what about Adam? The man covered his flat in Clingfilm and kept an index file of all his clothes, for Chrissake. If that wasn't stereotypical gay behaviour she didn't know what was. But because she knew Adam was straight, it had never occurred to her that *his* bizarre idiosyncrasies might have an adverse effect on Sam.

There was a tap on the door and Joe walked in.

'Wotcha,' he said with a tentative half-smile. Two years after their divorce, the hostility had gone, and in recent months, Rachel and Joe had been getting on better. But there was still a trace of awkwardness between them.

'Hello,' Rachel said, with an identical smile. 'Greg not with you? I thought you said . . .'

'Yeah, he's parking the car. He'll be up in a minute.'

'Well, I hope he's not going to be long,' Rachel said anxiously, as she continued to stack plates. 'I don't want Sam being late for school. Now look, I've packed his eczema cream. It's quite bad behind his knees. Please,

please make sure he puts it on before bed. And it occurred to me that maybe he should lay off dairy for a while. It seems to aggravate it.'

'Rache, will you stop being a Jewish mother for five minutes? Greg and I can cope, you know. He'll be fine.'

'Sorry,' she said, allowing a smile to creep onto her face. 'I worry about him when he's away, that's all.'

At that moment Sam ran in from his bedroom and threw himself into his father's arms. Joe kissed him and held him in a tight bear hug.

'Hi. So how's my boy?' he asked, letting Sam go and ruffling his hair.

'Brilliant,' he said. 'Listen, Dad, after school can we go to that old record shop we went to a few weeks ago – you know, the one in Finsbury Park? They might have some more Barbra LPs.'

'Yeah. Sure,' Joe said.

'Great. By the way, Mum says when she gets married to Adam I'm not allowed to invite Barbra Streisand to the wedding. She says she wouldn't come, but I think I should at least be allowed to write and ask her . . .'

'Whoa, Sam. Slow down.' Joe turned to Rachel. 'What, you and Adam finally got round to naming the day?'

'No, not quite,' Rachel said, shaking her head. 'It's just my mum getting ahead of herself and making announcements before there's anything to announce. Sam'll explain.'

'OK. So, Sam,' he said, ruffling his son's hair again, 'what makes you think Barbra Streisand would want to come to Mum's wedding?'

Before Sam had a chance to reply, the living-room door opened and Greg came in. God, Rachel thought, the man minced so much, cattle must shudder when he passed.

'Hiya,' he said to Sam, giving him a playful punch on the shoulder. He then air-kissed Rachel and presented her with a House of Fraser carrier bag.

'Oooh,' she said, 'what's this?' She looked inside. It was full of cosmetic samples.

'I always say beauty comes from within,' Greg twinkled. 'From within jars, tubes and palettes.'

'Greg, thanks,' Rachel gushed. 'These are wonderful. You are kind.'

'Yeah, well when you work on a cosmetics counter you can't move for freebies. I must confess I helped myself to the *Gommage Polissant* and the *Lift Jour Anti-Rides*, but I left the rest for you.'

She thanked him again. 'And, wow, Greg, that's some, er, fuchsia cashmere polo-neck you've got on.'

'Isn't it?' he said proudly. 'To be honest, it was a toss-up between the Valentino pink or the Yves St Laurent, but Joe persuaded me to go for the Valentino. I think he was right. It's just a tad softer with my skin tone.'

'Mmm . . . So,' she went on with faux breeziness, 'what else have you guys got planned for after school, apart from going hunting for old Barbra LPs?'

'Greg and I thought we might pop into that new kitchen shop in Hampstead,' Joe told her. 'We badly need a new set of frying pans.'

'And when we get back, Sam can help me season them,' Greg promised.

'Cool,' Sam piped up.

'Great. Marvellous,' Rachel said. 'Couldn't be better. And now you'd better get going – it's almost half past. Sam's stuff is in the hall.'

'Hi, it's only me,' Rachel called from the hall as she closed the Marxes' front door.

'Oh, hello Rachel,' Xantia shouted back. 'Come into the living-piazza. Otto and I are just finishing our meditation.'

Rachel hung her jacket in the clothes pod. As she made her way into the living-piazza she could hear the soft, slow beating of a drum and Xantia and Otto chanting the same word over and over again. She couldn't make it out, but it sounded a lot like 'Taramasalata'.

By the time she reached the living-piazza, their chanting had stopped and Xantia was sitting cross-legged on the floor, slowly rotating her head. Otto, who was on his feet, bent down to pick up the small African drum.

He shot Rachel a brief, distant smile before heading out of the living-piazza. Rachel couldn't make him out. On the one hand, Otto was this reserved, virtually silent artist who only became truly animated when other designers, or journalists like Nettle di Lucca from the

116

Sunday Tribune's 'Shitegeist' page came to the house to talk to him about his work. On the other hand, if she tried to imagine him without the purple clothes, what she saw was a very ordinary-looking, slightly overweight Jewish man in his mid-forties – not unlike a younger, balder version of her father. Like her father, too, Otto was an obsessive grazer and snacker.

Occasionally, Otto and Xantia spent the mornings at home working on interior design projects or sketching clothes for the new OP8 of the People range which was going to be launched in the New Year. It was quieter there than at their office in South Kensington – particularly with Rachel around to answer the phone and shield them from everything but the most dire of design emergencies.

Although Xantia would pop into the kitchen mid-morning to grab a yoghurt or a couple of Ryvitas, Otto seemed to be forever rooting through the cupboards and fridge for snacks. After a few minutes he would go back upstairs with a box of Jaffa Cakes, a packet of salt and vinegar crisps, or a couple of cheese and Marmite bagels and a glass of milk. An hour or so later, he would be back again with his snout in the fridge.

What Rachel found odd about Otto's snacking – apart from the amount – was that when she went upstairs to tidy the work-piazza after the Marxes finally left for the office, she could never see any empty wrappers or debris. Even odder was that although the Marxes were working on the first floor of an open-plan house where the slightest sound carried and could be picked up yards away, she never heard a peep from them. There was no chatter, no sound of them moving around; just silence. What was more, whenever she went upstairs to clean or put something away, they were never at their desks. At first she assumed one of them was in the loo and the other had popped out for a few minutes. But she never once heard the front door open, or the loo flush.

Funny, that.

'Now then,' Xantia said, as usual eyeing what Rachel was wearing (tight Lycra T-shirt, baggy drawstring trousers with dried-up baked bean down them) and wincing, 'the reason I asked you to come early today is that we're having guests tonight for dinner and I thought that to save me time, on top of the cleaning you could do some shopping and a bit of the food preparation. Naturally, I'll pay you extra.'

'Great,' Rachel said happily. 'I can always do with the money and I haven't got to dash home today to do the school run.'

'Excellent. You see, I always make it a rule to cook myself. I think catered dinner parties are so impersonal, don't you?'

'Oh, absolutely,' Rachel said, nodding. Of course she didn't have the remotest idea what she was talking about, never having been to anything catered that wasn't a wedding or a bar mitzvah – or once, in the case of her rich Uncle Sid who'd made it big in expandable document folders – a funeral.

'So,' Rachel continued, 'who's coming?'

'Oh, just the Blairs, the Prescotts and Joely . . . Richardson, that is,' Xantia said casually, sliding the Feng Shui coffee-table book to the other side of the coffee-table.

'Wow.'

'Yes, it is a bit. Security were here all day yesterday.'

'So, what are you cooking?' Rachel asked.

'Well,' Xantia enthused, 'I had this brilliant idea. I thought that seeing the Prescotts are northerners they would feel more at home if I served fish and chips.' She leaned over the coffee-table again and moved the Feng Shui book a fraction to the left. 'What do you think?'

'I thought it looked fine where it was to start with,' Rachel said.

'No, no,' Xantia said testily, 'not the book. My idea. What do you think?'

'Well, it's certainly plain,' Rachel said diplomatically. 'You can't go wrong really.'

'Precisely. Now then, the fish is being delivered later on, but I thought you could pop to Waitrose and get the potatoes, gherkins and guacamole.'

'Guacamole?' Rachel said, perplexed.

'Yes, you know, the green stuff. They always serve it with fish and chips.'

'Xantia, that's not guacamole, it's mushy peas.'

'Really? Goodness. Oh well, whatever. Get those then – and some sponge cakes, a drum of Birds custard and

119

a bottle of Emva Cream to make a sherry trifle. And I thought you could peel and chip the potatoes this morning and leave them in water in the fridge.'

'Fine. No problem,' Rachel said.

'Otto and I are going to work on some sketches up in the work-piazza for the next couple of hours and then we'll be off. I'll come and see how you're getting on before we go. Oh, I've left some money in the kitchen.'

With that, she adjusted her shroud and disappeared upstairs.

Rachel got back from Waitrose at about half ten. As she lugged four bags of shopping into the kitchen she almost collided with Otto, who was coming out. He had half a baguette filled with bacon in one hand and a can of Coke in the other. He offered to help her with the shopping. She thanked him, but said she was fine and he disappeared upstairs.

She had just begun chipping the potatoes when the doorbell rang. She rinsed the starch off her hands and trotted to the door wiping her hands down the front of her trousers as she went.

'Matt,' she said, surprised but inexplicably pleased to see him. 'Xantia didn't mention you were coming. Has the washing machine been playing up again?' She noticed he was wearing a trendy black windcheater over charcoal combats.

'No, no, the machine's fine.' He sounded a tad nervous, she thought. 'At least, I'm assuming it is. I mean, you'd know better than me as you work here. No . . . it's just that it occurred to me that Xantia may have lost the instruction manual for the Wiener. As I explained to you the other day, it's a pretty temperamental machine, the Wiener, and you need to know what you're doing. And as luck would have it I came across a spare manual while I was sorting through some papers. So I, er, thought I'd drop it round.'

'Oh, that's really kind,' she said, smiling and reaching out to take the booklet.

He smiled back.

She was suddenly aware that a) their eye-contact was lasting fractionally longer than it should between relative strangers and b) she was wearing no make-up.

'I'll . . . um . . . get Xantia, shall I? She's upstairs working.'

His face fell. 'What? She's here?' he said uneasily. 'It's just that I assumed . . . I mean, I thought she'd be at the office. Please don't disturb her. It really isn't that important. I just thought I'd bring the manual round, that's all.'

'Look,' Rachel said after a slightly awkward pause, 'I was just going to put the kettle on. Why don't you stay for a cuppa? I'm sure Xantia wouldn't mind after you've gone to so much trouble.'

He hesitated. For a moment she thought he was going to say yes.

'It's really kind of you, but I think Xantia might mind.

I don't want her to think you're slacking. Anyway, I'd better get going. I'm already running really late.'

Disappointment shot through her.

'But I'm sure she won't mind,' she persisted. 'Really.'

'No, honest. I should be off.'

'OK,' she said. Just then she heard the phone ringing in the kitchen. 'Oh, God, I'd better get that. Otto and Xantia have got me fielding their calls.'

'No problem,' he said.

'See you again maybe.'

'Yeah, sure,' he nodded.

She closed the front door and dashed towards the kitchen. On the way it occurred to her that Matt had only brought the washing-machine manual round as an excuse to see her, and that he might possibly fancy her. She blushed and couldn't help feeling mildly horny at the thought. That lopsided grin of his was very, very sexy. Then she remembered the blonde woman she'd seen him with at The Anarchist Bathmat. What was she thinking? The man had a girlfriend. A beautiful blonde one. He'd brought round the manual, she reasoned, simply because Xantia was a rich and famous client and it was important for him to keep her sweet. That way she wouldn't hesitate to recommend him to her rich and famous friends.

She picked up the phone. It was Kermit, Xantia's Parisian assistant at OP8, known affectionately as Kermit the Frog.

'Look, Kermit, if it's a real emergency,' she said, 'I'll

get her to the phone. But can you just give me some vague idea what it's about? . . . Woah, let me see if I've got that. Some avant-garde Austrian sculptor, yeah, is exhibiting his version of Lego at the Klagenfurt Design Fair, tomorrow, starting with a Build-Your-Own-Auschwitz kit. Even though it's meant to be an anti-fascist statement, you want to know if Otto and Xantia still want OP8 to have a stall there.'

She dashed up to the work-piazza. As usual, there was no sign of Otto or Xantia. It occurred to Rachel that maybe they'd nipped off for a quickie in the bed-piazza, but there were no sounds coming from behind the screen. She checked the bathroom, ran over the bridge, climbed the stairs to the next level and then the one after that. Everywhere was silent and empty. Finally she came downstairs, checked the main living-piazza and the front and back gardens. She could only assume they had gone off to work without saying goodbye. She went back to the phone intending to tell Kermit that the Marxes appeared to have left for the office, but she'd taken so long that he'd hung up.

'Rachel,' Xantia called from the hall, just as Rachel was putting the phone down. 'We're off now. See you tomorrow.'

Rachel jumped a foot in the air. Then she shot into the hall to confirm her ears weren't deceiving her. They weren't. Xantia was putting on a padded purple silk coat over her sari, Otto was coming down the stairs reading some papers. She couldn't make it out. A few minutes ago, Otto and Xantia hadn't been in the house. She'd looked everywhere. This was verging on the surreal. Where on earth had they sprung from? She didn't like to ask because she thought it would make her look stupid.

'Right, any messages?' Xantia said briskly, doing up the buttons on her coat. 'I know about Klagenfurt – Kermit just got me on my mobile. Anything else?'

'No, nothing . . . Oh yes, Matt Clapton popped round with a spare washing-machine manual. He thought you might have lost yours.'

'I think we probably have. Do you know, he is just so thoughtful. I tell you, the day he plumbed in our washing machine, some pipes burst and he stayed for two hours helping the workmen clear up the mess. I mean, it wasn't even his fault. But nothing is ever too much trouble for him. The man is a treasure.' She began staring wistfully into space. 'And he's so tall. And strong. There's this funny lopsided thing he does when he smiles. And he's got the tightest little butt . . .' She broke off, blushing, and cleared her throat. 'As I said, he's a treasure. An absolute treasure.'

After they'd gone, Rachel still couldn't fathom out where Otto and Xantia had got to while she was hunting for them. In the end all she could think was that they'd popped out and returned without her noticing.

Rachel got home just after four. She hung up her jacket, put her bag and keys on the hall table and glanced at the answer machine. One message.

'Hi, Rache, it's me, Ad. I'm at Manchester Airport. Listen, I've asked Barry the accountant to fax you over those Capital Gains Tax figures. I think you'll find they make very interesting reading. He really is the most brilliant tax accountant. Did I tell you they've named a loophole after him? Oh yeah, and by the way, I meant to tell you that when I was at the flat yesterday, I noticed your fridge had this rather fridgey smell. I've just put one of those egg-shaped deodoriser things in the post. You should get it in a couple of days. Speak to you soon. Bye.'

She smiled and shook her head.

'Adam, it's a fridge,' she said out loud. 'What did you expect it to smell of – tropical frangipani? Freshly baked bread? The Estée Lauder factory?'

CHAPTER 8

'. . . So Mrs Peach, the exercises the doctor gave you still not working then? Oh I know, life would be a lot easier for us women if you could lay a new pelvic floor like a new piece of twistpile. Look, I was wondering if I could speak to Sh . . . Soaked through? Every time you cough or sneeze? Half a dozen pairs a day? Oh, I quite agree, Mrs Peach, it's no life. I'd go for the operation if I were you . . . No, I *do* think so, really . . . A two-year waiting list? Gosh, that's scandalous . . . No, I'm sure they wouldn't make Elizabeth Taylor wait that long . . . Look, Mrs P., is Shelley around? I'd like to have a quick word if possible . . .'

Rachel, who was sitting at Xantia's kitchen table, mobile in hand, heard Mrs Peach call up the stairs.

The Flowtex commercial had been put back and Shelley had decided to go and stay with her mother for a few days. Rachel simply wanted a natter and to see if Shelley had any thoughts about how she might zap up her sex-life with Adam.

Xantia was adamant she should make no personal

calls during worktime, but since the Marxes' publicity machine had swung into action overnight and they'd flown off to the Klagenfurt Design Fair, where a posse of British broadsheet journalists and a BBC film crew were waiting to record their protest against the Lego Auschwitz, Rachel decided to take a break from clearing up last night's dinner-party mess and phone Shelley.

'OK, right,' Rachel said to Mrs Peach who had come back to the phone. 'Look, when she comes out of the shower, would you ask her to ring me? I'll be home in twenty minutes or so. Bye.' She stabbed the red button on her phone before Mrs Peach had a chance to go pelvic again.

Rachel finished at Xantia's just after one. She was double-locking the front door, aware of the bitter wind lashing at her bones, when she heard her name being called from the street. She swung round to see Matt heading towards the front gate. Her face broke into a broad smile.

'Oh, hi,' she called back, giving him a tiny wave. Pulling on her gloves, she started down the garden path towards him.

'Hi,' he said. He sounded nervous. Exactly as he had the day before. There was a tricky silence, which Rachel felt the need to fill.

'So, how are you?' she said, looking up at him, the smile still on her face. How she could ever have thought he was even remotely cross-eyed, she had no idea. His gentle, dark brown eyes were two of the least crossed eyes she'd ever seen.

'Oh, fine. Fine. Bit chilly, maybe.'

'Yeah, they said it's going to get even colder. Might even be a white Christmas.'

'Um.'

'It's nice to see you.' She wanted to ask whether he had stopped by for any particular reason, but couldn't quite work out a way of saying it without appearing rude.

'Yeah, you too,' he said.

'So, did you just happen to be passing or was there . . . ?'

'Sort of. I've just finished plumbing in a washer-drier down the road.'

'Oh right.'

'Miele.'

'Ooh, posh.'

'Yeah, two-thousand spin speed.'

'Right. Not quite as posh as the Wiener then.'

'No, not quite. The Wiener can do two thousand five hundred.'

'I know,' she grinned. 'I've been reading the manual.'

'Oh . . . good.'

She watched him take a deep breath and swallow.

'Look,' he continued, 'I hope you don't mind, but I got you something.'

She was taken aback to say the least. 'You have?' she said, giving him a bemused look. She paused. Then she started laughing. 'Oh hang on, let me guess. You've discovered the Wiener manual has a second volume.'

'No,' he said with a nervous chuckle. 'Not exactly. I bought you this.' From his jacket pocket, he produced a small oblong package wrapped in an old Tesco bag. 'Sorry about the carrier,' he said. 'It's all they could find in the shop.'

She opened the bag and took out an exceedingly battered and chewed paperback. She stared at the title. *Women in Comedy – from Music Hall to the Present.*

'You bought this for me?' She couldn't remember ever feeling quite so touched.

'Well, it didn't exactly cost a lot, but I thought you'd like it. I found it in a secondhand bookshop in Muswell Hill. It came out in the Eighties. It starts off with people like Marie Lloyd and ends round about Jo Brand. If you don't like it, you can always bin it. I won't be offended.'

'Matt, I love it,' she said, beaming with pleasure. 'Thank you. It's a sweet, sweet thought. Of course I'll keep it – I can't wait to read it. I've always wanted to know more about the early women comics. This is so up my street, I can't tell you.'

'You mean that?'

'Honest,' she nodded.

There was another silence.

'So,' he said eventually, 'what are you doing now?'

'I thought I'd go home, have a sandwich. I've got a meeting at my bank at half three, to discuss what the manager described in his letter as "the parlous state" of my account.'

'Sounds nasty,' Matt said. 'It's just that I was about to grab a quick bite. You wouldn't fancy keeping me company, would you?'

'I'd love to,' she found herself saying.

'Great,' he said. 'I'm parked up the road.'

She explained she had her car with her, but he offered to drop her back after they'd eaten and she saw no reason not to accept.

They didn't say much as they battled through the icy wind towards the corner. Finally Matt stopped beside a battered white Transit with *Clapton Domestic* printed on the side in large black letters.

'This is it,' he said, taking his car keys out of his trouser pocket. 'And please, no "born to be riled" white van man jokes.'

'I wouldn't dream of it,' she giggled.

'I have never suffered from road rage, I never knowingly cut anybody up and I always slow down before I go through a red light.' There was the lopsided grin again.

'That's OK, then,' she said.

'Oh, and by the way – it's called Morrison.'

'What is?'

'The van. You know, Van . . .'

'Yeah, I get it,' she said, grinning. It was a daft joke, but for some reason it rather appealed to her.

It also rather appealed to her that Van Morrison's dashboard was strewn with Biros, beaten-up map books, yellow stickies and McDonald's debris.

'So,' she said, as she did up her seat belt, 'doesn't your

girlfriend mind you buying presents for other women and then asking them out to lunch?'

'My girlfriend?' He gave her a puzzled look.

'Yes. The pretty blonde woman I saw you with at The Anarchist Bathmat.'

'What, Rosie, you mean? She's not a woman, she's my aunt.'

Rachel raised her eyebrows.

'No, honestly,' he said. 'She's my mum's kid sister. It's all a bit weird, but when my mum was expecting me, she discovered her own mother was pregnant with Rosie. We've always been close. She lives in Edinburgh now, but I always take her out when she's in town.'

'Oh, right,' Rachel said thoughtfully.

They decided to go for coffee and a sandwich at Bonjour Croissant in Highgate. On the drive over Matt asked her how she got into comedy. She told him about hating Fleet Street and it having been an ambition since she was a teenager.

'So, you gave up the journalism and just took a leap into the unknown. I really admire that.'

'You do?'

'Absolutely,' he said. 'You have to take risks in life. OK, you might fail at the end of the day – but at least you can say you gave it your best shot. I reckon there's nothing worse than waking up dead one morning, full of regrets.'

She nodded.

He went on to tell her his love of comedy had been

handed down to him from his father, a retired builder who had moonlighted as a pub comic in the Sixties and Seventies.

'He tended to mainline on those: "My-wife-is-so-frigid-every-time-she-opens-her-mouth-a-light-goes-on" gags. But it was definitely my dad who gave me a taste for comedy. By the time I was seventeen or eighteen I was hanging out at all the London comedy clubs.'

'Me too,' she said eagerly. 'I wonder if our paths ever crossed?'

The more they chatted, the more his shyness evaporated.

'Funny,' he said as they sat down at one of the small Formica tables at Bonjour Croissant. 'Can you imagine a café on the Left Bank called "Hello Crumpet"?'

She burst out laughing.

'So, where do you live?' she asked.

He told her he had a flat in Muswell Hill and that his best mate, who'd been living in New York for the last few months and got chucked out because he didn't have a Green Card, was staying with him for a few weeks.

'He keeps telling me he's looking for a job,' Matt explained, 'but I can't see much sign of it. Or of him paying any rent. All he does is sit at home all day, hatching these lunatic business schemes, none of which ever seem to work out.'

'Like what?'

'Oh, last month it was a chain of dog restaurants called *The Dogs' Diner*. Then there was his idea for a Biblical foods deli called *Cheeses of Nazareth*. Now he's working on some idea involving breakfast cereal. He did explain it, but to be honest I wasn't really listening.'

Rachel chuckled.

'I know he's a lazy bugger,' Matt went on, 'but he's my oldest mate and deep down, he's a really decent bloke. He's also desperate for a relationship. But he's absolutely hopeless with women. Comes on far too strong – you know, sounds like he swallowed a book of chat-up lines and then can't work out why women don't want to know.'

'So, what's his name, this friend of yours?'

'Tr . . . Dave.'

'Trdave?' she frowned. 'That's an unusual name.'

'No, it's not Trdave,' he explained. 'It's Dave. It's complicated. You see, he's got this nickname . . .'

Just then the waitress came to take their order.

'Anyway, that's enough of me going on about my problems,' he said after she'd gone. 'So, are you going in for the Joke for Europe Contest?' He told her he'd seen the posters advertising it at the Comedy Store.

She nodded. 'Assuming I get through the audition, that is.'

'Can't see that being a problem. You were fantastic the other night. Not only will the audition be a breeze, but you are going to wipe the floor with them at the contest.'

'Oh, I dunno about that,' she said, feeling herself start to blush.

They carried on chatting over sandwiches and several cappuccinos. Pretty soon she was telling him about Sam, her marriage to Joe and why it ended.

'Wow,' Matt said, putting down his tuna-fish sandwich.

'Yes, that's how I felt for while. But I'm OK with it now. Sam just takes having a gay father in his stride. He's amazing. I keep worrying he's going to get bullied at school, but so far there's been nothing.'

They'd been sitting talking for over two hours when Rachel suddenly remembered her appointment at the bank. She looked at her watch. It was almost half three.

'Oh God. Look, Matt, I am so sorry but I really do have to run. I'm due at the bank in about three minutes.'

She could see the disappointment in his face.

'Right, I'll drive you back to your car, then.'

She explained that the bank was just over the road and that she'd be fine walking back to her car afterwards. She reached into her bag and offered him some money towards lunch, but he wouldn't hear of it. She thanked him profusely.

'Look,' he said, a trace of hesitation creeping back into his voice, 'if your washing machine ever breaks down, this is where I am.'

He took a business card out of his wallet and handed it to her.

Rachel came out of the bank, virtually punching the air

with delight. Mr Lickdish, her avuncular bank manager, had given her a long lecture about cutting her coat according to her cloth before taking pity on her and saying that although the bank wasn't happy with the way she was managing her account, they were prepared to let her overdraft continue for the time being.

'What you have to understand, though,' Mr Lickdish had said, leaning forward over his desk and taking off his glasses, 'is that the bank isn't a charitable institution. At some stage in the not too distant future, we will have to insist that you put your house in order.'

'I understand,' she said with what she hoped was appropriate gravity. 'And thanks again.' She almost ran out of the office, petrified he would change his mind.

'Oh, one last thing, Miss Katz,' he called out as she was halfway down the corridor.

Rachel felt the colour drain from her cheeks. Mr Lickdish trotted along the corridor until he drew level with her.

'Here's a joke you could use in your act, and you can have it for free. I promise it won't appear on your statement.'

'Oh, right,' she said, mightily relieved. 'Go on.'

'Well,' he said, 'have you heard the Vatican has patented a new, low-fat communion wafer? It's called *I Can't Believe It's Not Jesus*.'

'Hilarious,' Rachel said, forcing a smile. 'Absolutely hilarious. Thank you *so* much.'

*   *   *

She felt like doing something to celebrate her reprieve from fiscal ruin, but couldn't think what. Shelley was away and most of her other friends were at work. In the end she decided to phone her parents and invite herself over for a cup of tea. It would be a chance to gently quiz her mother about Tiggy Bristol.

Faye answered the door, cordless clamped to her ear.

'No, you're right, Coral. I think there's a lot to be said for regression therapy.' She beckoned Rachel in, planted a kiss on her cheek and mouthed that she wouldn't be long.

'OK, so she hypnotised you, this woman. What then? . . . You became an Egyptian princess and then you drowned in a bath of asses' milk? Well, I tell you, it would certainly explain your allergy to dairy . . . Look, Coral, I got to go. Rachel's just arrived. Love to Ivan. I'll speak to you later.'

Faye stabbed the off button.

'You know,' she said thoughtfully, as they walked down the hall towards the kitchen, 'maybe *I* should have a go at this regression lark. How many years is it I've had that recurring nightmare about being with Captain Oates when he went for that final walk in the Antarctic? That could explain my phobia about shopping in freezer centres.'

They chatted about nothing in particular while her mother made tea.

'Oh, I meant to tell you,' Faye said, pouring milk into

mugs. 'Hylda Klompus phoned over the weekend to say she's prepared to knock off another five per cent if we make a quick decision.'

'Mum, please,' Rachel said firmly. 'You promised to let this Hylda Klompus thing drop.'

'OK, OK,' Faye came back defensively. 'I just wanted to tell you, that's all. I won't say another word.'

'So, Mum,' Rachel said casually, taking a sip of tea, 'you got any more plans to see that friend of yours – what's her name, Tiggy?'

'Maybe,' Faye said, looking and sounding distinctly shifty now. 'But she lives in the Midlands. It's such a long way for her to come.'

'Oh? Where in the Midlands, exactly?'

Just then Jack, dressed in tracksuit bottoms and a sweatshirt, staggered into the room, red, wheezing and breathless. Perspiration was pouring off his face and there was a huge wet patch on the back and front of his sweatshirt.

'Dad,' Rachel gasped. 'What on earth have you been doing?'

He pulled a chair out from under the kitchen table and sat down heavily. 'Jogging,' he said, between puffs.

Faye brought him a glass of water. 'Sure you're all right?' she said gently.

He nodded and began knocking back the water.

'But Dad, you never exercise.' Rachel was still shocked. 'In all the years I've known you, I've never seen you do anything more physically taxing than lift your hand to your mouth.'

'Well,' he announced, pausing to catch his breath, 'all that's changed.'

He put the glass down on the table and took hold of a roll of stomach flesh through his sweatshirt.

'I went for my check-up last week and the doctor says I could do with losing a few pounds. So I've started exercising. Don't worry, he said I'm up to it – and your mother's put me on a diet.'

At that moment the cordless went. Jack picked it up. 'Yes, she's here,' he said, turning towards Faye. 'Whom should I say is going to be listening?' He shot Faye a wicked grin. She returned it with a look which was seven-eighths glare and one-eighth amusement.

Jack covered up the mouthpiece with his hand. 'It's Simon.'

'Oh, right, excellent,' Faye said.

'Simon?' Rachel mouthed to her father.

'Yes, he's the upholsterer. He's got the fabric your mother ordered. She's recovering the three-piece.'

Although Rachel sensed an uneasiness in her mother's tone and facial expression, she failed to detect it in her father's.

Faye took the phone from Jack. 'Hello, Simon,' she simpered. 'Sorry about my husband. He's under the illusion he's got a sense of humour.' She walked over to the door and disappeared into the hall.

Rachel turned to Jack. 'But Mum's only just had

the suite recovered in that pink velvet Fleur de Lys,' she said, frowning. 'She loves it. She invited half the neighbourhood in to see it when it was done.'

Jack shrugged. 'She changed her mind. Said she wanted something a bit more contemporary.'

'But it must be costing a fortune to get it done again.'

Another shrug. 'If it makes her happy . . .' Jack stood up. 'Right, I think I'll pop up to the loo to see if maybe the exercise has got me going.'

'Dad, have you still not been? Did you mention it to the doctor?'

'Ach, doctors,' he said, waving a dismissive hand. 'What do they know?'

It was the line Jack always took. When Rachel was growing up, all the other children would be busy playing doctors while she was busy suing them for malpractice.

After he'd gone, Rachel put the kettle back on to boil. She'd just dropped tea bags into three mugs when she heard her mother giggling. Rachel sneaked across to the kitchen doorway to listen. The giggles were coming from the living room.

'You forgot to ask me what the other day? . . . How long have I been married? Well, Simon, let's put it this way – I'm on my fourth bottle of Tabasco sauce . . . No, really, I am . . . I don't? Ooh, flatterer. Well, I certainly feel it some days.' By now Faye's tone was positively coquettish. 'Yes, I think it's important to stay in shape. I try to get to the gym a couple of times a week.'

More giggles. Then: 'Friday?' Faye said, suddenly

lowering her voice. 'I'm not sure. It might be difficult . . . OK, I'll try. Look, I'll phone you if there's a problem . . . yes, me too. Me too. Friday at five-thirty, then . . . No, neither can I . . .'

Suddenly Shelley's words, 'Perhaps she's found herself a toy boy' began echoing around Rachel's head.

People flirted with each other all the time, Rachel kept telling herself on the drive home. It was nothing more than a bit of harmless fun. It didn't mean they were about to jump into bed. By the same token, her mother waxing her bikini line and buying expensive new clothes was probably nothing more than an effort to keep herself young and attractive.

The Tiggy Bristol issue, on the other hand, did bother her slightly. She was as certain as she could be with no real proof, that the woman was a fiction. Then again, she thought, Faye could have umpteen reasons for inventing her. Maybe she was 'up to something'. But whatever the 'something' was, it wasn't necessarily sinister and it certainly didn't have to be an affair. Apart from anything else the idea was far too hideous to contemplate. In the same way that parents didn't have sex, they most certainly didn't have affairs.

Rachel decided not to delve any further. Her mother would tell her what was going on, in her own time.

The first thing she did when she got home was check her answer machine. She hoped there might be a message from Shelley, but wasn't totally surprised to discover there wasn't. Mrs Peach was a sweet soul, but she was also one of the most self-obsessed individuals Rachel had ever met. She was in no doubt that she had completely forgotten to tell Shelley she'd phoned.

As she picked up Adam's fridge egg which had arrived this morning and which she'd unwrapped and left on the hall table, it occurred to her that she'd still had no word from him. This was completely out of character. Undemonstrative as he could be, Adam made a point of checking in with her every day – sometimes twice a day – whenever he was out of the country. She looked at her watch. It was nearly seven. Since there was no time difference to speak of in South Africa, he would probably be in his hotel room, getting ready to go out for dinner. Uncle Stan and his wife Millie had offered to put him up, but he'd politely declined. They lived in a luxurious but compact apartment and he thought things would get too crowded. Rachel also suspected that Adam feared their hygiene standards might not be up to his. She decided to phone him. She had the number written on a yellow stickie, which she'd put on the wall just above the phone. She peeled it off, sat down on the hall floor and dialled the number. The girl on the switchboard answered on the first ring. A few seconds later she was waiting to be connected to Adam's room.

'Yah?' It was a woman's voice. Very brusque. Very South African.

'Oh hello,' Rachel said tentatively, assuming she'd

been put through to the wrong room. 'Is that Mr Landsberg's room?'

There was a long pause.

'Mr Landsberg,' Rachel repeated. 'Mr Adam Landsberg.'

'Ah'm afraid Mr Landsberg isn't here raght now,' the voice said eventually.

'So this is his room then?' Rachel said, wondering who on earth this woman could be.

'Yes.'

'Well, do you know where he is?' Rachel was convinced she could hear the shower running in the distance.

'No,' the woman said. 'Ah'm afraid I have no idea. No idea at all.'

'Well, do you mind telling me who you are?' By now Rachel's suspicions about what Adam was getting up to behind her back were well and truly aroused.

'Me?' The woman sounded distinctly nervous now. 'Ah'm . . . Ah'm the hotel manager.'

'Really?' Rachel said, her tone distinctly sceptical.

There was another pause. 'Yes. You see, all the rooms on this floor have been invaded by a swarm of locusts.'

'Locusts,' Rachel repeated, frowning.

'Yah. In fact, the whole hotel has been invaded by locusts. They flew in from, er, Zimbabwe – or maybe it was Botswana – and, anyway, we've had to evacuate the entire building.'

Rachel was aware of the woman moving away from the phone. There was a loud thwack of what sounded like a rolled-up newspaper being brought down sharply onto a hard surface.

'Shit. Missed,' she heard the woman yell. Two more thwacks. More swearing. Then 'Aha. Gotcha.'

'What's that noise in the background?' Rachel asked. 'It sounds like a shower running.'

'No, no, no,' the woman said anxiously. 'It's not a shower. It's . . . it's the noise of the pest guys spraying insecticide.'

'What, with you in the room?'

'They're down the corridor.'

'I see,' Rachel said, dubiously. 'Sounds pretty dangerous to me.'

'Ach, it's not that bad. We've all got masks. The fumes should die down in a few hours. All being well, the guests will be able to move back into the hotel the day after tomorrow. Meanwhile we've got to find everybody alternative accommodation.'

'All right,' Rachel said. 'Not a lot I can do if Mr Landsberg's moved out. I'll just have to wait for him to contact me.'

She said goodbye and replaced the receiver. The most bizarre thought was occurring to her. But maybe it wasn't so bizarre. What *was* bizarre was the idea of a modern hotel, where the windows would be sealed for the air conditioning, being invaded by locusts. Loath as she was even to contemplate it, she couldn't dismiss the possibility that Adam was cheating on her. The way she saw it, the woman had clearly picked up the phone while Adam was in the shower, panicked when she heard Rachel's voice and made up this highly improbable story about locusts.

But Adam was desperate to marry her. It made no sense that the man who had been nagging her for months to set a wedding date, would go off and have an affair the moment her back was turned. It also made no sense that somebody would invent a tale as far-fetched as the locusts story and expect to be believed. It was so preposterous, Rachel decided, it simply had to be true. Maybe they'd come in through the air-conditioning ducts like something out of a horror film. She shuddered. Poor Adam. She wondered if locusts could eat through plastic. If not, then Adam's insistence on storing his socks, shirts and underwear in polythene bags might have paid off for once.

She took her glass of wine and the bottle into the living room. As she passed the small desk where the fax machine lived, she noticed a lengthy missive had arrived from Barry the accountant. She would look at it in the morning.

For the next couple of hours, she lay curled up on the sofa drinking wine. Having phoned Sam on the cordless and established that he was eating properly and that his eczema was under control, she tried Shelley, but there was no answer. She assumed Mr and Mrs Peach had taken her out to dinner.

Eventually she found her thoughts turning to Matt Clapton.

She couldn't get over how much she'd enjoyed their lunch. And the book. It had been such a kind thought. She was forced to admit she'd felt the kind of connection with Matt that she rarely experienced with Adam these days. And unlike Adam, Matt had been so encouraging about her entering the comedy contest.

She took a sip of wine. She barely knew Matt, she thought, and yet it felt like they'd been friends for ages. She reached into her trouser pocket and took out his business card. For a five full minutes she sat drinking and staring at it, without actually reading it. Instead she pictured his grin, his brown eyes, the rubbish on Van Morrison's dashboard.

She started to smile. OK, she found him attractive. And she had to admit she'd been strangely delighted to discover he didn't have a girlfriend. But so what? She wasn't a nun. She found loads of men attractive. Just because she was about to marry Adam, it didn't mean she had to stop fancying other blokes. It wasn't as if she'd ever cheat on Adam. She could never do that – except occasionally in her head when they were having sex. But that was OK because they both had mutually agreed fantasy people – Ralph Fiennes for her, Nurse Ratchet for him. He said it was the tall, blonde Teutonic thing, rather than the sadism.

Nevertheless she couldn't help thinking that she would give anything to hear Matt's voice. Her eyes focused on his phone number. It was his office number. If she phoned it, his machine would pick up. That way she could hear him without having to say anything. She carried on looking at the number, daring herself to do it. She dithered for a few seconds then, spurred on by the bottle of Fleurie she'd drunk on an empty stomach and which was now causing her head to spin, she grabbed the cordless and dialled.

Eight, nine, ten rings.

'Hello,' the voice said. She waited for the message to follow, but it didn't.

'Hello?' he said again.

Shit, it was him, not his answer machine. He clearly had his calls diverted.

'Oh, er hi, Matt,' she blurted. 'It's Kachel. Kachel Ratz.'

'Oh, hi Kachel, how are you?'

Unaware of her Spoonerism and his witticism, her addled brain battled to think of an excuse for phoning.

'I . . . er . . . you know you said I could call you if my washing machine ever broke down? Well, it has. It's making the most dreadful noise and I was wondering if you could take a look at it sometime. Any time will do. There's no hurry . . . What, now? Oh right, you're working in the neighbourhood. But it's gone nine . . . No, I was thinking of you, that's all. It's not inconvenient for me at all. Right, I'll see you in half an hour, then.'

Rachel stood in front of the washing machine and drained her wine glass. What on earth would she tell him when he arrived? There wasn't anything remotely wrong with the machine. It was virtually new. Her dad had bought it for her last year when her decrepit Indesit had finally conked out. She couldn't possibly confess to Matt she'd got him out on false pretences. He would be bound to think she was making a pass at him. She kicked the machine a few times in frustration. She supposed that when he arrived she could always backtrack slightly and say it was an intermittent fault. That way he wouldn't be too surprised to find the machine working perfectly and she would be saved any embarrassment. Short of sabotaging her own washing machine, she thought, what else could she do?

'Sabotage.' She repeated the word aloud. She stood thinking for a minute. Slowly her face lit up. 'Yesss,' she shrieked. Swaying slightly from the wine, she went into Sam's bedroom, pulled the rubber stopper out of his *Yentl* money box (Greg had found it at a flea market in Tel Aviv), and tipped the contents onto his bed. She picked up eight pound coins and returned to the kitchen. Then she opened the washing-machine door, tossed the coins into the drum on top of a load of dirty laundry waiting to be washed, threw in a couple of Persil tablets and pressed the on button.

CHAPTER 9

Seeing Matt standing in the doorway in his crumpled shirt and grubby Levis, she suddenly felt extremely horny. But then again, alcohol always did go straight to her clitoris.

'Hi,' she said with an awkward half-laugh, standing back to let him in. 'Thank you ever so much for coming over so quickly. I really appreciate it.'

'No problem,' he smiled. 'I'd been called out to an emergency in Highgate, so I was in the neighbourhood anyway. Sorry about my clothes – turned out to be a really messy job. This woman phoned me in a panic an hour ago, because her Siemens was leaking.'

'Oh, right. Does that happen to women too, then?' she found herself saying. She led him into the kitchen, aware that she was finding it difficult to walk in a straight line.

'There you go,' she said, pointing to the washing machine, which by now had finished its cycle. 'The moment I switched it on, it started making this horrendous slanking cound.'

She could see he was trying not to smile.

'Sorry, I meant clanking sound.' She felt herself redden. At the same time it occurred to her that it was late and that he probably hadn't eaten.

'God, you must be hungry. I can make you a sandwich . . .'

'Thanks, but I'm fine, really. I picked up a burger on the way over.' He turned to the machine. 'Right, let's take a look,' he said, putting his toolbox down on the floor. He pressed the on button. Almost at once there was an almighty racket from inside the machine.

'Blimey,' he said, switching it off again. 'Sounds like there's a load of loose change caught up in the works. Maybe you forgot to empty your pockets before you put in your last load.' He took off his jacket and put it down on the worktop.

'More than likely,' she smiled anxiously.

He knelt down and opened the washing-machine door. 'Mind if I take out the laundry?'

'Sure,' she said easily. She bent down towards the machine, intending to help him remove the laundry. What she hadn't noticed was Matt's hand moving towards the door at precisely the same time as hers. Their hands touched for a beat, maybe two. Their eyes met for a moment longer.

'Sorry,' she said, pulling her hand away and smiling an awkward smile. 'You carry on.'

A moment later, as she watched him reaching into the machine, she bitterly regretted uttering those last words. First out was her oldest, saggiest grey bra. This was followed by three pairs of Hampshire-sized, granny knickers – the ones she wore under her joggers on fat days, or while she sat in front of the telly stuffing her face with Galaxy when she had PMT.

'Where shall I, er . . . ?' Matt said, holding the wet underwear.

She could feel her cheeks burning. 'Oh, God. Sorry,' she said, grabbing the bra and knickers. 'Of course, they're not mine. They . . . er . . . they actually belong to my friend Shelley. She lives downstairs. Her washing machine's on the blink too, funnily enough. Strange how these things always happen in pairs. I mean washing-machine breakdowns, not knickers. I mean, yeah, they happen in pairs too, knickers. And . . .' Her fuddled brain suddenly went blank. She stood stuttering and stumbling for a few moments. 'And anyway, I offered to do a load for her. You might also find a pair of bedsocks, some winceyette pyjamas with teddies on them . . . oh, and a pink fluffy hot-water bottle cover. She's sweet, Shelley, but a bit dull. You know the type – wears a lot of fawn, never misses *Antiques Roadshow*.'

She stood looking round for the laundry basket. When she couldn't see it, she tossed the bras and knickers into the sink. While Matt knelt with his head in the drum, she asked him how he became a washing-machine repair man.

He told her it wasn't something he'd set out to do.

'After I left school, all I wanted to do was go to

drama school, but even though he was on the fringes of showbusiness, my dad wouldn't hear of it.'

'Why on earth not?'

'Money. Said actors spend most of their lives out of work. I dare say he was right, but I was furious at the time. Plus he'd seen how much time I used to spend as a kid messing about designing machines and gadgets. Still do, in fact. So, anyway, I went to university, got my engineering degree. Then after I graduated, I insisted on taking a gap year. A friend of my dad's took me on helping him repair washing machines and my gap year sort of turned into a gap life.'

'So, becoming a repair man was some kind of late onset teenage rebellion?'

'Pretty much.'

'Sud's law, eh,' she said with a hiccough.

Matt smiled.

'So, do you still want to go to drama school?'

He shook his head. 'I'm thirty five – it's probably too late now. Plus, I think I've moved on from that. Thing is, although I've never turned my nose up at making money, I've never really been into it in a big way. What I really want to do, and you'll probably think this sounds dead naive, is put my engineering skills to some really worthwhile practical use – in one of the developing countries, maybe. God, sorry. I sound like a Miss World contestant.'

She laughed. 'No, you don't. I know exactly what you mean.'

Rachel suddenly realised the wine was making her feel quite nauseous. She wasn't used to drinking a bottle to herself and she still hadn't eaten anything. The sicker she felt, the more impossible she found it to carry on chatting. While Matt wrestled the washing machine out of its housing, she moved away, sat herself down on a kitchen stool and rubbed her forehead with her hand.

'Rachel, you OK?' Matt asked.

'No, not really. I'm feeling a bit queasy. I think it might have been something I ate.'

She saw him eyeing the empty wine bottle on the worktop. He said nothing. Instead he picked up a glass from the drainer.

'Got any fizzy water?'

'Yeah, in the fridge.'

He walked across to the fridge, took out a bottle of Highland Spring and poured some into the glass.

'Here,' he said, handing it to her. 'This'll settle your stomach.'

'Thanks,' she said, looking at him as she took the glass. Sick as she felt, she couldn't help thinking he had the kind of sexy boyish face that could melt knicker elastic.

She took a sip. The cold, gassy water hitting her stomach made her feel worse. She grimaced.

'Look,' he said, 'why don't I finish off in here while you go and lie down.'

'No, I'll be all right, really. I'll just sit and watch.'

As he worked she sipped the water. Bit by bit the

nausea lifted and drowsiness kicked in. Eventually she could fight it no longer. She folded her arms on the worktop, laid her head down on top of them and passed out.

CHAPTER 10

Rachel groaned as the alarm went off, but made no attempt to open her eyes. Still lying on her stomach, she stuck her hand out from under the duvet and ran it over the bedside table, groping for the clock. She was vaguely aware that along the way her fingers brushed past a small metallic object she didn't recognise, but being half-asleep she was distinctly uncurious. Having found the alarm, she couldn't be bothered to locate the off switch. That would mean opening her eyes. Instead she stuffed the clock under her pillow. It would go off in a second or two.

She felt lousy. Her head was thumping and her tongue felt like a Body Shop foot sander. She lay still, waiting for the alarm to switch itself off. But it didn't. A minute later the muffled beep was still providing an excruciating backing track to the throbbing in her head. Finally she opened her eyes and propped herself up. Blinking against the light (she must have forgotten to pull the curtains), she pulled the clock out from under the pillow, thumbed the off switch and put the thing back down on the bedside table.

Rolling onto her back, she began making chewing motions in an effort to get her saliva flowing again. She stared up at the ceiling, feeling her mouth slowly rehydrate. It dawned on her that she had no memory of the previous night beyond arriving home, and sitting on the sofa drinking wine.

She turned her head towards the bedside table. The small metallic object she'd felt while trying to locate the alarm clock was in fact a stack of pound coins. How they'd got there she had no idea. She also had no idea why her blue plastic kitchen bucket was sitting on the floor next to the bed.

As she stretched across and picked up the coins, she noticed her arm was covered in white T-shirt sleeve. Yesterday's white T-shirt sleeve. She peeked under the duvet. Yesterday's trousers. Oh God. She could only assume she'd got so pissed last night, she'd forgotten to undress.

She held the coins in her open palm and counted them. There were eight. Her failure to undress she could understand; why she had gone to bed leaving eight pound coins on the table, she could not. She looked from coins to bucket and back again. She carried on like this for a while until images of the previous evening gradually began to return – in mortifying, Technicolor flashes.

Her face turned crimson as she remembered being drunk, phoning Matt's work number assuming she would get his machine, only to have him answer in person. She saw herself tossing the pound coins into the washing machine. She remembered him arriving and how sexy she'd found him.

'Omigod,' she muttered, covering her face with her hands. 'The knickers. He saw my granny knickers.'

She remembered their conversation about his former acting ambitions and his remark about having a gap life and how he wanted to do something useful to help the Third World.

After that her mind was a blank.

It remained a blank for a couple of minutes until bit by bit, another extremely clear and vivid picture emerged. She remembered falling asleep in the kitchen and half-waking as Matt scooped her into his arms, carried her into the bedroom and put her to bed.

Her face turned from crimson to purple. She was being struck by the most mortifying memory flash of all. She screwed up her face in horror as she recalled what happened next. As he'd covered her with the duvet she'd draped her arms round his neck, snuggled up to him and called him . . . and called him . . .

'Omigod,' she cried, turning to bury her face in the pillow. 'I only called him my Rinse Charming.'

Xantia rang just before eight to tell her not to bother coming in, as she and Otto were still in Klagenfurt and there would be nothing for her to do. It turned out that the only journalists waiting for them when they arrived at the Design Fair to protest against Lego Auschwitz were a man from the *Jewish Chronicle* and a film crew from *Eye-Witness News*, Zagreb. Enraged at not receiving the full broadsheet publicity they were convinced they deserved, the couple had decided to stay on an extra day in Klagenfurt to 'chivvy up' the newspaper editors back home. No doubt Xantia would sit on the phone for as long as it took, hectoring and bullying every editor in London, until they finally caved in and agreed to send their reporters to Klagenfurt.

More than a little relieved that she didn't have to go to work, Rachel put the kettle on and ran herself a bath. After a couple of mugs of tea and a long soak in hot water, her headache, although not her embarrassment, had virtually disappeared. She was just about to blow-dry her hair when the phone rang. It was Matt ringing to see how she was.

'Had a bit of a headache,' she said awkwardly, 'but that's gone now.'

'Didn't need the bucket then?' he joked.

'Oh, right. You put it there.'

'Yeah, just in case you chucked up in the night.'

'That was really thoughtful. And thanks for putting me to bed. I drank a bit too much on an empty stomach. I don't know what you must think of me.' She paused. 'And if I embarrassed you with anything I said, I'm really sorry.'

'There's nothing to be sorry for. You didn't say anything even remotely embarrassing. Honest.'

'That's not how I remember it,' she mumbled.

'Well, it's definitely how I remember it. You passed out and I put you to bed. You didn't even wake up.'

'Really?'

'Really. Now come on, let's forget it.'

'OK,' she sighed. 'If you're sure.'

'I'm sure.'

'Tell you what,' she heard herself say, 'how's about I cook you dinner tonight, to apologise?'

'Rachel, how many more times?' He was laughing, but there was a definite hint of frustration in his voice. 'You don't have to apologise.'

'I know, but I'd like to. Really. Please.'

'OK. Great,' he said kindly. 'I'd like that.'

'Eight o'clock?'

'Eight o'clock.'

She tried phoning Shelley a couple of times during the morning, but there was still no answer from the Peaches'. They must all have gone out – shopping for the baby probably. But Rachel couldn't help feeling uneasy. Even if she hadn't got yesterday's message, it was unlike Shelley not to phone for a chat.

She tried her again that afternoon when she got back from Waitrose with the ingredients for dinner, but there was still no reply. By now she was starting to panic: something had happened to Shelley or the baby. Then just before five, Mrs Peach rang and confirmed her suspicions. Rachel listened with her heart in her mouth as her friend's mother explained that just after Rachel had phoned the day before, Shelley had started having contractions.

'She kept saying it was nothing, but I insisted on driving her to Casualty. 'Course they take one look at her and decide she might be going into early labour. Then after a couple of hours it all stops. Anyway, they've been keeping her in, just for observation.'

'So she's all right – and the baby's OK?'

'They're both absolutely fine. But I was in a state for a few hours there. I mean, one minute there I was standing in the kitchen stuffing a couple of hearts for me and Mr Peach – not for Shelley 'cos as you know she's not a big meat-eater. Time and again I tell her it's not red meat that harms you, it's blue meat and green meat. But she never listens. Anyway, where was I? I've completely lost my train of—'

'When are they sending her home?' Rachel asked.

'Tomorrow, all being well. They've decided it was probably a false alarm and nothing to worry about. But they said she shouldn't take any chances. Even though she's seven months along, they don't want her going into early labour, if it can be avoided.'

'Will she stay with you?'

'Well, I want her to, but she says I fuss round her too much. She's insisting on coming back to the flat, so we'll drop her home tomorrow evening. Rachel, you will make sure she rests, won't you? If anything happens to her or this baby I don't know what . . .'

Rachel could hear Mrs Peach starting to cry.

'Mrs Peach, please, please don't worry. I'll look after her. Promise.'

Feeling much calmer now she knew Shelley was OK, Rachel made a start on dinner. Then she went to her wardrobe to find something to wear. She decided on her new Ghost dress. Everybody said how great she looked in it. After another bath and ages spent defuzzing, she carefully blowdried her hair and did her make-up.

It was only when she started hunting through her drawer for her best silk knickers and bra that she stopped short.

'What am I doing?' she said out loud. 'This is simply two friends having dinner. He is *not* going to be looking at my pants.'

Matt arrived on the dot, carrying a bottle of expensive red wine.

Rachel thanked him profusely. She thought about giving him a peck on the cheek, but thought it might make him feel awkward. He was wearing the same trendy black windcheater he'd worn when they'd had lunch at Bonjour Croissant, over a charcoal ribbed polo neck.

She took his jacket and hung it on the coat-stand.

'Why don't you come into the kitchen,' she said, 'and talk to me while I finish dinner.'

He followed her down the hall. 'Umm. Something smells good,' he said.

'Delia's roast lamb in Shrewsbury sauce.'

His face dropped.

'Oh God,' she said, feeling panic rise inside her. 'You're not veggie, are you?'

'No, it's not that. It's just that I had Shrewsburys for lunch.'

She stared at him blankly for a moment and then started to giggle.

While he uncorked the wine, she opened the oven and pulled out the tin of roast potatoes. Another twenty minutes, she thought.

'Oh, by the way,' he said, 'I thought you'd better have these back.'

He slipped his hand into the pocket of his khakis and took out a crumpled paper bag. Perplexed, she took it from him.

'I don't remember lending you anything,' she said, frowning. She peered into the bag. It contained a white lace G-string. *Her* white lace G string.

'How on earth did you get hold of this?' she said, feeling herself redden.

Matt said nothing. He simply finished pouring the wine. Finally he turned to face her, holding two glasses. He was smiling what she took to be a cryptic, knowing smile.

'Oh my God,' she said slowly. 'Last night . . . I, that is we . . . I mean we didn't, did we?'

He carried on smiling.

'Look, I know I was pretty slaughtered, but I'm sure I would have remembered if we'd . . . And I'm certain that when I woke up I still had my knickers on.'

'Rachel,' he said finally, 'it's OK. I'm just teasing. I found the G-string in my toolbox this morning. It must have fallen in when you chucked all that washing into the sink.'

'That was very cruel,' she said, trying her best to sound put out, but unable to stop herself smirking. 'For a moment there, I thought . . .'

'What?' he said, clearly still teasing her.

'C'mon,' she said, casting her eyes down to the floor. 'You know.' The wine was starting to go to her head.

Matt put down his glass and moved towards her. Then he took hers and put it down too. Placing his hand under her chin, he lifted her face so her eyes were level with his. A knowing glance passed between them. After a moment he pulled her towards him and kissed her on the mouth. For a second her body froze as she thought about Adam and their committed relationship based on mutual trust and honesty. But she couldn't help herself. She found herself wrapping her arms round Matt's neck and kissing him back.

'You have no idea how long I've been wanting to do that,' he said afterwards.

'How long?' she whispered, aware that her heart was racing.

'Oh, ever since you behaved like an imperious bloody cow that time at Xantia's.'

'Really?' she said, blushing.

'Really.'

He pulled her towards him again and began tracing

the outline of her lips with his tongue. He tasted of wine. As he parted her lips and his tongue came deep inside her, she felt a delicious shuddering inside her belly. She put her arms around his neck and moved her pelvis towards him. She could feel his erection against her. He carried on kissing her, probing her. She imagined his tongue between her legs. As he started running his hand over her bottom, she could feel herself getting more and more wet. She couldn't remember ever wanting anybody as much as she wanted him at that moment. Again she thought of Adam. She knew she should put a stop to this now. But she didn't have the strength to fight it.

As their kissing became more and more urgent, she was aware of him half-pushing and half-guiding her across the room. Eventually she realised her back was leaning against the cold metal of the washing machine. Still kissing her, he pulled up her dress and slid his hand underneath the skirt.

'Oh my God,' he whispered, running his finger over the wet patch on her pants. She let out a tiny whimper. He forced her legs apart with his hand and touched her a second time, tracing the outline of her labia. Her heart was beating even faster, her breathing slow and deep. He ran his tongue the length of her neck. The next moment he had found her mouth again.

'Blimey,' she said, pulling away in panic. 'What about my lamb in Shrewsbury sauce?'

'I told you,' he smiled. 'I'm all Shrewsburyed out.'

She reached out, just about managed to locate the oven dial and turned down the meat.

Somehow he managed to lift her onto the washing machine and at the same time pull her dress up round her waist She couldn't tell if it was his idea of a joke, or whether it was pure coincidence. Whatever the answer, she was far too turned on by now to stop and ask. He could pleasure her with the roller ball dispenser for all she cared.

As he began stroking the insides of her thighs, she leaned back onto the tiled wall, gripping the edge of the machine for support. He pulled the crotch of her pants to one side and allowed his fingers to brush over her skin. She let out a long soft moan and lifted her bottom as he tugged at her pants. When they were off he simply stood staring at her.

'Bring your legs up,' he whispered.

She lifted her feet up onto the top of the machine. She couldn't help thinking she must look as if she were about to give birth. Finally, when the ache between her legs was becoming unbearable, he gently pushed two fingers inside her. Deeper and deeper they went, feeling her, exploring her, but he made no attempt to touch her clitoris. Just as she was about to cry out and beg him to touch her, he bent down and began trailing his tongue over her swollen aching clitoris.

She arched her back and whimpered.

'Bloody hell, washing-machine man,' she said, 'I think you may just have found my Hotpoint.'

He looked up briefly and smiled.

Time after time when she thought she was about to come, he reduced the pressure on her clitoris to a featherlight touch. Every so often he stopped completely. Then he would push his fingers back inside her. She felt open, exposed and utterly helpless.

Glorious as his lovemaking was, she eventually became aware that her position on top of the washing machine wasn't ideal and that her back and legs were beginning to ache. As if reading her mind, he brought her legs back together and lifted her down onto the floor. She looked at him quizzically.

'Turn around,' he said.

She turned and he made her bend over the machine. She was aware of him moving away and looking round for something. Eventually he found it. Once again he pulled up her dress. A few seconds later she cried out in delight as she felt him squirt cold hand lotion onto her buttocks. He began massaging it into her skin, occasionally running his finger between her wet bottom cheeks and over her clitoris. She was just beginning to feel the quivering and shuddering building up in her vagina, when he stopped.

'I want to undress you properly,' he whispered.

He turned her to face him and reached for her dress.

'No,' she said, brushing his hand aside. 'You first.'

She kissed him and began tracing the outline of his erection with her finger. After a few moments she started undoing his belt and fly. He took off his sweater and tossed it onto the floor. His upper body was muscular, a can short of a six pack, maybe, but she detested overworked male bodies.

She tugged at his khakis. After he'd stepped out of them she did the same to his boxers. His thick erection sprang forward. She cupped his balls in her hand and began to stroke them. She watched his stomach muscles quiver, felt his fingers digging into her shoulders. She knelt on the floor and ran her tongue over his belly and down through his dark hair. A tiny seed pearl of sperm appeared on the tip of his penis. As she rubbed it away with her finger, he gasped. She began licking the top of his erection.

'Christ, that's good,' he groaned digging his fingers even harder into her shoulders.

She carried on like this for a couple of minutes until finally she took the entire length of his penis in her mouth. His whole body shuddered as her mouth went back and forth over the shaft.

'I think my legs are about to give out,' he whispered urgently.

'C'mon, let's go to bed,' she said.

'Now will you let me take off your dress?' he said as they stood by the bed. She nodded.

He pulled her dress up to her belly and held it there with one hand. The other he placed between her legs. A second later his fingers were probing deep inside her again. She lowered her head and let out a long low breath. Eventually he removed them and began spreading her juices over her stomach.

The dress off, he started biting and nipping her shoulders and the tops of her breasts. At the same time he managed to unhook her bra.

'You are so beautiful,' he said, staring at her breasts. He took each nipple in his mouth in turn until it was fully erect.

'Come here,' he said, taking her hand. He led her to the bed, took two pillows and placed them one on top of the other in the middle of the bed. She knew what he wanted her to do. She lay across the pillows, on her front and kneeling – her arse raised. She reached for another to put under her head. She was aware of him on the bed behind her. He stroked her oily buttocks again, occasionally flicking her clitoris, occasionally pushing his fingers inside her. She took a sharp breath.

He began to concentrate on her clitoris, rubbing it with firm circular strokes. She could feel herself beginning to drift away. She had no idea how long this went on. But by the end she was begging him to come inside her. But time and again he ignored her. When he did finally push himself into her it was almost unexpected and she cried out both with surprise and glorious delight. His thrusts were slow and deep. Occasionally they verged on painful, but all the time he kept stroking her clitoris, not leaving off for a second.

By now the pleasure was so intense that she was almost praying not to come. For the second time she felt the quivering build up inside her. At the same time, his thrusts become slower and even deeper. She was aware of him taking long gaps between each breath. Even then he didn't stop touching her. She came a moment or two after him, as he lay gasping, his head resting on her back.

When it happened, wondrous as it was, she couldn't help thinking how much it reminded her of a washing machine in the final juddering throes of its spin cycle.

'You know when I first realised you fancied me?' he said, putting down his knife and fork.

'When?' she asked, trailing her finger over the freckles on his nose.

'Last night, when you called me Rinse Charming.' He started to laugh.

'But you said . . .' She leaned across the table and punched him, not altogether playfully, on the arm.

Just then the phone rang in the hall.

'I'd better get that,' she said, getting up. 'There might be something the matter with Sam.' She tightened the belt on her dressing gown and dashed to the door, closing it behind her.

Shock and black guilt descended the second she heard his voice. 'Adam,' she said as quietly as she could. 'It's you . . . No, don't be daft, of course I'm pleased to hear from you. No, I am, really. You just caught me at a bad moment, that's all. What was I doing? I was, er, I was loading my shoes into that shoe rack you bought me and a trainer rolled under the bed. I crawled after it and when the phone rang it startled me and I bashed my head. Look, I'll speak to you tomorrow. OK. Night, bye . . . Yeah, me too.'

She walked back into the kitchen, head down, hands in her dressing-gown pockets. She'd just had the most mindblowing sex she'd experienced in years. But at the same time, she couldn't believe what she had just done to Adam.

'Rachel,' Matt said, looking at her quizzically, 'what on earth's up? Is there something the matter with Sam?'

'No, no,' she said, forcing a smile. 'It wasn't anything to do with Sam.'

'Something you want to talk about?'

'No. Just my neurotic Jewish mother phoning to see if I'm OK, that's all. You get used to it.'

'But it's half eleven,' he said, looking at his watch. 'Does she always phone so late?'

'Oh, sometimes she phones at one in the morning – just to check I'm asleep.'

It was only then that it registered with her that he was up and dressed.

'God, you're not going, are you?' she said.

'Rachel, please don't take this the wrong way. I've had a wonderful time tonight, and dinner was fantastic. But it's late and I have to be up at five.'

'Why so early?'

'Oh, I've been working on a design for a cheap washing machine which would cost virtually nothing to run – something I think might be really useful in the Third World. A mate of mine who works in engineering has agreed to help me build the prototype from bits and pieces of old machines. I've managed to get the government of Burkina Faso interested and a couple of chaps from their Embassy have agreed to come and see it. I promised it would be ready before Christmas, and we haven't even started assembling the damn thing yet.'

'God, just imagine if it worked out. I mean, with an invention like that, you'd be really famous . . .'

'Maybe,' he said smiling. 'Anyway, look I'm really sorry.'

'That's all right. I understand.'

He pulled her towards him and kissed her. 'I'll phone you tomorrow,' he said.

'OK,' she heard herself say.

CHAPTER 11

'So has he?'

'Has he what?' Rachel said vacantly, picking a tiny Mothercare Babygro up off the shelf and holding it in front of Shelley.

'Phoned you.' Shelley looked at the Babygro and screwed up her nose. 'Powder blue? Yeah, right. See if they do it in lime.'

Rachel groaned and put it down. Shelley's ex, Ted, had sent her £500 to buy baby things and she and Rachel had spent the afternoon trailing up and down Oxford Street in the freezing rain, failing to spend it because of Shelley's insistence that no baby of hers was about to make its debut in pastels.

'C'mon, you still haven't answered me,' Shelley persisted. 'Has he phoned you?'

'Two or three times,' Rachel said, 'but I let the answer machine pick up. I feel such a coward not speaking to him, but what can I do? Wonderful as the other night was, it was a huge bloody mistake.'

'I'm not surprised you did it though,' Shelley said, grinning.

'You're not? I bloody am.'

'Just look at the pressure Adam's been putting you under to give up the comedy, when he knows how important it is to you. Maybe at some level you're having second thoughts.'

'Don't be daft,' Rachel laughed, utterly unaware of the lack of conviction in her voice. 'You know how much I love Adam.'

Shelley didn't say anything. They carried on down the aisle, towards the steriliser units.

'So the sex was good then?' Shelley said casually.

Rachel reddened.

'Thought so,' her friend grinned. 'I swear,' she continued, 'there's nothing like treating yourself to a bit of rough from time to time.'

'Hang on,' Rachel came back at her. 'For your information, Matt is *not* a bit of rough. He's got a degree in engineering, as it happens.'

'Jackpot – a bit of rough with brains.' Shelley picked up a packet of rubber nipple shields, grimaced and put them back.

'Did I ever tell you,' she went on, 'I used to date this fireman called Terry? Two years I went out with him. God, the hours I spent stroking his helmet.' She headed off towards the pushchairs. Rachel followed.

'You know, from what you've told me, Matt sounds like a really great bloke.'

'He is, but I'm in love with Adam and I intend to marry him.'

'Oh yeah?' Shelley said provocatively. 'When?'

'Soon. In fact, I'm going to phone him in Durban tonight to discuss dates. I thought about Valentine's Day. It would be incredibly romantic.'

Shelley simply raised her eyebrows and began wandering down the line of pushchairs.

'Rache,' she said, stopping to pose beside one, 'does this buggy make me look fat?'

'Don't be daft,' Rachel said. 'How can a pushchair possibly make you look fat?'

'It's floral. Florals always make me look heavy.'

'Shelley, it's a pushchair – not a Laura Ashley puffa jacket.'

Shelley moved on up the line, stopping occasionally to scowl at the twee teddy and bunny-rabbit motifs.

'Look,' Rachel said eventually, 'we've been everywhere and you've seen absolutely nothing you like. Maybe it's time to accept that you are not going to find lime Babygros and a Cadillac-pink, rhinestone-encrusted pushchair with a detachable zebra-skin hood.'

'I don't want rhinestones, just something a bit more stylie, that's all. A bit less Croydon.'

'But when it comes to baby stuff,' Rachel said, 'people don't want style. They want Croydon. They feel comfortable with Croydon. They feel safe with Croydon. They do not want to be seen on the streets pushing a vehicle that looks like it was plundered from Elvis's tomb. Come on, you've been on your feet all afternoon. You know you should be resting. I promised your mum I wouldn't let you overdo things. How's about we go and get a cuppa and something to eat? My treat.'

It was dark outside now. The rain had turned to a fine drizzle, brilliantly illuminated by the street-lamps and cheesy Christmas lights. It was like walking through icy gossamer threads of tiny, twinkling beads.

Rachel put a protective arm through Shelley's and steered her round the puddles, past a crowd who had gathered in front of a bloke flogging foam rubber antlers and Santa hats from a suitcase, and guided her across the road to Selfridges. They headed for the coffee shop on the second floor. Like Oxford Street, it was mobbed with Christmas shoppers.

'They really should,' Shelley said once they'd finally found an empty table, 'think about having Christmas when the shops are less crowded.' She broke the seal on her bottle of mineral water and began pouring it into a plastic cup. 'Hey, and I still can't get over your news about the comedy competition. It's wonderful. Absolutely wonderful.'

Rachel blushed and smiled.

She'd called in at the Channel 6 offices the previous day, after she'd finished at Xantia's, and filled in the registration form for the comedy contest. It was the final day for entries, and they were holding the last of the auditions that afternoon. They squeezed her in at four and told her on the spot she'd qualified. She was still reeling with shock, both at how quickly it had happened, and the fact that she was in.

'God,' Shelley squealed, 'suppose you win and get your own show on Channel 6?'

'I know. Sometimes I reckon I stand about as much chance of winning the Joke for Europe Contest as a one-legged man at an arse-kicking competition. Then at other times I think, what if . . . ?'

Shelley took Rachel's hand and squeezed it. 'You are going to do brilliantly,' she said. 'I just know it.'

As Rachel thanked her, she was aware that Shelley wasn't listening. Instead she was staring into the distance.

'What?' Rachel said, stopping in mid-chew and frowning. 'What is it?'

'Right,' Shelley whispered, leaning across the table. 'I'm about to tell you something and after I've told you, I don't want you to move. OK?'

'Why?'

'Because she'll see you.'

'Who?'

'Your mother. She's sitting at a table by the exit. And she's with a bloke.'

Despite her best efforts to play down her mother's flirting on the phone with Simon the upholsterer, Rachel couldn't help having her doubts about it being nothing more than a bit of harmless fun. She'd mentioned it to Shelley last night. Her view had been that although it was impossible to rule out the possibility of an affair, it was highly unlikely bearing in mind Faye was in her sixties and, as far as anybody knew, happily married.

It had put Rachel's mind to rest, but only temporarily. This morning when Jack phoned to ask her if Sam would like a camera for Christmas, she hadn't been able to resist dropping Tiggy Bristol into the conversation.

'Who?' Jack had said, chortling at the daft-sounding name. 'Never heard of her.'

By the time she came off the phone, Rachel had been feeling distinctly troubled.

'You absolutely sure it's my mum?' she said now, twisting round in her seat.

'Of course I'm sure.'

'Where is she? I can't see her.' By now Rachel was almost on her feet. 'God, is she with Simon the uphol-sterer?'

'Well, he's not actually tacking chintz to his chair, but I suppose it could be him. Rache, for heaven's sake sit down or she'll see you!'

Rachel sat down and turned back towards Shelley. 'What day is it today?' she asked.

'Friday. Why?'

'That's the day they arranged to meet. Friday, at five-thirty.' She looked at her watch. It was a few minutes after.

'OK,' Shelley said, 'just take it easy. Now then, let's try again. She's at the table to the left of the exit sign. On my signal turn round very, very slowly. Right – go.'

Rachel turned. 'Oh, my God,' she said, in a whispered screech. 'He can't be more than thirty. Christ, you were right. My mum's got a toy boy.'

'You don't know that for certain. This could be completely innocent.' Shelley paused. 'Mind you,' she continued dreamily, 'he *is* gorgeous. If that's Simon, he can strip off my upholstery any night of the week.'

'Shelley,' Rachel was starting to get worked up now, 'this is no laughing matter. That is the man my mother could be about to leave my father for. I mean, just look at her. I swear that coat's brand new. And see the way he's gazing at her? Christ, you could pour that sickly sweet look on a waffle.'

Rachel swung back round to face Shelley. 'OK, what's he doing now?' she demanded.

'He's not doing anything. They're just talking. I have to say though, he looks nothing like an upholsterer to me. For a start his clothes are far too trendy.'

'What do you expect?' Rachel said. 'A brocade suit with fringes and tassels?'

'Not exactly. He just looks a bit too – I dunno – Soho House, I suppose. Look at that black rubbery mac thing he's wearing . . . Ooh, and that's a Paul Smith shoulder bag he's opening. I got the same one for my dad last Christmas.'

'What? You bought your dad a Paul Smith shoulder bag? But he's even older than my dad!'

'Yeah well, I got my mum a Vivienne Westwood bustier top and I didn't want him to feel left out.'

'Jeez, no wonder you're always hard up. So what do you think he is, if he isn't an upholsterer?'

'Something media-ish, I'd say. Probably TV.'

'Maybe he's a TV upholsterer,' Rachel said, giggling despite herself, 'with his own show. "And tonight, on *Loose Covers*, Simon the shagging sofa supremo stuffs Faye Katz from Chingford".'

Laughing, Shelley started pouring more Evian into her cup, but stopped. 'They seem to be leaving.'

Rachel swung round again. 'OK, so am I,' she said, scraping her chair back and getting up. 'I'm going to follow them. My mother is either having an affair or is about to, and I'm not going to sit back and let her chuck away forty years of marriage.' She began putting on her coat.

'Right, I'm coming too,' Shelley announced. 'But I'm telling you, Rache, this could all be perfectly innocent. If you've got it wrong, you're going to look such a twonk.'

'Believe me,' Rachel declared, 'I have not got it wrong.'

It was getting on for six o'clock and the crowds of shoppers had thinned considerably. Although this made it easy for the two women to follow their quarry through Selfridges, it also meant they stood a greater chance of being spotted.

They'd gone no more than a few yards when Faye and Simon stopped.

'Oh, no!' Rachel squealed in panic. 'They're coming back this way. Quick – freeze.'

'What d'you mean, "freeze"?'

'Pretend to be a mannequin.'

'Don't be stupid,' Shelley hissed. 'Your mother'll recognise us. Duck behind one of the garment rails.'

'No, look. Even better. The wig counter over there. We can make out we're trying on wigs.'

Rachel made a dash for the counter. Shelley trotted slowly behind her, supporting the underside of her bump with her hands. They each grabbed a wig, pulled it on and stood facing the mirror with their backs to the main thoroughfare.

Faye and Simon passed within feet of them.

'That was close,' Rachel whispered, aware that her heart was thumping.

'Tell me about it,' Shelley said breathlessly.

'You OK?'

'Rachel, stop fussing. I'm fine.'

As Shelley pulled off the bubble-cut wig she'd been wearing, she eyed Rachel's blonde bob, which she'd managed to put on backwards so that her face was completely obscured.

'Oh my God,' Shelley hooted, 'it's Cousin It.' Not many people could carry off that look. But, you know Rache? I think it's very you.' She parted the hair hanging down over Rachel's face and pushed it behind her ears.

'Funn-ee,' Rachel said, looking round urgently. 'Oh God, we've lost them.'

'No we haven't,' Shelley said calmly. 'There they are heading towards Lingerie.'

'Why does that not amaze me?' Rachel said, shaking her head slowly.

They watched from behind a seven-foot high Christmas tree decorated in scarlet and green sequinned bras and suspender belts, as Simon and Faye wandered leisurely around the stands. Occasionally one of them would stop to finger a pair of lace panties or a bra. At one point Simon held up a black lace G-string and grinned at Faye. Then Faye picked up a red Wonderbra. Simon grinned again and Faye burst into fits of giggles.

'Well,' Rachel muttered sarcastically, 'I'd say this all looks perfectly innocent, wouldn't you?'

Shelley looked at her a bit shame faced and said nothing.

In the end Faye and Simon appeared to decide on a La Perla bra and panty set in cream satin and lace. The two women watched as Simon took out his credit card and paid while Faye looked on, all coquettish smiles.

They followed the pair down to the ground floor, out through the revolving doors and into the freezing, damp evening. A second later Simon was hailing a cab.

'Oh no!' Rachel cried. 'We're going to lose them.'

She ran to the edge of the pavement, praying for a yellow light. Three or four taxis passed in quick succession, each with their lights off. By now Shelley had caught up with her.

'They've gone, Rache,' she said softly. 'Look.'

Rachel watched as the cab carrying Simon and her

mother did a U-turn and sped westwards towards Marble Arch.

Rachel had just finished slamming her foot into a large puddle when she turned round to see a woman in a trenchcoat and too much foundation standing next to her. Ramrod straight, she towered over Rachel.

'Excuse me, madam,' the woman said, adjusting her tan leather shoulder bag. 'Would you mind accompanying me back into the store?' She reached out and took Rachel's arm.

'Sorry?' Rachel stammered, utterly taken aback. She turned to Shelley as if to say, 'Do you mind telling me what's going on?'

'I think you may have some merchandise you haven't paid for,' the woman said.

'Omigod, Rache,' Shelley exclaimed. 'The Cousin It wig. You forgot to take it off.'

The store detective stood leaning against her desk, arms folded, listening patiently to the women's breathless, disjointed and rambling story about Faye's bush waxing, her lunches with the non-existent Tiggy Bristol, her affair with Simon the maybe TV upholsterer and the chase through the Lingerie Department which had called for urgent disguises. Five minutes in, her eyebrows were arched so high in disbelief, they looked like they were about to disappear under her hairline.

'Please, you have to believe me,' Rachel pleaded. 'I'm not a thief. I'm a stand-up comic. I can prove it.' She

told her the gag about the morning-after pill for men, but
the store detective's foundation didn't crack. Rachel was
pretty certain she hadn't even been listening. Clearly all
was lost.

The woman unfolded her arms.

'You know,' she said thoughtfully, placing her hands
on the desk, either side of her, 'if twenty-five years in
the police force taught me one thing, it's that genuine
shoplifters make some attempt to conceal the merchandise they are about to steal. At the very least they remove
the price tag. You did neither. You are either a highly
incompetent thief or the stress of Christmas shopping got
too much – you became confused and made a genuine
mistake.'

'Oh, I did,' Rachel gushed excitedly, sensing a reprieve
could be on the way. 'I got so confused. Very, very
confused. Didn't I, Shelley?'

Her friend nodded eagerly.

'Seeing as it's Christmas,' the detective said, allowing
her face to break into a smile, 'I'm prepared to give you
the benefit of the doubt.'

'You are?'

The woman nodded.

'Oh, thank you. Thank you so much,' Rachel said
breathlessly, adrenalin still pumping through her. 'You
see, I have this tendency to confusion. It runs in the
family. Goes back generations. My grandmother was the
worst. When she heard ninety per cent of crime happens
in the home, she moved house.'

At this point Shelley, smiling awkwardly at the store detective, took Rachel gently by the arm and began leading her to the door.

'Oh, and for years,' Rachel said, twisting round as she and Shelley reached the door, 'she thought a gargoyle was olive-flavoured mouthwash.'

CHAPTER 12

When Rachel arrived to do her usual weekly gig at The Gas Station in Islington, where the Joke for Europe Contest would be held, she was still reeling from the day's events. Seeing Faye with Simon had knocked her for six. As a result her timing was off and the audience had gone for her – big-time. When she described diaphragms as being a pain in the arse, some woman had yelled out, 'You're putting it in the wrong place.' Everybody roared. She struggled on until finally some bloke's mobile phone went off.

'It's my mate,' he announced, leaping to his feet, 'with some decent jokes for you.' There was a loud burst of applause at this and Rachel brought her set to a close as quickly as possible.

She trotted offstage, wiping the sweat from her forehead, and virtually collided with Lenny. He usually compèred at The Anarchist Bathmat, but tonight had been performing a ten-minute set along with all the other stand-ups.

'Hey, Rache,' he said, looking concerned, 'what went

wrong? You OK? I thought maybe you weren't feeling well or something.'

'No, I'm OK,' she said with a smile. 'Been one of those days, that's all – put me off my stride.'

'Oh, what – this bloke of yours giving you a hard time?'

'No, as it goes,' she said. 'My mum and dad.'

'Bugger,' he grinned. 'I thought I was in with a chance, at last.'

She laughed. She knew he was joking. He'd been living with his girlfriend for years. What was more, there had never been any sexual chemistry between them.

'That's better,' he said cheerfully. 'Come on, I'll buy you a beer. I have news.'

As they walked over to the bar, Lenny told her that the Channel 6 people had phoned him that morning to tell him he had been chosen to compère the Joke for Europe Contest.

'Lenny that's amazing, well done,' Rachel exclaimed. Lenny, who had been on the circuit far longer than Rachel, had taken her under his wing right from the moment she'd started out and she thought the world of him. She gave him a quick peck on the cheek and he blushed.

At the bar, the small gang of comics who'd been on in the first half – Rachel had known them all for years – were standing around bitching about who did or didn't stand a chance in the comedy competition.

While Lenny queued for their drinks, Rachel joined

the others. It was clear to her that tension was beginning to mount and that people were working their bollocks off on new material. When somebody turned to her and asked her how her writing was coming along, and she told them she hadn't started yet, they all looked at her as if she was either mad or lying.

'There you go,' Lenny said, handing her a bottle of Grolsch.

'Thanks, Len.'

He motioned her to a table. 'Rache, whatever you do, don't let this lot get to you. Panic is catching. Just keep your cool and you'll be fine. You know secretly everybody thinks you stand a good chance of winning this thing, don't you?'

'You reckon?' she said, looking down at her drink and sighing.

'I don't just reckon. I know,' he said.

They carried on chatting in the bar while everybody disappeared to watch the second half. Then, after a couple of minutes, Rachel became aware of tumultuous laughter coming from the audience.

'Jeez,' she said, 'somebody's going down well. Who is it?'

'Believe it or not, it's Pitsy.'

'Pitsy? When did she suddenly get funny? Mind if I go over to the door and listen?'

'Be my guest.'

Rachel stood up and went across to the double doors that led into The Gas Station's sizeable auditorium – it

189

had once been a theatre. Lenny followed. Pitsy was in full flood.

'. . . Of course, me and my boyfriend are totally incompatible. I'm a Virgo. He's an arsehole. I mean, we're lying in bed the other day and he announces he wants to do it. I tell him we've run out of condoms. To which he says, "Oh come on, I'll only put it in for a minute," and I go: "What do you think I am – a bloody microwave?"'

There was another burst of uproarious laughter.

'He also kept going on about what a gentleman he is. I said, "Why, because you get out of the bath to piss in the sink?"'

More laughter.

Rachel looked perplexed. 'I don't get it, Lenny. What on earth's going on? She almost sounds like a proper comic.'

He grunted. 'I have two words to say to you,' he said, picking a hair off his tartan trousers with a precise, pincer-like action.

'What?' she said.

'Noeleen Piccolo.'

'Come again?'

'Noeleen Piccolo – Australia's most popular female comic. It would seem that our Ms Carter has been nicking all her material.'

Rachel was aghast. 'You have to be kidding.'

'I'm not,' Lenny said. 'I was over at my mate Gary's house the other night – he's just got back from Oz. We'd sat down to eat our takeaway and I'd just put on this amazing three-hour video of the Kobe earthquake made by the Japanese Seismological Society, when he said did I fancy watching this tape he'd brought back of this stand-up called Noeleen Piccolo. I was a bit pissed off, but anyway, we watched it, and she was top. Then the next night, I'm compèring here and Pitsy goes on and does the same act – word for bloody word.'

'No. I don't believe it.'

'Honest. Gaz lent me the video. You can see it any time you like.'

'She's got some nerve,' Rachel said, slowly shaking her head.

There was a final burst of laughter and applause and Pitsy came offstage.

'Bloody hell, she's coming this way,' Rachel said. 'Right, I'm off. Thanks for the drink, Len. I'll see you at The Bathmat tomorrow.' She turned to go, but was a fraction of a second too late.

'Hi, Rache. Hi, Lenny,' Pitsy beamed, still speeding and breathless on adrenalin. As she lifted her hand to adjust one of her pigtails, Rachel couldn't help noticing her glistening armpit hair which was flecked with deodorant dandruff.

'Listen, Rache, I'm so sorry about the way your set went tonight. I mean, your material wasn't too bad, it was just your timing. Maybe we could get together sometime. I'd be happy to offer you a few pointers . . .'

Rachel had heard enough.

She shot Pitsy a filthy look and turned towards Lenny. 'Thanks again for the beer, Len. See ya.' She gave him another peck on the cheek and stomped off.

As Rachel got into her car, she decided that before heading home, she would phone Adam on her mobile. She couldn't wait to tell him about her plan for them to get married on Valentine's day. But when she got through to Durban he seemed distant and preoccupied.

'Am I keeping you from something?' she asked, hurt. 'You sound like you're trying to get me off the line.'

'No . . . no. I'm expecting room service with my dinner, that's all.'

'Oh, right,' she said quietly, only half convinced.

'I'm sorry if I sound a bit spaced out,' he went on. 'I'm just knackered.' He paused again. 'Right – that's the door. I really have to go. My dinner's arrived.'

'What are you having?'

'I . . . er. I dunno. I can't remember.'

'You can't remember? But you only just ordered it.'

'So I did,' he said nervously. 'Yeah. I'm having . . . I'm having springbok. That's it – carpaccio of springbok.'

'Nice,' she said sarcastically.

'Look, I have to get the door. Hang on.' She heard him put down the phone. A few seconds later she caught the sound of the room service waitress giggling about something.

He came back to the phone.

'She sounds happy,' Rachel said.

'Sorry?'

'The waitress,' she said.

'Oh. Yeah, apparently they don't get too many foreigners ordering springbok and she thinks it's dead funny. Now then, Rache, I must go. My dinner's getting cold and I'm starving.'

'Ad?'

'Yeah?'

'Is there something you're not telling me?'

'Not telling you? Like what?'

'It's just that every time I phone, there's a woman in your room.'

He laughed. A little too loudly, Rachel thought.

'Rache,' he said. His tone was gentle and soothing. 'I'm putting in sixteen-hour days at Uncle Stan's surgery. Do you mind telling me where I would find the time or the energy for other women? You know, I think all this worrying about your mother, plus the pressure of the comedy contest, is getting to you. It's making you irrational.'

'Yeah, you could be right,' she said. 'I'm sorry.'

'That's OK. Look, I really do have to go.'

'All right,' she said sadly. 'See you then. Love y—'

But he was gone. He hadn't even given her a chance to mention the wedding.

As she drove home down a side road, lined on both sides with parked cars, making it impossible for oncoming vehicles to pass each other, she was forced to reverse and pull into a space to let another car through. While she sat waiting for the car to go by she saw Matt's Transit parked on the other side of the road under a street-lamp.

'Gawd,' she said out loud. 'It's only bloody Van Morrison.'

All she needed now, she thought, was for Matt to appear. How would she explain not having returned his calls?

Naturally, he appeared at that moment, walking down the path of a nearby house. He reached the gate and turned back to wave at a couple standing at the door. In a flash her foot hit the accelerator and she was pulling away. She'd gone no more than a couple of yards down the road when a cat darted out in front of her, forcing her to slam on the brakes and stall. She turned the ignition key, but the car refused to start. She turned it again, still nothing. Twice more she tried to start it and twice more it refused. She couldn't bring herself to look in Matt's direction, but she was pretty sure that even if he hadn't seen it was her in the car, he would come over to offer his help.

A moment later he was tapping on her window. She turned towards him and wound it down.

'Rachel,' he said, suddenly realising who it was. 'What are you doing here?'

'Hi,' she said sheepishly, turning the engine again, but with no success. 'I'm on my way home from The Gas Station.'

'Oh, right. Listen, you'll flood the engine if you carry on like that. Give it a rest for a few moments.'

She took her hand off the ignition key and brought it to rest on her lap. 'So how are you?' she asked.

'Fine. Just had dinner with some friends.'

She nodded. 'Look, Matt,' she began anxiously, 'I'm sorry I haven't returned your calls . . .'

'Well,' he smiled, 'it did occur to me that maybe you were giving me the elbow, but I was pretty sure you enjoyed the other night as much as I did, so I assumed you were just busy.'

She looked at him, standing there shivering in the cold. He had a right to know the reason they couldn't carry on seeing each other. She had to tell him about Adam. She owed him that.

'Yeah, I was,' she said, 'but there's something else I think I should explain. I know it's late, but have you got time to pop round now? I'll make us some coffee.'

'Great,' he said chirpily. 'Right, try the engine again.'

She turned the ignition. Miraculously, it started.

CHAPTER 13

'Mmm, that feels good,' Rachel cried. 'Up, just a bit. Now, down a fraction. Stop. There. Oh, oh, yeah. That's the spot. *Oooh.*'

'You sure that's how you want me to do it?' Matt said.

'Ummm. Press just a fraction harder, maybe.'

'Like that?'

'Oh, yeah. That's it.'

'Do you want me to see if I can find another packet of frozen peas?' Matt asked. 'These have nearly melted.'

'OK, but you might have to make do with button sprouts.'

Matt stood up and headed towards the kitchen. Rachel lay on the sofa, attempting to turn her ankle and wincing.

While she and Matt were walking down the street towards her flat, Rachel had tripped on an uneven paving stone and twisted her ankle. The pain had been agonising. Matt was all for rushing her off to Casualty, but since she'd been able to wiggle her toes and could

SUE MARGOLIS

just about take her weight on that foot, she'd eventually
convinced him it was nothing more than a sprain. She'd
even wanted to walk upstairs to the flat, but before
she could try, Matt had scooped her into his arms and
carried her.

Despite the pain, as she put her arms round his neck
and breathed in his warm, slightly boozy smell, she'd
felt lust shoot through her. The Oxford Street Christmas
lights couldn't have been more turned on than she was at
that moment. Try as she might to fight her feelings, all
she'd wanted was for him to lay her on the bed, tear off
her clothes and make love to her. Instead he'd put her
down on the sofa, taken off her trainer and sock and set
to work on reducing the swelling to her ankle and foot
with a packet of Birds Eye Petits Pois.

'No more veg, I'm afraid,' he announced as he came
back into the room, 'so I've soaked a tea towel in
cold water. It should work almost as well as an ice
pack.'

He sat down on the edge of the sofa.

'Roll up your trouser leg a bit more,' he said. She
rolled.

As she watched his strong hands wind the cold wet
tea towel round her ankle, it was all she could do to
stop herself grabbing him and pulling him on top of
her. Instead she said, 'Be careful. Don't do it too tight
or you'll cut off my circulation.'

He looked up at her and smiled.

'Trust me,' he said gently. 'I'm a spin doctor.'

198

'Funn-ee,' she said, feeling her heart thumping and realising she was having what Shelley always referred to after a few glasses of Château No-shit as 'a Copydex moment'.

'So, you said there was something you wanted to tell me.'

'Yes,' she said softly, 'there is.' She closed her eyes and began rubbing the lids slowly with her fingers.

'What? What is it?' he asked anxiously.

She opened her eyes, reached out and took his hand. 'It's just that . . . well, I, er, I had my audition for the comedy contest yesterday and they told me I'm in.'

'That's great news. But I don't understand. Why on earth were you so nervous about telling me?'

She cast her eyes down. 'Well, you see,' she said uncomfortably, 'that's not all. There's something else, too.'

Just then the phone rang.

'Sorry,' she said, reaching for the cordless which was tucked down between her and the back of the sofa. It was Faye.

'Oh. Hi, Mum,' she said – a tad too briskly perhaps, but after the Selfridges incident, she was in no mood for casual chitchat with her mother.

'How are you? . . . What do you mean, I don't sound very pleased to hear from you? . . . 'Course I'm pleased to hear from you . . . No, I'm not getting my period. Look, if I sound a bit down, it's because I just sprained

my ankle . . . Mum, calm down! . . . No, really . . .
Please, it's OK . . . No, I don't need to see your Cousin
Michael the orthopaedic surgeon. It's just a sprain . . .
Yes, I'm resting it. Yes, I've got it strapped up . . .
Mum, it's nearly midnight. Why are you ringing so
late? . . . Aunty Who died? Jessie, God, yeah I remember
her – wasn't she the one who could do that amazing trick with soup? . . . I remember. She used to
weep borscht and try to convince us it was some kind
of stigmata . . . Look, Mum, if the funeral's tomorrow, I won't be able to get there on this ankle. Will
you apologise to everybody? OK . . . bye . . . Yes,
I'm OK. No, I'm not trying to get you off the phone.
No, Mum, *please* don't pop in with deli on the way
to the cemetery tomorrow. I've got plenty of food in.
I can manage. Sure I'm sure. Bye. Yeah. Love you
too.' She raised her eyes heavenwards and clicked off
the phone.

'You had an aunt who could weep borscht?' Matt said,
more than slightly taken aback.

'That's nothing for our family. My mother breastfed
me matzo balls.'

He chuckled. 'So, anyway,' he said. 'Back to whatever
this thing is you need to tell me.'

She sat looking into his warm brown eyes. He had
taken her hand and was smiling at her. She couldn't
do it. Not yet. She didn't have the courage to hurt
him. She'd get him to open a bottle of wine. Maybe it
wouldn't be so painful if she was pissed. She was just

about to ask him if he'd mind fetching the Fitou from the kitchen when he leaned forward and began running the back of his hand over her cheek.

'You really are beautiful.'

She turned scarlet.

'I want to make love to you,' he said, starting to kiss her.

She immediately pulled away. She couldn't let this happen. Not for a second time. She had to tell him. Right now.

'Matt, I can't.'

'Why? What's wrong?'

She closed her eyes for a moment and pinched the bridge of her nose. 'It's just that . . . just that . . .'

'What? Please, tell me what's the matter. What have I done? Why don't you want me to make love to you?'

'Because . . . because I . . .' She looked into his eyes again. 'Because I've been out all day. I haven't had a bath and I'm filthy.'

'Christ, is that all? You really had me going there for a minute. Rachel, this is not a problem.'

'Why?'

'Because,' he said, giving her a sexy grin, 'I'm going to give you a bath.'

'No – no, Matt!' she shot back urgently. 'You can't.'

'Why can't I?' he said easily, taking the beer bottle from her and putting it down on the coffee-table.

She knew she should tell him about Adam, that they couldn't go on seeing each other. She knew she should let him walk away. But try as she might, she couldn't. She wanted him far too much.

The next moment he had picked her up and was carrying her to the bathroom.

The bathroom was the best feature of the flat and was one of the main reasons Rachel had bought it. For a start it was very large – having been converted from a double bedroom – and although the previous owners had pretty much ignored the rest of the place, they'd spent a fortune doing up the bathroom. Rachel supposed it was a bit Eighties, with its giant Victorian four-legged bath with brass fittings, white tiles and deep blue tiled dado rail – Rachel's style, bathroom-wise, veered more towards sluiceroom chic with stainless steel everything – but there was no getting away from the fact that when the lights were off and she'd lit a few scented candles, it was incredibly romantic.

Matt sat her down on the ancient rose-pink brocade armchair which had stuffing pouring out of it and which Rachel still hadn't got round to recovering. Then he picked up a box of matches from a shelf next to the widow, went over to the low table at the foot of the bath and began lighting the thick chunky candles. There were a dozen or so, half melted most of them, with deeply cratered dusty centres.

He turned off the lights and Rachel sat watching as the tiny flames flickered and cast shadows on the tiled walls.

'That's better,' he said. He turned on the taps, and

picked up a couple of bottles of aromatherapy oil. 'Which one?' he said.

'Dunno,' she smiled. 'Why not try a few drops of each?'

Soon the room was filling up with lavender and jasmine-scented steam with a hint of vanilla coming from the candles.

'OK. Arms up,' he ordered gently.

She lifted them and he pulled off her Lycra T-shirt. Immediately he knelt down and began kissing her shoulders, and the tops of her breasts. She threw back her head in delight as he ran his tongue along her neck. Finally he began kissing her on the mouth. As his tongue came deep inside her, all she could think about was how desperately she wanted him to make love to her. Their kissing became more and more urgent.

'Wow,' he said when they finally came up for air. 'I meant to ask you last time – where on earth did you learn to kiss like that?'

'Oh, I used to be a tester at the bubble-gum factory.'

'Lucky bubble gum,' he said. He knelt down in front of her and began undoing her jeans zip. 'Help me get these off,' he said.

She lifted up her bottom and he began tugging at the denim. A moment later she was sitting there in nothing but her bra and pants. Matt knelt down and unhooked her bra and began sucking her nipples. Then he ran his tongue down her belly towards her pants. His fingers went just underneath the waistband. She thanked God she had on a pretty G-string and not her granny pants. He pulled back the elastic and trailed a finger through her pubic hair. She raised her bottom again and let him pull off the tiny lace triangle. Before she knew what was happening, he had spread her legs and was about to go down on her.

'Matt. Stop,' she cried, snapping them back together again. 'You can't. I'm smelley down there.'

But he simply looked up her and smiled. 'What, after one day without a bath? Of course you're not.'

For a second Adam shot into her mind. She tried to imagine him uttering those words. Christ, she thought, he'd have a nose bleed just thinking about making love to her if she hadn't douched first.

'Come on, now,' he said. 'Just relax.' He put his hands on her knees and tried to part her legs again but she resisted. 'Rachel, it's OK,' he told her tenderly. 'I promise.'

Finally she let him slide her down in the chair slightly and spread open her legs. For a few moments he did nothing but kneel there, gazing at her. She let out a long loud moan began running his tongue over her clitoris; so sublime was the sensation that she knew she would come in seconds. Clearly sensing this, he stopped.

'More later,' he whispered. 'I think the bath's ready.' He took off his watch and put it on the bathroom shelf. Then he bent down over the bath and swished his hand through the water, testing the temperature.

'Perfect,' he said, turning off the taps.

Rachel noticed that the swelling in her ankle was down slightly, but that the skin around it was turning blue.

'Don't worry,' Matt said. 'That's a good sign. Means the bruise is coming out.' He lifted her up, and as he lowered her into the bath, she immediately felt the hottish water soothing her ankle.

First he sprayed her hair with warm water, and spent what felt like ages expertly massaging her head with shampoo.

'Ummm, a brilliant masseur as well as a brilliant kisser,' she purred as she felt the tension drain away from her head and neck.

Having rinsed her hair, he told her to lie back. Then he squirted shower gel into his palm. He slid his hand back and forth over the length of her arm. She closed her eyes, savouring the sensation. Soon he moved to her breasts, and Rachel whimpered as she felt his hand slip and glide over her skin. Occasionally he would stop to trace circles over her nipples. Finally his hand disappeared under the water.

'Can you kneel up?' he whispered.

'I think so.' She took hold of the bath handles and taking great care, manoeuvred herself into a kneeling position.

'Bend over,' he said.

She did as he told her. He squirted the gel directly onto her buttocks. It was cold and she felt herself flinch. Ever so slowly he began massaging it into her skin. She closed her eyes again and gripped the handles for all she was

worth. Suddenly, with an exquisite lightness of touch he
was brushing his fingers between her buttocks. He slid
his hand down and began washing her crotch. She was
aware that a thick, gloopy foam had formed by now.
Then, without warning, he plunged two fingers deep
inside her. She threw her head back. It was as much
as she could do to stop herself screaming with the sheer
ecstasy. As he carried on exploring inside her, she begged
him to make her come.

'Soon,' he murmured, pushing his fingers even higher
and harder so that it almost hurt. 'Soon.'

He carried on like this for a while, her moaning and
moving up and down on the fingers. Finally he took them
out and went back to massaging her buttocks. Then he
reached down to her clitoris and began rubbing it in
small rhythmic circles. By now she was constantly letting
out small frantic gasps. Finally, she felt the quivering
sensation building up deep inside her.

But almost as soon as she came, she wanted more.
She was still desperate to feel him inside her. She virtually commanded him to get undressed and join her in
the bath.

'Come on,' she urged. 'There's loads of room for
two.'

He pulled off his T-shirt and stood up to unbutton
his fly. The moment it was open, she tugged on his
combats and pants. His erection sprang out. She put
her hands on his buttocks, drew him towards her and
took the entire length of his penis in her mouth. As she

moved her head slowly back and forth, at the same time caressing the tip with her tongue, he stood looking down at her, moaning softly.

Then, just as she sensed he was about to come, she stopped. She beckoned him into the bath. Careful to avoid touching her ankle, he climbed in at the tap end and sat in front of her, his legs bent up.

'Bring your legs down,' she said.

'There's not enough room,' he protested.

'There is if we do it this way – come on.'

As he lowered his legs, she moved herself forward on her knees and straddled him.

'OK, now lie down.' He lay back, the big brass mixer tap just above his head.

She took his penis in her hand and guided it towards her vagina. For a few moments all she did was slide it repeatedly across the opening. Occasionally she let it slip a millimetre or two inside and then immediately removed it. He gasped, begged her to let him come inside her, but she wouldn't let him. She saw no reason not to tease him the way he'd teased her. She carried on sliding and teasing until neither of them could bear it any longer. Finally, she lowered herself down onto his erection. Gripping one of the bath handles for support she began to move herself slowly up and down on him. Feeling him finally penetrate her was exquisite. He did his best to reach for her clitoris, but the angle was wrong. Instead he lay there holding her arse and moaning as he watched her pleasure herself.

She carried on riding him faster and faster, great waves of water tumbling over the side of the bath.

They came together a few moments later.

'God. God. Oh God,' he moaned.

Because her eyes were closed, Rachel assumed he was crying out in ecstasy. Without opening her eyes she lay herself down on top of him and began kissing his cheek. Matt carried on oh God-ing.

'Well, I've no need to ask if that was good for you,' she whispered dreamily. She started smiling to herself as a thought occurred to her. 'Have you ever wondered,' she said thoughtfully, between kisses, 'what atheists shout when they reach orgasm? I mean it wouldn't sound quite right, yelling: "Oh random, Oh chance, Oh casual fortuitousness", would it?'

'Rachel, I hate to disappoint you, but this isn't ecstasy I'm experiencing. It's pain.'

Her eyes shot open and she saw his hand was clamped to his forehead.

'I bashed it on the mixer tap.'

'Oh, no,' she gasped, sitting up. 'Here, let me have a look.' She pulled his hand away. The skin wasn't broken, but a shiny cherry-tomato lump was already forming.

'What's it look like?' he said.

'It's going to be sore, but it's not too bad. I'll bathe it in some cold water.'

Very gingerly she climbed out of the bath. Then she wrapped herself in a towel and took a bag of cottonwool balls from the cupboard under the basin.

'I dunno,' she said, shaking her head as she wet a cotton ball under the cold tap, 'your head, my ankle. What do we look like, the pair of us? Jack and bloody Jill.'

She knelt down on the floor beside the bath and began bathing his lump. He winced as she touched it.

'Oh, stop being such a baby,' she chided. 'It's only a tiny bump.' She tried to carry on dabbing at it, but he grabbed her wrist and smiled a sexy smile.

'Come here,' he said softly, pulling her towards him and starting to kiss her.

After they pulled away she didn't move. She simply stayed there, gazing into his eyes. It was only now, as she knelt beside the bath, dabbing at the lump on Matt's head, that she was finally able to admit to herself that she did have feelings for him. Deep, powerful feelings.

CHAPTER 14

'So, I take it we're talking the L word here,' Shelley said, picking up her spoon and stabbing at the lemon in her hot water and lemon.

Rachel shrugged. 'I dunno. Yes. No. Maybe. All I know is that as I knelt there dabbing his head, I could hear this voice telling me it would be wrong to walk away.'

'So, did you tell him how you felt?'

''Course I didn't. I mean, how could I sit there and say, "Oh, by the way, I think I might be falling in love with you. Just one teensy problem, though – I'm planning to marry somebody else".'

Shelley nodded sympathetically.

'I dunno, why isn't Adam enough for me?' Rachel fretted. 'He's attractive, successful. He cares about me . . .' Her voice trailed off. 'Shelley,' she said, doing her best to sound casual, 'do you think Adam's capable of having an affair?'

'What?' Shelley burst out laughing. 'Don't be mad. He'd only have to think about cheating on you and he'd get one of his nose bleeds.'

Rachel told her about the women in Adam's hotel room. Shelley considered for a few moments.

'I suppose it's just possible he's got someone,' she said slowly.

'I'm pretty certain he has.'

Shelley asked her how she felt about it.

'Well, even though I've been seeing Matt I still can't help feeling hurt. But it's not the overwhelming desperate hurt I always imagined I'd feel if Adam cheated on me. Do you know the emotion I'm feeling most of all?'

Shelley shook her head.

'Relief.' She picked up Shelley's spoon and began prodding at the sugar in the bowl. 'At least if he's seeing somebody I can stop feeling so guilty about Matt.'

Just then the intercom buzzer went. Rachel looked up. 'That'll be my parents on the way to Great-aunt Jessie's funeral.'

'Stay where you are,' Shelley said. 'I'll get it.' She disappeared, returned thirty seconds later and nodded. 'Your mum's on her way up. Your dad's gone off to park the car. I've left the door open.'

'Oh God,' Rachel sighed, 'it was bad enough on the phone last night. How do I handle my mum? After that spectacle in Selfridges, how can I just sit here and carry on as if nothing's happened?'

'You just do, OK?' Shelley said simply. 'For the last time, Rache, their marriage is not your problem. I know it's hard, but you really don't have any choice.'

Rachel nodded. 'Oh, and by the way,' she warned her

friend, 'don't say anything to my mum about how you thought you were in labour the other day – not unless you fancy hearing a gasp by Last Rites account of her seventy-two-hour labour with me, the climax of which is a gruesomely detailed description of her inside-out placenta and her post-partum perineum which swelled to the size, shape and colour of a Frankfurter.'

Shelley screwed up her face. 'Eeuuch.'

'Just don't mention the word "labour" and you'll be fine. Promise.'

'Don't worry,' Shelley promised. 'I won't.'

Faye walked into the kitchen, mobile pressed to her ear.

'No, listen, Coral – you'll be fine. If the nurse said it was nothing, then it's nothing. Just go home and take it easy. Look, I'm at Rachel's now. I gotta go . . . OK, bye. Speak to you later. Love to Ivan.'

She put her mobile in her bag and turned to Rachel. 'I dunno, if anybody else got tired and thirsty shopping at Brent Cross two weeks before Christmas, what would they do? They'd sit down and have a drink. Not Coral. She gets on the phone to NHS Direct to check she's not diabetic.'

'Hi, Mum,' Rachel smiled.

'Oh, my poor baby,' Faye gasped, seeing Rachel sitting at the kitchen table with her foot resting on a chair. She rushed over, threw her arms round Rachel's neck, and kissed her.

'Sweetie, how do you feel? Is it painful? Can you

walk on it? Are you sure we shouldn't get it X-rayed? Maybe you should take off the bandage – it restricts the bloodflow, you know. Look, let me take it off.' She bent down.

'Mum, please leave it alone. It's fine, really.'

'OK, but just let me take a look at it.'

'Mum, it's much better today. It doesn't need looking at.'

'Well, if you're sure.'

'I'm sure.'

'Hi, Mrs K,' Shelley said perkily.

Faye swung round. 'Oh Shelley, darling. Sorry, I didn't see you standing over there.' Faye went over and kissed her hello. 'So, not long to the big day,' she said excitedly, taking off her coat. 'How's it all going?'

'Fine,' Shelley beamed. 'Couldn't be better.'

Faye hung her coat over the back of a kitchen chair and then waved her hand in front of her.

'Huh, you may be fine now, but you wait until you go into labour. You should have seen me – seventy-two hours it took me to get Rachel out. Excruciating it was. I tell you, afterwards did I swell up down there. It looked like a—'

'Thank you, Mum, but I don't think Shelley really wants to know how your undercarriage assumed the size and shape of a Frankfurter.'

'Frankfurter?' Faye exclaimed. 'It felt a damned sight bigger than a Frankfurter. I tell you, Shelley, for three weeks after I had Rachel, it was like trying to walk with a marrow between my legs.'

'I'll put the kettle on,' Shelley said, by way of changing the subject.

Just then Jack appeared carrying two bulging carrier bags. He put them down on the kitchen table, greeted Shelley with a kiss and went across to do the same to Rachel.

'Hi, sweetie. How's the ankle?' he said, taking off his coat and hanging it on top of Faye's.

'Bit easier today. Doesn't hurt quite so much when I walk.'

'So, there's nothing broken. Thank the Lord for that.'

'How are things with you, Dad? Any – you know – *movement*?'

'Nothing for two days,' he said morosely. 'Not a dickie bird.' He began rubbing his hands together. 'It's bitter out there. I don't think the sun'll even attempt to come out today.'

'Who can blame it?' Faye said. 'Would *you* come out on a day like this? Right, Jack,' she continued briskly, 'let's unload this shopping. Rachel, Daddy and I stopped off at the Shalom in Gants Hill on the way over. There's two dozen bagels, a couple of pounds of smoked salmon, two tubs of cream cheese, some pickled cucs and a big bag of Danish – enough to keep you going for a day or so.'

'But Mum, that's masses. I'll never get through it. You'll have to take some home.'

'Don't be silly. Of course you'll eat it,' she said, taking

215

the cheese and salmon over to the fridge. 'I daren't give your father the Danish or the cream cheese – he's actually dropped two or three pounds in the last week.'

'Yeah,' Jack said dolefully as he put the Danish and bagels into Rachel's bread bin. 'I'm starving myself to death so that I can live a little longer.'

'You know, Rachel,' Faye said, 'this fridge really could do with a clean-out. There's mould growing on the sides. Why don't I get a bucket of Flash and—'

'Mum, please,' Rachel said, far more loudly than she intended. 'Just leave it, eh? I'll get round to it eventually.'

'All right, darling,' Faye said, looking hurt. 'I was only trying to help.'

Shelley handed out mugs of tea and they all joined Rachel at the table.

'Shelley,' Jack whispered, giving her a wink. 'Fetch the Danish – there's a good girl.'

Giving him a conspiratorial smile, Shelley went over to the bread bin and brought back the bag of pastries. He put his hand inside, took one out and put it to his lips.

'Jack,' Faye snapped. 'What are you doing? You've lost three pounds this week.'

'Yeah, and if I go on at that rate, in eighteen months I'll have disappeared completely. Tell me, is that what you want?' He popped the pastry into his mouth.

'OK, eat then. See if I care,' Faye said, turning to Rachel. 'So,' she went on, 'I've been having a few more thoughts about the wedding reception.'

Rachel winced. She and Shelley exchanged glances.

'I've done a rough seating plan which I'll show you when we've got more time to go over it. But not only that, I've had this fabulous idea.' She paused for effect.

'I thought,' she continued, 'it would be a hoot, seeing as Adam's a dentist, to name each of the tables after teeth.' Another pause.

'So,' she said, positively brimming over with excitement now, 'you could have Incisor, Molar, Wisdom – the old people could sit at that one. I thought it was such an original idea. What do you reckon?'

Rachel closed her eyes and pinched the bridge of her nose.

'Mum, quite frankly, along with the idea of Sam wearing a pageboy suit, I think it's the most . . .'

'Well, I think it's a great idea, Mrs K.,' Shelley leapt in, clearly trying to keep the peace. 'Really witty.'

'You do? Wonderful. And what do you think, Rachel?'

Rachel looked at Shelley whose eyebrows were raised in an arc of expectation.

'Very humorous,' she said flatly.

'There you go, Jack,' Faye said, elbowing him in the ribs. 'I told you people would like it.'

Jack shrugged. 'OK,' he said, 'just so long as your Cousin Avril doesn't completely lower the tone by standing up after dinner and telling that joke of hers about how she used to go out with a dentist and the first time they had sex, she didn't feel a thing.'

'What's wrong with that?' Faye came back at him. 'It's funny.'

'No, it isn't. It's crude.'

Faye said it was only crude because it was a member of her family telling it and that if it were somebody from his side, it would be hysterical.

'That's ridiculous.'

'Is it?' Faye said heatedly. 'I don't think so.'

Her parents' bickering was, of course, no worse than usual, but for Rachel it was yet more evidence – not that more was required – that their marriage was over. Suddenly deciding to ignore Shelley's advice about not interfering, she took a deep breath and opened her mouth to speak.

Seeing this, Shelley shot Rachel a glance and cleared her throat noisily.

'So, er, Mrs Katz, how did Aunty Jessie pass away? Old age, was it?'

'Well, she was pretty ancient,' Faye agreed, 'but actually it was more complicated than that. Turns out she'd had pneumonia and had been at death's door for ages. Apparently it was only machines and tubes keeping her going. Then one morning, the hospital cleaner comes in and unplugs her life support to use the hoover. Five minutes later, poor Jessie's gone. Terrible tragedy.'

Rachel started laughing first and pretty soon they were all corpsing. After a couple of minutes, Faye said if she didn't get to the loo she was going to wet herself.

'So, Shelley,' Jack said after Faye had disappeared

and the laughter had died down, 'you going in for this natural childbirth thing then?'

'Yes, I'm hoping to give birth in a pool.'

'Oh, I've read about that. I can see it must be great for you and the baby, but don't the rest of the people find it all a bit unpleasant?'

Shelley looked puzzled, not knowing whether she was meant to laugh or take him seriously.

'It's OK, Shelley,' Rachel explained, straight faced. 'It's just one of his jokes.'

'Oh, right,' Shelley said, giving a polite giggle.

Just then Faye returned from the loo.

'Look, Rachel,' she said, 'we'd better get going. We're due at Bushey in forty minutes, and you know how slow your dad drives. Plus he's got no sense of direction.'

'Faye, don't start. I've had to replace the clutch on the car twice this year. Whose fault's is that, do you mind telling me?'

'Don't look at me,' she said indignantly. 'I don't use the clutch.'

Rachel could still hear them squabbling as they went down the stairs.

'All right, all right,' Faye said to Jack, once they were in the car, 'I didn't mean to criticise your driving. I'm sorry. Forgive me?'

'When have I ever not forgiven you?' he said, putting his hand on her thigh and grinning at her.

She leaned across, put her arms round him and kissed him on the cheek.

'You know, Jack,' she said, afterwards. 'I'm worried.'

'Worried? What about?'

'There's something going on there,' she said, looking out of the car window towards Rachel's flat.

'What do you mean?' Jack said, starting up the engine. 'What sort of something?'

'I found a watch in the bathroom.'

'So?'

'Jack, it was a man's watch.'

'So?'

'So . . . don't you think it's odd. Adam's away and there's a man's watch in the bathroom.'

'Why is it odd? Maybe she had a plumber in to do a repair and he took his watch off.'

'She'd have mentioned it if she'd had a workman in. It's the kind of stuff we talk about. No, she's seeing somebody – she's cheating on Adam, I just know it. How could she do this, Jack? How could she do it? She'll break poor Adam's heart. Not to mention Sam's. Oh God, Jack, what'll I tell Hylda? Her special offer finishes on the fifth of January. She wants a deposit for the reception.'

'Sod bloody Hylda. You'll just have to stall her. If Rachel's having second thoughts about Adam, don't you start pressurising her about wedding receptions.'

'Jack,' Faye said, taking mild offence, 'as if I'd do that.'

'And what's more, don't say anything to her about the watch.'

'But I have to,' she shot back. 'I'm her mother. I can't just sit back and let her end it with Adam and ruin her life. I have to say something.'

Jack turned off the engine and took his wife's hand. 'Faye, listen to me,' he said gravely. 'Just remember what we're involved in at the moment. How would you feel if Rachel found out about it and started interfering? I mean, she'd be bloody furious if she knew. She wouldn't give us a moment's peace. By the same token, she won't welcome you interfering in her relationship with Adam. Leave it, Faye. Her love-life is her business. We have no right to interfere.'

CHAPTER 15

Rachel put down her notes and cleared her throat.

'OK, right,' she said, taking another bite of Marmite toast. 'Has it ever occurred to you there are certain things you'll never hear a man say and certain things you'll never hear a woman say? For instance, who's ever heard of a bloke turning to his girlfriend and going, "I think we have a problem with our relationship"? or a woman gazing at her naked fella and uttering the words, "My, what an attractive scrotum"?'

She took another bite of toast.

'Yeah. That'll work,' she said contentedly. She sat back in her chair, folded her arms and smiled.

Rachel's comedy writing was coming on extremely well – probably, she decided, because it provided a welcome escape from the Adam-Matt issue. She couldn't get over how quickly the ideas had started to flow. By yesterday evening, she'd printed out her first draft. She knew it needed a bit of editing and polishing, but she was pretty sure she had the basis for her five-minute comedy contest set. She hadn't dared to think it up till now, but it was starting to occur to her – particularly after what Lenny had said the other day about her being the best known *un*known on the circuit – that she might just stand a chance of winning this competition.

She folded up the notes and put them in her bag, which was on the kitchen table. Then she looked at her watch. It was gone half-eight. She had less than half an hour to get to Xantia's. Having missed two days' work because of her sprained ankle – the news of which had irritated Xantia no end – she didn't want to be late.

It was only as she stood up that she realised she had nothing on her feet. Her ankle was virtually painfree now, but still pretty bruised and puffy. Discovering late last night that she couldn't even begin to fit her foot into her trainer, she'd phoned Shelley in a panic to see if she owned some Wellington boots or a pair of galoshes. She didn't. The best she could come up with was a pair of multi-coloured Bolivian yak-wool slippersocks with ten knitted toes and ankle tassels. Her mother had given them to her one Christmas – round about 1983 – and she'd never worn them. Ridiculous as they were, the slippersocks, being warm, stretchy and having a grippy rubber sole – were perfect.

Rachel dashed into the bedroom, picked a sock up off the bed and put it on over her bad foot. She then looked at herself in the full-length mirror. The effect of the slipper sock and her combats was hideous, to say the least. She dithered about whether or not to wear the other one, but decided she'd look even odder in non-matching footwear.

She went back into the kitchen to fetch her bag and keys. Then, sticking a cold triangle of Marmite toast between her teeth, she headed towards the front door.

'Hi, it's only me!' Rachel called out as she let herself in chez Marx. When she got no reply, she assumed Otto and Xantia had left for the day.

She began in the kitchen, wiping over the worktops and emptying the dishwasher. Then she went upstairs to the first floor-piazza to change the bed linen and clean the bathroom. When she'd finished, she took the Dyson, the dusters and polish to the top of the house and started cleaning her way back down to the bottom. An hour or so later she'd dusted and vacuumed the entire house. There wasn't a corner she'd missed. Finally she went back into the kitchen to fetch a bucket of water. Having vacuumed the wooden floors, she now had to mop them. She was standing at the sink, squirting wood cleaner into the bucket when she suddenly became aware of somebody behind her. She shot round.

'Xantia,' Rachel cried, her spare hand leaping to her chest. 'God, you made me jump.' She put down the bottle of wood cleaner and turned off the hot tap.

'Did I?' Xantia said with an easy smile. 'Sorry.'

'Forgive me,' Rachel said, still breathless with shock, 'but I'm a bit confused. I've just cleaned the whole of upstairs and I didn't see you. Or Otto. And you didn't reply when I called out to say I was here. I don't get it. Where were you exactly?'

Xantia cleared her throat, a touch nervously, Rachel thought.

'But darling,' she gushed, pushing a stray dreadlock back inside her shroud, 'Otto and I have been in the work-piazza, working. Surely you saw us?'

'But I've just dusted and vacuumed the office,' Rachel protested. 'You weren't there, either of you.'

'I can assure you we were,' Xantia said a little testily. 'I bet the doctor prescribed you strong painkillers for that ankle of yours. If you're anything like me, they play havoc with the memory.'

'But I'm not on painkillers.'

'Oh well, I don't know then,' she said dismissively. 'But we were definitely there.'

Rachel shrugged and shook her head. She could see no point in getting into an argument. But there was no doubt in her mind that when she went into the office to dust, Xantia and Otto had *not* been there.

'So how *is* the ankle,' Xantia said, her face oozing mock concern. 'Still painful?'

'No, the pain's gone. But it's still a bit swoll—'

'Excellent, because I need to ask you something. Otto and I are giving our annual pre-Christmas lunch party on Wednesday the eighteenth, and I was wondering whether you'd be available to take coats and help serve drinks and nibbles?'

'Sure,' Rachel said. 'So long as I can get some

childcare, 'cos Sam will have broken up from school by then. But it shouldn't be a problem.'

'Wonderful.' Xantia moved to go and then turned back. 'By the way,' she said, 'are you going in for the Joke for Europe Contest?'

'Yes,' Rachel replied, slightly taken aback. 'I am. How did you know about that?'

'I was on the phone to my niece – well, she's Otto's niece really – and she told me that she was entering. Surely you've come across Vanessa? She's been on the London circuit for ages.'

Rachel stood and thought. Vanessa. No, the name meant nothing to her, which was odd since she was sure she knew all the London comics entering the contest.

'No,' she said, shaking her head. 'Don't think I have.'

'You really should keep a lookout for her. Hugely talented young woman. She told me that when she finished her audition at Channel 6, the panel actually stood up and applauded. Just between you and me, I think she'll walk all over the competition.'

'Really?' Rachel said, trying and failing to keep the iciness from her voice.

'Oh yes. Otto and I went to see her at the Comedy Café on Saturday night and she was the only one there with anything even approaching star quality. I mean, I'm sure you're quite good too, but Vanessa's an absolute natural. Her parents haven't got much money, so we've been supporting her while she's been struggling to make a name for herself. But her talent is so immense, I'm sure she would have made it even if we hadn't been around to help.'

She paused and shook her head. 'I just can't believe your paths haven't crossed.'

'No, neither can I,' Rachel said, forcing a smile.

As Rachel stood there deciding that even though she'd never met this Vanessa woman, she already hated her, Xantia was busy staring at Rachel's feet. It seemed to have taken her until now to notice them.

'Umm, interesting footwear,' she sniggered. 'I had no idea the slippersock had made a comeback in the suburbs.'

Just as Rachel was considering strangling Xantia with one of her dreadlocks, Otto appeared. He was wearing a lavender silk kimono over baggy white trousers and a matching T-shirt.

'You know, my darling,' he said, opening one of the kitchen cupboards, 'you shouldn't be so dismissive about the slippersock.'

'I shouldn't?' Xantia said, frowning and tilting her shrouded head coquettishly to one side.

'Absolutely not.' He took out a packet of Penguins and started opening it. 'You see,' he went on, biting off half a Penguin, 'what you are failing to appreciate is that there is something intensely intrepid and courageous about the way Rachel is disregarding contemporary style and fashion in favour of these obsolete, laughably absurd *objets trouvés*.'

He paused to shove the last half of Penguin into his mouth.

'I would suggest furthermore,' he went on, 'that there is an irrational, iconoclastic, almost neo-Dadaist quality to this display of hers. Moreover, the blaze of hugely contrasting colours used on the toes of the slippersocks leaves me in little doubt that in her efforts to establish a new artistic language, she has fallen under the powerful influence of the Fauvism School as well as *Art Informel*.'

He finished eating the Penguin and started to unwrap another while Xantia looked thoughtfully at Rachel's slippersocks.

'Do you know, Otto,' she said eventually, 'I think you're right. And would I be correct in thinking I also detect a subtle nod towards *Art Brut*?'

Rachel recognised this term from A-level art. It referred to works of art created by criminals and the insane. But because she was being so supremely entertained by the Marxes' pretension and stupidity, she was no more than mildly offended.

'Very possibly,' he said, nodding solemnly. 'Ve-ry possibly.'

'So, do you think we should ask Rachel to wear the slippersocks to the party? Or even better, perhaps we could get all the waiters and waitresses to wear them. The likes of Charles Saatchi and Damien Hurst would think it was just *so* witty.'

'Superb,' he declared, starting on a third Penguin.

'And why don't we even go a stage further by giving a pair of slippersocks to each of our guests as a Christmas present?'

'That is inspired,' Xantia declared. 'Utterly inspired. Otto, you are a genius . . . don't you think so, Rachel?'

'Oh, definitely,' Rachel said, laughter hovering at her lips. 'Definitely.'

Otto and Xantia disappeared into the hall, busily debating how they would get two hundred pairs of slippersocks knitted in time. A few minutes later Rachel heard their driver beep and the front door close.

She decided to put the kettle on. As she waited for it to boil she found herself smiling at the extent of Xantia's and Otto's affectation. After a moment or two, her smile turned to a puzzled frown as she pictured cleaning the couple's office. They *hadn't* been there. They just hadn't. There wasn't an iota of doubt in her mind. This constant vanishing act of theirs was starting to trouble her. Where in the name of buggery did they go? And why?

As usual she finished work just after one. Instead of going home she was meeting Lenny. He'd heard about her ankle from Chris the booker at The Bathmat and had rung to see how she was. As they chatted they realised they wouldn't be seeing each other before the contest as neither of them had any more gigs booked.

'Tell you what,' Lenny had said, 'I've got nothing on tomorrow lunchtime. How's about I buy you a pie and a pint?'

They arranged to meet at The Red House, around the corner from Rachel's flat. Being close to home, it didn't involve her ankle in any extra driving. 'It's easy to find,' she told Lenny. 'It's right next to the Kall-Kwik photocopying place.'

The pub was pretty packed. There were the men in suits sitting alone with their pints and plates of Terry the landlord's homemade Pad Thai, the groups of girlies sipping spritzers and a few old codgers reading the racing pages, determined to make one glass of Guinness last well into the afternoon. Lenny was nowhere to be seen. Rachel looked at her watch. Even though she'd stopped home to change out of the slippersocks and into a pair of summer flip flops, she was a few minutes early. She decided to get a drink. As it was gone half one and approaching the end of the lunch-hour, the initial rush for drinks and food was over and the area round the bar was nearly deserted. The two barmaids were busy clearing away empties and Terry was standing chatting to a customer while he polished glasses with a tea towel.

''ere, Tel,' the bloke sitting at the bar was saying, in a broad Liverpool accent which Rachel found strangely familiar. 'Have you heard about these new Viagra eye-drops? They do nothing for your sex-life, but they make you look hard.'

Terry chuckled. 'Nice one,' he said, hanging a couple of wine glasses on the rack above his head.

Rachel stood still for a moment, taking in the bloke's

blue velvet jacket and the wild hair which looked like it had a family of starlings camping in it.

'Oh no,' she murmured. 'It's him.'

It was Tractor, the irritating but amusing leather-trousered wally who had tried to pick her up the night she'd come in to buy a carton of orange juice for Sam. Just as he had that night, he was sitting with a copy of the *Sun* in front of him.

'Says here,' he said, draining his pint glass, 'some explorer bloke froze to death at the North Pole. Makes you think. I mean, if you froze to death and went to hell, wouldn't there be some point along the way you'd be really comfortable?'

She found herself smiling and shaking her head at the same time. If she went up to the bar he would probably recognise her and start coming on to her again. She decided to sit herself down at a table in the corner and wait for Lenny. He could fetch the drinks and save her the embarrassment of another encounter with Tractor. But the only free table was a couple of feet from the bar. Reluctantly she took it. She sat down with her body turned away from the bar. Then she took her comedy notes out of her bag and started reading through them, but she couldn't concentrate. Terry and Tractor's conversation kept bursting in on her thoughts.

'So,' Terry was saying, 'any sign of a job yet?'

'Nah. You see, most employers want you to take a written maths and English test. 'Cos I'm dyslexic, that's where I fall down. But apparently they're advertising for lifeguards at the indoor pool down the road. Thought I might give that a go.'

Terry laughed again. 'Do me a favour, Tractor. You've got the body of a whippet with growth-hormone deficiency. Plus you told me ages ago you couldn't swim. Correct me if I'm wrong, but I always thought that was a major requirement of a lifeguard.'

'Yeah, I know, but you don't half get some fit birds up there.'

'True,' Terry said, still laughing, 'and when one of them starts drowning in the deep end, she's really going to let you give her the kiss of life after you've dived in to rescue her wearing your Flipper rubber ring.'

'All right,' Tractor said dejectedly. 'I get the point.' He licked his finger and turned over the page in the newspaper. 'Look,' he said, stabbing at a picture, 'there's that actress – you know, the one with malumbas so large she couldn't ring your doorbell without backing up first. God, what's her name? Anyway, she's had twins. Girls.'

He turned the paper round to show Terry. 'Look.'

Terry, who had four teenagers, merely grimaced.

'You know, Tel,' Tractor said wistfully, 'I'd love to have a baby.'

'What, yer biological clock ticking, is it?' Terry chortled.

'You know what I mean. I'd like to be a dad one day, that's all – after I've finally settled down. I reckon kids really brighten up a home.'

'Yeah, they never turn off any bloody lights.' Terry

paused. 'So you haven't got any other ideas for a job, then?'

'Nah,' Tractor said. 'Not that it really matters because I'm expecting to hear from the Kelloggs people any day now. I tell you mate, once I get the Kelloggs money – wey hey!'

'What Kelloggs money?'

'Didn't I tell you?'

'Don't think so.'

'This is just between you and me, right?' he said, lowering his voice, but not enough so that Rachel couldn't hear perfectly well. 'The thing is, I've invented this new breakfast cereal. Well, not the cereal itself, not the ingredients – more the shape of the bits. It's got a Roman theme.'

'Roman,' Terry repeated.

'Yeah. What I did was design a whole load of these wheaty bits in the shape of chariots, gladiators, slaves, lions and the Emperor Nero with his thumb down. Then I sent the drawings off to the chairman of Kellogg's to offer him first refusal on the idea which, even though I do say it myself, I am in no doubt he will accept. What is more, Terry, my old son – I have come up with this stellar brand name. Get this – you'll love it. *Imperial Cereal*.'

'Imperial Cereal. Yeah,' Terry said, straight faced. 'Yeah, I suppose it's got a certain ring about it.'

'Too right it blinkin' has,' Tractor said emphatically. 'But this is just between us, right? You're not to breathe a word, Tel. Not a word. This could be worth millions, mate. Absolute millions.'

'Don't worry,' Terry said, clearly humouring him. 'My lips are sealed.'

Rachel put down her comedy notes and frowned. For some reason Tractor's cereal invention rang a bell with her. She vaguely remembered somebody telling her about a friend of theirs doing something similar, but for the life of her she couldn't think who.

Just then a particularly pretty twenty-something woman wearing a Lycra top and no bra got up from a table of other twenty-something women and headed towards the bar. Rachel turned round slowly in her seat, unable to resist getting an eyeful of what she knew would happen next.

She watched Tractor giving the woman the once-over, take *The Clitorati* out of his pocket and place it beside him on the bar. When she failed to notice the book, he tapped the cover.

'Brilliant book,' he said, drawing on his fag. 'In my opinion it's a profound and thought-provoking historical analysis of gender conflict from the eighteenth century to—'

'Really?' she cut across him. 'I'm impressed. But if you take another look at the quote on the back, I think you'll find it says "searing historical analysis" – not "profound".'

'Oh,' he said, giving her a wink. 'So you've learned it as well, have you?'

'Not exactly. I wrote it.' She turned the book over. 'You see after the quote it says, Rosie Lloyd – *New Society*. Well, that's me. I'm Rosie Lloyd.'

She turned to Terry and ordered a Perrier, while Tractor, not even remotely humiliated or put off his stroke, started asking her if she fancied going out for a curry.

'It'd be on me,' he called after her as she went back to her seat. 'You could have a starter and everything.'

Rachel was chuckling away quietly to herself when she felt somebody tapping her shoulder. She jumped and swung round to see Pitsy beaming at her. Rachel groaned inwardly. As far as she knew, Pitsy lived in Clapham. She was miles off her patch.

'Rachel, hi. What are you doing here?'

'I live just round the corner. I'm meeting Lenny for lunch. What about you?'

Pitsy pulled out a chair and sat down. She explained, as she took a sip from her Guinness, that she was meeting a girlfriend who also lived in the neighbourhood.

'Listen, Rache, I am just so sorry to hear about what happened to your ankle.'

'Thanks.'

'Must be painful.'

'It was. But it's much better now.'

'So, how's the writing going?'

'Oh not bad,' Rachel said, forcing a smile. 'Getting there. You know.' She folded the papers in half, slipped them inside her bag and put the bag at her feet.

'Well, I've said it before and I'll say it again. If there's anything I can do to help . . .'

Rachel felt inclined to ask Pitsy how she had the bare-faced effrontery to offer her help, when she was so hard up for decent material herself that she was stealing it from Noeleen Piccolo. But she didn't. It would only cause a scene.

'So how's *your* writing going, Janeece?' Rachel asked, through gritted teeth.

'Well you know what it's like when you write all your own material,' Pitsy replied with a deep shrug that had the effect of sending her half of Guinness, which she appeared to have quite forgotten she was holding, almost entirely down Rachel's front.

Rachel let out a shocked cry and leapt out of her seat. Her T-shirt was soaked through.

'Oh, just look at me,' she squealed, pulling her shirt away from her bra and shaking it. 'I'm drenched.'

'Rachel, I really am terribly—'

But Rachel wasn't listening. She was already running to the loo.

Muttering about Pitsy being clumsy as well as stupid and dishonest, Rachel dabbed at her front with paper towels. Her T-shirt was now covered in a very large, very brown stain. The only way she was going to get it out was to soak it in bleach when she got home. All she could do now was attempt to dry it. She spent the next ten minutes standing with her breasts thrust under the hot air hand-drier. She figured that if Lenny arrived, Pitsy would explain what had happened.

As Rachel returned to the bar, she saw Pitsy standing at the table, putting on her coat.

'Hi, Lizzie,' she called out to a woman coming towards her. It was clearly the friend she'd been waiting for. Rachel watched them hug each other hello. Then Pitsy took the woman's arm and guided her, rather briskly, Rachel thought, towards the door.

'She might at least have waited until I got back before running off,' she said to herself. '*And* she's left my handbag on the floor.'

Rachel was too busy darting over to retrieve her bag to notice the one Pitsy was now carrying. It was a Kall-Kwik carrier.

Pitsy had been gone no more than a few seconds when Lenny appeared.

'Christ, sorry I'm late. I got carried away in a seismology chatroom. Then the traffic was murder. Did you know they've found some really interesting new tektites in the Czech Republic? By the way, you'll never guess who I saw walking down the street.'

'Pitsy,' Rachel said glumly. 'She was making a quick exit. She just spilled Guinness down me.'

'It wouldn't surprise me if that was deliberate,' Lenny said.

'Nah,' Rachel replied. 'She's just an all-purpose klutz.

Before I forget – does the name Vanessa Marx mean anything to you? She's meant to be some shit-hot new comic and I've never heard of her.'

Lenny shook his head. 'Me neither.'

'You sure?'

'Absolutely. Why?'

Rachel explained about her being Xantia's niece.

'Come on, Rache, you know how people exaggerate, particularly relatives. She's probably just a Red Coat at Butlins or something.'

'But Xantia was adamant about her entering the competition.'

'Maybe she is. But if we've never heard of her, she's nothing to worry about.'

'I'm not worried exactly. I just hate not knowing who I'm up against.'

'I know,' he said kindly. 'But you have to believe me when I tell you that nobody's got a better chance of at least getting in the top five than you. And anyone who's there or thereabouts will be made.'

'Oh, come off it,' she said, feeling herself going red with embarrassment.

'If only you'd stop being so bloody modest. You know I'm right about the competition, don't you?'

She shrugged. 'Maybe.'

'That's better,' he said, smiling. 'Now, what are you having to drink?'

Joe brought Sam home just after eight.

'Mum, Mum, I've missed you!' he squealed, charging at her and virtually knocking her off her feet.

'Whoa,' Rachel cried out as she hugged him, at the same time doing her best to steady herself. 'Mind my bad ankle. Come on, I think we'd better sit down. Has he been OK?' she asked Joe as she sat on the sofa with Sam, who seemed perfectly content to sit on her lap while she kissed him and rocked him back and forth in her arms like a two year old.

'Absolutely fine,' Joe said. 'Apart from all the Barbra stuff.'

'So, have you heard from her yet?' Rachel said, smiling at Sam and brushing his fringe out of his eyes.

'No, not yet. But I know I will. I'm just certain.'

Rachel shook her head good-naturedly.

'And Mum, you'll never guess what. Greg let me use his blow-torch.'

'His blow-torch?' Rachel exclaimed. 'Gosh, I hope you wore goggles. So what were you doing – burning off old paintwork?'

'Derrr,' Sam said, looking at her as if she were a bit simple. 'We were making crème brûlée.'

CHAPTER 16

Rachel and Shelley carried on down the road, falling about with laughter. In an attempt to enter the Christmas spirit, the owners of the Korean mini-market on the corner had on display in their window a three-foot-tall fibreglass Santa Claus – *nailed to a cross*.

They were on their way to the Post Office to pick up Shelley's new vibrator. She'd broken her last one getting rid of a spider. It had been crawling across the bedroom carpet towards the bed, which she was in at the time. Having once watched a nature documentary which had explained that spiders always run away from loud noise, she had made a grab for the vibrator which she kept on her bedside table. In her extreme panic, however, she'd forgotten to turn the thing on and simply thrown it at the spider. She'd scored a bull's eye arachnid-wise, but had destroyed the vibrator.

Shopping around on the Internet, she'd discovered the Vibromax Turbo 2000, made in Des Moines, had three times been voted Vibrator of the Year.

She'd arrived home from the Flowtex Menstrual Mats

shoot just before one o'clock. A faulty camera had interrupted filming earlier in the week and forced the actors and crew to work Saturday, but the director had taken pity on everybody by twelve and decided to call it a day. When she opened the front door, Shelley had found a card from the Post Office informing her that the postman had attempted to deliver a package that morning. It was now waiting to be picked up at the local depot.

Over the moon that the Vibromax had finally arrived – her pregnancy hormones were making her exceedingly horny and she couldn't wait to give it a test run – she immediately dashed upstairs to ask Rachel if she'd come along with her to collect it.

'That way I get some moral support,' she said.

'Why on earth do you need moral support?'

'Well, it might not come wrapped in plain paper. Can you imagine standing in the queue and being handed a package with *Al's Vibrator Shack* printed all over it? I'd want the ground to swallow me up. If you're there too, you can help me pretend we're putting on a play and it's a prop.'

Rachel had made the point that it was only a week until the comedy competition and she was up to her eyes editing and polishing her material, but Shelley had offered to buy her a cappuccino and a sarnie at Starbucks and so she'd given in.

By now they'd almost reached the Post Office.

'So are you going to tell Matt how you feel about him?'

Rachel stopped briefly and ran her foot through a pile of brown crispy leaves.

'Yep. I just hope he feels the same way, that's all.'

Shelley raised her eyebrows.

'OK, OK. I know he fancies me, but that doesn't mean he's in love with me. Suppose all he's after is a casual affair?'

'It's possible, but from what you've told me about him, I doubt it. So, you've finally decided to end it with Adam, then?'

Rachel nodded. 'I have to – even if I don't get it together with Matt. Things haven't been right between us for ages. If I'm honest, they probably never were. Being with Matt finally made me face up to it.'

Shelley reached out, took Rachel's gloved hand and squeezed it.

'Come on,' she said. 'We're here.'

The bloke behind the collection depot counter looked down at the card Shelley had handed him.

'Ooh,' he said, shaking his head and tweaking a ginger beard hair between grubby nails. 'I'm not sure we're going to have much luck finding this. You can see what a mess we're in.'

Indeed they could. Apparently a mains water pipe had burst the day before and the area behind the counter where all the parcels were stored had been flooded. The smell of wet cardboard hung in the air, and on top of trestle tables stood umpteen untidy piles of sodden, half-open packages – many of them minus their address labels.

'What did you say the parcel had in it?' the chap said to Shelley.

'Oh, erm . . . it's . . .' She cleared her throat nervously. 'What would you say it is, Rachel?'

'Electrical goods,' her friend obliged.

'What – as in a kitchen appliance?'

'More bedroom, really,' Rachel said.

Shelley coloured up and dug her in the ribs.

'What – you mean like a bedside light?'

'Er . . . a bit more animated than that,' Shelley replied.

'Look, we're going round in circles here,' the Post Office bloke said. 'You tell me what it is and I'll do my best to find it.'

Just then Rachel spotted an oblong parcel with the name of their road just about discernible.

'Oh, look,' she said. 'That's it – over there.'

The chap went to fetch it.

'Then again it does look a bit big,' Rachel whispered, 'for a . . . you know.'

'It'll just be the packing,' Shelley told her.

'Um,' Ginger Beard said slowly, putting the package on the counter, 'the road name's there all right, but the number's been washed away. We'd better open it, just to check it's yours.'

'Oh no!' Shelley shot back, colouring up. 'That really won't be necessary. I'm sure it's my parcel.'

But the chap insisted. Apparently under these circumstances it was Post Office regulations.

As Shelley's face grew redder and redder, he carefully opened the parcel. Half a minute later its contents were sitting on the counter.

'Ooh,' he enthused. 'The wife would just love this. She's been nagging me for ages. You see when I'm on earlies, I'm up at five. That means leaving before I have a chance to give her one. This would give her a real thrill.'

He paused. 'So this is definitely your package then?' he asked Shelley.

'Oh, yes,' she said, swallowing hard. 'Definitely.'

The next minute she was making a beeline for the door, the Teasmaid under her arm.

'But it's not yours – you can't keep it,' Rachel panted once she caught up with her.

'I know,' Shelley said. 'I'll drop it back later and say there's been a mistake.'

Shelley was trying to convince Rachel to come back with her and create a diversion by pretending to faint so that she could nip behind the counter, locate the vibrator and run off without Ginger Beard noticing, when they heard somebody calling from across the road.

'It's Matt,' Rachel said, smiling and waving. He was carrying a bulging Waitrose bag in one hand.

'God, he is gor-geous,' Shelley squealed as she watched Matt darting through the traffic towards them. 'He could put his hand inside my drum any night of the week.'

'Hi,' Matt said to Rachel, bending down to give her a quick peck. He smelled deliciously of the cold.

'Hi, you,' she purred, kissing him back.

'How's the ankle?' he enquired.

'Fine. Almost back to normal.'

'So, Rache,' Shelley said, her eyes glued to Matt, 'aren't you going to introduce us?'

Rachel performed the introductions.

'Hello,' Shelley simpered, her voice several dozen octaves lower than usual. She stood still gazing at him, her mouth slightly open, her eyes beginning to glaze over. In the end, Rachel brought her to by standing on her foot.

'Oh, right. Well, I'd best be going. I've . . . er, I've got to go and see a man about a vibrator. Nice to meet you, Matt.' Then she walked away, clearly having no idea what she'd said.

'So *that's* Shelley,' Matt said, putting an arm round Rachel as they began walking down the street.

She nodded.

'Your friend, the spinster who wears fawn and never misses *Antiques Roadshow*?'

Rachel gave him an uneasy smile.

'But she's pregnant, wearing a zebra print coat and seems to have no qualms about telling a perfect stranger she uses a vibrator.'

'I know,' Rachel said innocently. 'It's amazing how much she's come out of herself recently.'

As it was lunchtime and she was missing out on her cappuccino and sarnie, she invited Matt back to the flat for a bite to eat.

'Great,' he said. 'Then I can pick up my watch. I left it in the bathroom when we . . .' His voice trailed off. He took her arm, forcing her to stop. Then he kissed her on the lips.

Back at the flat, Rachel got busy making coffee.

'So, how's the writing going?' Matt asked with genuine interest.

She explained she'd pretty much finished and that it was simply a question of editing and memorising her material now.

'I'd love to take a look at what you've written,' he said.

She coloured up. 'God, I couldn't possibly let you see,' she said.

'Oh, go on – please?'

It took him a few more minutes of gentle persuasion before she finally gave in and went to fetch the printout of her set.

As Matt read through it, every so often he would burst out laughing and repeat bits back to her.

'This is fantastic,' he said when he'd got to the end. 'Absolutely fantastic. I am so proud of you.'

She blushed a second time.

'Come here,' he said, pulling her towards him. 'I want you.'

They had just started to kiss when the intercom went.

'Oh, I forgot. That's Sam back from swimming.'

'Look,' he said, 'if you're not ready for me to meet him yet, I'll go.'

247

Rachel's mind began racing. As far as Sam was concerned she was about to marry Adam. Letting him think she had a new boyfriend would only cause complications – particularly as she couldn't be certain as to the precise nature of her relationship with Matt.

'Could we just pretend you've come to mend the washing machine?' she asked.

'No problem.'

'Hey, Sam,' she called out as her son dashed past her towards his bedroom. 'Don't dump your wet things in the hall. Pick them up and take them to the laundry basket.'

He trotted back obediently, his wet fringe matted and plastered to his forehead.

'Who's that in the kitchen?' he asked.

She told her white lie. Apparently satisfied, he disappeared with his bag of swimming things.

Rachel decided to go and fetch Matt's watch which she'd put in her dressing table for safekeeping. In the end it took her a few minutes to find it. The dressing table had three drawers and she couldn't for the life of her remember which one she'd put it in.

When she came back to the kitchen, Matt was still sitting at the kitchen table, but he had been joined by Sam. Having clearly introduced themselves, they now appeared to be deep in conversation. Rachel stood just inside the doorway, watching them, not wanting to interrupt. It occurred to her that in the two years he had known Sam, Adam had never really sat down and talked to him.

'So how long have you been into Streisand, then?' Matt was saying.

'Oh, I dunno – a year or so. I know all her songs off by heart.'

'Really? My old dad's a huge fan. He's got loads of her records.'

'Me too, but I bet he hasn't got *Pins and Needles*, the 1962 album. Or *Color Me Barbra*, the original 1966 version.'

'No,' Matt said. 'I don't think he has.'

'My dad got *Color Me Barbra* for me last week from this secondhand record shop we go to in Finsbury Park. I've got it in my room. I'll play it for you, if you like.' Sam jumped up from his chair.

'Come on, Sam,' Rachel said, walking into the room. 'Matt's got to look at the washing machine. I'm sure he hasn't got time for—'

'Oh, I can always find a few minutes to listen to some vintage Streisand,' Matt said, standing up. 'Right, Sam. You lead the way.'

As Matt passed her she slipped his watch into his hand and he put it in his jeans pocket.

A few minutes later, Matt came back to the kitchen having left Sam still playing records in his room.

'Great kid,' he said.

Rachel beamed as she poured fresh coffee into mugs.

'It's funny,' he said, sitting back down at the table and taking one of the mugs, 'I've got this cousin – Dudley, his name is. About fifteen years older than me. For years he worked as a small town solicitor, somewhere in Leicestershire, doing divorces and conveyancing. Then in the mid-Eighties he left his wife and took himself off to California. Apparently he did a law conversion course and family rumour has it that he's now some hotshot Hollywood lawyer. Don't know if I quite believe it, but according to my dad, he's Barbra Streisand's attorney.'

'Sounds a bit farfetched to me,' Rachel said.

'Yeah, probably,' Matt said with a shrug.

Rachel took a sip of her coffee.

'Matt – look, I want to apologise for Sam. He's gets a bit carried away with this Barbra thing. It's actually becoming something of an obsession. Joe just encourages it. I wish he wouldn't.'

Matt laughed. 'Do you know, I can't help thinking how much Sam reminds me of myself.'

'What, you were into Barbra Streisand?'

'No. Torvill and Dean.'

Rachel almost choked on her coffee.

'Of course I was a fair bit older than Sam – nearly fifteen. But every time they came on the TV, I just sat there captivated. There can't have been many teenage boys asking their mothers for ice-skating lessons. I even made her buy me one of those Lycra all-in-one suit things. My dad did his nut, of course. Started calling me a poof. I don't think we exchanged a civil word for six months.'

'God, that's awful. How can a parent be so cruel?'

'Oh, you have to see it in context,' Matt said. 'My dad was a builder. Even now, he's a great big hulking bear of a man. All his drinking mates were brickies and scaffolders. Can you imagine the grief they'd have given him if they'd discovered he had a gay son?'

'S'pose,' she shrugged. 'But that's as long as it lasted then, your obsession with Torvill and Dean – just six months?'

'Yeah, I think in the end I just got bored.'

'Oh well, that's good to know.' She gave a nervous laugh.

He began looking at her quizzically. 'Rachel, are you really worried about Sam and this Barbra thing?'

'Worried?' she said defensively. 'Why should I be worried?'

'I dunno. You just seem a bit tense all of a sudden.'

She stared into her coffee.

'You think Sam's going to turn out gay like his dad, don't you?' he said.

'Don't be ridiculous,' she shot back. 'He's only ten. He isn't anything.'

'I agree. But you *do* think he could be gay, right?'

She looked up. 'Sometimes,' she said, almost in a whisper. 'I know it shouldn't matter how he grows up, but I can't help worrying. There's so much prejudice out there and I just want him to have a regular, straightforward life. Is that so wrong?'

'No,' he said, reaching across the table and taking her hand. ''Course it's not wrong.'

'You know, you're the first person I've told about all this.'

'I thought I might be,' he smiled.

'You think I'm stupid and ignorant, don't you – for feeling the way I do?'

'Rachel, that's the last thing I'm thinking. You're not stupid *or* ignorant. But you have to stop worrying. It's probably only a phase he's going through – a phase that has nothing whatsoever to do with his sexuality.'

'Yeah. That's what I keep telling myself, but it's hard . . .'

'I know,' he said gently.

They sat in easy silence for a few moments. She suddenly felt closer to him than ever. She decided to seize the moment, tell him she loved him. The worst that could happen was that he'd tell her he only wanted a casual relationship. She could bear that – for the time being at least. She was just about to open her mouth to speak when he stood up and said he had to get back to his Third World washing-machine invention which was finished but refusing to start.

'But I was going to make you lunch,' she protested.

'I'm sorry, but I really should get going.'

Just then Sam appeared, a Barbra LP in his hand. 'Here, I thought your dad might like *Pins and Needles*. I've got two copies.'

'Gosh, Sam. That's really kind of you, but I'm not sure . . .' He looked up at Rachel.

'No, it's OK. Please, take it,' she said.

'Thanks,' Matt said, ruffling Sam's hair. 'That is really kind of you. He'll love it. I just know he will.'

Sam beamed with pleasure.

Matt bent down and gave Rachel a fractionally sustained peck on the lips.

'I'll phone you,' he said. 'Bye, Sam. And thanks.'

'He's cool,' Sam announced as they walked back into the kitchen. 'He told me this wicked joke about two buckets of sick on a bus.'

She chuckled. 'What do you want for lunch?' she said.

Sam shrugged and sat himself down at the table. 'He isn't really the washing-machine repair man, is he?' he said, dipping his finger in the sugar bowl and licking it.

'What do you mean?' Rachel said, snatching away the sugar bowl. 'Of course he is.'

'Then why didn't he look at the machine?'

'He did. While you were in your bedroom.'

'I didn't hear it going.'

'You probably had your headphones on.'

He didn't say anything for a moment. Then: 'OK, but why did he kiss you?'

'Kiss me?' she said with more than a hint of discomfort in her voice. 'Well, he's . . . he's sort of a friend as well as being the washing-machine repair man,' she said weakly.

'Friends don't kiss you on the lips. Kissing on the lips is like snogging – unless it's your mum or your grandma doing it to you. And you only snog people you want to have sex with.'

'Sam, that's enough. Matt is a friend, that's all. Just a friend.'

'So you're not going to marry him then – instead of boring Adam.'

He was raising too many issues – issues she was nowhere near ready to discuss with him.

'Of course I'm not going to marry him,' she said edgily.

'Wish you were. Matt's a laugh.'

'Yes, I know,' she smiled.

She paused and took a deep breath.

'Tell you what,' she went on in her best deal-brokering tone, 'why don't you phone one of your mates and see if they want to come over and play after lunch. Or even stay the night. And if you're good I'll get Chinese for supper.'

'OK,' Sam shrugged. 'I'll phone Charlie . . . So you're definitely not going to marry Matt then?'

'Definitely. Now off you go and phone Charlie.'

A few moments later, Rachel heard Sam on the phone.

'. . . anyway one bucket of sick turns to the other and says, "You look miserable," and the other one says, "Yeah, I always get sad when the bus gets to this spot – it's where I was brought up".'

Because Charlie's mother was temporarily without a car and couldn't deliver her son to Rachel's, she said it would suit her better if Sam came to their house. She said he could even stay the night.

Rachel dropped Sam off at Charlie's just after two.

On an impulse she decided to go to her mother's. It occurred to her that Faye just might be ready to talk about her relationship with Simon. She'd been feeling fractionally better disposed towards her mother in recent days. When she'd finally plucked up the courage to tell her she'd passed the audition for the Joke for Europe Contest, Faye's eyes had filled with tears.

'But darling, I'd never realised you were this good. I mean, I always thought you were funny, but deep down I just assumed you were kidding yourself. Daddy didn't, though. He always said you had it in you to be a success.'

'Of course, it may all come to nothing,' Rachel warned her.

'It doesn't matter,' Faye had said, patting the back of her daughter's hand. 'You got this far – that's what counts. Oh sweetie, I am so proud of you.' She'd then put her arms round Rachel and hugged her.

Rachel knew her mother would be at home. Every Saturday afternoon her father went to see West Ham, leaving his wife at home with a face pack, a Maisie Mosco novel and a box of Ferrero Rocher.

The moment she pulled up outside the house, she noticed the bedroom curtains were closed. She frowned.

They couldn't be. They wouldn't. Not in the bed Faye had shared with Jack for forty years. It was unimaginable. Wasn't it? She could hear Shelley telling her not to interfere, but she couldn't stop herself. She just had to find out what was going on.

With surprising calmness, Rachel got out of the car, locked it and walked up the garden path. Deciding there was no point ringing the bell because her mother was hardly likely to answer, she went rummaging in her bag for the spare set of house keys her parents had given her in case of an emergency. And if this wasn't an emergency – albeit a marital emergency – she had no idea what was.

It was only as she turned the key that it occurred to her there could be other, perfectly innocent reasons for the bedroom curtains being closed. Maybe Faye wasn't well and had taken herself off to bed. Or maybe her father was in bed. Or maybe they were in bed together. She couldn't simply barge in. She might make a complete fool of herself. Still determined to find out what was going on, she tiptoed into the hall and up the stairs.

She was about halfway up, when she heard voices and laughter coming from her parents' bedroom. She stopped to listen. The first voice was unmistakably her mother's. The second was male. She didn't recognise it. She decided it had to be Simon. So, she'd been right after all. Her mother *was* in bed with him. Feeling distinctly nauseous, she started up the stairs again. She could hear more laughter. Strange – it belonged to a woman, but not her mother. Rachel paused and frowned. Suddenly a man joined in. It sounded like her father. What on earth was going on in there?

The only possible explanation she could come up with was that she'd made a dreadful mistake, that the voice she'd thought was Simon's wasn't Simon's at all, and that her parents had done something like put in new fitted wardrobes and were busy showing them off to friends. But why they would show off new fitted wardrobes with the curtains drawn, she had not the remotest idea.

She reached the landing and edged her way along it slowly, her back and palms pressed against the oyster silk wall, Bruce Willis style. As she got close to her parents' bedroom, she could see the door was open a crack. By now her heart was going like the clappers. The overwhelming likelihood was that her parents were in the bedroom innocently premièring their latest home improvement. What would she say if they caught her spying on them?

Her thoughts were interrupted by the voice she'd originally thought was Simon's and then decided wasn't.

'So what I'd like you to do, Faye, darling, is just relax and perhaps put your legs up a bit – yeah, just like that. Oh, that's fantastic. Just fantastic. Now I've got a glimpse of your bottom and so has Tom. That all right for you Tom?'

Tom? Who was he? And why in the name of buggery was he looking at her mother's bottom? Suddenly she was in no doubt that whatever was going on in that room had nothing to do with fitted wardrobes.

By now Rachel had reached the bedroom door. Blood pounding in her ears, she dared herself to peek through the crack. She must have looked for no more than a few seconds, but it was long enough.

It wasn't her mother and Simon she saw lying half-naked on the bed, their arms and legs entwined, her mother wearing the skimpy cream satin bra and pants Simon had bought her in Selfridges – it was her mother and father. But her relief was shortlived. Kneeling at their feet was Simon – fully clothed and leering. Sitting at the end of the bed, watching Simon watch her parents, sat a puffy, pasty-to-the-point-of-bleached, sixty-something couple. Her immense baggy breasts were tumbling out of a fuchsia lace Wonderbra. His paunch was draped over white Aertex Y-fronts. He was also holding a large pink ostrich feather.

She recognised them at once. It was Coral and Ivan Finkel.

She tiptoed back down the stairs and, silently, let herself out.

CHAPTER 17

'Swingers?' Shelley hooted. 'Don't be ridiculous. Rachel, your parents are elderly Jewish people. Take it from me, they are *not* swingers.'

'But they were in bed with another couple.'

'Hang on, hang on.' Shelley, took a cushion from the end of the sofa and shoved it into the small of her back. 'A minute ago you said they were "on" the bed, not "in" it.'

'In bed, on the bed,' Rachel said with a dismissive wave of her arm as she continued pacing round Shelley's living room like a demented leopard in a cage, 'what's the difference? They're still swingers.' She drained her glass of Château No-shit.

'But were your mum and dad actually doing, you know – *stuff* – with this Coral and Ivan?'

'Well, no,' Rachel conceded. 'Not at that exact moment.'

'And what about Simon? What was he doing?'

'Just kneeling there,' she said, pulling a disgusted face, 'drooling.' Then there was this Tom creep, but I couldn't see him.'

'So, Simon wasn't touching either of them?'

'No, but he was watching. That's almost as bad.'

'And what about your parents? Can you remember precisely what they were doing?'

'I dunno. Cuddling, I suppose.'

'Just cuddling. So, you didn't actually see anybody do anything to anybody?'

'Shelley,' Rachel said, exasperation creeping into her voice, 'my parents and their friends were lying half-naked on the bed. Isn't that enough? What do you think they were about to do – examine each other's bodies for signs of melanoma?' She picked up the bottle of Château No-shit from the coffee-table and refilled her glass.

'So,' Shelley said, 'you legged it without really seeing anything?'

'I didn't need to *see* anything. Look, if they're not swingers, what are they?'

'I dunno,' Shelley was clearly struggling to come up with an answer. 'Maybe they're just . . .'

'Face it – *they're swingers.*' Rachel knocked back some wine. 'Ivan Finkel even had an ostrich feather in his hand. Is that perverted or what?'

'Nah. Perverted's the whole ostrich.'

Rachel giggled despite herself.

'Look,' she said, taking another mouthful of wine, 'this really isn't funny. These are my parents we're talking about.'

'I know,' Shelley said, trying to keep a straight face. 'I'm sorry. I realise you've had a shock today, but I can't help thinking you're getting this whole thing out of proportion. I mean, so what that in their more advanced years, your parents have become . . .'

'Swingers.'

'I was going to say, "become interested in a bit of Bohemian eroticism".'

Rachel gave her a withering look. 'They're perverts. I have perverts for parents.'

'All right, all right. Let's accept, just for a moment, that they *are* swingers. So what? They're doing no harm to anybody. I mean, swinging's a bit naff – a bit Weybridge maybe, but if that's what you're into . . .'

'If it were anybody else,' Rachel said tersely, 'I'd agree with you. But it's my mum and dad. It's bad enough thinking of them having sex at all. But this . . . this *debauchery* at their age. It's disgusting. I mean, why can't they just . . . ?'

'What? Sit on their commodes playing dot-to-dot with their liver spots? Rachel, leave them alone. At least you know now that your mother's not cheating on your dad.'

Rachel gave a tiny shrug. 'I guess,' she sighed.

By now it was late and Shelley, who was finding it almost impossible to stay awake past nine o'clock these days, started yawning. Rachel took the hint.

'Oh, by the way, I didn't tell you,' Rachel said as Shelley opened the front door to let her out. 'I saw that Tractor bloke in the pub again the other night.'

'Oh right,' Shelley said, perking up. 'The joker with

the stylie Seventies' gear and pale skin? I'd really like to meet him.'

'Believe me, you wouldn't,' Rachel said. Tractor was harmless and vaguely entertaining, she supposed. But there was no doubt in her mind that Shelley could do far better. 'For a start he's still trying to pick up women with that ridiculous book. And he doesn't have a job. From what I can tell, all he does is sit in The Red House reading the *Sun* and inventing ludicrous get-rich-quick schemes.'

'Oh,' Shelley said, grinning. 'Like what?'

'OK, get this. He invents breakfast cereals. Apparently his latest has a Roman theme.'

'What, you mean like wheaty, sugarcoated centurions and gladiators?'

'Yeah, he calls it "Imperial Cereal". He's actually sent the idea off to the chairman of Kelloggs. I mean, is that sad or what? Look, I'll speak to you tomorrow.'

She thanked her for the wine and stepped out onto the landing.

'It's OK,' Shelley said. 'And please try to calm down about this swingers thing. It is just possible you've got hold of the wrong end of the stick.'

'Yeah, right,' Rachel said with a doubtful laugh. She turned and started to walk away.

Shelley closed the door. 'Imperial Cereal,' she giggled to herself, leaning her back against the door. 'That's really funny.'

* * *

The phone started ringing the moment Rachel walked into the flat.

'Hi, darling, it's only me.'

'Ah,' she said. 'Mum.'

'You know the thing I love about phoning you, Rachel? You always sound so pleased to hear from me.'

'No, it's not that. I am pleased,' Rachel blustered, running her fingers through her hair. 'It's just that . . .' Blimey, she thought, how do you chit-chat with your mother, when only a few hours earlier you caught her swinging with Coral and Ivan Finkel?

'Rachel, you sound peculiar. What's the matter? Are you ill? Omigod, don't tell me. It's Sam – Sam's ill. What is it? Is it serious? Have you called the doctor?'

'No, no, Mum. It's OK. We're fine. I . . . er . . . It always startles me when the phone goes late at night, that's all.'

'But sweetheart, it's only just gone ten. It's not that late. Are you sure you're all right?'

'Yes, really,' Rachel said, doing her level best to convince herself that her parents' sexual preferences were none of her business, that she had no right to judge them and that to do anything other than have a perfectly normal conversation with her mother would be narrow-minded to the point of bigotry. 'So, how are you and Dad? You two been up to anything interesting?'

She instantly slapped her hand against her mouth. She'd uttered those words before she could stop herself. Now her mother would think she was prying.

'I mean,' she gabbled, 'not that you've probably been up to anything much at all. Probably just had a regular, boring ostrich . . . I mean day.'

'Rachel. Have you been drinking?'

'Me? No. Well, I may have had a couple of glasses of wine at Shelley's. But I think I'm just a bit tired. I've been working really hard learning all my material for Sunday, that's all.'

'I hope you're not overdoing it,' Faye said, sounding distinctly troubled. 'Look, I'm phoning because I want to talk to you about Adam.'

'Adam?' Rachel said, a tad uneasily.

'Yes. Now listen to me,' Faye said, lowering her voice to a virtual whisper. 'I know sometimes the grass can seem greener on the other side of the street, but the thing is, as soon as you set foot on that grass and sample the forbidden fruit, you stand a real risk of setting the cat well and truly among the pigeons.'

'Sorry, can you run that by me again?'

Of course Rachel had understood every word. By getting her mother to repeat herself, she was simply playing for time. Somehow, she hadn't the vaguest notion how, Faye had got an inkling she was cheating on Adam and she had to work out what she was going to say. She couldn't tell her the truth, that she was about to end her relationship with Adam. Faye would only start begging her not to ruin her life. Then she'd burst into tears, hyperventilate with emotion and Jack would have to sit her down and make her breathe into a paper bag. Rachel wasn't ready for all that. Not yet. At the same time, she didn't want to lie. Her only option, she decided, was to get her mother off the line. But how?

It was a few moments before the solution hit her. While Faye prattled on about what a lovely boy Adam was, how she loved him like a son and what a wonderful husband he would make, Rachel rammed the phone between her chin and shoulder and began climbing onto the slightly rickety hall table. Very gingerly she stood up. Her back pressed against the wall for support, she reached up and stabbed the red tester button on the smoke alarm. The earpiercing shriek came instantly.

'Rachel,' Faye squeaked, 'is that the smoke alarm? What's happened? What's going on?'

'It's OK!' Rachel bellowed above the din, as she eased herself down from the table. 'Nothing to worry about. Sam woke up with the munchies, put a slice of bread in the toaster and burned it.' To illustrate her point, she let out a couple of highly theatrical coughs.

'Look . . . *cough* . . . I gotta go . . . *cough* . . . and open some windows. There's smoke everywhere. No, nothing's alight. Mum, listen to me – there's absolutely no need to call the fire brigade. Everything's under control.' She moved her head away from the phone. 'OK, Sam,' she called out, 'I'm coming! Look, Mum, I really have to go.'

With that she put down the phone.

CHAPTER 18

The Dalai Lama smiled and raised his hand in polite refusal as Rachel offered him some deep-fried alligator goujons from her tray. He then returned to his conversation with Anthea Turner.

'My dear Miss Turner,' Rachel heard him say as she moved away, 'I must thank you. I am truly humbled by your insight. I have been Dalai Lama for two thousand years and in all that time, I don't think I have ever perceived enlightenment in quite that way before.'

Rachel watched the Dalai Lama bestow another beatific smile on the TV presenter, give a brief nod and move on.

'Mr Winner,' she heard him cry a few seconds later. 'This is a both a pleasure and an honour . . .'

As Rachel continued to wander through Otto and Xantia's celebrity-packed living-piazza with her tray, earwigging snippets of conversation, she realised she was the only person there she hadn't heard of. She was in no doubt that if all the guests dropped dead at that moment, Parliament, the entire British media, fashion and entertainment industries, not to mention The Ivy and The Priory Hospital, would be forced to close.

Of all the guests invited to the lunch party, the only one Rachel had truly wanted to meet was Xantia's niece Vanessa, but apparently she'd phoned at the last minute to say she was too busy preparing for the comedy contest to come.

'Such a conscientious girl,' Xantia had said in a way that made Rachel feel like an absolute wastrel.

It was gone three now and Rachel, like all the other waiters and waitresses who had been on their feet since the party began at midday, was starting to get backache. The multi-coloured slippersocks, which they had all been forced to wear (the Marxes' OP8 of the People factory having managed to rush them out just in time for the party), although comfortable, failed to offer the support of proper shoes.

Rachel was aware that Otto had spent much of the do standing by the Christmas tree, a ten-foot-high mass of tangled silver wires lit by hundreds of tiny tungsten lights, talking earnestly to Charles Saatchi. From the bored expression on Charles Saatchi's face, Rachel assumed Otto was expounding his slippersock theory. At one point they were interrupted by a call coming through on Otto's mobile. If Otto's slippersock theory had failed to impress Charles Saatchi, the phone call surely made up for it.

'Kofi, Kofi . . . a pleasure as always,' Rachel had

heard Otto gush. 'Such a shame you couldn't be here.' He covered up the mouthpiece. 'I won't be a minute, Charles – the Secretary General of the United Nations is thinking of building a conservatory and wants to pick my brains.'

Xantia, on the other hand, had glided around in a lavender silk sari, her wrists loaded down with silver bangles, working the room like the social operator she was, cold shouldering guests she considered to be of little use to her socially or professionally – Ainsley Harriot, Fern Britton, the Archbishop of Canterbury – while assuming the kind of genuflectory demeanour before others – the Blairs, the Stings, the Amises – which would have done Uriah Heep proud.

Just as Rachel was heading back to the kitchen with her empty tray, Xantia came up to her and said that as it was well after three, people would be starting to leave soon and that Rachel should stay in the hall and be ready to retrieve coats from the master bed-piazza.

Rachel had just deposited her tray in the kitchen and returned to the hall, when the front doorbell went.

'Blimey, that can't be Shelley already,' she muttered. Rachel's car had refused to start that morning because the battery was flat, and she'd had to cadge a lift from Shelley.

'Tell you what,' Shelley had said as Rachel got out of the car, 'I'll pick you up if you like – but only if I can have a nose round the house.'

Deciding that with all the people milling round, Otto and Xantia were hardly likely to notice one more, Rachel agreed.

'You're an hour early,' Rachel hissed as she opened the door.

'Yeah, I know,' Shelley said, stepping inside. 'But I wanted to take my time. You know, get a decent butcher's . . .'

Rachel watched as Shelley's eyes darted round the hall.

'Oh my God,' she said slowly. 'Is this stylie, or is this stylie?'

Rachel explained that the party hadn't finished yet and asked her if she felt up to helping with the coats. 'That way I can show you upstairs.'

'Fine,' Shelley said vacantly, gazing up at the glass ceiling dome.

Eventually the first dozen or so people came into the hall and handed in their numbered coat tickets.

A few moments later, Shelley was following Rachel upstairs.

'Here, Rache,' she muttered, 'did you see that last bloke who handed me a ticket?'

'Yeah – dark chap. What about him?'

'That's him. The one from that film we saw.'

'Which one? From which film?'

'Oh, you remember . . . in the end Richard E. Grant eats him. He's married to that woman – you know, the one out of *E.R.* . . . with the hair.'

At one end of the master bed-piazza two hanging rails on wheels stood loaded with coats.

'Right, come on,' Rachel said to Shelley. 'Help me match the numbers on the coats to the tickets.'

But Shelley wasn't listening. She was too busy standing in the middle of the piazza letting out one gasp of delight after another as she turned slowly through 360 degrees.

'God, Rache, this whole house is awesome. Just awesome.'

'Yeah, I know,' Rachel said, as she began piling coats on the bed. 'But I really could do with some help.'

By now, Shelley was stroking surfaces and opening drawers.

'Shelley, leave the drawers alone. If Xantia came up here and caught you snooping, she'd have a fit.'

But Shelley took no notice and continued to wander round the room.

Having given up all hope of Shelley helping her, Rachel got on with finding coats. As she stood by the hanging rails, getting more and more frustrated with a couple of tickets which appeared not to have partners, she was unaware of Shelley pulling open the milky opaque glass door of Xantia's vast walk-in wardrobe and disappearing inside.

It was only when Rachel finally got all the coats together on the bed and looked round for Shelley to help her carry them downstairs, that she realised her friend had vanished.

'OK, very funny,' she said good-humouredly. 'Come

on, stop playing games. Where are you? I really do need some help now.'

There was no answer.

'Shelley! Hello!'

'I'm in here,' Shelley's muffled voice came back.

'Where?'

'Here. In the wardrobe.'

'OK, come out then,' Rachel said.

'No, you come here. There's something you just have to see.'

'Shelley, that's Xantia's wardrobe. I can't go—'

'Just come,' Shelley commanded.

Rachel went over to the wardrobe and peered in through the open door. But there was no sign of her friend.

'All right,' Rachel said. 'So where are you?'

'Over here.' Shelley's voice was still faint. It sounded almost like it was coming from behind a wall. Rachel stepped into the wardrobe, which was lit from above by two spotlights. There were clothes rails on either side of her. Shelley's voice seemed to be coming from beyond the rail on her right. Rachel pushed some clothes aside to make a gap, bent down and stepped through. All that met her was the side of the wardrobe.

Rachel was exceedingly confused by now. 'Where on earth are you?' she called.

'Here,' Shelley repeated.

'Where's here? Narnia?'

Just as she said the word 'Narnia' the wardrobe side

slid open. Suddenly Shelley was standing in front of her grinning.

Rachel yelped with shock, leapt backwards, bumped her head on the hanging rail and fell onto the wardrobe floor.

'God, you scared me,' she panted as she sat rubbing her head and blinking. By now the partition, door or whatever it was had closed again. 'Do you mind telling me what's going on?'

'Get up. Get up,' Shelley said excitedly as she bent down and took her friend's arm. 'You have got to see this, Rache. It'll freak you out.' She helped her to her feet. 'Now hold on to me and close your eyes.'

Rachel closed her eyes.

'Right now,' Shelley said. 'There's a button here somewhere . . . OK, got it.'

Rachel heard an electronic sliding sound.

'Now then,' Shelley said. 'Mind the step.'

Rachel put her foot down, on to thick carpet.

'Now you can open your eyes.'

Rachel stood, gawping. She could actually feel her jaw dropping.

Shelley had led her into a brightly lit, windowless room about the size of her parents' living room, she supposed. The floor was covered with the gaudiest of purple and gold swirly carpet. The walls were magnolia anaglypta. There was a York stone fireplace, a matching York stone-clad bar, a rose-pink velvet three-piece with fringes and tassels. In one corner, next to the largest and ugliest widescreen TV Rachel had ever seen was a waste-paper bin, also covered in pink velvet. On the imitation Chippendale coffee-table stood a large glass bowl full of fruit, with a pair of filigree grape-cutters on top. There were several nests of tables, identical to the coffee-table, but smaller. On two of these stood gold and onyx lamp with rose-pink pleated shades. Hanging from the walls, between the bookcases packed with false books, were cheap Canaletto prints in heavy imitation-gold frames.

'Oh my God,' Rachel said slowly. 'Oh my God.'

'What is it?' Shelley asked. 'Some kind of ironic joke?'

'So this is where they come,' Rachel whispered to herself, turning her nose up at a plate of stale pizza crusts on the velvet arm of a chair, and a discarded Pizza Hut box on the floor next to it.

'What do you mean, "where they come"?'

'Here. The Deep Pan Pizza-Piazza.'

Shelley gave her a bewildered look. Rachel started to wander round the room gasping, just as Shelley had a few minutes ago in the bed-piazza. Occasionally she would stop to pick up a filigree photograph tree or run her fingers over a china King Charles spaniel.

'Rache,' Shelley said with a puzzled frown, sitting herself down on the pink velvet pouffée, 'come on, you still haven't told me. What *is* this place?'

Rachel finally turned to look at her. 'I'm not sure,' she said.

She explained about Otto and Xantia's disappearing

act and how she would clean the house, certain that they were out, only to have them appear from nowhere.

'When I challenged Xantia about it, she just said they'd been in the office all the time and I'd missed them. I mean, how can you clean a small office and miss two people sitting there? But she was so adamant. I tell you, I was beginning to think I was going mad. At least now I know what's been going on.'

Suddenly Rachel heard footsteps. She swung round. Standing in the doorway, wide-eyed with shock, was Xantia.

'Ah,' she said, swallowing hard. 'So . . . you and your friend have discovered our um . . . our little secret.'

Rachel couldn't help noticing how spectacularly her crimson face was clashing with her purple sari.

'Er, no. Yes,' Rachel spluttered in shocked confusion. 'I mean, it's very amusing, very witty.'

'It is?' Xantia asked, doubtfully.

'Yes. Very ironic.'

Xantia gave a puzzled frown. Then almost at once her face brightened.

'Oh, yes it is, isn't it? It's . . . a project Otto and I have been working on in secret for months.' Her voice was shaking. She paused, clearly trying to construct the rest of her story. 'It's . . . it's a monument to the aesthetic illiteracy of lower-middle-class, middle-aged suburban existence. The . . . er . . . the Tate Modern commissioned it. Of course, we didn't want the press finding out about it until it was ready to be unveiled, so

we decided to create our vision here. In the New Year all
the furniture and ornaments will be moved to the gallery
and we will reassemble our opus.'

She smiled an awkward smile.

Rachel nodded. 'Look, Xantia,' she said, 'we really
didn't mean to intrude like this. My friend, Shelley
discovered the room by accident.'

'Yes,' Shelley piped up. 'It was all my fault. It had
nothing to do with Rachel. I was looking through your
wardrobe. I know it was wrong and I'm truly, truly
sorry. Then I accidentally pressed the button, the partition slid back and . . .'

Just then they heard Otto's voice coming from the
bed-piazza.

'Rachel,' he called. 'Where are you? I've got a hundred people downstairs waiting for their coats.'

'Otto, darling,' Xantia called. 'We're in here.'

Otto came into the room, took one look at Rachel and
Shelley and visibly blanched.

'So I see,' he said softly.

'It would seem,' Xantia continued, 'that Rachel and
her friend have been doing some exploring.'

'Good God,' he hissed, 'what are we going to do? I
mean, if the press get hold of this, we'll be fin—'

'Oh, do be quiet, dahling,' Xantia cut across him
with a nervous giggle. 'The press will be delighted by
our ironic tableau, except we don't want them to hear
about it just yet. And I'm sure Rachel won't say anything
to anyone about our project.'

Otto looked at Xantia and frowned. 'Project?' he said. 'What project?'

'You know, Otto,' she said, '*This* project. The room. I've just been explaining to Rachel how it's about to go on display at the Tate Modern.'

'Oh,' he said. 'Right. No. I'm sure they won't say anything.'

'No, no, of course we won't. I promise. Why would we? And we really are sorry, Xantia, about being here. It won't happen again.'

'No, it won't,' Xantia said, a distinct quiver still in her voice. 'Rachel, you invited a friend here today without my permission. If that wasn't enough, the pair of you have been snooping and going through my things. I'm just not sure I can trust you any more. I'm sorry, but I think you should leave.'

'What? You mean you're sacking me?'

Xantia nodded.

'But,' Rachel pleaded, 'I really didn't mean . . .'

'I think you should go.'

'Xantia, please,' Shelley said. 'It was my fault, not Rachel's.'

Xantia didn't say anything. She simply stared at the floor.

Rachel and Shelley trudged past the Marxes without saying another word. Otto stepped out through the wardrobe after them and began gathering up coats.

As she drove Rachel home, Shelley did nothing but apologise.

'Come on, Shelley,' Rachel said eventually. 'Enough's enough. It wasn't all your fault. It was partly mine. I was the one who said you could look round the house. I should have asked Xantia first.'

'Wouldn't have made much difference. I'd still have found the secret room.'

'You do realise,' Rachel said, 'there's no way it was commissioned by the Tate Modern.'

'Yeah, the thought had occurred to me. If it really were for the Tate, there'd be a Damien Hirst-type pickled sheep's head on the coffee-table. Something gross, to shock people. And if it was simply some kind of art installation, why were they so embarrassed?'

'You know,' Rachel said reflectively, 'I remember reading an article once a few years back about Otto and Xantia being brought up in Gants Hill.'

'Get away,' Shelley giggled. 'What – they're from Essex? Don't be daft.'

'No, it's true. If I remember rightly they were both brought up in Thirties' terraced houses off Woodford Avenue.'

'All right, but so what? They went to St Martin's and became design icons. The rest is history.'

'Maybe not,' Rachel said thoughtfully. 'Just suppose that room isn't a piece of art, but a refuge, a sort of retreat into a past life. Somewhere they feel really at ease and comfortable.'

Shelley burst out laughing. 'That's an absurd idea,' she said. 'They love that house. It's breathtaking.'

'So's the Taj Mahal. It doesn't mean I'd want to live there. Think about it. There isn't one comfortable chair or sofa in the place.'

Shelley considered for a moment.

'So they just pretend to adore it? Really the secret room is the place they love?'

'Yeah,' Rachel said eagerly. 'And that would explain why Otto was so desperate for us not to go to the papers. Can you imagine what would happen if Nettle di Lucca wrote about them having a secret lounge with velvet furniture and Canaletto prints on the walls?'

'But they'd just tell the press what they told us – that it was a whimsical art installation and the whole thing would end up a triumph.'

'Probably. But you have to look at it from their point of view. The way they see it, once their Essex connection is added to the equation, people in that élitist, rarefied world of theirs might think twice before they believed them. Otto and Xantia are worried that they could be denounced as phonies and end up a laughing stock – not to mention totally ruined.'

'God,' Shelley said, her eyes widening. 'You could make a fortune if you went to the papers. Aren't you even a bit tempted?'

'Nah,' Rachel said. 'The Marxes may be the worst kind of pretentious snobs, but I couldn't help feeling a bit sorry for Xantia this afternoon. She seemed so . . . I dunno – vulnerable, almost. No, I could never do the dirty on them.'

CHAPTER 19

'OK,' Rachel continued, as she lay in the bath making shampoo horns with her hair. 'Have you ever thought how different things would have been if the Twelve Apostles had been gay?' She paused and counted three beats for a ripple of laughter. 'The Last Supper would have been brunch. The water at the wedding feast of Canaan wouldn't have been turned into wine, but Bombay Sapphire Martinis with a touch of Curaçao for colour. And the Sermon on the Mount would have been a musical.'

'Yesss . . . finally,' she said out loud.

Until now her delivery had been a tad too fast, but suddenly, despite her nerves and the Joke for Europe Contest being less than three hours away she felt she'd got it just about right.

Every so often over the last couple of days, particularly when she was worrying about the speed of her delivery, her confidence had started to flag, but each time – as if by some miracle – Lenny or Matt would phone to give her pep talks and remind her what an excellent chance she stood of winning the contest. Even Adam had made encouraging noises on the phone from Durban.

Occasionally, like now, she allowed herself to imagine what that would mean. Not only would she get to take part in the Eurovision Comedy Contest finals in Helsinki, but – far more importantly – she would be given her own comedy show on Channel 6. The enormity of this was almost too much for her to take in. She wondered how it would feel to wake up one morning to discover she was famous. Most mornings, the only thing she discovered when she woke up was that she was half an hour late.

She'd have agents, writers, producers, stylists, lawyers. People. People who would speak to other people's people. She giggled.

She'd be recognised in the street. And she'd have money. Real money. Several times she'd fantasised about swanning into the bank and parading her TV contract in front of Mr Lickdish.

She swished the foamy water round her and just for a second tried to imagine what it would be like to have all that and Matt too.

It wasn't simply pep talks from Lenny and Matt, however, which had boosted her confidence.

Two nights ago, after she'd finished her set at The Flicker and Firkin in Chiswick, where her material, albeit old stuff, had gone down a storm, a painfully trendy middle-aged chap wearing strange wiry German glasses and a black suit with a mandarin collar had come up to her in the bar and introduced himself as Robin

Metcalf, the programme controller of Channel 6. He must have spent a full five minutes telling her how talented he thought she was and how much the Channel 6 producers who saw her audition had been raving about her.

'You know,' he said as he turned to go, 'we all have high hopes of you on Sunday. Incredibly high hopes.'

Rachel had thanked him and said something suitably self-deprecating about wishing she shared his confidence, but had secretly felt considerably buoyed up.

She'd also been buoyed up, although nothing like to the same extent she'd been after her meeting with Robin Metcalf, by discovering that the middle classes in north-west London were just as desperate for dailies as they'd always been. She'd only put her postcard in the newsagent's window yesterday and already had half a dozen interviews lined up.

Since Xantia's party she'd met Matt once – for lunch. He offered to go round and sabotage Xantia's Wiener when she told him about getting the sack. Then he'd roared when she told him about the secret room. She'd tried to tell him how she felt about him, but they were in a crowded, noisy pub and it hadn't seemed the right moment.

During this time, there was one thing she'd tried desperately – but failed – to keep out of her mind: Adam was due home on the day of the contest.

She'd decided she couldn't tell him their relationship was over on the phone. Even if he were having an affair, she felt she owed it to him to tell him face to face. But when? She knew she couldn't even begin to cope with the emotional trauma of ending it with Adam and going in for the comedy contest on the same day. Her only option was to pretend everything was OK between them until the competition was over.

That meant she was then faced with the problem of how to keep Adam and Matt apart since they would both be there. Short of running between them like some demented character in a bedroom farce, she hadn't the faintest idea how she was going to prevent them meeting. She'd also been worried about keeping Matt and her parents apart, but that had been resolved by her parents' decision to have Sam for the night and watch the contest on TV.

Then last night, out of the blue, Adam had rung to say one of the dentists who worked for his Uncle Stan had walked out and Stan needed him to fill in until he found a replacement.

'I'm so, so sorry, Rachel,' he'd said. 'I know how much me being there meant to you, but I can't just abandon Stan. He really needs me.'

He'd sounded tentative and nervous. It was obvious to Rachel that he'd been geared up for tears and tantrums. When she didn't cry or make a fuss and told him quite cheerily that she understood and that he shouldn't feel guilty, he was clearly extremely confused by how well she was taking it.

Wrapped in a towel, her hair dripping onto her shoulders, she went into the bedroom and paused to look at the vase of sunflowers sitting on her dressing table. Jack and Faye had sent them that morning to wish her good luck. She was suddenly aware of just how much she loved her mum and dad. Swingers they might be, she found herself thinking, but they were still the same caring, adoring parents they'd always been. What was more, they weren't about to split up. What they did in bed – and with whom – was none of her business. She resolved to bury the memories of what she'd seen the other day – although burying the memory of Ivan Finkel and the ostrich feather was going to take some doing – and try to carry on her relationship with them as if nothing had happened.

Her outfit was lying on the bed. Faye had insisted on paying for it, but having insisted on paying, she'd also hinted heavily at how much pleasure it would give her to come along with Rachel and help her choose it. Rachel had been reluctant to say the least. Their worst fights had happened in Top Shop when she was a teenager, and they'd rarely been shopping together since. She just knew that if Faye came with her, history would be bound to repeat itself. But in the end she decided it would be ungrateful to refuse and they'd met up at Brent Cross on Friday afternoon.

It had occurred to her that Faye might use the occasion as an opportunity to carry on fishing for information about the state of her relationship with Adam, but she didn't. Rachel assumed she'd picked up on how nervous she was about the competition and decided to back off. The nearest she got to bringing up the subject was in Karen Millen when she told Rachel how disappointed she was Adam couldn't make it to the contest.

'I suppose if he's busy, he's busy,' Faye said. Rachel couldn't be sure if she was imagining it, but she was almost certain she detected a hint of annoyance in her mother's tone. It was the first time Faye had ever been anything other than gushingly approving of Adam and all things Adamian.

Once again she'd considered telling her mother about Matt, but decided against it. She wasn't up to stemming the lava flow of maternal shock, tears and cross-questioning which were certain to follow – and little more than twenty-four hours before the most important night of her career, she was especially not up to it. Instead she'd gone on about Adam's Uncle Stan's angina and how Adam felt he just couldn't let him down. Then she'd changed the subject. Faye, clearly seeing the conversation was going nowhere, had taken the hint and carried on looking down the rails.

'Oh!' she'd squealed, a few moments later. 'Just look at this.'

Rachel looked and pulled a face.

'But something sparkly would be just the thing to get you noticed,' Faye enthused, holding the strappy, split-to-the-thigh silver lurex dress up against Rachel.

She'd been on the point of saying, 'Yeah, and maybe we could accessorise it with a kerb and a police prosecution,' but she'd held back because she thought Faye might take offence. Instead she'd smiled and said it wasn't quite the look she was going for.

In the end they compromised on black satin Capri pants, a shiny fuchsia top with a slash neck and threequarter sleeves, and a pair of matching pink suede mules with kitten heels.

Rachel spent the next half-hour carefully blow-drying her hair, doing her make-up and getting dressed. Her outfit was still a bit tarty, she decided – not so much urban chic as Romford chick.

She put this to Shelley when she popped in a few minutes later to wish her good luck.

'Don't be so silly,' Shelley said, her voice oozing calm and reassurance. 'You look fantastic. Now, just go out there and knock 'em dead. Me and Matt'll be there cheering you on.'

'Thanks,' Rachel said warmly, giving her friend a hug. 'You know – for always being there. I don't know what I'd do without you.'

Rachel got to The Gas Station just before seven. Parked outside, as there had been yesterday when she and the other contestants arrived for a technical rehearsal, were three enormous Outside Broadcast vans with dozens of thick electrical cables spilling from their rear doors and snaking over the pavement. Treading carefully, Rachel followed the cables inside. The lobby was packed with puffing, sweating blokes in T-shirts, humping equipment and bumping beer guts. As she stood watching them, the

SUE MARGOLIS

reality of what was about to happen – that she was going to appear live on national TV – suddenly dawned. Feeling desperately alone, she started to shake.

'Oh, hi. Can I have your name, please?'

Rachel spun round to see a smiling girl in a black puffa jacket carrying a clipboard. Hanging from a chain round her neck was her Channel 6 pass. Rachel identified herself. The girl scanned her list, ticked Rachel's name and directed her upstairs to the green room.

It was brimful of smoke and nervous chatter. Most people were lounging around in small groups, either on the floor or on red plastic chairs. Anyone who didn't have a fag in their hand was clutching a bottle of Perrier. Several people were pacing up and down looking pale and alone. Among these was a male ventriloquist carrying a dummy. Both were dressed as Nana Mouskouri.

At one end there was a long buffet table full of sandwiches and soft drinks. Above this were three TV monitors. Thinking a can of Coke might settle her stomach, Rachel headed towards the table, smiling and saying hi to people as she went. She was taking her first sip, when she saw Lenny coming towards her.

'Hiya, Rache. How you doing?' He kissed her on the cheek.

'Oh, fine – apart from feeling I'm going to chuck up any minute . . . you?'

'Same,' he said with a feeble smile. He reached for a Seven-Up.

Lenny had just suggested they went outside for some fresh air when the clipboard girl came in to collect half a dozen people – including Lenny – and take them off to make-up.

As Lenny disappeared out of the door, Pitsy walked in. She saw Rachel immediately and waved. She was wearing a short scarlet satin dress, red ribbons in her pigtails and matching clumpy platforms. Rachel looked to see if she'd shaved off her tarantulas. She had. Clearly somebody at Channel 6 had taken her to one side and had a quiet word.

'God, Rache,' Pitsy said, joining her at the table, 'you look a bit green. You're not nervous, are you?'

'Oh well, you know,' Rachel smiled, taking another sip of her Coke. 'Maybe just a bit.'

'Really? Of course I've never suffered from nerves. That's because I'm always so confident about my material. I think people only get nervous when they're not sure their stuff's up to it.'

She was considering pouring her Coke over Pitsy's head, when the clipboard girl returned and called Rachel's name.

Rachel, along with all the other contestants, had known her position in the competition running order for some days. She was due on last. The advantage of this was that when it came to the voting, she would still be fresh in the judges' minds. The disadvantage was that she had to wait an hour and a half to go on.

Once the contest had started, she couldn't bear to stay in the green room watching the other comics on the monitors in case they were absolutely brilliant and undermined her confidence completely.

Instead she paced up and down outside until she got too cold, or sat alone in the bar next to the auditorium, reading through her material and listening to the laughter coming from the audience. It was while she was sitting in the bar, twenty minutes or so before she was due to go on, feeling sicker than ever that she realised there was no longer any point reading through her material. If she didn't know it now, she never would. If it was crap, it was too late to change it.

For a few moments, she sat staring into space. Then she started looking for displacement activities. Anything to ease her rising panic. First she began flicking crisp crumbs off the table. When all the crumbs had disappeared onto the floor, she reached into her bag for her make-up mirror. Her face looked fine. Then, as she put the mirror back, she noticed a comedy contest programme lying on the chair opposite her. She leaned across the table and picked it up. The centre pages contained a list of contestants. Underneath each name was a five- or six-line biography. It was only as she scanned the columns of names that she realised Vanessa Marx wasn't listed. Rachel thought it distinctly odd, since Xantia had made such a song and dance about her niece appearing in the contest.

She shrugged. She could only assume Vanessa had

pulled out or that Xantia had got her wires crossed in some way. Shoving the piece of paper into her bag, she thought no more about it.

By a quarter to ten, she decided to go back up to the green room and watch Pitsy, who was on immediately before her, on the TV monitor. Assuming she didn't have the nerve to use her stolen Noeleen Piccolo material tonight, she would therefore be back on her usual submediocre form, Rachel couldn't wait to see her. The woman was clearly about to make a complete fool of herself.

But Rachel never made it to the green room. Instead she was grabbed by the now frantic clipboard girl who had been looking for her everywhere. She led Rachel through some doors and along a corridor towards the stage.

The pair stood in the wings, Clipboard in front, a few feet nearer the stage, holding Rachel's handbag. After a minute or so the make-up girl turned up, wearing a gormless smile and a hat like an inverted flower pot over short blonde ringlets. She began dusting Rachel's face with powder and spraying lacquer onto her hair. On stage, Lenny was doing a few minutes compèring before Pitsy came on.

'Thank you, Dennis,' he was saying, referring to the previous comic, 'for that rare insight into the British and their bogs. Of course, where I come from we don't wash our hands after going to the lavvy. In fact, we don't wash them after unblocking the lavvy . . .'

There was a burst of laughter from the audience. A moment later he was introducing Pitsy.

The make-up girl continued to faff with Rachel's hair. Despite her nerves, she managed a quiet snigger. If anybody was about to get their comeuppence it was Pitsy bloody Carter.

'I've been going out with this bloke for the last year or so,' she began. 'Of course we're totally incompatible. I'm a Virgo. He's an arsehole . . .'

As the audience roared, Rachel let out a loud gasp.

Clipboard swung round and hissed at her to be quiet.

Rachel couldn't apologise on account of her mouth being wide open and her hand over it. With no thought to the make-up girl, who was still busy spraying and arranging her hair, she moved a few paces closer to the stage.

'He's always going on about what a gentleman he is. To which I say, "Why? Because you get out of the bath to piss in the sink?"'

Another huge laugh.

Rachel couldn't believe Pitsy's audacity – not to mention recklessness. She was going live on national television with Noeleen Piccolo's material. She carried on with her routine – then suddenly it changed.

'So anyway, have you ever thought how different things would have been if the Twelve Apostles had been gay?'

Rachel's stomach gave one almighty lurch. Assuming her ears were deceiving her, she simply stood there listening and blinking.

'The Last Supper would have been brunch. The water at the wedding feast of Canaan . . .' Rachel's stomach lurched a second time. She opened her mouth to speak, but all that came out was a tiny muffled yelp. She tried again. Her jaw moved up and down, but still no words came. Instead she stood there in gobsmacked, wide-eyed shock and amazement.

'And the Sermon on the Mount would have been a musical.'

A roar – with clapping – could be heard from the audience.

Finally Rachel managed to blurt out a few words. 'Omigod,' she said in a strangulated gasp. 'That's my material. Pitsy's stolen my material. She's fucking stolen it.'

Clipboard swung round for a second time. 'For heaven's sake, will you please be quiet.'

'But you don't understand. She's—'

'Look, you're just having a last-minute panic,' Clipboard soothed. 'Try to relax. You'll be fine when you get out there.'

Pitsy was getting into her stride by now.

'. . . like, who's ever heard of a bloke telling his girlfriend: "I think we have a problem with our relationship"? Or a woman gazing at a guy and saying: "Jeez, what a cute scrotum"?'

Another surge of laughter from the audience.

By now Rachel was hyperventilating and quite literally tearing at her hair. Seeing this, the make-up girl let out a distraught squeal and came at her with a brush.

'Look, just piss off, will you?' Rachel hissed. The startled girl leapt six feet backwards.

'You don't understand – it's *mine*. That's my set,' Rachel said in a whispered shriek. 'Every word. Every sodding bloody buggering word.'

It occurred to Rachel to march out on stage and put a stop to Pitsy's set. But enraged as she was, she had the sense to realise that nobody would believe her. She would come across as a jealous, ranting madwoman and end up being removed by Security. Added to that, her career would be over. As if it wasn't already.

So she just stood there, continuing to tug at her hair and jump up and down with fury. If she got hold of Pitsy she would kill her. No, first she would phone Noeleen Piccolo and the two of them would kill her. Then they'd throw her body to the dingos.

It wasn't long before Rachel's rage gave way to panic. She had no material to go on stage with. Nothing. It was all she could do to stop herself bursting into tears. There was nothing for it, she'd just have to go on and perform old stuff. She took a deep breath. OK . . . OK, she thought, doing her best to calm down and focus. What would she use for an opener? But her mind was a blank. A complete and utter blank.

She looked at the stage. Pitsy had finished her set and had left, presumably from the far side. The applause was deafening. She turned her head towards the audience.

People were standing up, whooping and cheering. The vote was a mere formality, Rachel thought. Pitsy had won. Pitsy had stolen her material and won. Rachel's head started to spin. She felt sick. Thinking her legs were about to give way, she grabbed the stage curtain for support.

Finally the applause died down and Lenny started telling the audience that he was about to put on a slide show. There was more loud laughter and applause when a moment later the back of the stage was lit up with pictures of children's playground slides.

The next moment Lenny was announcing Rachel's name.

'Right,' Clipboard said. 'Remember what we told you in rehearsal – just go out there, have fun and ignore the cameras.'

Then she dug her clipboard in Rachel's back. Rachel frequently got the jitters before going on, but she'd never experienced anything like this. Numb with fright, she didn't move. Clipboard dug a second time. After a moment or two, she took a couple of faltering steps towards the stage. She was about to take a third when she felt somebody grab her arm.

'Rachel. No. You can't.'

She turned. It was Matt. Shelley was standing by his side. Both of them looked breathless and utterly distraught. Matt drew her back into the wings.

'She stole my material,' Rachel blurted out. 'That woman who was on before, she stole it.'

'I know,' he said, putting his arms round her. 'Shelley and I saw everything.'

'Look,' Clipboard cried out, her voice a mixture of panic and exasperation, 'will somebody just explain to me what's going on? Who stole what? Rachel, you have to get out there. Please. They're waiting.'

'She's not going anywhere,' Shelley announced, reaching out and grabbing Rachel's handbag off Clipboard. 'Except home.'

'Rachel Katz . . .' Lenny announced anxiously for the second time. And for a second time her music struck up.

By now Matt and Shelley were virtually frogmarching Rachel past the bewildered technicians and backstage people towards the stairs which led down to the stage door.

'Please. You can't leave,' Clipboard called frantically as she and the make-up girl came after them. 'Come back!'

'Rachel Katz . . .' Lenny announced again with a nervous laugh and a loud clearing of his throat. More music.

'Oooh,' Rachel heard the make-up girl squeal. 'It's just like that scene in *The Sound of Music* when the Von Trapps do a bunk to Switzerland.'

Choking back tears, Rachel did her best to think of a few of her favourite things, but couldn't.

CHAPTER 20

It was a few seconds later, as they reached the stage door, that Rachel finally broke down. For a full five minutes she sobbed uncontrollably into Matt's shoulder, while Shelley patted her gently on the back.

'Come on, sweetheart,' Shelley said eventually, 'let's get out of here. There's nothing you can do now.'

Rachel sniffed. Then she suddenly raised her head and broke free from Matt's embrace. 'That's just where you're wrong,' she said, her face etched in grim determination.

Before Matt and Shelley could stop her, she was charging back up the stairs towards the green room where she knew all the contestants would be glued to the TV monitors, as one by one the panels from thirty regions nationwide announced their results. She threw open the door and charged in, looking positively thunderous. Everybody turned round, startled. She could tell by their awkward expressions that they'd been gossiping about her and why she had apparently lost her bottle. She searched round frantically for Pitsy, but couldn't see her.

'*Pitsy,*' Rachel's voice boomed. 'Where the bloody hell is that bitch? Come on, tell me: where is she?'

Nobody spoke. They simply gawped at this raving, panting woman, boiling over with fury, who had quite obviously lost her grip in the minutes leading up to her performance and had now progressed to some kind of frenzied psychosis.

'She's not here,' somebody said tentatively, clearly trying to placate the madwoman. 'We haven't seen her. Try the loo.'

Rachel spun round on her heel and virtually collided with Shelley and Matt.

'Rachel, please. Stop this,' Matt implored her, taking hold of her arm. 'Shelley's tried the loo. She isn't there.'

But Rachel wasn't listening. She yanked her arm away, ran down the corridor and charged into the Ladies. If she got hold of Pitsy she would rip out her intestines and wrap them round her pointless, scrawny little neck.

Like some deranged, pre-menstrual Kung Fu fighter, she kicked open every cubicle door. Nothing. Pitsy had clearly gone into temporary hiding. Only to emerge, no doubt when the final score was announced and she was declared the winner.

A second later she was running up and down the corridor shaking door handles and yelling Pitsy's name.

'Janeece, I'm going to get you, you marsupial-fucking, kleptomaniac bitch.'

Every room was locked. She could think of nowhere

else to look. Frustrated and defeated, she stood bashing her head slowly against one of the doors.

'Come on, Rache,' Matt whispered, putting his hands on her shoulders. 'Why don't we all go back to my place and get monumentally slaughtered.'

She let him put an arm round her.

'No, the two of you go,' Shelley said diplomatically. She handed Rachel her bag. 'I'll go back upstairs and wait for Lenny to come offstage. Someone should tell the poor guy what's been going on. Then I'll go home and phone your mum and dad and Joe – let them know you're OK. I'll say you'll phone them tomorrow. You're not up to it now.'

She gave Rachel a hug, shot Matt an affectionate smile and headed towards the door. Rachel stared after her, full of gratitude. It was true – she was in no fit state to talk to any of them. Not yet.

Once they'd got going and the van warmed up, Rachel began to calm down a little. She started thinking about how Pitsy might have got hold of her material.

'Oh my God,' she said slowly after a minute or so. 'I know how she did it.'

She gave Matt the lowdown on Pitsy and how she'd stolen Noeleen Piccolo's material. Then she told him about the day she'd been at The Red House waiting for Lenny, when Pitsy had turned up.

'She spilled her Guinness down me. I went to the loo to sort myself out, leaving my bag at the table. My notes were inside. I must have been gone a good ten minutes.

Christ, she had time to read through everything – write stuff down, even.'

'Perhaps she didn't have to write it down,' Matt said thoughtfully. 'Maybe she photocopied it. My flatmate drinks at The Red House. I've been there to pick him up a couple of times when he's got legless, and I've noticed there's a Kall-Kwik right next door. Thing is, why would she do it?'

'Same reason she stole Noeleen Piccolo's material. Pitsy's deeply untalented and she knows it, but she's also pathologically desperate to be famous. What do you do when you're as desperate – not to say barking – as she clearly is and you can't come up with your own gags? You pinch somebody else's.'

Matt simply shook his head in disbelief.

'Thank you for being there,' she said, managing a smile. 'I can't tell you how much it means to me. If you and Shelley hadn't rescued me, I'd have gone out there and made a complete arse of myself.'

He squeezed her knee. 'Look,' he said warmly, 'I know everything seems bleak and hopeless right now, but you *will* get your career back on track. And with talent like yours, you will make it to the top. It's just going to take a bit longer than you thought, that's all.'

'Yeah, maybe,' she said softly, to please him more than anything.

Neither of them spoke for a moment or two.

'You know,' Matt said thoughtfully, 'there must be some way of exposing this Pitsy creature.'

'How? There's no copyright on jokes. And even if there were, I'd have no way of proving the material she used tonight was mine.'

'Yes, you would. I read it. I came to your flat last week – the day I met Sam – and read it.'

She smiled again and rubbed his arm affectionately. 'And who do you think's going to believe you? You're sleeping with me – you're bound to say that.'

Reluctantly, he took her point.

Although it was the Sunday before Christmas, there was virtually no traffic and they reached Matt's flat in Muswell Hill in less than twenty minutes. It was at the top of a large, slightly rundown Thirties' block.

While he fetched some whisky tumblers from the kitchen, Rachel went into the living room and sat herself down on the battered aubergine leatherette sofa, removing what she assumed was part of a washing-machine motor from the small of her back. She began looking round the room – at the smoked-glass coffee table, covered in smears, half-full mugs, old newspapers and more mechanical odds and sods, the balding, crusty brown carpet, the Andy Worhol *Campbell's Soup* print, the G-Plan-style fire surround with a bottle of Eau Sauvage on top – Matt's flatmate's, she assumed – the torn vertical blinds at the window. The whole place gave the impression of having been put together round about 1974 and not having seen a hoover or can of Pledge since. All it lacked was a stainless steel fondue set and a bowl of stuffed olives gathering dust on the sideboard. God, she thought, Adam would demand one of those anti-germ warfare suits before he'd set foot in here. She, on the other hand, although she wouldn't have wanted to live there, couldn't help finding it all rather bloke-ish and appealing.

'You know, Shelley would love this room,' she said when he came back with the glasses and a bag of ice.

'This? It's a pit.' He went over to the white melamine wall unit and opened the fold-down door of the cocktail cabinet.

'Yeah, but it is just so retro.' Like the chief mourner at a wake, Rachel felt relieved to be discussing something mundane for a few moments. 'Shelley adores anything like this. You haven't seen her flat. It's amazing. A bit over the top colour-wise, maybe, but she's got a real feel for design. If you were OK with hanging onto the furniture and keeping the Seventies' theme, she could really make something of this room.'

'Funny you should say that,' he said. 'I've got the decorators coming in tomorrow to give me an estimate to do the whole place. They said they could work through Christmas and finish it in time for when my mum comes to stay in the New Year.'

Rachel looked at him, frowning.

'You've found people to work through Christmas?'

'Sikhs,' he said.

'Oh. Right. Well, why don't I come tomorrow and bring Shelley. She's bound to have some bright ideas.'

He came over and handed her a glass of Scotch. 'You sure you're going to feel up to it?'

'Probably not,' she smiled. 'But I'll only sit at home obsessing about Pitsy if I don't.'

'OK. Great,' he said. 'I was going to ask the two of you over anyway. I'm planning to test-drive my Third World invention. It's finally finished. The Burkina Faso trade delegation are coming to see it at the beginning of January and with a bit of luck they'll . . . well, you never know.' He sat himself down next to her on the sofa.

'That's fantastic, Matt,' she said, pulling him towards her and kissing him. 'I wouldn't miss it for the world.'

She glanced at her watch. 'The voting must be over by now,' she said. Before he could stop her she'd stabbed the remote. 'Call it morbid curiosity,' she said, taking a glug of Scotch. 'But I have to be certain she won.'

The TV screen was filled with shots of a jubilant Pitsy in the green room surrounded by all the other contestants, swinging her winner's trophy in the air and swigging champagne from a magnum bottle.

A tear rolled down Rachel's cheek.

'Surprise. Surprise,' she murmured. She turned to Matt. 'That should have been me.'

'I know,' Matt said softly, wiping away the tear with his finger. He got up, came back with the whisky bottle and topped up her glass.

'Of course,' Pitsy was trilling to some TV reporter Rachel didn't recognise, 'I couldn't have done it without my aunt and uncle who have supported me in my career ever since I left Australia.'

'I didn't know she had an aunt and uncle over here,' Rachel said.

Pitsy was immediately joined by two more people.

'Oh my God,' Rachel yelped, almost choking on her Scotch, 'it's Xantia and Otto. Pitsy's their niece?' She watched as they both hugged and kissed Pitsy. 'I don't get it. Xantia said her niece's name was Vanessa.'

The sight of Pitsy and the Marxes posing for the press photographers was suddenly more than Rachel could bear. She turned off the TV.

'Hang on. Hang on,' Matt said, leaning towards the coffee-table and picking up the *Radio Times*. 'I'm sure there was a piece about the contest in here.' He flicked through the pages. 'Yeah, right. Here it is.'

He passed her the magazine. A double page was filled with individual pictures of all the contestants – Rachel included. Underneath each one was a short biography.

'I never knew about this,' she said, shaking her head. She found Pitsy's picture almost immediately and began reading the blurb.

' . . . "born Killadingo, Queensland, 1974 . . . blah, blah, blah . . . proud parents Roy and Nadine Carter . . . British-born Nadine is sister of the world-famous interior designer, Otto Marx". Right, here it is: "her parents named her Vanessa, but since turning professional in 1999, she has opted to use her second name, Janeece".'

She tossed the magazine back onto the table.

'So,' Matt said, 'do you think the Marxes have any idea what she's been up to?'

'Dunno. I mean the Marxes are pillocks, but I can't imagine them actually being part of something like this.' She leaned back against the sofa and began rubbing her eyes.

'Come on, you're knackered,' Matt said. 'Why don't you get some sleep now?'

This time she didn't argue.

Matt's bedroom was strewn with clothes, newspapers and even more bits of metal and mechanical junk.

'Sheets are clean though,' he said as she took a pile of circuit boards off the bed and put them on the floor.

He pulled her to him. 'We will sort this out, you know,' he said softly. 'Somehow. I promise.'

'We?' she said. 'How d'you mean, "we"?'

He paused and took a deep breath. 'I mean,' he said, holding her eyes in his, 'I love you.'

'You do?'

He nodded. 'You sound surprised,' he said.

'Well, I thought maybe you might, but I wasn't sure.'

She sat down on the bed. He came and sat next to her. Then with his hand on her chin, he turned her face towards him.

'So, do you feel the same way?'

She gazed back at him. 'Definitely,' she said.

Their deep, tender kiss seemed to go on for ever. Afterwards he hugged her so tight she could barely breathe. She knew full well she should tell him about

Adam and that she was planning to end it the moment he got back from South Africa, but she couldn't. She was afraid he might be angry with her for not being straight with him, and after the night she'd had, she felt utterly incapable of dealing with it.

After he'd let her go, he opened the chest of drawers and gave her a neatly folded shirt to put on. Then he insisted on making her hot milk.

When he came back, she was already in bed. He handed her the milk in a South Park mug. When she'd finished, he lay down beside her, stripped to his boxers, holding her and stroking her head.

'Night,' he said, kissing her forehead.

Despite the whisky, the hot milk, and him holding her, she couldn't drop off.

'Matt, you awake?' she said after ten minutes or so.

'Just about,' he mumbled.

'I can't sleep,' she said. 'I just keep going over and over what happened tonight. You haven't got any sleeping pills, have you?'

He propped himself up onto his elbow and switched on the bedside light.

'No, but I've got something far better,' he grinned.

'Oh Matt, I'm knackered. I really don't feel like . . .'

The next thing she knew he had thrown off the duvet. Slowly he began unbuttoning the shirt she had on, nipping and kissing her breasts as he went.

'Right, take it off,' he said, 'and roll over onto your stomach.'

A few moments later he was straddling her and she could feel oil being drizzled over her back. There was a powerful smell of lavender.

Slowly and expertly he began massaging her neck and shoulders, pressing his fingers into the hard, knotted muscles. A couple of times she flinched with pain. Then, very gradually the discomfort began to ease and she could feel herself starting to relax.

'Oh, you are good at this,' she whispered. 'Very good.'

He carried on like this for a while. Then he began kissing her neck and shoulders. Lying beside her now, he trailed his fingers along her spine. Soon he was stroking her bottom through the cotton of her pants. As he ran his finger between her buttocks, she quivered with delight.

She turned over and let him pull off her pants. By now she could feel moisture seeping out of her. His fingers found it. Moments later they were gliding over her clitoris.

'Just let go,' he urged her softly. She felt herself drifting away, floating on a sea of pure pleasure. Soon she felt the first spasm and then another.

Afterwards he planted tiny kisses all over her face, stomach and breasts.

'Now sleep,' he commanded kindly, pushing her fringe out of her eyes.

'Thanks again for being there tonight,' she said, starting to feel drowsy now.

'I'll always be there,' he whispered.

*　　*　　*

The moment she woke up, the memory of what had happened at the comedy contest hit Rachel like a wrecker's ball. But at the same time, she felt oddly, irrationally buoyant. Then she remembered Matt had told her he loved her. She let out a couple of contented little sighs and turned over to put an arm round him, but he wasn't there. Almost at once she heard his voice coming from the living room. There was a second voice, too. Also male. Bound to be his flatmate, she thought. She listened, but couldn't make out what they were saying.

As she examined her feelings about last night more closely, she realised that her fury had by no means disappeared. What had disappeared, however, was the feeling of hopelessness – the fear that her career was over. It had been replaced, probably as a result of Matt's positive thinking rubbing off on her, she decided, with an overpowering determination to expose Pitsy and get even with her.

She stared up at the ceiling. Maybe she should start with the obvious – find Pitsy, appeal to her better nature and beg her to admit publicly what she'd done. She laughed out loud. The idea was absurd. First Pitsy was barking and didn't have a better nature. Second she would have gone to ground by now and be impossible to find.

The only alternative was to speak to Xantia. Deeply buried as it was, Rachel was certain the woman did have a more human side. She'd seen glimmerings of it when she and Shelley discovered the secret room. For a few moments Xantia's haughty eloquence had given way to bumbling, beetroot-faced embarrassment. But whether her human side extended to her possessing feelings for anybody other than herself, it was hard to say.

But there was a chance – albeit slim to the point of being waiflike – that she might be able to convince Xantia of what Pitsy had done, and that Xantia might respond by being so outraged that she would agree to put Rachel's case to the people at Channel 6. She was bound to have contacts there. She probably even knew Robin Metcalf, the programme controller who'd introduced himself to Rachel at The Flicker and Firkin in Chiswick.

Rachel knew it would be impossible for her to be declared the winner of the contest in Pitsy's place. It would be far too complicated, not to say embarrassing for Channel 6. All she wanted was for her reputation with them to remain intact. That way they might at least consider offering her some television work in the future.

The only problem with her plan – apart from Xantia refusing to see her or refusing to believe her story – was that since the Marxes always spent Christmas in Venice, she wouldn't be able to get to her until the New Year. Monumentally frustrating as it was going to be to sit out Christmas worrying and speculating about what her reaction might be, she had no choice.

Eager to hear what Matt thought of her plan, she got

out of bed, put on the dressing gown he'd left out for her and headed into the hall. As she stood there doing up the dressing-gown belt, she could hear Matt's voice quite clearly now. He was having a go at his flatmate about the mess in the living room and in particular some empty curry cartons which hadn't been thrown away. After a moment or two she heard the second voice. Her hand flew to her mouth.

'Look, I'm sorry, mate,' the voice with the unmistakable Liverpool accent was saying. 'I was going to clear it up last night when I'd finished, but it was gone two by then and I was feeling dead miserable. I'd had to ditch me blind date. She turned out to have eyes like two limpid pools – which was brilliant – except she had a nose like a diving board.'

'Tractor?' Rachel murmured to herself in utter disbelief. 'Matt's flatmate is *Tractor*?'

She opened the door a crack and peered in, to check her ears weren't deceiving her. They weren't. There he was, lying outstretched on the sofa. He was reading the paper and drawing on a fag, wearing nothing but his leather trousers. Matt was standing by the dining table, gathering up curry containers.

'And what about all this crap on the floor?'

She could see that the floor immediately surrounding the table was a sea of small objects which looked like they were made of paper.

'It's me origami.'

'I'll pick it up then, shall I?' Matt said sarcastically.

'Look, I've said I'm sorry. Just leave it. I'll do it later.'

Matt bent down and began sweeping the bits of origami together with his hand. Then he picked one up and began staring at it. She could just about see it was petal-shaped with lots of folds.

'So, what are they?' Matt said, shoving his finger inside one of the folds.

'Cunts,' Tractor said.

'Who are?'

'Me bits of origami. The thing is, I can't get 'em quite right. I worked on them for hours after I got in last night, but me outer labia keep prolapsing.'

Outside the door, Rachel was choking as she tried to avoid bursting out laughing.

'For Chrissake, Tractor,' Matt groaned. 'I've brought Rachel back. She had a terrible shock last night. Somebody stole her material and she's feeling pretty wretched. The last thing she wants to walk into is a pile of origami, er . . .' Matt hesitated.

'Cunts,' Tractor obliged.

Shaking his head, Matt began picking up the bits of paper.

'So where is she then, your bird?' Tractor asked.

'Rachel,' he said, emphasising her name, 'is still in bed.'

'Right. Oh, by the way, I didn't tell you. I got a letter from the Kelloggs people this morning.'

'Oh yeah – saying what exactly?'

'Well, it was only a compliments slip really, but it thanked me for my Imperial Cereal proposal and said they would be writing to me in due course.'

'Fantastic,' Matt said disdainfully, ramming several failed origami genitalia into the remains of a chicken tikka masala.

Tractor took another drag on his cigarette.

'Here,' he said, holding up the paper which Rachel could now see was the *Radio Times*. 'You see these pictures of all the Joke for Europe contestants? Well, I know one of them.'

'Who?' Matt said, coming over to look at the picture.

'Her. I've met her.'

'Tractor, that's Rachel. How do you know her?'

'Oh, I tried to pick her up a few weeks ago in The Red House. Don't get all aerated, it was ages ago.' He began gently scratching his chest.

At this point Rachel made her silent entrance.

'She made out she wasn't interested,' Tractor continued, 'but just between you and me, I reckon she really had the hots for me.'

'Hi, Tractor,' Rachel said, beaming.

Tractor leapt off the sofa and stood in front of her, red in the face. Then he bent down towards the coffee-table and stubbed out his cigarette in the ashtray. It came as a complete surprise to her that he was even remotely capable of embarrassment. Despite herself, she couldn't help finding it ever so slightly endearing.

'Hi,' he said awkwardly, crossing his arms in front of

him to cover up his nipples. 'Sorry about what happened last night. Matt told me somebody stole your material. You must feel like shit.'

'Yeah, something like that,' she said breezily, noticing Matt whisking the curry cartons off the table and hiding them behind his back.

'Well,' Tractor began sheepishly, 'I was just about to get in the shower. Anyway, nice to see you again, Rachel.'

'And you, Tractor.'

'Here,' Matt said. 'I think these are yours.' He took the curry cartons from behind his back and handed them to his friend.

Tractor turned to go, but Matt called him back and placed the ashtray full of cigarette butts on top of one of the cartons.

They watched him walk to the door, where he stopped, lowered his head and sniffed his armpits. When he finally left the room he was muttering something about always ending up smelling like a packet of Vesta curry whenever he had an Indian.

Matt closed his eyes and pressed his eyeballs with his fingers.

'Rachel, I'm sorry. I had no idea Tractor tried to pick you up. Oh God . . . Don't tell me he pulled that *Clitorati* stunt of his.'

'OK, then I won't,' Rachel teased.

Matt gave a brief grin. 'I know you think Tractor's an absolute tosser, but he's not a bad bloke—'

He broke off. Coming from the bathroom were the loud, atonal sounds of Tractor singing. ('*Furry, cross the mercy . . . dah . . . da da da dah*').

Matt rolled his eyes. 'It's just that he hasn't got the first idea how to handle women.'

'You don't say.'

Matt leaned over the back of the sofa and picked up a pair of Y-fronts.

'And OK, he's a bit of a layabout.' He rammed the underpants into his jeans pocket. 'But I make allowances for him because he's been through a really rough time lately. The reason he disappeared to New York was to get over a broken heart. He'd finally managed to meet a woman and then, when he was really starting to fall for her, it turns out she only wanted him for his sperm. If he hadn't got up in the middle of the night and gone hunting through the deep freeze for a couple of fish fingers to put in a sandwich, he'd never have found out.'

'What? You mean she was a sperm napper?'

Matt nodded. 'Deep freeze was chocka with his used . . .'

'All right, enough,' she giggled. 'I get the picture.'

He came over to her and ran his fingers across her smiling lips. 'You know, I think your sense of humour might be returning,' he said.

'Oh, I wouldn't go that far,' she said. 'It's just that I am determined not to let Pitsy sodding Carter get the better of me, that's all.'

She explained about her plan to go and see Xantia.

He said it was probably a long shot, but definitely worth a try.

'You just wait,' Rachel said with a positively evil grin. 'When I've finished with Pitsy, she'll be begging for mercy.' She reached out, took an apple from the fruit bowl and bit into it. Hard.

'You know,' he said, 'that's one of the things I adore about you.'

'What? My grit and steely determination in the face of adversity?'

'No,' he said. 'The way you chew. Like a rabbit, with your front teeth. It's really sweet.'

'I do not,' she squealed indignantly, reaching for a cushion and bashing him playfully over the head with it.

CHAPTER 21

'So how are you bearing up, darling?' Faye asked, in that painfully concerned tone she always used at times of great personal suffering like funerals or the time Coral's new kitchen units finally turned up – after a four-month wait – with Sandringham rosewood doors when she'd ordered the Balmoral teak.

'Mum, I'm fine – just like I was when you rang an hour ago and an hour before that.'

'Are you sure? I mean, how can you be fine after the trauma you've been through? Coral says you could be in denial. She thinks maybe you should get some counselling – you know, to help you unleash your anger and start grieving for your lost jokes. She saw somebody a few years back, when she got that obsessive compulsive thing. Mind you it didn't do her any good. Every time she went, she spent the hour tidying the therapist's room.'

'Mum, I don't need therapy. I'm OK, honestly . . . No, and there's nothing you or Dad can do . . . No, please don't go to the police. They won't be the remotest bit interested. Can you imagine Nick Ross on *Crimewatch* saying: "If you've seen the woman who stole these jokes, police are waiting to hear from you"?'

'All right, but your father's still going to speak to Henry, our solicitor. I'll phone you tonight and let you know what he says.'

'OK, Mum. Whatever. Speak to you later.' Rolling her eyes, Rachel pressed the off button on her mobile and put it down on the dashboard.

Shelley, who was sitting in the passenger seat, started laughing. 'They do say,' she said, 'that all women eventually turn into their mothers.'

'God, I just hope that's not true,' Rachel said.

'Yeah, me too. Mine's always fancied Michael Fish.'

It was just after two and Rachel and Shelley were on their way to Matt's washing-machine unveiling in Rachel's car. The drive from Crouch End to Muswell Hill shouldn't have taken more than five minutes, but being Christmas Eve, the roads were jammed with traffic heading out of London and they'd hardly moved for a quarter of an hour.

Shelley turned up the radio, which was playing Christmas carols, and started singing along to 'Silent Night'. Rachel joined in with the descant even though she knew she could sit on a Chubb lock and still not be in key. By the time they reached the final 'Slee-eep in heavenly peace', not even Shelley could reach the high note and they burst into a fit of giggles.

It was a while before Rachel realised that Shelley had stopped laughing and instead was inhaling sharply through her teeth. Rachel turned to look at her. She was grimacing and both hands were clamped to her bump.

'You OK?' Rachel asked.

Shelley let out a long slow breath and smiled. 'Yeah. I'm fine. It's these Braxton Hicks practice contractions. I've been getting them all night.'

Rachel looked at her with concern.

'You sure they're just practice contractions? I got them with Sam, but I don't remember them hurting that much. You're only a month off your due date, you know. After what happened a few weeks ago, shouldn't we go to the hospital and get you checked out?'

'Nah, stop fussing. I'm fine. It's gone now.'

'You sure?'

'Positive. These pains feel exactly the same as they did when I went to hospital the first time. It was a false alarm back then – it'll be the same now. I'm not making a fool of myself again. Let's just change the subject. So, now that you and Matt have finally got round to telling each other how you feel, when are you going to give Adam his marching orders?'

'As soon as he gets home, whenever that is. Could be weeks before—' She broke off a second time. Now Shelley was making tiny blowing sounds.

'That does it,' Rachel declared, seeing her friend's contorted face. 'I'm getting you to hospital. Braxton Hicks contractions don't hurt like that. You, my friend, are in labour.'

'Rachel,' Shelley cried out in exasperation. 'Will you

stop this? I'm not in labour. The pains are only lasting a moment or two. See? It's gone again.'

Her face broke into a grin. 'Anyway,' she went on, 'I categorically refuse to drop this baby until I've met the gorgeous Tractor. I can't believe he's Matt's flat-mate.'

'Shelley, for Chrissake, what are you like? Here you are, probably in the first stages of labour and all you can think about is going on the pull.'

'Look, for the last time, I am NOT in labour. These are just practice contractions – OK?'

'Fine. If you say so,' she said.

The traffic was so bad that it took them another half-hour to get to Muswell Hill. On the way, Shelley had two more 'practice contractions'. She had another as they stood outside Matt's block waiting for him to answer the intercom. Rachel said nothing this time, deciding there was no point arguing. If the pains really were Braxton Hicks, they would go off eventually. If Shelley was in real labour, she'd know soon enough.

'It's us,' Rachel said, once Matt had answered the intercom.

'Hi. Tractor's not with you, by any chance, is he?'

'No, haven't seen him.'

'Oh. It's just that he should have been back here an hour ago, that's all.'

The buzzer went, Shelley pushed open the door and they stepped into the lobby. Then, just as the door clicked shut behind them, they heard a voice outside.

'Oh, come on, Demi,' the voice pleaded. 'Come on, sweetheart. A few more paces, just for me.'

'That's Tractor,' Rachel said with a puzzled frown.

'You sure?' Shelley said, sounding distinctly downcast. 'Seems like he's got a girlfriend.'

'Must be his blind date from last night,' Rachel said. 'But I'm sure I heard him say he dumped her.'

'Look, Demi, don't give me a hard time. Come on, how's about some Liquorice Allsorts?'

The two women exchanged bewildered glances.

Suddenly there was a clip-clopping sound.

'Good girl, Demi. That's a good girl.'

Clip, clop. Clip, clop.

'Rachel,' Shelley said, 'is it just me, or do you hear *hooves*?'

Shaking her head with puzzlement, Rachel opened the door. Tractor was heading up the path towards them. He was pulling on a rope. The rope was attached to an exceedingly motheaten, elderly donkey.

'Oh my God,' Rachel muttered. 'What is that?'

'It's a donkey,' Shelley tittered.

'I can see it's a donkey,' Rachel said. 'I mean, what's it for? In case you hadn't noticed, there's not a lot of call for beasts of burden in Muswell Hill.'

Shelley ignored the remark. She was too busy eyeing up Tractor's brown velvet suit with its very fitted, very wide-lapelled jacket and flared trousers.

'God,' Shelley whispered. 'You were right about his pale skin. Is he gorgeous or is he gorgeous?'

Rachel rolled her eyes.

A moment later Tractor and the mangy Demi were standing in front of them.

'Hi, Tractor,' Rachel said. 'Nice donkey.'

'Yeah. Demi belongs to my Aunty Pam. She runs a sanctuary in Kent. I've just been to collect her.' He began stroking the animal's nose.

'Must have caused a stir, a donkey on the bus.'

'Very funny. I borrowed Van Morrison and hired a horse-box.'

By now he had noticed Shelley.

'So, Rachel,' he said, smiling, 'you haven't introduced me to your friend?'

'Oh, right. Sorry. This is Shelley. She lives downstairs from me . . . But I still don't fully understand. What are you doing bringing a donkey into a block of flats?'

He ignored her.

'Hi, Shelley,' he said. 'I'm Dave, but my friends call me Tractor.'

'Oh, why's that, then?'

'Shelley,' Rachel muttered testily, 'you know why it is. I've told you.'

Shelley stamped hard on Rachel's foot.

'Well,' Tractor said, unaware of the muttering and foot-stamping, 'David Brown – that's my full name – is the biggest-selling make of tractor in Cornwall. I was born down there and as soon as I went to school everybody started calling me Tractor. Then when I was nine, we moved up to Liverpool, but by then all my family called me Tractor too. I guess the name just stuck. So when's the baby due?'

'Four weeks,' Shelley simpered, running her hands over the tight purple and emerald striped sweater encasing her bump.

'What do you want? A boy or a girl?'

'Don't mind.'

'I love babies.'

'Really?'

'Yeah. I think it's because I used to be one.'

Rachel stared in disbelief as Shelley burst out laughing.

'Course, I was dead ugly when I was born. In fact, the police have still got an arrest warrant out for the stork.'

Shelley laughed a second time.

'So what brings you to London?' she asked through her giggles.

'Oh, I've lived here off and on for years. Spent the last few months in the States, though – pursuing various business interests. Now I'm back, I'm thinking about diversifying. Right now I'm in negotiation with one of the major food conglomerates. They've put several significant offers on the table, but I'm still considering my options.'

'Several significant offers, my arse,' Rachel muttered.

Shelley dug her in the ribs.

'Well if you ask me,' Shelley said, 'the only really expanding market foodwise is organic produce and health foods.'

'I dunno about that. Health foods killed my grand-father, you know.'

'Killed him?' Shelley said in astonishment. 'Good God. How?'

'They were in the lorry that ran him over.'

Shelley laughed so hard she started snorting.

'Look,' Rachel butted in, 'when the two of you have quite finished guffawing, can we please establish what this donkey is doing here?'

Tractor turned to Rachel. 'Didn't Matt tell you?'

'Er, no.'

'Well,' he said, patting Demi's flank, 'this washing machine of his is designed for use in villages in the Third World – where there's no electricity, right?'

'Right.'

'So if it can't run on electric, then it's got to be powered somehow, right?'

'Dunno – s'pose.'

'Take my word for it. It has. Well, a washing-machine drum full of water's far too heavy for a human being to turn, but not for your average beast of burden – like Demi here. She's going to test it out.'

'What?' Rachel gasped. 'You're actually going to take her up to the flat? What about the smell?'

'Don't worry, she'll get used to it.'

Ignoring Rachel's gobsmacked silence, Tractor gave Demi's rope another tug. She reared her head, let out a couple of loud braying noises and finally moved forward a couple of paces. Tractor had just manoeuvred her into the doorway when a Parcel Force delivery man trotted up to the door, carrying four shoebox-sized packages wrapped in brown paper.

'Delivery for number forty,' he announced, hovering behind Demi. 'Don't think I can quite squeeze . . .'

'Oh, right,' Tractor said. 'That'll be for Polly the aromatherapist who lives in the flat opposite me and Matt. Don't worry, mate. I'll take them.'

Seeing Tractor had only one hand free, because the other was still holding the rope, Rachel reached across Demi and took the packages.

'A donkey,' the Parcel Force man chortled, patting Demi's rear. 'If I'd have thought, I'd have got one for the wife for Christmas. She's always nagging me to get her some help around the house.'

No sooner had he disappeared than the decorator arrived. Rachel recognised him because he was wearing a turban. He'd brought his two sons with him – twins, Rachel suspected – aged about twelve, also in turbans.

'Hi, I'm Sadu Singh. I'm looking for Mr Clapton's flat.'

'He lives at thirty-eight,' Rachel said, smiling at Mr Singh. 'But don't worry, we're all headed up there – once we can get the donkey through the door.'

'Perhaps I can be of some assistance?' Mr Singh said with the kind of polite smile which suggested he came across donkeys blocking doorways every day of the week.

Rachel was about to explain the animal's presence

when Demi, braying loudly, took several paces back onto the outside path and dropped a steamy, heady payload onto the flowerbed.

'Eeuurch, gross,' the twins shouted in unison.

Mr Singh was whispering to them to be quiet when Rachel saw Matt coming down the stairs. He trotted over to them, kissed Rachel briefly on the cheek and said, 'Hi,' to Shelley.

'Ah,' he said, seeing Tractor tugging at Demi's rope, to no avail. 'I was wondering where everybody had got to. Now I get it. Look, we have to get her into the lift and upstairs to the flat or else the neighbours will see and have a fit. Mr Singh, I know you probably think we're completely mad, but I'll explain everything as soon as we get upstairs.'

With that he began pulling on Demi's harness, while Matt carried on tugging at the rope. They pulled as hard as they could, but Demi steadfastly refused to move.

'Look,' Rachel said eventually, 'how's about I take the other side of the harness?'

'OK,' Tractor said.

She handed a parcel each to Mr Singh and the twins. The fourth she put down on the floor. But the moment Rachel touched the donkey's harness, it began braying louder than ever. There was still no sign whatsoever of her putting one hoof in front of another. It was only when Tractor suggested Matt and Rachel move away and he try to cajole her on his own that she ambled through the doorway and into the lobby. At least then the Singhs could come in out of the biting cold.

'Good girl. Good girl,' Tractor smiled, holding out a palmful of Liquorice Allsorts. Demi licked them up eagerly.

'Right. Just a few more feet, my darling. Just a few more feet.'

Demi looked at him, farted and refused point blank to go any further.

Everybody was so taken up with getting Demi into the lift, that no one heard old Mrs Liebowitz, who lived on the first floor with Mr Liebowitz, creep down the stairs to see what all the commotion was about.

Anybody else seeing the pregnant woman, the man tugging at the donkey and the three men in turbans carrying parcels might well have assumed that being Christmas Eve, somebody in the block was holding a children's Christmas party and that the people gathered in the lobby were the hired entertainment, who were about to perform a particularly life-like Nativity Play, but were having trouble convincing the most lifelike element to take part. Not Mrs Liebowitz.

As a consequence of her having spent most of the morning with her Catholic neighbour Mrs O'Rourke, stuffing her face with mince pies and – more to the point – knocking back half a dozen large schooners of Harvey's Bristol Cream, Mrs Liebowitz – who never usually drank, apart from a glass or two of Israeli dessert wine at Passover – reached a different conclusion. A very different conclusion.

As she peeked over the banister and surveyed the scene in the lobby, she gasped, let out a couple of 'Omigods' and gasped again.

The excitement, not to mention the sudden palpitations in her chest, were too much for her to bear. She rummaged in her cardigan pocket for the spare angina pill she always kept wrapped in a piece of toilet paper. Her clumsy arthritic fingers going as fast as they could, she eventually managed to unfold the paper and place the pill under her tongue.

Dry-mouthed and breathless, she climbed back upstairs as fast as her heart and short, varicosed legs would allow.

'Harry, Harry,' she shrieked as she stood panting in the kitchen doorway. 'Come quick. You'll never believe what's going on downstairs in the lobby.'

Mr Liebowitz, who was sitting at the blue Formica kitchen table and who had, until that moment been reading the *Evening Standard* and peeling a satsuma, didn't look up.

'What now?' he sighed wearily, breaking off a satsuma segment and popping it into his mouth. 'What is it I won't believe?'

'Look, if I tell you, you won't believe it. You have to come and see. Harry, for God's sake put down that orange. You have to come. Please.'

Harry Liebowitz broke off a second segment and stared at his wife over his glasses.

'Ada, you look flushed. How many glasses of sherry did that Maggie O'Rourke give you?'

'A few, but I feel fine, honestly. Please. I'm begging you. Put that orange down and come with me.'

'You still haven't told me what's going on.'

'OK, wait for it.' She paused for dramatic effect. 'Downstairs in the lobby there's a pregnant woman, a man pulling a donkey – I think he might be one of those nice boys from upstairs, but I couldn't make him out properly because I forgot my glasses. AND three men in turbans. Carrying gifts.'

'Really,' he said flatly. 'You'll be telling me next they couldn't find room at the Holiday Inn.'

He guffawed at the cleverness of his own joke.

'Ada, you had too much to drink, you fell asleep in the chair and you've been dreaming.'

He went back to his newspaper. 'Oh, for crying out loud,' he moaned. 'Look at this – Christmas Day films: *The Great Escape*. Every bloody year it's the same. What's the matter with these TV people? Don't they watch television?'

'Harry – please, you have to believe me. There's a donkey. They're trying to get a donkey in the lift.'

'Ach, why would anybody put a donkey in a lift?'

'I dunno. Maybe it can't manage the stairs. Do you want to know what I think?'

'No.'

'I think . . .' She paused for dramatic effect. 'I think The Second Coming's come.'

'The Second Coming,' he repeated.

'Yes, I'm sure of it.'

'Fine. Whatever,' he said vacantly, running his finger down the list of BBC programmes for Boxing Day. 'Little and bloody Large,' he muttered to himself. 'That's the best they can come up with.'

'Harry,' Mrs Liebowitz implored. 'I said I think it could be The Second Coming. Don't you think that's at least worth looking up from your paper for?'

'But you're saying one of them might be one of the fellas upstairs, only you're not sure because you didn't have your glasses? Actually, come to think of it, this could be something, couldn't it? If you're right, then you'll be in the next edition of the Bible. The Gospel according to Ada Who Forgot Her Glasses. The Book of Liebowitz the Tipsy. "And there did cometh to the Hill that is Muswell several strangers who the people could not quite make out, for their eyes were dim and they had forgotteneth their bifocals".'

He paused to break off yet another satsuma segment.

'Anyway,' he continued with a shrug. 'So what it's The Second Coming? We're Jewish. The First Coming meant nothing to our lot. Why should the Second?'

'But maybe that's the whole point. Don't you see? Maybe God was so angry that the Jews ignored the First Coming that He's sent another one.'

'To Vayzemere Mansions, Muswell Hill?' Mr Liebowitz chortled. 'Makes perfect sense . . . My God, then there's Cannon and sodding Ball.'

330

'Harry, please. This is no joke.'

'Who's laughing?'

'Oh, please come downstairs, Harry,' Mrs Liebowitz begged, almost in tears now.

He let out a long, lung-evacuating sigh. 'All right. All right.' Gripping the table top, Harry Liebowitz, who was no lightweight, heaved himself slowly off the chair.

'Quick,' she cried urgently. 'Quick.'

The pair creaked down the stairs. Then they looked over the banister down to the lobby.

'See, there's nobody there,' Mr Liebowitz declared. 'I told you, it's the drink. Ada, accept it – you fell asleep. You've been dreaming.'

'For the last time, I was NOT asleep,' Mrs Liebowitz insisted. 'I didn't dream it.'

Shrugging, Harry began to trudge back up the stairs. Desperate to find something to prove to her husband she hadn't been dreaming, Mrs Liebowitz carried on down. When she reached the bottom, she noticed a brown paper parcel lying in the middle of the lobby. She walked over to it. Realising it was identical to the parcels carried by the Three Wise Men, she bent down slowly, one hand in the small of her back, and picked it up. Without stopping to see if there was an address or a label to indicate what it might contain, she ripped into the package. Had she stopped to look she would have seen it was meant for Polly, the aromatherapist who lived at number forty. (What with all the clapping and cheering as they'd finally got Demi to walk across the lobby and into the lift, Rachel had forgotten to pick it up.)

Inside she found two tiny blue glass bottles, wrapped in tissue and packed in polystyrene balls. Mrs Liebowitz unwrapped one and then the other. Because she wasn't wearing her glasses, she had to hold them at arm's length to read the labels. For a moment she simply stood there open-mouthed and blinking. She virtually sprinted back up the stairs.

'Harry,' she screeched as she reached her front door, 'I don't know what to do now. The Three Wise Men, they left their Frankincense and Myrrh downstairs.'

'Don't worry,' Harry's voice came from the toilet. 'They'll come back for it.'

Once inside, Matt led everybody, including the Singhs, who had dropped the three boxes of aromatherapy oils off at number forty, along the hallway towards the kitchen. Demi had stopped giving trouble and was clip-clopping happily behind Tractor and Shelley, who were deep in conversation about babies.

Soon everybody had piled into the tiny kitchen. The washing machine was standing in the middle, covered by a blanket. Sticking out from underneath it was an enormous, black metal handle bent into a strange configuration which ended in a large U-shape with padding around it. Next to it was a large bucket of water, and next to that, what seemed to be an old, mechanical gym treadmill. A thick green hose led from under the blanket to the sink.

The Singh twins were clearly underwhelmed by all this and asked if they could go into the living room and watch TV. Mr Singh, however, appeared genuinely intrigued as Matt explained that he was about to see a demonstration of the first washing machine designed for remote villages in the Third World.

'All right, let's get started,' Matt said. Then, like a conjuror whisking away a tablecloth from under a pile of crockery, he tugged at the blanket.

'Ladies and gentlemen,' he announced, beaming, 'I give you the Donkulator Mark One.' The other end of the mysterious handle, it turned out, disappeared into a large aluminium box bolted to the side of the shell of an old white enamel top-loader, clearly dating from the Sixties.

Once everybody had stopped clapping, Demi allowed Tractor to lead her onto the treadmill and put the U-shaped end of the handle round her neck as a harness. This done, Matt opened the washing-machine lid and filled the drum with water from the bucket. A moment later Tractor gave Demi a handful of the pink beaded Liquorice Allsorts, which the donkey apparently favoured, and she promptly began walking at a gentle unhurried pace.

The handle, and then the washing-machine drum, immediately started turning.

'Now what you have to imagine,' Matt said above the purposeful whirring noise, 'is that out in the villages, Demi here wouldn't be on a treadmill, but walking around a pole. Yet the principle is identical. The connecting rod between her and the machine would still enter the gearbox here' – he indicated the aluminium box on the machine's side – 'and create via a patented mechanism the turning motion in the drum . . . here. It's a high-ratio gearbox, which only requires Demi to break into a brisk walk like so . . .' he stroked Demi's flank and whispered to her ' . . . to create a full, albeit relatively slow spin-cycle.'

Demi speeded up on her treadmill, and the whirring noise from the gearbox grew to a clatter, swiftly followed by the familiar sound of a washing-machine drum spinning at a respectable pace.

Matt's face broke into a broad smile. Rachel turned and hugged him.

'It's absolutely brilliant,' she squealed excitedly. 'I am so proud of you.'

'Yeah, well done, mate,' Tractor said, slapping Matt on the back.

But Rachel and Matt were now too busy kissing to notice his congratulations.

'I love you,' Rachel said when they finally pulled away.

'I love you too,' Matt smiled, giving her one last peck on the lips.

'The Donkulator is going to make you world-famous,' she said. 'You're going to get the Nobel Prize for Laundry. I just know it. *I just know it!*'

'Well,' Matt said over the din, 'we'll have to see if

the guys from the Burkina Faso trade mission like it first when they come to see it next week. It's all been a bit seat-of-the-pants these last few weeks. I only got the drain cycle sorted a couple of days ago, and I still haven't gone the full donkey with it yet.'

With that, with a massive gurgling and burping sound, the hosepipe in the sink began gushing water.

'Oh yess,' Matt cried. 'Oh yes.'

'Oh no,' Shelley cried. 'Oh no.'

Everybody shot round to look at her.

Shelley cleared her throat nervously. 'Sorry,' she said, looking down at the tiny puddle at her feet. 'But I think my waters have broken in sympathy.'

She then screwed up her face in pain and collapsed onto a kitchen chair as another contraction arrived, followed less than a minute later by another.

Rachel said she thought Shelley could be about to give birth, in which case they should call an ambulance. No ordinary vehicle stood a chance of getting through the Christmas Eve traffic and Shelley to hospital on time.

While Matt dialled 999, Rachel and Tractor helped Shelley into Matt's bedroom.

'Mr Singh,' Matt said as he picked up the phone, 'I'm terribly sorry about all this. Maybe it would be better for you to come back after Christmas. In the meantime, would you mind unharnessing Demi and taking her out onto the balcony? You'll find some fresh hay there.'

'It was a walk of no more than a dozen paces to the bedroom. On the way, Shelley had three more violent contraction that left her drained.

'Don't worry,' Tractor told her confidently after the last one. 'I know all about delivering babies. I didn't tell you, but our mam had all six of my brothers and sisters at home. When she went into labour the last time, with our Eugene, the midwife didn't arrive until it was all over. Me dad had taken the other kids out for the day to give her a break so I was the only one there to help her.'

'What?' Shelley said, looking at him all doe-eyed. 'You delivered your baby brother, all on your own?'

He nodded.

Rachel frowned. She couldn't work out if this was another Tractor tall story, like his fictional negotiations with the 'major food conglomerate'.

'So, how old were you?' Shelley asked him.

''Bout thirteen. But I wasn't quite on my own. I had the lady from the emergency services on the phone talking me through it.'

The moment Shelley sat down on the bed, another contraction came. This time she almost screamed the place down.

'Rache, I think it's coming. I think it's coming.'

Rachel could feel panic rising inside her, not helped by Demi who, out on the balcony, suddenly seemed to fancy herself as a contestant in the Eurovision Braying Contest.

'OK, sweetheart,' Rachel said, trying to hide her

panic, 'just hold my hand and breathe. Christ, where is that bloody ambulance?'

Even if Tractor did know something about delivering babies, she reasoned, it couldn't possibly be as much as the paramedics.

By now Tractor had plumped up three pillows and arranged them against the headboard. Gingerly, Shelley lifted her feet off the floor and eased herself along the bed.

'Rachel,' Tractor said, 'why don't you go to the linen cupboard and get some towels.'

'OK,' she said, letting go of Shelley's hand. 'Don't worry,' she whispered, stroking her friend's head. 'I'll only be a minute.'

'Eeeeeuuuuuurch,' Shelley groaned.

'Eyyooore, eyyoore,' came the response from the balcony.

'Omigod,' Rachel muttered. 'The donkey thinks she's found a friend.'

'All right, Shelley, mate,' Tractor said calmly. 'Just breathe through it. Blow, blow, blow. That's it. Excellent. Good girl.'

Rachel had to ask Matt where the linen cupboard was. He led her to the end of the hall.

'Ambulance is on its way,' he said. 'And the Singhs have got Demi in hand.'

She nodded. 'Look,' she said, taking in his pale, anxious face. 'Why don't you put the kettle on?'

'Oh yeah,' he said shakily. 'Boiling water. You always

need boiling water when babies are being born. Why is that?'

'I've no idea,' she chuckled. 'I was just thinking you look like you could do with a cuppa and I'm sure Mr Singh could. He must be freezing to death out there on the balcony.'

By the time Rachel came back with the towels, Shelley's lower half was naked and her knees were bent up. Tractor had taken off his jacket, rolled up his shirtsleeves and was kneeling on the bed at her feet.

'Christ,' she was yelling, her face contorted in pain. 'I want to push. I want to push.'

'Shit, Tractor,' Rachel said, starting to feel really scared now. 'I can see the head. What do we do? Why isn't the bloody ambulance here? Are they having their bloody Christmas party or what?'

'Rachel, will you take it easy?' Tractor said evenly. 'You're no use to anybody if you start panicking. Now just give me the towels and go back to holding Shelley's hand.'

She handed him the towels, a couple of which he slipped underneath Shelley.

'It's going to be all right, I promise,' Rachel whispered to Shelley, kissing her on her damp forehead. 'In a few minutes you're going to have a beautiful, beautiful baby.'

'Right, when you feel the next contraction,' Tractor said, 'I don't want you to push, I want you to pant. I'm just going to check the cord's not caught round the baby's neck.'

The next contraction came. Shelley dug her nails into Rachel's hand, screwed up her face and panted for all she was worth.

'OK,' Tractor announced. 'It all seems to be fine. Right, next time, push. Push really hard.'

Her chin on her chest and still gripping Rachel's hand, Shelley pushed. By now her spiky red hair was plastered to her head with sweat. Rachel picked up one of the spare towels and wiped her face.

Shelley looked at her briefly and managed a smile. The contraction passed and another took its place.

'You're doing brilliantly,' Tractor urged. 'Come on, just a couple more pushes and we're there. You can do it girl.'

Two gargantuan pushes later, the head emerged.

A few moments after that, Satchmo Peach slid into the world, bawling his head off.

CHAPTER 22

Mrs Peach, a small woman with a large red patent handbag and bleached highlights the width of tagliatelle, arrived at Shelley's hospital bedside in a flap.

'Oh love,' she panted, leaning over to kiss her, 'I'm sorry it's taken us so long to get here, but the traffic was murder. Then, you'll never believe it, there was this terrible accident on the Southend Road. Four cars burned out. Lord knows how many fire engines. I counted six bodies. Your dad reckons there were eight. Thing is, we couldn't pass by without getting the Panasonic out, so now we've run the batteries right down, and used up all the tape. There's none left to film the baby.'

'Don't worry, Mum,' Shelley said cheerfully. 'I mean, a four-car inferno and charred corpses on the Southend Road is a once-in-a-lifetime video opportunity. Unlike the birth of your first grandchild.'

'Oh, I'm so glad you understand. Anyway, to make up for being late, your dad's downstairs buying up half the hospital florist's . . . So, are you all right? Is the baby OK?'

'Yes,' Shelley smiled. 'We're both fine.'

'Are they positive the baby's OK?'

'Absolutely. Seven pounds and completely healthy.'

Mrs Peach brought her hand to her chest and let out a long sigh of relief.

'Oh, thank heavens,' she said. 'Your dad and I were so worried, what with it being born so suddenly and in someone's flat like that. Whose place was it, anyway?'

Shelley explained that it was a long story, and she'd tell her another time. For the moment, the doctors wanted to keep her and the baby in hospital for a couple of days just to make certain they were both all right.

It was only then that Mrs Peach noticed Rachel, who was sitting in a high-backed plastic armchair on the other side of Shelley's bed.

'Rachel,' Mrs Peach cried. 'I didn't see you sitting there. Look, thank you so much for everything you did this afternoon. Heaven only knows what would have happened if you hadn't been there.'

'Oh, I didn't do a lot,' Rachel said, blushing ever so slightly. 'So, Mrs P., how are you?'

The instant Rachel uttered those last words, she wished she hadn't. It was clear that Shelley, who had closed her eyes and was pressing the lids with her fingers, shared her wish.

'How am I?' Mrs Peach said with a caustic, chesty laugh as she plonked herself down at the end of the bed and began rummaging through her handbag. 'Have you got an hour or six?'

'Mum,' Shelley hissed, as her mother pulled out a box of ten Benson & Hedges. 'Put them away. This is a bloody maternity ward.'

'Oh right. Sorry,' Mrs Peach said sheepishly. 'It's all this excitement. I wasn't thinking.'

She put the fags back and snapped her bag shut. 'So anyway, what was I saying? Oh yes. How am I? Well, I tell you, Rachel, everything's got so bad now – you know, *down below* – that I can't even laugh without leaking. I've had to completely give up watching *The Vicar of Dibley*. See, Shelley, be warned – that's what having babies does to a woman's body. Now then, where's that grandson of mine?'

'Oh, I was wondering when you'd get round to asking,' Shelley said with a sarcastic smile. 'He's here.'

She pointed to the crib, which was on Rachel's side of the bed. Mrs Peach tiptoed round.

'Ooh, who's a little darling, then?' she squealed, stroking Satchmo's tiny bald head. 'Who is? Come on, tell Nana – who's a little darling, then? Oh Shelley, he's gorgeous.' She reached out and took her daughter's hand.

'Yeah, he is, isn't he?' Shelley beamed proudly. 'I can hardly believe I've got him.'

'Oh, you will,' Mrs Peach said, 'the first time he's up screaming all night.' She turned back to the crib. 'Aren't you bootiful? Oh, yes you are. Ooh, come to Nana, little man. Come to Nana.'

Moving her handbag along her arm, Mrs Peach gently

picked the sleeping infant out of the crib and sat cradling him on the edge of the bed.

'Satchmo,' she said, smiling at Shelley. 'That's what they called Louis Armstrong, wasn't it? Of course "It's a Wonderful World" is one of my favourites, but I didn't know you were a fan.'

'I'm not. I just like the name.'

'It's certainly unusual, I'll give you that. Have you thought about a second name? It might be an idea to make that something a bit more conventional. Then if he doesn't like Satchmo, he can use his second name instead.'

'Mum, please don't start. I really like Satchmo. I think it's kinda boho.'

'Do you, dear? Oh well, it's your choice. I'm sure we'll get used to it, anyway. What do you think, Rachel? Do you think Satchmo's got boho?'

'Oh definitely,' Rachel lied. Privately, she was with Mrs Peach on this one. In her opinion the poor little mite was going to get teased mercilessly when he started school, but she wouldn't have dreamed of hurting Shelley by saying so.

Mrs Peach gave a good-natured shrug. 'Your father and I were hoping you'd go for something a bit traditional. In fact, just between you, me and the gatepost, he was secretly hoping you'd name him after your paternal grandfather.'

'Yeah, right. Like I was going to call a child of mine Enoch.'

Just then Satchmo began howling.

'Oh, has my little man got the windy pops then?' Mrs Peach cooed. Carefully, she put Satchmo over her shoulder and began rubbing his back.

'Come on,' she said, standing up. 'Your mummy needs to rest. I'll take you for a little walk. Why don't we go and look at the pretty Christmas tree?'

With that Mrs Peach pootled off up the ward.

'You know, Rache,' Shelley said, taking her hand, 'I am so glad you and Matt finally got it together. You are just so right for each other. You're going to have a wonderful future.'

Rachel felt a lump in her throat. 'Yeah, I think so, too. Look, I'd better get going – Matt said he'd come round later. I'll see you tomorrow. Sam's spending Christmas at Joe's, and he and Greg have invited me over for lunch. I'll pop in and see you on my way there, OK?'

'Yeah. Great,' Shelley said sleepily. 'And Rache – thanks again for everything.'

'Come on, I didn't do anything really, other than panic. It was all down to Tractor.' She walked to the end of the bed and picked up her jacket.

'Rache,' Shelley said, a slight hesitation in her voice.

Rachel looked up.

'I know you haven't got much time for Tractor, but after what he did today, you have to admit he's pretty special.'

Rachel was forced to admit he probably was.

* * *

The moment she got back to the car, her mobile went. It was Sam.

'Oh hi, darling,' she said cheerily. 'I was just about to phone you. How you doing?'

'I'm fine. Mum – I'm really, really sorry about what happened last night. I reckon that woman should go to prison for what she did.'

'Yeah, too bloomin' right,' Rachel agreed.

'Dad said he'd stick a red-hot poker up her bum if he got hold of her.'

'Did he really? Oh, that's so sweet. Tell him I appreciate it, will you?'

They carried on chatting for a couple of minutes. She asked him what he'd been up to and he told her he'd spent the afternoon watching a video of *Beaches* with Greg.

'That's nice,' was all she said. 'Oh, by the way, Shelley had her baby.'

'Cool.'

'Little boy – called Satchmo.'

'Satchmo? That's pants.'

She told him off for being rude, but only half-heartedly.

On the drive home, she decided she couldn't put off telling Matt about Adam any longer. Once again it occurred to her he might be angry with her for not being honest with him. But surely, she thought, once she had reassured him how much she loved him and made it absolutely clear it was over between her and

Adam – even though she hadn't actually told Adam yet – he would come round. Nevertheless, as she pulled up outside her flat, she was aware that the ferrets which she usually only felt before a gig, were performing backflips in her stomach.

She'd just opened a bottle of wine when Matt arrived.

'Perfect timing,' she declared, brandishing the bottle. She kissed him, took his jacket and hung it up.

'Rache,' Matt said, looking at her and frowning, 'you seem tense. You OK?'

'Yeah, fine,' she twittered, realising she wasn't as good at hiding her nerves as she thought she was.

'So how are Shelley and the baby?' he asked as they walked into the living room.

'Great,' she said. 'Tractor's popping in to see her later.'

Matt laughed and sat down on the sofa. 'I think he's really fallen for Shelley, you know,' he said.

Kneeling down by the coffee-table, she picked up a wine glass and began filling it.

'Matt,' she said, handing him the glass, 'there's something important I need to tell you.'

'Oh my God,' he said with a theatrical gasp, 'don't tell me you found Pitsy, did her in with a meat cleaver, and packed her dismembered body into half a dozen black bin-liners, which you're hoping I might dispose of in Epping Forest.'

'Nice thought,' she laughed. 'But, no.'

'She took a large gulp of wine.

'It's just that I haven't been completely honest with you.' She was looking directly into his eyes now. Her pulse-rate had rocketed.

'The thing is . . .' She swallowed hard and decided to just come out with it. 'All the time I've been seeing you, I've been sort of engaged to somebody else.'

'What?' he said, screwing up his face in shocked confusion, more than anger. He put his wine glass down on the coffee-table and waited for her to continue.

As she told him about Adam, he sat rubbing his hand over his chin.

'But you have to understand it's over,' she said finally, getting up and coming to sit next to him on the sofa. 'Matt, I have never loved anybody like I love you.'

He didn't say anything.

'Look, I know I haven't been straight with you, but it was really hard for me. When I first started seeing you – even when we started sleeping together, I was still trying to convince myself I was in love with Adam. It took me ages to sort my head out and realise what I was feeling. Ask Shelley. She'll tell you what a state I was in.'

Grimfaced, he stood up and walked over to the window.

'Rachel,' he said, keeping his back to her, 'what sort of a future do we have if we can't be honest with each other?'

'Matt, I'm sorry. It was wrong. But I was just so confused. I promise I will never, ever keep anything from you again.'

He turned to look at her. She could tell from his tight-lipped expression, he was furious with her. She'd never seen him angry before and she couldn't help thinking how sexy she found it.

'How do I know it's really over between you and this Adam?'

'Because I say it is. Plus I'm pretty sure he's been seeing somebody else in South Africa.'

'And how do I know you're not going out with me just to get back at him?'

She felt barely able to dignify his question with an answer.

'You know that's not true,' she said in what was little more than a whisper. She watched his face soften. He came back to the sofa and sat down next to her.

'Rachel.' His tone was kinder suddenly, more gentle. 'You were planning to marry the bloke. You've said yourself how confused you've been. Maybe you're kidding yourself when you think you have no feelings left for him. You might not find it as easy to walk away as you think.'

'But I've already walked away . . . in my mind at least.'

'You haven't actually told him it's over, have you?'

'No, but that's because he's in South Africa and I want to tell him face to face. Even though I think he's cheating on me, I feel I owe him that.'

'Or maybe it's because you still love him and you can't bring yourself to tell him it's finished.'

'Matt, that's just not how it is,' she said, desperately trying to stop herself crying.

He arched his eyebrows.

'OK, I admit finishing with him will be painful, but there's no way I'm about to back out.'

'Look,' he said taking her hand, 'I think I should give you some space to sort out your feelings.'

'But my feelings *are* sorted.' Her eyes were starting to sting with tears.

'So you keep saying, but I need to be certain you're certain.' He paused. 'Tell you what, why don't you take Christmas to think things over one last time? Then maybe you should speak to Adam. Phone me in the New Year.'

He leaned over, kissed her briefly and stood up. Then without so much as a 'Merry Christmas' he was gone, leaving Rachel bewildered, but at the same time wanting to kick herself.

She ran her fingers through her hair. The moment she'd started to have feelings for Matt she should have taken stock of her relationship with Adam, faced up to the fact it wasn't working and finished it. That way Matt wouldn't have been hurt, he wouldn't be furious with her for being dishonest, and by now everything would have been sorted out.

She had no choice, she decided, but to call Adam immediately and find out when he was coming home. If it was within a few days she would wait and tell him it was over face to face, as she'd always intended. If he was planning to stay any longer she would just have to end it on the phone.

She imagined Matt's reaction once she'd told him she'd done the deed. He would wrap her in his arms, tell her she was forgiven and how sorry he was for doubting her. Then they'd have spectacular make-up sex and be back on track again.

Not that finishing with Adam was going to be remotely easy – or anything but sad.

Two glasses of wine inside her for Dutch courage (in case it turned out he was staying on in South Africa and she had to finish with him now), she went into the hall and dialled his hotel.

'Ah'm sorry,' the chap on reception said. 'Mr Landsberg and his friends have all gone to a Christmas Eve wildebeest roast. Ah'm not sure when he'll be back.'

CHAPTER 23

'Anus-ol,' Tractor said, picking Shelley's haemorrhoid cream up off her hospital locker and studying the name. 'That's disgusting. I mean, what they've done, is put the words "anus" and "hole" together. So, if you think about it, they've named the stuff "arsehole".'

'No, they haven't,' Rachel said witheringly. 'You don't pronounce it anus-ol. It's anyusol. The "sol" bit means solve.'

Shelley had gone to the loo, leaving Tractor and Rachel sitting by her bed. Satchmo was asleep in his crib.

'Oh, right,' Tractor said slowly as the penny dropped. 'I get it. But you'd think they'd've come up with something a bit sexier – like, say, PileDriver. I mean, Arsehole's not exactly an easy concept to market, is it?'

'Unlike Imperial Cereal, of course.'

'You may mock,' he said, waving his finger at Rachel, 'but you and Matt will be laughing the other side of your smug faces when I get the call from Kelloggs.'

'Maybe,' Rachel giggled. She was getting to like Tractor. There was something about his wackiness and almost childlike optimism which she found appealing.

She hesitated a moment. 'Tractor, have you spoken to Matt this morning?'

He said he'd seen him briefly, just as he was leaving for Nottingham. One of his mother's sisters lived there and his family always spent Christmas with her.

'I thought he wasn't going this year because he wanted to spend time with you, but he changed his mind at the last minute. Rachel, has something happened between the two of you?'

'Sort of.' She explained.

''Course, you know why he reacted like that, don't you?'

She frowned and shook her head.

'It's happened to him before – women not being upfront with him. A few years ago he got involved with this nurse. Gorgeous she was, bum on her like two perfectly formed . . . anyway, she was married. A year they'd been going out before she told him. And then it was only to kiss him goodbye and say she was staying with her husband. I know none of us likes not being given the complete picture, but Matt's got a real thing about it.'

'God,' Rachel said, looking particularly troubled now. 'I had no idea.'

Just then Shelley reappeared.

'Who's got a real thing about what?' she asked, climbing back into bed.

Rachel told her story for a second time.

'Look,' Tractor said when she'd finished, 'you two sit and have a natter. I'm having me dinner at our Bridget's in Feltham. I'd better get moving.'

He stood up, kissed Shelley on the cheek and said, 'Tara,' to Rachel. as he walked past Satchmo's crib he paused to look in.

'You know, Shelley,' he said, winking, 'he's got your chins.'

'What d'you mean "chins"?' she said, feigning offence. 'Bloody cheek. Now bugger off.'

But he didn't move. He looked back down at the baby.

'Tell you what my old Scalextric's just sitting in our mam's loft doing nothing. Maybe I should drive up to Liverpool after Christmas and get it. Kids love it.'

'Tractor, that's really kind, but Satchmo's really busy between feeds at the moment, what with him playing Subbuteo with my dad.'

She and Rachel looked at each other and started giggling. Eventually Tractor saw the joke.

'Oh right,' he said. 'Maybe I should wait until he's a bit bigger.'

'I think that might be best,' Shelley said, still laughing.

He turned to go.

'Oh, Tractor,' she called after him. 'By the way, thanks again for the choccies.'

'My pleasure,' he smiled.

'Tractor's got such a brilliant sense of humour,' Shelley said once he'd gone. 'He arrived at the crack this morning and for two hours I don't think I've stopped laughing. I mean, just look at these.'

She reached down, opened the locker and brought out a cellophane-wrapped box of novelty chocolates.

''Course,' she said, 'I probably won't eat them – they're full of E numbers. But it's the thought that counts.'

She put the box down by her side.

'Rache, don't worry about Matt. He adores you. Once you've finished with Adam, he'll come round. I know he will.'

'God, I hope so,' Rachel said gloomily.

Shelley's face broke into a smile. 'Come on, it's Christmas. Sod the E numbers. How d'you fancy a chocolate willy?'

'So did Shelley like the giant bogey you got her?'

'Sam, for your information that bogey set me back thirty-five quid – and yes, she loved it.'

Joe looked curiously at Rachel. She explained she'd bought Shelley a silver ring for Christmas.

'And stuck to the band there's this huge nugget of translucent fluorescent green plastic. It's all sort of jagged and pitted.'

'You're right, Sam,' Joe said, winking at him. 'Does sound exactly like a giant bogey.'

'Will you two just shut up taking the mick,' Rachel

said, hitting Joe playfully on the shoulder with a cushion.

'No, please. Don't hit me,' Joe pleaded. 'I feel sick. I shouldn't have had that third helping of Armagnac soufflé.'

Rachel jeered and promptly bashed him again.

It was nearly four and Greg's magnificent, much fretted over 'fusion' Christmas lunch of crab and prawn wanton laksa, perfectly cooked turkey served on individual vegetable mountains, and a Sri Lankan syrup and cashew nut cake thing as well as the Armagnac soufflé and Christmas pud, was finally over.

Greg, whose hostess flush had developed into a severe post-culinary stress headache and who had been forced to down three Nurofen as a result, was loading the dishwasher, having steadfastly refused all offers of help. Rachel and Joe, weary and bloated from all the eating and boozing, were lolling on the white Conran sofa with Sam between them.

Rachel couldn't believe what a thoroughly enjoyable and relaxed day she'd had. Not only had Joe and Greg refused to let her lift a finger, but they hadn't stopped going on about what they would do to Pitsy if they got hold of her. For the first time Rachel was aware that the residual anger she felt towards Joe had all but disappeared. She had decided not to say anything about what was going on with Matt because she didn't want to spoil the jolly atmosphere.

'You know, Greg,' Rachel said as he reappeared, carrying a tray of coffee and truffles, 'that lunch wasn't so much a meal as an edible art form. That prune and Armagnac soufflé . . .'

Greg blushed with pleasure as he put the tray down on the coffee-table.

'Yes, and although I say it myself, the turkey rather tickled the palate too.'

'That's because you left the bloody feathers on,' Joe said, winking at Rachel.

Greg started pouring coffee in a mock huff, but everybody else, including Sam, collapsed with laughter.

While the adults sat drinking their coffee, Sam started to become boisterous and irritating. When he wasn't clambering over Rachel or Joe, he was telling unfunny jokes or trying to get their attention with daft riddles and tedious 'OK-which-hand's-it-in?' magic tricks.

'Come on, Sam,' Joe said eventually, 'why don't you go back on the Internet. There must be some Barbra sites you haven't found yet.'

The three of them had clubbed together to buy Sam a computer for Christmas. Overjoyed, he'd spent the whole morning in his bedroom at Joe's surfing the Internet. Now, because he was tired and wanted attention after all the adult conversation, he was reluctant to go back.

'You just want to get rid of me, don't you?' he sulked.

It took them nearly ten minutes to convince him they didn't. Finally, muttering something about not having asked to be born, he disappeared into his bedroom.

'You know, Rache,' Joe said, 'it's amazing. He'll be a stroppy teenager before we know it.'

When they'd finished coffee, Greg suggested a walk. 'Might clear my head,' he said.

'I'm in,' Joe said. 'Rache?'

'Do you mind if I don't? I'd rather lie here and have a nap, if that's OK.'

Joe called to Sam to ask him if he wanted to come, but by now he was so engrossed in the Internet that all Joe got by way of reply was, 'Ssh. Go away. I'm busy.'

Rachel dozed off almost immediately.

'Mum.'

She had no idea how long she'd been asleep, when she became vaguely aware of Sam's voice somewhere in the distance.

'What?' she said drowsily. She half opened her eyes. He was standing at the foot of the sofa.

'Mum. Do you think we're going to get snow?'

'Oh, I don't know,' Rachel groaned, putting a cushion over her head.

'But Mum, they've got six feet up in London.'

'Sam, no jokes now, darling, I'm asleep.'

'No, Mum, Mum. My friend Emily's dad had to dig them out of their house yesterday.'

'You haven't got a friend called Emily.'

'I have. She's really nice. We've been telling each other jokes. She said maybe we could go to the movies some time.'

'Oh God, why do you kids insist on using that word. We're English – we go to the cinema.'

'Whatever, but can I go?'

'I suppose. Find out exactly where she lives. And why she's telling you weird stories about snow.'

He trotted off. A minute later he was back.

'Cobble Hills,' he announced. 'Is that anywhere near Muswell Hill?'

She took the cushion off her head.

'Er, not as such,' she said. 'I think you'll probably find she lives in the other London. It's in Canada. That would explain the snow.'

Sam's face fell. 'Oh right,' he said dejectedly. 'She sent me a photograph. She looks really pretty. I thought maybe she could be my girlfriend. She's thirteen, so I said I was twelve.'

Rachel giggled. 'Oh, Sam. What a shame she's so far away.'

He disappeared back to the computer, no doubt to give Emily the bad news that the trip to the movies was off.

Rachel sat up. It was a moment before the full impact of her son's brief encounter on the Internet hit her. Emily was a girl. Sam thought she was pretty. He wanted to go to the pictures with her, this older woman. He'd even lied about his age.

'Way to go, kiddo,' Rachel murmured to herself. 'Way to go.'

She carried on sitting there, a gormless smile on her face. She didn't hear the front door open, or Greg and Joe walk back into the room.

'Rachel. Come in, Rachel,' Joe said, waving his hand in front of her face.

'Oh what? Sorry,' she said vacantly. 'I was miles away.'

'You OK?' Joe asked. 'You look a bit flushed.'

'No, I'm fine, absolutely fine. Couldn't be better.' She paused. 'Joe?'

'Yeah?'

'This may sound an odd question, but how old were you when you hit puberty?'

'Me?' He looked puzzled. 'God knows. Although I do remember having my first wet dream about Bradley Lebetkin when we were still at primary school So, I suppose I'd have been about ten, going on eleven.'

'So, deep down you were always certain about your sexuality – even though you married me?'

'Pretty much, though I didn't admit it to myself. Why?'

'Oh, no reason,' she said.

Rachel got home about ten, having left Sam behind. He was staying on with Joe and Greg for another few days. It was only as she stood in the hall taking off her coat that she saw the red light flashing on her answer machine.

She flicked the switch and rewound the tape.

There was a message from her mother wanting to know how she was and another from Lenny asking the same. He also said he'd had a go at trying to find Pitsy, but hadn't had any luck.

'Her flatmate said she hadn't seen her since yesterday. Meanwhile, I managed to find an email address for

Noeleen Piccolo. I've messaged her, telling her all about Pitsy and to keep a lookout for her on the Sydney circuit. It occurred to me that our hairy friend may be so scared of you finding her that she's hot-footed it back to Oz for a few weeks until her Channel 6 show starts. I don't know if anything'll come of it, but Pitsy is such a vicious cow, I couldn't just sit back and do nothing.'

She wished he were there so that she could hug him.

'You are a star, Lenny,' she said aloud. 'Do you know that? A bloomin' star.'

The third message was from Adam. Apparently he'd been trying to reach her ever since the competition to find out how it went, but since all he'd been getting was her answer machine he'd ended up phoning Faye. She'd told him about Pitsy.

'What a bitch. How could somebody do such a thing? It's evil. Pure evil. You must be devastated . . . Look, I have some news, too. I'm coming home. Miracle of miracles, Uncle Stan has found a friend of a friend to fill in at the surgery from next week. So I'll be home tomorrow, Boxing Day. My plane gets in at one, but don't bother coming to meet me, I'm getting the Shuttle straight up to Manchester. One of the partners in the practice is having a drinks do in the evening and since I've been away so long, I really ought to show my face. I'll drive down to you first thing the following morning. There's something really important I need to discuss with you.'

It immediately occurred to her that he wanted to tell her he'd met somebody else and that their relationship was over. That would make what she had to say so much easier. On the other hand, she wished she didn't have to wait an extra day to see him. She was already pretty anxious about this meeting. More hanging around, rehearsing and re-rehearsing what she was going to say to him, would only make her worse. It took a few moments before the solution hit her. Being Boxing Day, he would probably have to wait ages for the Manchester flight. She would meet him at the airport and speak to him before he caught the Shuttle.

CHAPTER 24

'Blimey,' Rachel muttered, staring at the bloke in the Panama hat and cream three-piece suit with a purple silk handkerchief spilling out of the breast pocket. 'Where's that berk off to – tea with Oscar Wilde?'

It was several seconds before she realised the 'berk' was Adam. She shook her head in disbelief. Adam had superb taste in clothes. He was one of the chic-est, most understated dressers she knew. He was certainly no poseur. As she watched him push his trolley past the first few dozen people standing by the customs exit waiting for friends and relatives, she wondered what could possibly have caused such a bizarre sartorial metamorphosis.

Must be what *le tout Durban* is wearing this season, she thought to herself, knowing how easy it is when you're abroad to go native fashionwise. What about that poncho she'd bought in Guatemala? It never did quite work when she got back to Crouch End.

By now her heart was pounding. Last night in bed she'd gone over her goodbye speech a dozen times and she still wasn't sure what she was going to say.

She began waving at him tentatively, as if he were a black cab and she couldn't quite make out if he had his light on, but he didn't see her. He'd stopped and turned to speak to the young woman following him, also pushing a trolley. Judging by all the shared laughter and eye-contact, they knew each other pretty well.

'It's her,' Rachel whispered to herself. The woman was bony, verging on angular, immaculately pressed and coiffed, wearing thin-rimmed gold spectacles and a grey business suit.

Maybe because she'd never been 100 per cent certain Adam was seeing somebody else, it hadn't occurred to Rachel that he might bring her home with him.

'No wonder he didn't want me meeting him at the airport,' she said to herself.

Adam and the woman carried on walking and chatting, clearly not realising they were heading straight towards Rachel.

When they were only yards from her, a holdall suddenly fell off the woman's trolley. Adam bent down, picked it up and stacked it back on top of her pile of cases. Then with a flourish of his Panama hat he performed a deep, theatrical bow. While Rachel screwed up her face – half laughing, half squirming – the woman burst into fits of giggles. He then puckered up in that Mick Jagger impersonating a goldfish way of his and planted little kisses over her face.

Rachel walked forward a few paces and tapped Adam on the back.

'Hiya,' she said brightly. 'Hope I'm not disturbing anything.'

Adam shot round. 'God . . . Rachel,' he gasped. 'I wasn't expecting you.'

'So I see,' she said. 'Aren't you going to introduce me to your friend?' She knew she shouldn't tease him, but she just couldn't resist it. She beamed at the woman who was hovering awkwardly and visibly shocked, next to Adam.

'Er, erm, yes,' he spluttered. 'This is Yootha. She's my Uncle Stan's dental hygienist.'

'I am so pleased to meet you,' Rachel gushed, noticing how well her thin wiry lips accessorised her glasses. 'Adam must have been *so* grateful to have had you around during that terrible locust invasion.'

Ivana Trump caught buying Birkenstocks couldn't have looked more humiliated than poor Yootha did at that moment.

Before Yootha had a chance to say anything, they had both turned to look at Adam who had started fumbling in his trouser pocket and swearing to himself. Blood was trickling gently out of his nose and down his chin.

In a second Yootha had produced a wad of tissues from her bag.

'OK, Addy, just put your head back and pinch the bridge of your nose.'

After a few moments he brought the tissues down from his nose and sniffed. 'I think it's stopped. Look,

Aardvark, Rachel and I need to have a talk. Why don't you go and have a wander round Boots. You could check out the different types of dental floss. I'll come and find you later.'

'All right, Addy, if you're sure you're OK.'

He assured her he was and she walked off, pushing her trolley.

'Addy and his little aardvark,' Rachel said, grinning at Adam. 'How sweet.'

They found an empty row of seats. Adam took off the hat and sat swinging it between his knees.

'Look, Rache,' he said, 'I'm really sorry. I didn't mean you to find out like this. I wanted to sit down with you and explain.'

She nodded slowly. 'So, you and Yootha – it's pretty serious then?'

'It's early days yet but yes, I think it is. We clicked from the instant we met. You know, we have so much in common. She irons her underwear, just like me.'

'Yeah, once she's starched it,' Rachel said, smiling and batting her eyes innocently.

'And she's made me change my entire wardrobe. She reckons a man hitting early middle age should look more distinguished.'

Rachel didn't say anything. Early middle age, she thought. He was only thirty-six, for crying out loud.

'You know,' Adam went on, putting the hat down on the empty seat next to him and turning to face her. 'I'd been dreading telling you. I've spent days psyching myself up to tears and a huge scene. But you seem to be taking it incredibly well.'

'Ah. Well, you see there's a reason for that . . .'

As she told him about Matt, his shock and incredulity gradually gave way to relief.

'You know, Rache,' he said finally, 'we were kidding ourselves thinking we could ever make each other happy. We are such different people. You with your comedy, me with my . . .'

'Trouser-press?' she volunteered helpfully.

He gave a half-laugh. 'I thought that once we were married, I could change you, make you more like me. But deep down I've known for ages we were wrong for each other.'

'That would certainly explain why you went off sex,' she said.

'I'm sorry. I should have said something.'

She patted his knee and said it didn't matter now.

'So, you really love this Matt, then?'

'Oh, yes.'

He put his arm round her shoulders and told her how happy he was she'd found someone. She said she was happy for him, too.

'I'm going to miss you,' he said.

'Yeah, me too.'

A tear rolled down her face. He wiped it away. Then he hugged her, but only briefly. She sensed his emotions were starting to get the better of him, too.

He let go of her and stood up.

'I'd better get moving. Yootha will be wondering what happened to me.'

She reached out and squeezed his hand. 'Take care,' she said.

'Yeah, you too. Give my love to Sam.'

She nodded.

He turned to pick up his hat, but an exceedingly fat, moley woman in flesh-coloured polyester slacks and a T-shirt that said *Pittsburgh: City of Dreams* now occupied the seat on which he'd left it.

Feeling a mixture of sadness and enormous relief, Rachel headed off across the concourse towards the car park. It was only when she wandered into Departures and found herself standing next to the Qantas check-in desk, that she realised she'd been walking in completely the wrong direction. She had just turned round and begun retracing her steps when she noticed a tiny woman with pigtails heading away from the desk towards the departure lounge.

Rachel's face turned Dulux white.

'Fuck,' she exclaimed, her hand forming an involuntary fist. 'It's Pitsy.'

Rachel's walk turned to a trot.

'Janeece,' she yelled across the concourse. 'Come back here. Come – back – here!'

The moment Pitsy turned round and saw Rachel, a look of sheer horror appeared on her face. In a second she was running towards the departure gate. Rachel started running too, shouting after her as she went. When Pitsy refused to stop, she began yelling at passers-by.

'Stop that woman, please. Somebody stop that woman.'

Pitsy was sprinting by now; Rachel was falling behind.

'Please somebody, stop her,' she shrieked. 'She stole my jokes.'

By now people were stopping to stare at the crazy woman. One member of a group of laughing Japanese businessmen hurriedly put a video camera up to his eye.

Rachel stopped and gasped for breath as, ahead of her, Pitsy showed her ticket and passport to the chap at the Departures entrance.

'Stop her,' she bellowed. 'She's a thief. Don't let her through.'

But it was too late. Pitsy had gone. As Rachel wheezed her way up to the desk, she could see Pitsy heading towards passport control.

'She stole my jokes,' Rachel sobbed quietly. 'She stole my jokes.'

Rachel stood there for a few seconds, her head in her hands, digging her fingers into her scalp with frustration. When she finally looked up, she let out a tiny, terrified yelp. Looming over her were four policemen in bullet-proof vests, machine guns across their chests.

Rachel's hands shot into the air in surrender.

One of the policemen, a middle-aged chap, stepped forward.

'It's all right, love,' he said with a gentle smile. 'Put your hands down. You just come along with us and we'll tell you some brilliant jokes.'

He reached out and took Rachel's arm.

'No, you don't understand,' she pleaded frantically, doing her best and failing to release her arm from his powerful grip. 'That woman really did steal my jokes. Honestly. You have to believe me.'

'Oh, we do. We do,' he soothed. 'Come along and you can tell us all about it.' Escorted by his three colleagues, he led her away from the crowd which had started to gather.

'Move along now,' one of the cops said. 'The show's over. There's nothing left to see.'

'Now then, can you remember what medication you're on?' the middle-aged policeman asked Rachel.

'I'm not on any medication,' she howled. 'I'm a comic. I'm a stand-up comic.'

''Course you are,' the policeman said genially. ''Course you are. Now did you hear the one about Saddam Hussein, Carol Vorderman and a camel?'

CHAPTER 25

The moment she got back from Heathrow – the police having released her after she'd finally persuaded them to phone Lenny and Joe, who confirmed her story about Pitsy – Rachel tried ringing Matt. She was desperate to tell him it was over between her and Adam, but there was no reply either from the home number or his mobile.

The following day she tried again and got Tractor who said he hadn't heard from Matt either, although he did remember him saying something about maybe staying on in Nottingham for a week or so. She asked if he had a contact number. He hadn't. On top of that he'd left his mobile at home.

'Look,' Tractor said, 'he wasn't expecting to hear from you until after the New Year. He probably just fancies a complete rest after working so hard on the Donkulator. Anyway, he can't stay away too long, he's got the Burkina Faso trade delegation coming next week. I'm sure he'll get in touch. Stop worrying.'

But she couldn't. By the third day she'd convinced herself that Matt was now so angry with her for keeping her relationship with Adam a secret, that he never wanted to speak to her or see her again.

By the end of the week she was aching for him so much that she wasn't eating or sleeping. She even took her mobile with her on New Year's Eve to Polly the aromatherapist's party – to which Tractor had got himself, Shelley and Rachel invited. This was just in case he decided to call at midnight and wish her A Happy New Year. But he didn't.

At 2 a.m. everybody decided to do a Conga down the street. Rachel was last in line, mobile clamped to her ear. By now she was so slaughtered, she was dialling numbers at random in the hope of finding him. Most people hung up on her, but she had a particularly pleasant few minutes exchanging New Year's greetings with a Mormon family in the Wirral.

The only thing preventing her falling into a complete decline was the thought of meeting Xantia and the possibility – however remote – that her former employer might help her get her career back on track.

She assumed Xantia would return from Venice around 3 or 4 January. There seemed little point in calling first to arrange an appointment. That way Rachel would be forced to state her case over the phone and Xantia would probably refuse to listen and hang up. Her best bet, she decided, was to keep driving over to the house, on the off-chance of catching her.

There was nobody home on 3 or 4 January.

On the morning of the fifth, just as she was about to

head off to Xantia's for the third time, the phone rang. It was Tractor to say he'd found a note from Matt on the kitchen table.

'It was under the Marmite jar. He must have written it before he went away. Thing is, this place is such a tip, plus I've been off Marmite recently so I missed it. Anyway it says to tell you that before you go and see Xantia you should ring his mate Phil.'

Rachel frowned. The name meant nothing to her. 'That's all?'

'Yeah, and there's a number.' He read it out to her. 'Look, I'm sorry if it's important, but I've only just noticed it. Let me know how you get on. Tara, kid.'

'God, Rache, that's amazing,' Shelley said as she sat at her kitchen table attempting to do her mascara, eat toast and breastfeed Satchmo at the same time. She was due at the film studio at eleven and was running late. Both Rachel and Tractor had begged her not to go back to work so soon after having Satchmo, but the Flowtex people had decided to make a second commercial as a follow-up to the first and the money, not to mention them being perfectly happy to let her bring Satchmo with her, had been far too tempting to turn down. 'You mean this mate of Matt's actually *built* Otto and Xantia's secret room?'

'Yep,' Rachel said, 'while he was renovating the house for them. All my instincts were right. According to Phil, their love affair with the house is a complete sham. They loathe it. They both think it's utterly cold and bleak. The secret room is where they go to slob out and get comfortable. Apparently Otto ended up offering Phil and his workmen five hundred quid each to keep quiet about it.'

'You'll certainly have no trouble getting Xantia on your side now. All you have to do is threaten to tell the papers about the secret room. Easy. She'll crumble like a slice of stale cheese . . . Do my lashes look OK?'

'They're fine. What do you mean, all I've got to do is threaten to tell the papers? That'd be blackmail. I'd be descending to Pitsy's level.'

'Rache,' Shelley said, strapping Satchmo into his portable car seat, 'when we discovered the secret room, you said you couldn't hurt the Marxes, but things have changed. It's your career on the line here. Pitsy has to get her come-uppance.' She got up and walked over to the fridge.

Rachel sat thinking.' 'I know,' she began, 'but . . .'

She broke off. Shelley had just opened a Tupperware container and was now stuffing two large green leaves into her bra cups.

'Cabbage,' she said, seeing the quizzical look on Rachel's face. 'Great for cracked nipples.'

Just then Shelley's cordless went off. It was Tractor phoning to wish her good luck and offering to come round in the evening and heat up a couple of Tesco organic pizzas.

'So how are you two?' Rachel grinned, as Shelley put

the phone back down on the table. 'Have you – you know . . . ?'

'Leave off,' Shelley laughed. 'I only had a baby ten days ago. Now I know exactly what your mum meant about walking around with a marrow between her legs. No, we're just taking things really slowly.'

Rachel nodded approvingly.

'So,' Shelley went on, 'are you going to come on heavy with Xantia or not?'

'Not. I just don't have the stomach to start threatening her.'

'Well,' Shelley said, still arranging cabbage leaves in her bra cups, 'it's up to you, but unless the woman's undergone a lobotomy and complete personality change over Christmas, I think it might be your only option.'

Almost as soon as she'd rung the bell, Rachel heard the clack of stilettos on limestone. Xantia's new daily, she assumed.

The door was answered by a tarty-looking middle-aged woman wearing skintight red satin trousers and black patent heels. A giant gold hoop hung from each earlobe.

Rachel introduced herself and explained she used to work for Xantia.

'I know she's probably very busy, but I was just wondering if she might be able to spare me a couple of minutes. There's something important I need to discuss with her.'

The woman said nothing. Instead she stood looking at Rachel, a vague smile on her lips, her head bent slightly to one side. The silence was making Rachel feel awkward. She smiled back sheepishly, taking in the woman's platinum-blonde bob and tight black Lycra top. Across the front was an embossed red and gold tiger's head – mouth open, teeth bared. She couldn't put a finger on it, but there was something vaguely familiar about her.

'Hello, Rachel,' the woman said eventually. 'I've been expecting you.'

Rachel recognised that haughty tone at once.

'Omigod. Xantia?' she said in gobsmacked amazement. 'Is that you?'

'Yes, dahling,' she squealed, her voice suddenly brimming over with childish excitement, 'it's me. The new me. Or should I say . . . the *real* me.'

She did a twirl, followed it with another and then stood back to let Rachel in. Still blinking in stunned amazement, Rachel stepped into the hall.

'I don't get it. What on earth's . . . ?'

But before she could finish her sentence, the two of them were suddenly surrounded by a small group of people. In her confused state, it took Rachel a few seconds to take in the cameras and lights and realise it was a TV crew.

'OK, people,' Xantia said, clapping her hands. 'Take five, will you? There's something important I simply must attend to.'

Somebody said, 'Cut,' and the cameras and lights were switched off.

As Xantia led her into the kitchen, Rachel couldn't help noticing she'd developed a sexy wiggle in her walk.

Xantia motioned Rachel to sit down.

'Nescaff?' she said, brandishing the jar.

Rachel shook her head and said she was fine.

'Oh well, I think I will.'

'Xantia, please, you have to tell me. What's happened? What's going on?'

'Well . . .' She began spooning instant coffee granules into a mug. 'Otto and I have decided to come out of the closet – well, out of our secret room, anyway.' She paused for dramatic effect, staring at the jar of Coffee Mate she was now holding, as if it were Yorick's head, 'And tell the world that we are bourgeois vulgarians – and proud of it.'

A whispered, 'Blimey' was about all Rachel could muster.

'Otto's even designed a lapel ribbon – black, covered with tiny gold sovereigns.'

She poured boiling water into the mug.

'You see, we know there are others like us out there – cutting-edge designers who in order to protect their reputations, not to mention their livelihoods, are forced to live in soulless art-installation surroundings like these, when secretly they are crying out for magnolia lounges, Laura Ashley chintz and fretwork radiator covers.'

She came and sat down opposite Rachel.

'Our mission,' she continued, 'is to help stop these pour souls denying their true selves. God gave us cocktail cabinets that play "Nessun Dorma". What right do we have to throw them back in His face?'

'So what made you and Otto decide to come out?' Rachel asked.

'Ever since we built the secret room, Otto and I have lived in fear of it being discovered and the two of us being blackmailed.'

'But Xantia,' Rachel cut across her, 'I would never have done anything like that.'

'Oh no, not you, dahling,' she laughed. 'You're far too principled. Once I'd thought about it, I knew you'd never have the stomach for it.'

'Oh thanks,' Rachel said peevishly.

'Anyway, when you and your friend discovered the room, we realised what a relief it was. The stress of keeping it secret, along with maintaining the pretence about Otto's lineage, had been driving us both mad.'

'You mean he isn't related to Karl Marx?'

'Good God, no. His family were in buttons.'

She paused again.

'So anyway, we've decided to sell up and move to Weybridge. Just yesterday Otto and I saw this truly amazing house. It used to be owned by some Page Three model or other. There's a state-of-the-art gym, a wood-panelled snooker room with stags' heads all over the walls and a bar done out like a country pub. It's to die for, Rachel. Just to die for.'

'Yes, I can see that,' Rachel said.

Xantia was looking dreamily into the distance.

'And don't tell me – the film crew is here to follow you and Otto on the road to damask?'

'Yes. In fact, there's another crew out with Otto. He's gone off to buy one of those huge American camper bus things. We thought we might take it down to Newquay in the spring.'

'And what about the business?' Rachel asked.

'Well, obviously we can't carry on selling style we don't believe in. Otto thinks we should diversify into commemorative chinaware.'

Rachel chuckled. Bonkers as they were, she couldn't help rather admiring the Marxes.

They fell silent for a moment or two. Rachel wondered if this might be the time to bring up Pitsy.

'Xantia, I haven't told you the reason I'm here.'

'But I know why you're here. I said when you arrived that I'd been expecting you.'

Rachel looked at her, puzzled.

'A friend of yours – Lenny, the chap who compèred the comedy contest – was here a few minutes ago. He brought this with him.'

She turned in her chair and picked a video-cassette up off the worktop.

'He's a very persuasive young man, Lenny. Refused to go until I'd watched it. It's a recording of an Australian comic called Noeleen Piccolo. At first I hoped it was this Noeleen who had stolen material from Janeece, but deep down I knew it was the other way round. Although we never admitted it, we always suspected Janeece wasn't particularly talented. I'm ashamed to say this, but the only reason she got any engagements at all was because Otto and I bribed the bookers.'

Rachel nodded. 'I see,' she said.

'It was Otto's idea. His sister leads a bit of dog's life married to some ne'er-do-well in Killadingo and he just wanted to do something for her. She was so proud when she thought Vanessa, or Janeece, or whatever name she goes by now, was making it. But Rachel, you have to believe me when I say that before Lenny came to see me with the tape, I had no idea that my niece was stealing material. I can't begin to tell you how sorry I am. Otto and I haven't seen or spoken to Vanessa since the contest. We have no idea where she is. All I can say is that I hope she gets the punishment due to her.'

She reached out and took Rachel's hand in both of hers. 'Just before you got here I spoke to Robin Metcalf at Channel 6 and explained everything.'

'You did? Oh my God, Xantia, that's amazing. What did he say?'

'He said he'd seen you perform a few weeks ago and already knew how talented you are, but assumed you got stage-fright the other night and decided he couldn't risk having you appear in any future live shows in case it happened again. I assured him you *hadn't* been suffering from stage-fright. He's going to call you, either today or tomorrow.'

Rachel got up, walked round to Xantia and hugged her.

'Thank you,' she said, kissing her on the cheek. 'Thank you so much.'

Clearly not used to being the object of sudden, ostentatious displays of affection, Xantia's face turned precisely the same colour as her satin trousers.

Rachel danced down the garden path, into the street and straight into Lenny.

'Omigod, Len,' she cried out in excitement, 'I was just about to phone you. What are you doing here?'

He explained he'd seen her arrive at Xantia's, assumed she was planning to talk to her about Pitsy and decided to hang around to find out the outcome.

'It's sorted,' Rachel said. 'Xantia's fixed things with Channel 6 – and it's all because of you. Lenny, you saved my life. How am I ever going to thank you?'

She flung her arms round him, almost knocking him off his feet.

'You can buy me a pie and chips,' he said, laughing.

'Done,' she replied, shoving her arm through his and forcing him to dance down the street with her.

They were sitting in the pub drinking pints of Guinness while they waited for their pie and chips, discussing all the offers of TV work which had come Lenny's way since the comedy contest, when suddenly he broke off.

'Oh, by the way,' he said, his face breaking into a grin, 'I was saving this. I've got something to show you.'

'God, Len,' she giggled, 'I'm not sure I can cope with any more surprises today.'

'Ooh, I think you'll cope with this one.' He reached into his coat pocket and pulled out a folded newspaper. He handed it to Rachel. 'It's the *Sydney Morning Herald*. Brilliant front page, eh?'

She read the headline. *COMIC GETS VEGEMITED AND FEATHERED.*

Underneath was a large colour picture of Pitsy being attacked by a furious, hysterical woman armed with a jar of Vegemite. She gazed at it for a few seconds in disbelief. Then she let out a loud, high-pitched squeal of delight.

'Kakking kangaroos, it's Noeleen getting her revenge.' She laughed so hard, people turned and stared.

Lenny explained: 'Seems like as soon as Pitsy got back to Sydney, she got up at some comedy club open-mike night and did her Noeleen Piccolo material. And guess who just happened to be in the audience?'

'Ms Piccolo, having read your warning email . . . Lenny, what can I say? This is just amazing. Just amazing.'

She threw her arms round him and planted a huge smacker on his forehead.

'You know,' she said thoughtfully, sitting back in her chair, 'there's one thing I still don't understand. The only way Pitsy was able to use my material on the night of the comedy contest was because she came before me in the running order. How on earth did she arrange it?'

'Yeah, the same thought occurred to me. I've got this

mate who's a floor manager at Channel 6 and I got him to do some asking around. Turns out that after she went for her original audition one of the assistant producers asked her out. It's over now, but apparently they were seeing each other for several weeks.'

Rachel shook her head slowly, taking in what he'd told her. 'And during that time, Pitsy nobbled him.'

'Well, that's one word for it, I suppose,' Lenny said, grinning.

They'd just finished eating when Rachel's mobile started ringing. It was Shelley, calling from the film studio.

'I've only got a second because I'm due on set,' she said, breathless with excitement, but you must get down here – now. There's something you *have* to see.'

'What? What is it?'

'Your mum and dad. They're here.'

'Mum and Dad? Don't be daft. What would they be doing at a film studio?'

'Rachel, they're here. I promise.'

'But why? I don't understand.'

'You soon will. I haven't got time to explain. Just get in your car and come.' She gave Rachel the address in Archway.

Looking extremely puzzled, Rachel made her excuses to Lenny, promising to take him out for a posh dinner very soon, to say thank you properly for everything he'd done. Then she quickly gathered up her coat and bag and headed for the door.

CHAPTER 26

'At seventy-two,' Jack said with a wicked smile, 'I still feel like a twenty year old. The thing is, there's never one around.'

Faye laughed too loud and bashed him playfully on the shoulder.

'Oh, take no notice,' she said. 'He doesn't mean that. I think what my husband is trying to say is that just because there's snow on the roof, it doesn't mean there's no fire in the house. We may be getting on a bit, but Jack and I are still just as much in love and attracted to one another as we were on our wedding day. I adore him.'

Rachel and Shelley were standing at the back of the soundstage, watching Faye and Jack sitting on a chintz sofa being interviewed on camera.

'Look,' Rachel hissed to Shelley, 'do you mind telling me what the hell's going on. Why are my parents being filmed?'

Shelley said nothing. She simply gave a knowing smile.

'There's still no man who can give me goose pimples the way Jack can,' Faye continued.

She turned to look at him. They gazed into each other's eyes, then Jack took her in his arms and kissed her passionately on the lips.

'And cut.' It was the director's voice. Although Rachel could hear him, she couldn't see him because he had his back to her.

'Faye, Jack,' he continued, 'that was fabulous. Simply fabulous. Is that okay for you, Tom?'

The cameraman nodded.

Faye and Jack got up from the sofa.

'You really think we were all right, Simon?' Faye said, blushing. 'I mean, you can cut the bit about him fancying twenty-year-olds, can't you?'

Rachel looked at Shelley and blinked. 'What? That's Simon? *The* Simon? Simon the pervy TV upholsterer?'

'Well, his name is certainly Simon,' Shelley said, laughing.

At that moment Faye noticed Rachel.

'Oh good Gawd,' she exclaimed. 'Jack, it's Rachel.'

She came running across, nearly tripping over a cable as she went. Shelley beat a tactful retreat to the back of the soundstage where Satchmo was asleep in his car seat, being guarded by one of the floor managers.

'Rachel,' Faye said, smiling anxiously. 'Whatever are you doing here?'

'Er, I could ask you the same thing. Mum, why are you and Dad giving interviews about your sex-life?'

Faye and Jack exchanged a glance.

'Look, sweetie,' Jack began, 'your mother and I were

going to tell you, but we thought you'd try to stop us doing it.'

'Doing what?' Rachel said. 'I don't understand.'

'We replied to an advertisement in the *Guardian*. Simon over there makes TV documentaries. We're taking part in a six-part series, advising older couples on sex. *Love in the Time of Rheumatism* it's called. It's all very respectable and above board. We even managed to persuade Coral and Ivan Finkel to take part.'

Suddenly her father's exercising, the diet, not to mention what she'd seen going on in her parents' bedroom made sense. Realising they weren't swingers, relief shot through Rachel.

'So, it's a kind of self-help thing?'

'Yes,' Faye said timidly. 'You mean you don't mind?'

'Mind? Why should I mind? "Mind" is when you discover your parents are . . . I dunno, senile swingers or something. This is . . . wonderful. Gross, but wonderful.'

'The thing is,' Faye carried on, 'there's some film of us in bed together and we're not wearing very much. Nothing happens, of course – it's all very tasteful. I get to wear some really sexy underwear. Simon took me to Selfridges to choose it.'

'Good for you, Mum. Good for you both. I am so relieved – no, I mean I am so, er, *proud*. Really, really proud.'

'What?' Rachel said to Sam, as she came into the kitchen

to start his tea. 'You told Robin Metcalf I was on the loo?'

He nodded.

She made a soft snorting sound.

'Well, you were. I didn't tell him – you know – what you were doing or anything.'

She supposed she should be grateful for small mercies.

'I just said, "She's on the loo and she'll phone you back". What's wrong with that? I even remembered to get his number, just like you always tell me to.' He handed her a scrap of paper.

'OK, well done,' she said, ruffling his hair. 'You did fine. It's just that Robin Metcalf's a pretty big cheese and it might have been better to say I'd popped out, that's all.'

Sam shrugged, took a packet of salt and vinegar crisps out of the kitchen cupboard and headed back to his bedroom.

Rachel took several deep breaths, went into the hall and dialled Robin Metcalf's direct line.

He greeted her warmly, spent a minute or so telling her how sorry he was about what had happened at the comedy contest, and then revealed that since speaking to Xantia he had spent a couple of hours with his Head of Light Entertainment and several producers discussing how the Channel might make some kind of amends.

They had decided there was no question of Pitsy being

given her own show or appearing at the Eurovision Joke
Contest in Helsinki. Instead they would tell the press she
had gone down with some chronic debilitating lergy and
award her prizes to the runner-up.

Rachel immediately saw the fairness in this. Even
though it was her material that had won the contest,
she hadn't actually appeared on the night and had no
right to usurp the runner-up.

'But meanwhile,' Robin Metcalf continued, 'there is a
new live comedy show featuring all our best stand-ups,
beginning on Channel 6 this Saturday. But we have a
problem. Our top of the bill has gone down with flu and
has been forced to pull out so we were wondering if you
would be able to fill her place?'

What? Come up with new material in two days? She
couldn't. It was impossible, ridiculous, madness. Was
this guy touched or something?

'OK, you're on,' she said eagerly. 'And thank you so
much for this opportunity. I won't let you down.'

An hour later, her excitement began to subside. How
she was going to come up with a brand new five-minute
set in forty-eight hours, she hadn't the foggiest idea.
As panic rose inside her, she wanted Matt more than
ever. She wanted him to wrap her in his arms and
tell her not to be scared because he loved her and
he knew she could do it. She wanted him to come
round with curries to keep her going while she wrote.
But more than anything she wanted to tell him she'd

ended it with Adam and that she loved him to the moon and back.

She picked up the receiver again and dialled his number. All she got was the answer machine.

CHAPTER 27

'So, yeah anyway – I'm thirty-four and my mother is desperate for me to get married. She thinks settling down is what you should be doing at thirty-four. How would she like it if I turned to her the day she hits eighty and said, "Hey, Mum, when are you going to break your hip? All your friends are breaking theirs"?'

Once again the audience roared, whooped and banged their beer bottles on the tables. Rachel stood in front of them, beaming. In her industrial Levi hipsters and psychedelic halter-neck top, tiny diamanté clips in her hair, she was unrecognisable from the panic-stricken, grubby-pyjama-ed woman who had spent the last two days praying for inspiration as she sat at her computer, comfort-eating pumpernickel and marshmallow fluff and necking bottles of Rescue Remedy like they were vodka miniatures.

Her nights had been spent lying awake, willing Matt to come back to her.

But somehow she'd managed to come up with a brand new five-minute set in forty-eight hours. And here she was, topping the bill, live on national TV. What was more the audience – which included her parents, Shelley and Tractor – were loving every minute of her set. More important still, Robin Metcalf was loving it. For the last four minutes he'd been standing at the back laughing and cheering with the rest of the punters. As she waited for the applause to die down, Rachel felt about as high as it was possible to get without the aid of an illegal substance.

'Thing is, I don't have much luck with boyfriends.'

'Aah,' the audience came back.

She giggled. 'Yeah. I've had so many failed blind dates, my mates clubbed together to buy me a guide dog.'

More laughter.

'Then when I do manage to start a relationship it's usually with a guy who can't get in touch with his emotions. There was this bloke I went out with a few years back. I used to snuggle up beside him on the sofa and tell him I loved him. And all he'd say was, "Shut up, I can't hear the game". After him there was the one who turned out to be a bank robber. God knows how I missed the signs. I thought his crowbar was something he was saving up for the third date. Apparently he'd spent his childhood in and out of detention centres. The only picture his parents had of him was a police mugshot in a gold frame.

'Then there was this last bloke I was seeing. He was . . . He was . . .'

The shock made her heart nearly skip a beat. How

she had missed him for the best part of five minutes, she had no idea. But he was right there at the front – looking straight at her. He wasn't laughing or clapping like the rest of them. He was just sitting there, taking the occasional sip from a bottle of Budvar. And watching. She carried on looking directly into the audience. If she turned towards him, made eye-contact, it would throw her completely.

'Anyway, this bloke . . . He . . . er . . .'

She stood there swallowing hard and clearing her throat.

Why had he come? She could only assume it was to tell her it was over.

The audience was chuckling. They clearly thought her sudden uneasiness was part of the act. She looked at Robin Metcalf who was smiling expectantly. Then, unable to stop herself, she turned towards Matt. In a second her eyes were locked onto his and all she could think was how much she loved him and ached for him and how the thought of losing him was unbearable. By now she was aware that the audience chuckles had turned to uncomfortable coughing. Somebody shouted, 'Get on with it.' She strongly suspected that if she looked to the back of the audience she would see Robin Metcalf with his head in his hands.

She'd promised not to let him down, but she was doing precisely that. As the seconds went by and still she said nothing, she realised she could probably kiss goodbye to her career once and for all. In that case, she thought, she had nothing to lose. She might as well come out and say what was on her mind.

'You see,' she said quietly, 'this last bloke I was seeing, I loved him. I still do. But I did something stupid. I wasn't straight with him – there were some important things about myself I held back – and now he doesn't trust me.'

There were a few more awkward giggles from the audience.

'He went away last week and I've spent the whole time waiting for him to call me, but he hasn't. I've tried phoning him, to tell him how much I love him and miss him, but he hasn't been answering his mobile. Now I don't know if he ever wants to see me again. I'm pretty sure I've blown it.'

She turned back to the audience.

'Pretty stupid, eh?' she said.

Once again she looked at Robin Metcalf. There was this pained, pleading expression on his face as if to say, 'Please, please let this be going somewhere.'

She didn't notice Matt slowly get up.

'Rachel,' he said, 'you haven't blown it. I love you.'

She stood stock-still, hardly able to believe what she was hearing. Then she turned to face him.

'You do?'

He nodded. 'I do.'

She swung round to face the audience.

'He does,' she squealed.

The next moment she'd dropped her mike and, oblivious

to the TV cameras following her, she went charging into his arms.

The applause was deafening. By now people were standing up and cheering. Others were whistling and stamping their feet. A few of the women had tears in their eyes.

'Oh my God,' she said, laughing and crying at the same time, as he wrapped her in his arms. 'You've just announced you love me on live television.'

'Well,' he grinned, 'now I'm going to snog you on live television, too.'

For the next few minutes as the credits rolled on the nation's television screens, the couple stood there in front of the stage hugging and kissing, unaware of all the people coming up to them, slapping them both on the back and wishing them good luck. It was only Robin Metcalf laying his hand heavily on Rachel's shoulder that brought her back to earth with a jolt.

'Oh God, Robin . . . I'm so terribly sorry. I saw Matt sitting there and I just lost it.'

'It's OK, love. You were brilliant tonight and the audience loved you. And I think you're going to find the publicity launches you into the stratosphere within a few hours. I just want to tell you your future is absolutely assured with us. But I would be grateful – and so would my nerves – if any subsequent reconciliations between the pair of you took place in private.'

With that he kissed her on both cheeks and told her

that she would be topping the bill for the whole ten-week series. Then he headed off to the bar.

'Omigod,' Rachel said quietly, utterly stunned. 'I've got it. The whole ten-week series – I've got it.'

Matt pulled her to him.

'I am so proud of you,' he said softly, looking into her eyes. Then he kissed her again.

In the end the only place they could find to talk without being mobbed by wellwishers was the tiny, two-cubicle, Ladies.

Matt stood with his back to the door and every few seconds, as women tried to get in, Rachel would call out that it was occupied.

'You see, when you went off to Nottingham without leaving your number,' Rachel said, leaning against a wash basin, 'I assumed you were really angry and never wanted to see me again.'

'The irony is, I did leave a number. I left it on Tractor's mobile.'

'I never got it.'

'I know that now. Tractor only just told me he doesn't know how to access his messages. And he's never read the instruction book because it's propping up the broken leg of his bed. I know I should have phoned you with my number, instead of relying on Tractor, but I was scared.'

'Scared? Of what?'

He paused. 'That I'd find out you were planning to go back to Adam.'

He explained that it wasn't until he'd got home a few hours earlier to meet the Burkina Faso trade delegation that Tractor told him she'd finished with Adam.

'I love you,' he said again, stroking her cheek. 'And I'm sorry if I overreacted to the whole Adam thing. It was just that I could see history repeating itself, that's all.'

'I know. Tractor told me all about this married woman you went out with. I'm really, really sorry I wasn't upfront with you right from the beginning. So, tell me. What did they say, the Burkina Faso people?'

'Oh,' he said casually, 'only that they loved the Donkulator. And with the help of a grant from the World Health Organisation, they're planning to buy a thousand of them at five hundred dollars a piece. And apparently other Third World countries have seen the design and are showing an interest, too. Tractor reckons we could be making them full-time before very long. We'll need staff and a factory and everything.'

'Matt,' she gasped, throwing her arms round him again. 'You're famous. You're going to be famous. You really will get the Nobel Prize for Laundry.'

By now there was a queue of desperate, full-bladdered women outside the loo, bashing on the door demanding to be let in. But rising above the irate female voices was one male voice.

'Er, excuse me . . . we're press, come to interview Ms Katz. Mind your backs . . . *Daily Mail* coming through.'

'It's Tractor pretending he's from the papers,' Rachel giggled.

Matt opened the door a few inches and Tractor and Shelley squeezed in. More hugs, backslapping and whoops of congratulation followed.

'Far be it for me to rain on your parade, my friends, but I too have news,' Tractor said eventually.

Tractor was wearing what appeared to be a brand new, secondhand Seventies velvet suit. He and Shelley exchanged knowing glances.

'I thought you might be interested to know I've just had an email from the Kelloggs people. They love the Imperial Cereal idea. In fact, they adore it. They said it was just what they were looking for — described my designs as pure genius. They're going to start test-marketing it in a few months. We're talking hundreds of thousands here.'

Rachel and Matt looked at each other, not sure if this was a wind-up.

'Oh ye of little faith,' he said, clocking their expressions. He reached into his pocket, produced a printout of the email and handed it to Matt.

'Look,' he said, leaning over Matt's shoulder and pointing to the last paragraph. 'They're offering me a two-cereal deal.'

Outside, the full-bladdered women were getting crosser and more mutinous. In between their thumping and threats to bash down the door, they seemed to be having an argument with a woman who was trying to push to the front.

'No, no, you don't understand,' the woman was saying

indignantly. 'I can't wait my turn . . . and nor can my husband. This is urgent. You see, that's my daughter in there. She's locked in with some strange man.'

She started banging on the door.

'Darling, it's me. Come out, please. You have to tell us what's going on. What's happened to Adam? I mean, should I be telling Hylda Klompus to forget the heart-shaped salmon mousses?'

Rachel turned to Matt and smiled a strained smile.

'Matt,' she said, 'this isn't quite the setting I had in mind, but I think maybe the time has come for you to meet my mum and dad.'

As she opened the door, the queue of women burst in like *Titanic* escapees heading for the lifeboats, leaving a terror-stricken Faye and Jack outside, pinned to the wall.

'You know, Rachel,' Matt said as they drove back to her flat in Van Morrison, 'I really like your parents – particularly your mum.'

'What, even when she said that bit about when the light catches you at a certain angle you could be Jewish?'

'Even then,' he grinned.

CHAPTER 28

It was a sweltering July day and Hampstead Register Office was filling up with wedding guests.

Faye and Jack had been in their seats for twenty minutes. Faye had spent most of that time on the mobile to Hylda Klompus.

'So everything's under control, Hylda? Nothing's been left out to sweat in this heat – the Hollandaise sauce for the salmon is still in the fridge? God forbid we should have an outbreak of salmonella . . . No, I'm fine. My ankles have swollen up like tree trunks, but apart from that, I'm OK.'

'Faye,' Jack hissed. 'Come off that bloody phone. They'll be starting in a few minutes.'

'How will they be starting? The bride and groom are still standing outside. Doesn't Rachel look lovely? I'm so glad she went for the ivory. The pure white did nothing for her complexion.'

She dug Jack in the ribs. 'I knew I was right about that watch I found in Rachel's bathroom. There was definitely something going on. And then when Adam didn't show up at the comedy contest . . .'

She turned round to see Shelley walking in with Tractor who had Satchmo strapped to his front in a baby harness.

'Lord, I hope Shelley keeps that baby quiet. She'll be the next one to get married. They're like that, her and this Tractor. According to Rachel he's a very substantial fella now. She's giving up acting and he's financing this health-food chain she's opening.'

At that moment Joe and Greg came in with Sam. Following close behind were Adam and a visibly pregnant Yootha.

'Ach, will you look at her with that *schmo*, Adam. She looks like a stick insect with a beer gut. But doesn't Sam look lovely in that navy suit I got him. I'd have preferred the kilt and frilly shirt, but he wouldn't hear of it.'

'How can you blame the kid. What are we, the bloody Clan McKatz?'

'Jack?' Faye lowered her voice as she sat contemplating Joe and Greg. 'I wonder which one of them is the woman?'

'Oh Faye, for crying out loud.'

'All right. I was just curious, that's all.'

'What's keeping them?' Jack said irritably, running his finger round the inside of his collar.

Faye turned round and craned her neck.

'There's something going on outside. I think that might be them coming in . . . Oh no. I'm wrong. It's somebody else.'

She paused.

'Oh my God,' she squealed. 'Oh my God. It's *her*.'

'Who?'

'Jack, turn round.'

He turned. 'I can't see without my glasses,' he said.

She opened her bag and handed him hers. He put them on.

'I just know it's her. Jack – I just know it.'

'Who?' he said, sounding exasperated.

'Her. It's Barbra Streisand. She came. She actually came.'

'Faye, calm down. It'll be a lookalike. Rachel and Matt will have hired her to keep Sam happy.'

'It's not a lookalike. Look at the nose, the eyes.'

Before Jack could stop her, Faye had leapt out of her seat. The woman she thought was Barbra Streisand was sitting down at the back of the room.

'Er, hello,' she said, virtually curtseying.

The woman looked up and smiled.

'I'm Faye Katz, the bride's mother. Can I just say what an honour and a pleasure it is to meet you and that I saw *Yentl* six times.'

The woman carried on smiling a cryptic smile.

'It *is* you, isn't it? You *are* Barbra? My husband thinks you're a lookalike, but I'm convinced you're you.'

The woman winked, tapped the side of her nose with her finger and continued fanning herself with a Concorde ticket.

EPILOGUE

The Eurovision Comedy Contest had been held in Helsinki the previous March. It was won by the Norwegian comic with a routine based on Ibsen, Grieg – and a Matjes herring.

Sisteria

Sue Margolis

'A tremendously funny, colourful and gripping read' *Mail on Sunday*

If Beverley Littlestone knew what was good for her, she would steer clear of her sister Naomi, who's just got in touch after a five-year silence. Hasn't Beverley got enough to contend with – like her husband Melvin, invariably engaged in a lunatic scheme with 'failure' written all over it in mile-high neon. Not to mention her daughter Natalie, for whom PMT means Permanent Menstrual Tension.

But Beverley can't say no to her sister – and Naomi's self-serving plans are going to launch Beverley out of suburbia and into a whole new world of drama and desire . . .

0 7472 5774 4

headline

Something for the Weekend

Pauline McLynn

When private investigator Leo Street is sent away to County Kildare to spy on the supposedly cheating wife of a loathsome client, she's delighted to be getting away from rainy Dublin and her hopeless, permanently resting actor boyfriend Barry. The one catch is that she has to masquerade as a member of a cookery course and the only piece of culinary equipment Leo can handle is a tin opener – Weekend Entertaining Part One is daunting to say the least.

As she strips away layers of marital infidelity – not to mention several other scandalous secrets – she battles with bread-making and brûlée. But where will it all end – in triumph or tragedy?

'*Something for the Weekend* introduces an amiable anti-heroine who clearly has a great deal of life in her' *The Times*

'A fabulously funny novel' *Sunday Independent*

'Packed with cheeky sarcasm and wit' *Company*

'An upbeat, chatty novel' *Daily Mail*

'A novel that demonstrates a sure ear for dialogue' *Marie Claire*

'Lively characters . . . satisfying authenticity' *Image*

0 7472 6397 3

headline

Now you can buy any of these other bestselling
Headline books from your bookshop or
direct from the publisher.

FREE P&P AND UK DELIVERY
(Overseas and Ireland £3.50 per book)

Olivia's Luck	Catherine Alliott	£5.99
Backpack	Emily Barr	£5.99
Girlfriend 44	Mark Barrowcliffe	£5.99
Seven-Week Itch	Victoria Corby	£5.99
Two Kinds of Wonderful	Isla Dewar	£6.99
Fly-Fishing	Sarah Harvey	£5.99
Bad Heir Day	Wendy Holden	£5.99
Good at Games	Jill Mansell	£5.99
Sisteria	Sue Margolis	£5.99
For Better, For Worse	Carole Matthews	£5.99
Something For the Weekend		
	Pauline McLynn	£5.99
Far From Over	Sheila O'Flanagan	£5.99

TO ORDER SIMPLY CALL THIS NUMBER

01235 400 414

or e-mail <u>orders@bookpoint.co.uk</u>

Prices and availability subject to change without notice.